"I will now turn to my colleague to explain the reason behind our decision."

A small figure, definitely feminine stood.

"Thank you, Sir." She said in a high thin voice, "This decision has not been entered into, ahhh, lightly." She spoke very slowly and it was easy to tell that she would have been much more comfortable speaking a Chinese dialect than English. "We are placing a high priority on reaching outward from our planet and we must, ahhh, present a united front, when we meet those from other worlds, outside of our own." She sat down with a sigh. Obviously speaking English or just speaking to a large group was a chore for her.

A man rose from the end of the shadowed table. "We are not as technologically advanced as some of you. I am here to tell you that with this alliance, we, my countrymen, will finally be able to share with those of you who are advanced, to achieve those goals that have been far out of our reach." The well-modulated deep voice of an African nation stopped speaking momentarily as his head turned to look around at those with whom he shared the table.

"We have a large population available to learn, assist, and participate at all levels of this alliance, this new government, as they are needed."

The man who had begun the meeting began to speak again.

"While you have not heard from all of those at this table, you have heard from those that represent two of the largest population areas on the globe. They stand with us. There are those who presently work for us, who hate us, on a fundamental level. Yet for their own reasons, mostly monetary, they have agreed to our terms, at least for the time being. They are not sitting here tonight, or should I say this morning, but they do understand and have been told that if they make any effort to undermine, thwart, elude, or in any way stop the forward motion of this action they will be dealt with immediately, unceremoniously, and completely."

"In other words," the man chuckled, "we don't trust them and they kn⸺ ⸺ They know very little about us, other than we supply them at ⸺ other times with funds. They are so cc ⸺ beliefs that they cannot understand anything beyond their own agendas. That can and will be useful for us in the short term, but make no mistake, it will not be tolerated in the long term. However, as I stated earlier, the timeline begins when this meeting is over and I cannot stress enough that any and all options, including terrorist actions that could cause great loss of life are sanctioned to keep this timeline maintained at all costs. Anyone who attempts to stop this movement will be dealt with swiftly.

"As you depart this room, your personal assignments, procedural codes, and any other information each of you might need are waiting for you. When you leave the front door, kindly deposit your handout and the red folders in the appropriate receptacles. Thank you all for your attention and attendance."

Ed looked at his watch. He had been in the building barely a half hour and now he knew the decision and he knew why. The how would be different for each of them and as he stepped to the door to exit he took his folded paper from its customary slot in the long wooden file box that was always there when they left a meeting.

He lined up with others in the hallway standing against the wall as each looked, read and carefully digested their assignments. Some moved their mouths as they committed the words to memory, others read and re-read as if to etch the words on the backs of their eyelids. Whatever the method, all were done in less than two minutes and wordlessly trooped out the front door, papers in a covered cylindrical bucket on the right, red folders in a similar one on the left. It was always the same.

Ten minutes later he was back on the road, returning to Washington, the White House. Several cars that had been in the parking lot either passed or remained behind his, he didn't care. Although he was glad that finally the move was being made to head well out into space beyond the present short range goals of NASA, the price that so many innocent people might have to pay to achieve that end was monumental.

Ed changed back into his uniform and returned the nondescript tie, shirt and jacket to the carryon. Although he was accustomed to long hours and sleepless nights, he felt weary from the stress of the previous day and the outcome of the meeting. Now, he had to prepare a report for the President. He had been advised to tell him only the bare bones.

He had the unhappy duty of keeping tabs on a president who was not trusted by the small group of people who actually made the policy of the nation.

The president had come to Washington as the Vice-President three years ago. Then, President Chapman had succumbed to an aneurysm one evening after dinner, only months into his presidency. Michael Stapleton had been sworn in less than an hour later. He had been briefed for days on where things stood in regard to foreign policies, Congressmen and Senators foibles and strong points, diplomats prepared to come and pay homage. But when it was Colonel Ed Gately's turn to walk in and tell the new President what his role really was in the scheme of things, the scene had been less of a briefing and more of an explanation of how the world and the United States was run.

Stapleton could not, and would not believe that he was not in control of the country. He refused to listen to the advice of those who told him what had to be done, when and how. He persisted in issuing statements, having meetings and following through on agendas, which were not considered in the best interests of the country. Finally, after several weeks of blunders, media laughter, and an approval rating of less than a grade B movie, he was advised by one of his 'friends' to take a trip.

Stapleton took the trip and wound up in the middle of a meeting of the most powerful men in the world. They promptly took him in hand and issued the direst of warnings, along with explanations and orders of what he should be doing. Stapleton returned to the White House a changed man, who finally listened to advisors and issued statements as prepared.

Colonel Gately felt sorry for the man. Sure, he had been tough to get along with, but now the man was a mere shadow himself. Now he would stay up for hours, memorizing everything that he had been given for the coming weeks as to policies that were not according to his belief, plans in which he had no part, and actions totally against who he was.

Ed Gately knew the next morning was going to be worse than anything he had ever been through, when presenting the future plans of the group to the President. He also didn't agree with how they were going to achieve their goals, the estimated loss of life was frightening, but he only had to deliver the message, he didn't have to be responsible for carrying it out.

Gately left the limousine, returned to his basement office, closed the door and locked it. After taking off his jacket and loosening his tie, he laid down on the couch he'd dragged in months ago from a dusty storage room, for these long nights to get a couple of hours of down time. But his mind wouldn't let him sleep. It kept playing and replaying the words from the paper. If his job wasn't completed, perhaps, just perhaps, it would delay, or stop this insane plan.

Finally he knew what had to be done and got up. He put on his uniform jacket and cap, left the room, the White House, went out into the dawn and hailed a cab. When he arrived at his home, he woke his wife.

"Evelyn. Evelyn, honey, pack a bag, now. We have to take a trip."

"A trip? A bag?" She said as she began to sit up, a slim hand tousling her short brown hair.

"Now. We'll get breakfast on the way." He was already pulling his own black leather carryon from the closet.

"What do I need?" She asked as she stumbled toward the bathroom.

"Just for an overnight, hon, you know, slacks, a pullover, nothing dressy." He was used to directing her, letting her know if she had to be ready for a special occasion. He pulled a dark sweater over his head, and took a tweed jacket from the closet before leaving the bedroom.

"Okay, give me a couple of minutes."

"That's all you have. I'll be waiting for you at the door." Ed ran down the stairs and into his study next to the kitchen. He bent down in the corner behind his desk and pressed a wall panel, which slid back to reveal a safe. When he opened it, he pulled out passports and emptied it of large bundles of cash. He pulled his belt off and pulled a long cloth pouch from his pocket and slipped the bundles inside it, yanked his sweater up and wrapped the pouch tight around his waist.

He slammed the safe closed, slid the panel back and left the room, putting on his jacket as he went. As required, his wife was just leaving the bottom step, with her own small bag. They went out the side door and into the garage. He had only been in the house just over ten minutes. The glint of sun was stronger now in the October sky.

The colonel drove the rest of that day. While back in Washington as the sun set, his former colleagues began to search his office and then his house. The group from the log house sent out a directive that when he and his wife were found, their unexpected vacation would be made permanent.

Sarah touched his cheek, and ran a thin finger down his neck and up under his chin. Her brown eyes looked into his blue ones, but he didn't return her gaze.

"Gotta go, Sarah." He said, matching action to words, he swung his bare legs from under the sheets and reached down to gather his clothes from where they had been dropped hours before.

"Why? It's early, Barry. I thought we could talk. Spend some time together. I haven't seen you in over a week."

"You do love to talk, don't you, Sarah. Well, I have to get going. My son's got a basketball game tonight and I promised him." He stared at his face in the mirror, same square jaw, body still fairly tight, thanks to those extra workouts he'd been putting himself through lately.

"You've begged off before."

"Yeah. This one's a playoff. You know, special," he said, as he fastened his shirt.

"Well, the least you can do is kiss me good bye." she said as she pouted at his back.

He stopped for a moment and stared at both their reflections in the mirror, then, making up his mind he turned around and looked at her.

"This is the last time. Sarah."

"What? The last time?" She brought herself to her knees, coyness forgotten as she tried to assimilate his words. "What do you mean this is the last time?"

"I've been thinking about this a while. We've had a pleasant few years. I'm sure you must have realized, Sarah, sooner or later we'd have to go our separate ways. Well, today is that day. The last time for us."

"That's where you're wrong, Mr. Barry fuckin' Senator!" Sarah's voice began to rise along with the flush of color in her cheeks. "Your child will make sure this isn't the last time."

"Leave my son out of this!"

"I'm not talking about your precious son! I'm talking about the baby you and I are having!" Sarah was shrieking now.

"Don't pull that shit on me." He said, his voice a snarl, as he turned on her. "You know better than that. There is no baby." He picked up his jacket from where it was thrown over the back of a chair. "I'm leaving now, and I don't expect to hear another thing from you about any fake baby."

Sarah had left the bed, her blonde hair, usually perfectly styled was matted to her head, her silk robe wrapped around her small body. "You don't have to believe me!" She opened the drawer of the nightstand. "Here, here's the paper from the doctor. Maybe you'll believe her!"

Barry Danner, his face now contorted in anger, snatched the paper from her hand. He gave it a cursory glance and tossed it on the floor. "You expect me to believe some phony piece of paper? You're crazy. You need to grow up little girl. This is the major arena. Your small town tactics don't work here. You better head back home." Without a backward glance he left the bedroom, went down the hall and out of the apartment.

Sarah's hand went to her mouth, stifling a scream, sobbing, she fell back across the bed. She actually thought she loved him, that he loved her. How had she let herself get involved with him? Hours later she awoke to find it dark outside and the bedside clock glowed nine-thirty.

She got up, went in the bathroom, took a shower, her hair wrapped in a towel and her petite body wrapped in a white terry robe, bare feet padded into the kitchen. Her mind was numb. Why couldn't Barry believe her? What was going on? She'd noticed a change in him the last three or four weeks. Then last week, instead of getting together for dinner as usual on Wednesday, he'd called on Tuesday afternoon, telling her there'd been an emergency and he had to be away on Wednesday.

Thursday, yet another phone call, then nothing, until last night, when he called and asked if he could see her today. Here. On a Sunday. No, nothing had been normal. They'd been seeing each other for several years and nothing like this had ever happened. She didn't feel like making anything to eat. So she rummaged around in the cabinets until she found some peanut butter and crackers. She nibbled half-heartedly on the snack as she leaned on the counter staring into space. Then she looked down at the plate, disgusted, threw the last of the crackers in the garbage and went to bed.

The next morning Sarah went to work. But when she arrived, Becky, the receptionist told her that Mary Fleming wanted to see her as soon as she came in. Sarah looked at Becky in surprise, because Mary Fleming never spoke to any of the staff below her own level of Director.

Sarah walked down the hall and knocked on the paneled door.

"Come." The lilt of the voice belied the caustic person beyond.

Sarah opened the door, "Becky said you wanted to see me, Ms. Fleming?"

"Oh, yes. Sarah. Thank you for being so prompt. I do wish it was under better circumstances." The tall older woman with salt and pepper hair got up, walked around the desk, and rested a slim, beige suited hip against the polished desk facing her.

Sarah stood in the middle of the floor, flanked by two inviting leather armchairs, staring at the woman. "Better circumstances?"

"Yes. Sit down. Sit down. You realize I'm sure that the economy has taken a down turn. This office works primarily on donations, which have fallen off drastically. I have to let go everyone hired within the last three years. That's only the beginning. I'm really not sure at this point whether even that will be enough."

Sarah sat on the edge of one of the chairs. "But Ms. Fleming, only five people were hired after me and I've been here almost four years.

There are at least five hundred people working in this office. This doesn't make any sense at all. The small salaries of a few researchers won't help."

Mary Fleming stared at the younger woman for a moment, then, left her perch on the desk, her sling backed heels clicked on the wood between the oriental rugs as she sat down behind the desk.

She hesitated a moment, pushed back a stray hair into the bun at the back of her head, "I've misjudged you, Sarah. Well, I guess I might as well tell you, your job no longer exists. Your position was specially funded within our organization. That funding, um, that grant has been withdrawn. I have no opening for you to continue somewhere else within the organization right now. I might down the road. But there is nothing here now."

"What do you mean specially funded? I thought I worked for the Denton Group. What have I been doing? All that research? If not for Denton then for who, for what?" Sarah couldn't begin to fathom what this woman had just told her. "What kind of nonsense is this?"

"To tell you the truth, Sarah, that's why I'm handling this instead of your immediate supervisor. Denton Group was specifically requested to hire you. We have now been directed to let you go. Might I add, I'm informed your severance package is most generous. But there is a stipulation." Ms. Flemings' hands, clasping and unclasping in front of her belied her calm voice.

"A stipulation as well? I'm being let go and you're giving me a stipulation?" Sarah was fighting back tears, and she could hear the tremor in her voice, but she was determined that the well groomed woman across from her would not see her break down.

"Just a small one, and that is that you return home immediately."

"Return home? Return home? Why should I? I have a perfect right to stay here in Washington. I thought I could work here in Washington, help out, help my country in some small way. I thought my research for Denton Group was at least a way to start. Now I find out I don't even know who I was working for and I'm out on the street. Well, I suppose I might as well go home to Seattle. At least those are people I can trust."

"Well, you're not destitute. You've been an excellent employee and

I've given you a good reference. Your desk has been cleared out and your personal items will be sent to your apartment. I've been requested to give you this," Mary Fleming said, as she handed a thick envelope to Sarah across the desk. My understanding is that the contents will help you out until you can find something else."

Sarah stood up realizing she had been dismissed. She took the manila envelope, thanked the woman and left the office. She went to the ladies room and in a cubicle opened the envelope. Inside was a reference from Ms. Fleming, a cashier's check for fifteen thousand dollars and a one-way ticket in her name for a flight to Seattle. She pulled out a stapled document and unfolded it to reveal an insurance policy stating that she had personal health insurance for one year.

On her way back to her apartment she deposited the check in her bank account. When she got home she called the special number she had for Barry and left a message. Then she called home and chatted with her mom for a while, telling her she would be returning home in a few days.

Barry called her back later that afternoon, "Sarah, I'm so sorry. I wasn't thinking straight, so much on my mind. You had every right to be angry."

"I wanted to tell you about the baby last week, but I didn't see you. Then you seemed so distant I didn't know whether I should."

"Can I make it up to you? Please, Sarah. Let's go out to dinner tonight. Okay?"

"Uh, well, all right." She said hesitantly. She hadn't wanted to give in to him so quickly, but as usual, despite her feelings to the contrary, she agreed to meet him at one of his favorite restaurants at 7:30.

Sarah caught a cab in front of her building at seven. When she went into the restaurant she was greeted by the maitre d' who informed her that Barry would be unable to join her. She stood there, shocked, her cheeks flaming with embarrassment, not knowing what to do. She turned toward the door, hesitated, turned back to speak to the man, but he was already escorting the couple, that had been behind her, into the restaurant.

Sarah went back out and began to look for another cab. A limousine pulled up, and the uniformed driver jumped out.

"Ms. Martin?" He said as he walked around the back of the car.

Sarah looked up, surprised to see Barry's driver standing there.

"He asked me to bring you to a different restaurant and told me I was to apologize to you for his changing things at the last minute."

"Oh? Well, all right, Jim. Thank you. Apology accepted."

The elderly driver helped her into the back and returned to the driver's seat. He drove away from the downtown section of Washington and into the suburbs of Arlington. On a side road he pulled over and stopped.

"Please wait just a moment, miss." He said as he got out of the car.

Sarah turned and looked out of the back window, where nothing but a street light met her gaze. She looked out of the tinted side windows and saw only trees. She couldn't even see the driver in the darkness.

The doors on each side of her opened and two hooded figures jumped in each grabbing her by the arm. Another figure jumped in the vacated driver's seat and the limousine sped away into the darkness.

Sarah immediately began to scream and twist violently against the pressure on her arms, but suddenly her mouth was roughly taped over, her arms bound behind her back, and she was rolled off the seat onto the floor of the car. While she lay there a sweet smelling cloth was held over her nose and she lost consciousness.

An hour later the car stopped on a deserted bridge and the unconscious young woman was thrown over the side into the fast moving current of the river below. The limousine hadn't stopped more than forty-five seconds before it took off on the return trip to Washington. It stopped yet again in Arlington and the regular driver returned to the vehicle and drove back to the underground garage where all the limousines, private cars and drivers waited for the people above to finish the business of governing the country in yet another late night session.

Early the next morning at the Dulles Airport, an attractive blonde young woman took a flight to Seattle. Her name on the passenger list was Sarah Martin. Upon arrival at the airport in Seattle, she disappeared into the city.

A week later, an anonymous tip was received by police about a car floating in the Potomac River. Three men were found stuffed in the back seat. All had been shot in the back of the head. Newspapers went into a frenzy of headlines about a possible mob hit in the Capital. Congressmen and Senators made loud statements about not allowing such mob activity in the city that housed the seat of government for the greatest nation in the world.

A week later a call was received by Mary Fleming in the offices of the Denton Group, the oil lobbying research firm for which Sarah Martin worked.

"Ms. Fleming, I'm really sorry to bother you, I'm Doreen Martin, when I asked for Sarah they insisted upon getting you on the phone."

"You mean Sarah Martin?"

"Yes. She's my daughter."

"Oh. She was going home to Seattle, Mrs. Martin. Although I'm not sure exactly when, she hasn't worked here for about two weeks now."

"Yes, I know, she said she was leaving the job, but when I couldn't reach her at her apartment, I thought I'd try her there."

"I can understand your concerns, Mrs. Martin. I wish I could help you but I knew nothing about her plans except that she was expecting to return home. I haven't seen her since she left my office her last day here."

"All right. I'll have to call the police then I guess. I appreciate your help, Ms. Fleming."

"No problem at all. She probably just took a short vacation for herself. She received an excellent severance package. You know she probably took a little trip and will be in touch with you shortly."

"You may be right, but that wasn't her plan when I spoke with her. Well, thank you again, Ms. Fleming. Good bye."

Immediately after Mrs. Martin hung up Mary Fleming dialed a number, reached in her top desk drawer and flicked on a switch.

A masculine voice answered. Mary Fleming spoke urgently "Sarah Martin's mother just called here. She said her daughter never made it home to Seattle. You wouldn't know anything about that would you?"

"Just thought I would ask. That girl was a great researcher, super worker. I can't understand why you didn't want her to continue."

"Right. It's none of my business. Well, you asked me to let you know if anyone came around asking about her. I've done my job." She hung up the phone, reached into the desk drawer and took out a small recorder. Mary stood up and went over to the matching wood credenza, took out her handbag, threw the machine into it, took her coat from the stand behind the door and left the office. As she walked past her startled secretary, she said, "I don't feel well, Hope. I'm going home. If I had any appointments for the afternoon, cancel them, please."

Mary Fleming took the elevator down to the garage, got in her car and left the city. When she reached home she walked into her small house in Chevy Chase, threw the days mail on a table in the living room and went up the stairs. She knew when she took the extra money to hire Sarah Martin it stunk to high heaven and now the stench had turned putrid. She had always known something would happen and she was ready for it.

She unlocked the desk drawer beside her PC and took out some media mailers. A few of the brown padded envelopes had been addressed and stamped, ready to go for months. She dropped a disc in each mailer, sealed the envelopes and stuffed them in her large handbag. That done, she looked around at the neat home office, went down the hall, looked into her bedroom, the bed still made as she had left it that morning. She walked down the stairs and left by the back door.

Her blue compact car was still sitting in the driveway an hour later when the house burst into flames. By the time firemen reached the house it was fully involved and burning white hot. A neighbor across the street told the firemen she had seen Mary come home early. She must be inside. But in searching the rubble of Mary Fleming's house after it had cooled, no body was found.

When arson investigators questioned the elderly neighbor later she told them she had seen a man walking down the street. He was young, about forty. He had knocked on Mary's door, but hadn't gone in. But then she hadn't stayed to watch everything that went on in the neighborhood. She was in her kitchen when she heard something like a "loud poof" she said. While she was checking around her own house, she happened to look across the street and saw the house in flames.

When they asked her how long had it been between the time she'd seen the man at the door and she'd heard the noise, she said 'only about five minutes, I guess.' The investigator nodded, made a note in his book, thanked the woman and left.

The firemen continued with their investigation while the rest of the neighborhood stood by and speculated on what had happened.

Ed Gately and his wife checked into a small hotel in Buggiba, Malta, overlooking the Mediterranean. During the three hour layover at Heathrow, he exchanged Canadian money for British pounds, and he and his wife purchased a few more clothes. Evelyn hadn't stopped exclaiming over the beauty of the Alps as the Air Malta plane flew over the snowfields and villages. When she saw the Mediterranean suddenly appear she gasped in surprise.

He loved his wife dearly, but he worried that people might remember the woman who had kept her eyes so glued to the window that she barely noticed when the stewardess brought their meal or the hot towels to wipe their hands. Her delicate face and brown eyes always made his heart melt, even now. Although they'd never been able to have children, she never pushed him to adopt, she always said it was much easier for them to move about quickly when he was transferred, without children to worry about. They'd had a cat for a while, but he'd run off one summer and hadn't returned.

No, it was always just the two of them. It was perfect now. No explanations to family. No need to call a son or daughter. Both their parents were dead. Sometimes he wondered about the strange games life played on one.

"Ed? Do you want to go for a walk? You know to check out some of the local sites?" Evelyn called from the balcony.

"Sure. I have a friend here on the island I want to get in touch with. I'll try to call him from the phones downstairs, while you get some information."

The two went downstairs together from their second floor room and parted in the lobby. Evelyn asked the desk clerk about places of interest and looked over the brochures he pointed out. A few minutes later Ed joined her.

"Did you get hold of your friend?" She asked as she closed up a colorful circular.

"Yep. Talk about luck. He was just about to leave his house. We can meet him in the capital, Valletta."

"Oh, that's wonderful! The clerk was telling me that we can get a bus right around the corner to take us anywhere we want to go. There's a station there."

Ed and his wife walked hand in hand down the brick sidewalk, one side was jammed with tourist shops, open stalls and grocery stores, on the other a narrow roadway bordered a promenade next to the sea. They had only gone three blocks when they found a large circular drive filled with bright orange busses, not one less than twenty years old.

"You have got to be kidding." Ed said to his wife.

"Come on. We have to look for bus twenty-five. That's the one he said goes into the capital."

"Okay, if you insist. But these things don't look as if they'll get around the block never mind around the island." He realized his wife thought they were truly on vacation and was enjoying herself.

Laughing, his wife grabbed his hand and they walked over to the little kiosk to get the correct change. They looked at the lettered cardboard signs in the windshield of each until they found the right bus, which looked about forty years old. Other tourists and locals were already on the bus, so they took separate seats. The cushioned seats had lost their color and the thick, old foam stuffing of cushions was shredding onto the floor.

The ride to Valletta went around one curve after another, then down a steep hill headed straight toward the open sea, with a swift right turn at the last minute. Ed was glad he was alone so he could memorize the route in case of an emergency later on. He had been in Malta years ago and had forgotten about the treacherous narrow roads. If he had to stay more than a day he would have to rent a car and learn them as quickly as possible in case the Leader traced them here. Philippe could help him with that as well as any weapons he might need.

Rents were reasonable here and they needed an apartment quickly. He had already made the list in his head. He knew he'd have to leave Evelyn. But this was the one place in the world he felt she'd be safe by herself for a while.

Finally the bus pulled up to the gates outside of Valletta and everyone slowly inched their way off the bus.

"Ed. This is incredible, a walled gated city," Evelyn said, as she took his arm.

"Well, that's part of the attraction of this island. It's so different from any other western country. We're meeting my friend in the square in front of St John's Co-operative Cathedral. Maybe he'll give us a guided tour."

"That would be perfect. I'm already overwhelmed." She said as she breathed in the odors of spices from the cubbyhole restaurants wedged in along the outer wall.

They walked through the gates onto the main street, surrounded by shops, American fast food restaurants, and past several missionaries. Young men dressed in crisp white shirts with name tags, black ties and wearing back packs, stopped the Maltese youth and tried to engage them in conversation.

The two kept walking down the narrow main street as Evelyn stared in wonder at the number of jewelry and lace stores. Each store was barely wider than the entrance door. Finally there was a sign for the Cathedral pointing down a side street to the right. Ed said laughing, "You'll have plenty of time to shop and look. After all we just got here."

Evelyn laughed with him. "I've just never seen things like this before. This is wonderful. We should have come here years ago."

"The army never sends us to great places like this. You should know that by now."

"Ed!" A tall, blonde young man stepped toward them from the shadow of one of the pillars in front of the church.

"Philippe! Good to see you. Thanks for meeting us on such short notice. This is my wife, Evelyn."

"Nice to meet you, Evelyn. Why don't we go inside where it's cool, quiet," he said as he stepped between them.

The three walked into the enormous building. Evelyn moved slightly ahead of them looking at the many tombs that formed the floor. "We have to talk and now," Ed hissed close to the ear of his friend.

Philippe nodded. "I want to show Ed something, if you don't mind, Evelyn. I've waited years to get him over here. You might like to walk around, there are several beautiful chapels on each side and of course a gift shop."

"Oh. No, problem. It will give me time to wander around at my own pace. I'll meet you two back here," she said, her voice hushed in deference to the holy place.

The two men walked quickly up the left side of the church and disappeared through a chapel door that led to the burial vaults of the Knights of St. John. They walked down the steps into one of the vaults and through an iron gate, which Philippe closed quietly behind them.

"What's happened to bring you here, Ed? I don't hear from you for years and then out of the blue you're on my doorstep."

"The world is about to go crazy, Philippe. Completely crazy. I walked out on my job and by now they're probably looking to kill me for what's in my head."

"What the hell could you be mixed up in that someone would want to kill you? Who is looking for you? Who are they?"

Quickly Ed brought Philippe up to date on the events of the last few years. Then he began to tell him of the events of the last seventy-two hours.

"I didn't think anything of the meeting at all. Granted, I was surprised at the people they had talk to us. Representatives from other countries, but as usual we were given no names or even what country they represented. It was when we were given our procedural sheets that I found out what they were really planning."

"Don't keep me in suspense, Ed. You never cut and run from anything. What could be so bad?"

"I have trouble even putting it into words." He paused and walked around the center tomb, touching the cold stone. "These people believe that to reach their goals a certain number of people will be lost, an acceptable loss. In any great endeavor to move the world forward, whether war, or even some of the large building projects like dams, bridges, people are lost. But not like this, Philippe. Never like this. Not in America.

"I was supposed to inform the President that within the next several months there would be several aggressive acts on the American people and civilians around the world by terrorists. But that this would all start within the next month. They have already placed their plans in motion and the losses would reach well into the thousands."

Philippe gasped and his face blanched under his tan. "If they know why don't they stop them?"

"They, this supposedly altruistic group I joined, paid terrorists to perform these acts to bring the American people and the rest of the world together in a strong unity that would be fortified by the strength of millions. They consider the losses to be minimal. When the terrorists have completed their work, they will be terminated immediately."

Philippe sat down on the side of a tomb, unable to continue to stand under the weight of what he had just heard. He shook his head from side to side. "No wonder they want to kill you, walking around with this kind of knowledge. Do you know what the exact plans are?"

"No. Only when the first one, whatever it is, is going to happen. That will be the largest with the largest loss of life. They're looking for several thousands. The others will be smaller, but all over the world. At precisely staggered intervals. Just enough to ensure that everyone, all countries pull together. I can't believe how cold that sounds, Philippe.

"Regulating how much bloodshed is enough to pull the world

together. What the hell kind of group is this? What kind of people are they? What did you do when you found out?"

"Nothing immediately. I just followed normal procedure. But I just couldn't take it. I was gone several hours I'm sure, before they noticed me missing. I figure I had at best a six to eight hour head start."

"Okay, Ed, how can I help you? What do you need from me?"

"Get Evelyn an apartment here, sign the lease for a year in the safest place on this island you can find." He slid his hand into a side pocket of his jacket and came out with a handful of large bills.

"No problem, I can do that today."

"Well, this one will be a problem. I need fresh identification. I've used two different sets already just to hide us getting here. Here is the name that you will rent the apartment under for Evelyn. It's safer for her to stay there without me." He pulled a slip of paper from his breast pocket and handed it to his friend. "I need at least three sets of ID for myself. I don't want to stay on this island longer than forty-eight hours unless I have to. We've already been here for five."

"I can do this. I have friends with properties and they have other friends. The safest place is Mdina. I'll see if I can get her in there by tomorrow. I'll get you out of here by tomorrow night with your ID. Where do you want to go?"

"I think it's best to hide in plain sight, but I need to start in Greece. But here's what I would like someone to do for me. Someone you can trust who is about my height and build. You know the drill. Use this passport and have them fly from the Caribbean to South America and move about several different countries as quickly as possible. Can you get that done?" The dark blue folder with the eagle slipped from hand to hand in the dim light.

"Ed, that's the easy part. Say about twelve to twenty-four hours in each country should lay enough notice around for them to follow. Then we reach Mexico and destroy this passport and begin the long trip home."

"Less than twelve if possible. Just long enough to go through customs than out again. You and I need to keep in touch somehow, what's the best way? We left our cell phones back at home in the states."

"Post office box and I'll give you a special phone number. No problem." Philippe wrote down a name address and phone number on a pad, tore off the sheet and gave it to Ed. "Call this phone number tonight at 8pm no earlier, I will make sure you have a safe cell to use before you leave. Here is where you have your wife go in the morning and this is where you should meet me late tomorrow afternoon. Have you told her anything of this?"

"No. She thinks I was given a vacation and surprised her with this trip. I'll have to tell her some of the truth or at least something plausible, otherwise she'll never agree to stay here by herself."

"Good wife material, Ed. Never asks questions."

"Sometimes I wish she would. But don't get me wrong. She's just so damn supportive of everything I do. She thinks of me like... like one of these knights, I guess. Even after twenty years." He said gesturing to the tomb they were now both leaning on.

"Keep an eye on her for me, Philippe. I don't think I'm going to get out of this alive."

"I'll have my wife meet her, introduce her to people. That will be the easiest way. But so far you're ahead of them and you've got a plan. I'll do my best to keep you both alive."

"Okay. I guess that's it. I just wish I had some weapons for defense. You can't get a paper clip through Heathrow."

"Done. I have enough connections to get you set up and out of here tomorrow night with everything you need."

"Thanks, Philippe. I hated springing this on you like this, but, I had no one else I could trust."

"After what you did for me I owe you, Ed. I wouldn't be alive now. I told you then, anytime, anything. I meant it." He clapped his friend on the back and they started from the underground vault.

"Where can I take Evelyn for a nice dinner tonight?"

"You're staying in Buggiba right?"

"Yep."

"There's a hotel there with a great restaurant, fantastic food, view of the sea, The Dolce. If you took the bus here it's next to the bus depot."

"I remember seeing it. Perfect. Thanks again, Philippe."

They chatted quietly as they walked back toward the entrance of the church. Ed looked around keeping an eye out for Evelyn, and raised a hand in a wave when he saw her stroll under the arches looking at murals.

"An attractive woman, Ed. No wonder you want to keep an eye out for her."

"Up to now, friend, I've been exceptionally lucky. Let's hope it holds out."

Evelyn came up to the two men. She looked from one to the other, a question in her eyes, on her face, but she said nothing. She simply took her husband's arm and held it tightly.

"It's been wonderful meeting you, Evelyn. I have to run. Business you know. But I'll be seeing you both tomorrow." Philippe said. He turned and walked out of the door.

"Darling. I think jet lag is catching up with me." Evelyn said to her husband. "Could we just go back to the hotel?"

"Sure. Good idea. Philippe told me there is an excellent restaurant in that hotel next to the bus stop. We can have a quiet dinner there later."

"Fine. Right now I just need to take a nap." She said as they left the cool of the church and stepped into the bright sunlight.

The man sat in his favorite of the many leather chairs in his study. Beside him on the table was a manila folder. Across the cover the word 'confidential' was stamped in red. The man's angular face was flushed nearly the color of the stamp, his anger was so great. He didn't want to speak to the younger man standing at attention, near the door, until he was once again under control.

The adage about 'not shooting the messenger' popped into his mind and helped to calm him.

"Michael," he said his voice quiet, "do you know anything about this situation?" He tapped the folder.

"No, Sir. I was told to bring that to you. I'm not cleared to read anything directed to you."

I'll bet. The man thought to himself. But aloud he said, "Excellent. Tell Sir James we will be meeting at the third place tomorrow night, usual time."

"Yes, Sir. Good night, sir." The impeccably dressed man left, closing the door quietly.

He hated to have meetings so close together. But these sudden disappearances, and that fool Danner. They had to clip his wings. What the hell was that man thinking to pull that kind of nonsense? There was too much riding on this action to allow these kinds of problems to cause delays or undermine the project.

He felt safe in his haven, locked behind three foot thick walls, in a mansion built in the late 1800's by one of the railroad magnates. In the winter, he could stay here isolated by the mountains and the snow. But now that NASA had assured them of the signal they had to get prepared and that meant showing the outsiders a united front. They only had two years to bring the world together. If that meant innocent people had to be sacrificed to help unity, so be it. They had to expand, grow, and lead the world now.

Their ancestors had agreed long, long ago, when this group had been started, to do whatever necessary for the good of the earth and all of mankind. Each father prepared, schooled and shared with the son or in some cases daughter, or niece or nephew, the need to continue this group and its mission. The work of the group was to plan and operate behind the scenes to move the governments of the world forward and together for the greater good. Over two hundred and fifty years, the leading families had managed to keep friendships, and in many cases seeing scions of families marrying the daughters of others.

Outsiders were only brought in by permanent members to perform necessary day to day defined assignments. All outsiders were vetted and had the capability of fluency in several languages, the highest academic scores, and noted for their ability to remember any and all given information accurately. All were expected to have regular jobs, and in some cases assisted in obtaining the right job that would ultimately assist the group.

Now this was threatened with exposure. They had misjudged Gately, an outsider. Attacks of conscience always ruined the best people. All of his other assignments had been carried out with such immediacy that this aberration was most uncharacteristic. Suddenly, the man's face became animated, "I wonder." He said out loud.

The diamonds of his Rolex twinkled in the light of the desk lamp as he grabbed the phone and punched a button. "Ah, General. Good to find you at your post. Would you be kind enough to be at my door in two hours? I have some questions for you." He dropped the phone into its cradle, not waiting for a response.

Two hours later General Anders was being shown into the study of the one man in the world he feared.

"I'm glad you were able to come."

"You know I'm always available for you, Sir," the general said still standing just inside the door.

"Good. Good. Now, General, be so good as to sit down there," the great man gestured to an isolated chair facing him, "and tell me about your Colonel Edward Colin Gately. Tell me all about him, everything, no matter how insignificant." That said the leader of the secret group swiveled his chair around so that the only way Anders knew he was there was from the aromatic cigar smoke circling overhead.

"Ah, Ah. You have a dossier on him, Sir. When I brought him in to the group, I told you about him then, Sir."

The chair whirled around and the leader stood up, "General Anders, if I wanted to know what you had given me already I wouldn't have you in front of me. I have made a request and I expect you to follow through. Now!" Blotches of color had flushed his cheeks, his anger had returned full force. General Anders lurched up from his chair as if struck, "Yes, Sir. Right away, Sir."

Standing on his feet he began to tell the story of what he knew of Ed Gately. He was second in his class at high school in Middleton, Illinois. He made top ten in his class at Northwestern. On and on Anders voice droned, reciting almost verbatim what was in the file.

"You learned your lessons well, General, now tell me what's not in the files. Tell me about his parents, his wife, his friends, his hobbies."

"Uh. He's married, Sir. His wife's name is Evelyn. They've been married twenty-two years. I…I…uh…think his parents are both dead. Never saw him play golf or tennis, Sir."

"Well, General Anders, I think you have been very remiss in bringing someone about whom you know so very little into our fold. I'd like you to find out quite a bit more about our Colonel Gately. Quite a bit. Oh, and General, you have forty-eight hours in which to complete your task." With that he left the room, quietly closing the door on the startled General.

The General looked at his watch. Three thirty in the afternoon. By the time he made it back to the office two hours at least would be gone. He half ran to the front door so quickly that the butler barely had time to open it for him and hand him his cap. He ran down the stone steps to his car and jumped in.

"Put the sirens on as soon as you leave the gate. I have to be back at the office faster than you've ever made it," he yelled to the driver.

Then he grabbed the cell phone from its charger, and punched in his secretary's line.

"Nell, thank goodness you're there. I've got a problem and you're going to need to work overtime. Call your hubby and tell him to look for you in a couple of days. We have a crises and I need you to make these calls before I get back there." He began listing places and people for her to call.

She was protesting on the other end that he was going too fast. "I don't have time to slow down. Just get it done."

He hung up and began another call, this one wouldn't go through, the circuits were busy. The car's siren was like a chant in the background that minutes and seconds had already been lost.

Damn. He'd been so sure of Gately. Career man. Upstanding, straight arrow. He'd even checked to see why they had no children. Pulled the medical records and found it had been the wife. Everything had been right up front. He should have checked the parents at least to know whether they were alive or dead. If dead he was expected to know how they died. But he'd been in such an all fired hurry to bring Gately in. The man was so damned brilliant, had a mind like the proverbial steel trap. There wasn't a thing you could talk about that he didn't already know quite a bit about. What had sent him running for the hills? He knew when Gately was found he'd be terminated, but right now he knew that within forty-eight hours if he didn't have something on Gately's background he himself would be terminated. Never mind just something, he had to know what kind of toothpaste his grandfather preferred.

He slammed the door of the car before it had completely stopped and ran up the steps of the office building. He barely acknowledged the salutes of those he passed as he was waved through security and slid his arm into a closing elevator door.

His secretary had apparently been called by the driver or security that he was on his way because she met him as he stepped off the elevator. Her voice was chattering at his ear as he strode toward his office, her heels barely keeping pace with him.

When he reached his desk he looked at her for the first time, "Good job as usual, now just finish the rest of that list, and if anyone wants me I can't be disturbed."

"Yes, Sir," Nell said and left the office.

There were three phones on his desk, he picked up one and punched in a number.

"Peg, Darling, you remember the talk we had when we were on vacation, well it's time to sell that car now." He paused, "Yes, dear, I know you love that old car, but it's time for it to go." He said no more and hung up the phone. He knew that his wife would immediately pack up the children and leave for a predetermined destination. If anyone were listening they would think he was talking about the '67 Chevy he always kept in mint condition. Probably think he'd had an offer. He didn't want Peg and the kids anywhere near Washington if he didn't win this fight.

For the first time he understood Gately's disappearance. The man simply realized he couldn't be a party to mass murder as a way to global unity. Anders stared at the gold desk set. It's inscription mocking him, "Honor Above All Else". He had long ago ceased to be an honorable man. He believed in the cause of global unity, order and peace. But the price was escalating even beyond his own capability to stomach and now it was too close to home.

Bud Anders turned in his swivel chair and opened the credenza behind him under the window. The blinds were drawn against dark skies. Rain was predicted for tonight. He pulled Gately's confidential file from the locked inner safe and spread the contents out on his desk. He checked and rechecked looking for any connections he had missed.

Friends, only one or two showed up and both had been killed. One in a car accident in Germany and the other in the last days of the Gulf war. Not good odds to be his friend. The man had always kept to himself. Even his wife didn't join the usual groups or committees.

Neighbors when questioned hardly saw them. The lawn service was paid monthly, the cleaning service, everything was paid by check and on time. When their bank account was frozen only fifty dollars remained in both the savings and checking. No safety deposit boxes. Gately and his wife were almost non-existent. They had one credit card and it was only used to fill the gas tanks of their personal cars. There wasn't even any liquor in the house when they searched it only hours after realizing he'd disappeared.

Who was he? Who was Gately? There had to be something here. Something he was missing. That was usually the way these things turned up, right in front of you all the time.

Anders pushed the few papers around in the folder and looked again at the information on Gately's high school background. No great athlete, two years of track, played baseball freshman and sophomore years, a member of the debating team, graduated salutatorian, national honor society. Perfect college material. No fraternities in college, graduated summa cum laude. They had already talked to his advisors and professors in college only to find out that his girlfriend, who later became his wife, was also his closest friend.

Bud Anders slammed the folder on his desk, disgusted. He went over to the coffee pot and poured a cup. Nell always had it ready. He hoped she wouldn't be pulled into his mess. She had been loyal to him for the last fifteen years he'd been in the Pentagon. But she didn't know the first thing about…about… He couldn't even bring himself to think the name of the group that would be his demise.

He called Nell on the phone. "Any word back from your calls yet? Time's wasting, Nell."

"I know, Sir. Um… Can I see you for a minute with some of these? Just to go over them?"

"Sure, come on in." She must have something and someone was nearby.

Thirty seconds later, Nell walked in. Her unlined brown face belied her age. He knew she was a grandmother. Despite having a figure that would be considered chunky by some, she always dressed to enhance her best features, playing down her size. Based on what he knew of other assistants in this place Nell was among the best and the brightest.

She closed the door quietly. "I don't quite know how to say this, Sir, but something very strange is going on."

"What do you mean strange?"

"Anytime I've ever called one of these people, usually they get right on the phone, today they are all on their way out the door on an emergency, unavailable to speak with you as they are in a confidential meeting, or say 'I'll have to get back to him'. One I called, Tom Dickson, his wife answered, she was hysterical, in tears, saying her husband had just been killed in a car accident. He was backing out of their driveway and a truck ran right into the driver's side door."

Anders craggy face blanched when he heard what happened to Tom. Now he knew he was in major trouble. They weren't even giving him the time, or allowing him access to the people who might help him. The word had gone out. He knew how it worked, he'd done it himself many times. He didn't like being on the receiving end.

"What do you want me to do, Sir? Other than what I told you earlier about security arrangements and surveillance around Colonel Gately's house and office during the time after he disappeared I have nothing else."

"There's nothing else you can do, Nell. You might as well go home. No sense in hanging around then. You got each name on the list I gave you?"

"Yes, sir. It was the same everywhere." She handed him a hand written sheet with multiple check marks and notations running down the paper.

"Right. Well, call your hubby and let him know you're on the way home after all." His voice had quieted and sounded older than it had earlier.

"Yes, sir. If you're sure there's nothing I can help you with. You said it was a crises." She frowned, her face showing concern.

"It is. But I… uh, it's more top secret than your classification, so I'll have to deal with the rest of the calls on my own. Thanks, Nell."

The woman had turned to leave when Anders spoke up, "Why don't you take the rest of the week off. Put in for a couple of weeks' vacation before you leave, I'll sign and route it for you."

"Thank you, Sir," she said surprise in her tone and on her face.

When she left, Anders pulled a form from his desk drawer, filled it out to request a bonus for his secretary. That with the vacation time would ease finding herself without a job come Monday. She would get the usual government pension, but this would help tide her over until she could decide what she wanted to do.

He completed the paperwork slid it into an interoffice envelope, went out to Nell's desk, signed her vacation request and put both items in the box for late pick-up. He returned to his office, drew his hand down across his face, sighed tiredly, and looked at the file yet again. Were those friends really dead? He booted up his computer and began the task he hated most, searching. Probably why he hadn't done the job before. He could only rely on himself now that Tom was dead. The man had pulled more of his irons out of the fire than he could think of.

Finally, the access screen. He punched in the names of the two friends. The one who was killed in Germany in the car accident in 2007, Karl Lieske. He had also been in intelligence in the army. Had gone to Germany on holiday with his wife. Both killed in a pileup on the Autobahn in the fog. He was working for Molson Securities at that time as Director of their Acquisitions Department. Whatever that was.

Paul Landers had been killed only days before the final pull out from the Gulf. He had been a 22-year old sergeant, at the end of his second eighteen month stint. Stepped on a land mine, identified by his dog tags, sent home in a body bag. Parent's had been divorced. Mother had claimed the body, buried in some backwater town in Maine.

Anders continued the search to see if either parent was still alive. His search reached a dead end when he found that Lander's mother had died of cancer only three years after burying her son. The father had disappeared while his son was still in grade school.

Anders sat at his desk, collar loosened to reveal curly grey hairs slipping out of his white undershirt as he doggedly continued for another hour, searching through Gately's and Landers' military records, but without success. He knew how easy it would have been to change tags if someone had wanted to disappear. He didn't have the time to get bodies exhumed for DNA testing to see if mother and son were indeed a match. But he had a hunch that was the one he wanted. But when he found pictures of both Landers and Lieske, he knew that was also a dead end.

He printed the last picture of the young man and the few details he'd been able to get from the record. That in hand, along with Gately's file he left the office for what could be the last time.

He signed out a car for himself in the basement garage and left the city. If he was unable to reach the last person on his list, the only name he hadn't given Nell then he might as well give up. He couldn't check these things out alone. Not with someone looking over his shoulder, watching every move. He needed help and he certainly wouldn't get it in Washington.

Once he got home to his now empty house, he turned on the television. He wanted to see if there was any information about his friend Tom's death. He waited for the eleven o'clock news to come on while he ate a plate of lasagna Peg had left in the oven for him. When he saw a picture of the driver of the truck being interviewed after the accident that had killed his friend, Anders shot up out of his chair and spilled the plate into the floor.

The small house was shrouded in a darkness only the heavily leafed trees of an old forest could provide. A tall man dressed in a dark coat, moved slowly from the car into the house, stopped just inside the door and the house was flooded with light. He closed the door quietly and waited. Just the two of them tonight. He hated this house. No room to move about. But there was no need in opening up one of the lodges for this meeting.

When Michael had returned from delivering the message he said the Leader had been very angry. Even though he spoke quietly as always afterwards, Michael had noticed the sudden flush of his face while he read the document. Thank heaven Michael was not only discreet, but blessed with good common sense and an observant eye.

Sir James Galston, like his father, grandfather and great-grandfathers before him, was a leading member of the group. As the direct descendant of one of the founding fathers he had almost as much power as the man he was waiting for, yet he preferred his silent position, one step behind the Leader. Galston's elegance and bearing belied the ruthlessness of the man. He demanded and received absolute loyalty from his staff. Even more now since the incarceration of the two young gardeners who after having been overheard gossiping about the comings and goings at his home, he'd had their homes raided by police, who conveniently found several ounces of cocaine.

He had few vices, one of which was smoking a pipe, which was now stuck unlit in the corner of his thin lipped mouth. Security demanded that no smoking materials were ever used at a meeting place. The distinct odor of a cigar, pipe or cigarettes could linger for an observant searcher.

He heard the quiet engine of a car, just before it shut down and coasted onto the gravel at the front of the house. He retreated further into the small house, peering from an alcove he could see the front door, but still slip out the back door if needed.

The door opened. "Sir James?" The leader called out. "Still up to your games of hide and seek?"

"I was just checking to make sure it was only you." Sir James answered as he left concealment and walked toward the newcomer.

"Caution is highly commendable, my friend. Well, let's get down to business. I'm sure your time is too short as well to waste on these problems."

The two men sat down on the only two cushioned chairs in the room.

"Have you found Gately?" Sir James asked quietly.

"No. It's as if he and his wife dropped off the earth. Our bigger problem right now is this nonsense with Danner. As one of the members of our core group we have to accord him certain status, but this mess he's gotten mixed up in far outweighs anything any of our members has done so far. Do you have any ideas?"

"His son is too young to enlist to keep his place. No nephews either or anyone to take his place. Should we just hold a place open until his son is old enough?"

"From what you're saying, Sir James, You consider him deceased. Am I right?"

"Some sadly unfortunate accident, skiing, car, hit and run. The worrisome part is the woman who was working for him. She's also disappeared."

"Let her. It's impossible for her to know anything of us. I think she's scared of him."

"True. He has always been difficult to keep in line. He's been warned before about his dalliances and rough tactics. Nothing like his father, although John did warn us that he was headstrong."

"Hah! Headstrong!" The leader almost spat the words. "Sir James, that man is beyond headstrong. We've been more than lenient. He's playing in our back yard and leaving his stinking garbage."

"Then we are in agreement."

"Yes."

"I can easily have something prepared if you wish."

"Sir James, anything you decide to prepare will be at your discretion. All I ask is that the timetable is not too far out. We have too many things upcoming in the near future."

"True. Was there anything else?"

"Yes. General Bud Anders. We have a real sticky problem there as well. He brought Gately in for White House liason."

"Right. What else has happened?"

"I've had all of our people working on that disappearance with no luck. Usually there is something. It's been only days but they should have been seen somewhere. So when I questioned Anders further about our mutual friend. He knew less about him than I did."

"Was he crazy bringing him in without a thorough check?"

"Let's call it forgetful. He has forty-eight hours to find out something and get us something to go on. Unfortunately, he will not be receiving any help from his friends. He is completely on his own, Sir James. If he gets what's needed fine, but if not, then, well, I think he'll be going to some very remote place to complete his tour of duty. Unfortunately, it will only be less than a week."

"Ah. Good work. That should keep him quite busy."

"According to surveillance he's extremely busy. He only has twenty-four hours left."

Just then a small buzzing sounded in the otherwise quiet room. Sir James pulled out his phone. One graying eyebrow raised as he read the message on the tiny screen.

"Well, well, well. Our man Gately has been spotted in St John in the Caribbean getting on an airplane bound for Belize. Alone."

"So he dumped the wife somewhere and is now on the run. We have pictures of the wife. She's probably down there sunning herself and we'll easily pick her up. That will bring him up by the short hairs."

"I'll take care of that at the same time I'm working out the other problem."

"Excellent, Sir James. You know I think you and I get so much more done between the two of us than when the rest are here."

"By the way. Any news from NASA recently?" Sir James asked as he walked to the door.

"Only that our invitation has been accepted and they will be here during "our Pleiades" as they put it, in two years. They have certain criteria for landing and meeting which they have asked us to prepare. They will be sending us that information shortly."

"So the plans are definitely a go. This is an historical time for all of us." Sir James said. "Let's hope we can keep a tight rein on everything."

"That's why we have to get rid of any glitches now, Sir James. We can't allow these problems to stall the motion of progress."

"Never. Good night." The squire of Badgely Manor left the small cabin in the woods, went to his car and drove off into the night.

The leader stayed behind, checking the entire building, even the cushions for telltale signs that they had been there. But as usual there was nothing. Both were the most cautious of men. They kept their enviable place in the group because neither ever left anything to chance and each covered the others tracks. It had even been that way in school.

Anthony Morris Vanderlin, as he was known then, had gone to school in England, meeting James Galston there. Being the foreigner, Vanderlin was always the guest of the Galstons at Badgely Manor during school holidays. When it came time for college, James Galston came to America and was always the guest of the Vanderlins at their estate in Connecticut.

Only when the two had graduated did they find out that their friendship was not a chance meeting and their entire schooling had been designed to forward the needs of the group. They each earned higher degrees at Harvard, traveled together around the world for almost two years, before

Galston's father died. Sir James was immediately inducted into the group, but Anthony had to wait a few more years. Despite that fact, upon his entrance into the group he became a force to be reckoned with.

Now, some forty years later, no one, not even Sir James uttered his name. He was known only as the Leader. Vanderlin trusts, money, foundations, stocks and real estate were so enmeshed in the fabric of the United States and the world that with every twenty-four hour period he earned almost twenty million dollars. Few people ever heard the Vanderlin name mentioned anymore. Their Connecticut estate had been sold soon after Anthony's father died. His mother had been moved to a small cottage of fifteen rooms on Cape Cod.

Anthony worked at finding a wife that would look good on his arm, educated, have little or no family and not mind where he was or with whom. When he finally found her, he was forty-four years old. Although she was a very attractive woman, she had never been very healthy. She became pregnant four years into the marriage and died from toxemia, giving birth, but they were able to save his heir, a girl.

Now his daughter was finishing high school in Switzerland and ready to go to college. She had been accepted to several. But his plans, as his father's, were to be followed. She would go to Yale.

The leader turned out the lights and left the house. He hated the lonely drive home from here. But he did not allow the chauffeur near this house, or any of the others. He always drove himself. It was already one-thirty in the morning and while he didn't require much sleep, he'd had an exhausting day.

Minutes later, a shadowy figure wearing camouflage emerged from the woods, and moved stealthily toward the house. He opened the door, stayed low to the ground, and as the leader before him, checked the entire area with the aid of a small flashlight attached to his cap, in case even a piece of tobacco from his boss' pipe had fallen. Once, many years before, during such a check he'd found a button that someone had lost. He'd turned it in the next morning to Sir James. Sir James had given him a substantial raise and told him that he was to continue the practice after each meeting. But Sir James had never shared that fact with the Leader. He preferred to keep many things to himself.

The apartment in Mdina was beautiful. The graceful roof overhung the small balconies of the bedroom and living room. It came comfortably furnished, with the electricity included. Evelyn loved the apartment, but that was all she was happy about.

After dinner, the night before, as the couple walked and then stood by the Mediterranean Ed told his wife as much of the truth as he could. It had been one of the hardest things he'd ever had to do in his life. But for some strange reason she still looked at him with the same trust and love in her eyes. He couldn't believe that she hadn't ranted and raved and cried and screamed at him for bringing her to a strange country and abandoning her. That she hadn't berated him with the lie he'd been living. He knew he would never understand this wonderful woman he'd been fortunate enough to marry.

Now here they were at lunch in a small restaurant, just outside the walls of Mdina, with lace curtains at the windows overlooking the streets and parking area.

"You're sure you like that place? We can look at another one. There's time."

"No. That one is perfect, Ed. It's high enough to see everything, yet only two flights down to the street. Plus with the balconies I can sit out and read during the day." She held his hand in her own smaller one. "I can't believe you're leaving though." She brought his hand up to her lips, then held it against her cheek.

"I explained...

"I know, I know. I'm hoping this all works out and you'll get back here safely and soon."

"Believe me, darling, so do I. Once I get back we can stay right here. I just want to make sure of that."

"Yes. As usual you have to check everything out for yourself."

"That's the only way not to have a mistake made. If you make it you have no one to blame for it but yourself. So I triple check, because I don't want to blame me."

They both laughed but it was strained. Ed paid the check and they returned to the narrow streets of the city. They had to wait, while a horse and buggy turned a corner, then they climbed up the hill to the apartment.

Once inside, Ed pulled out his money belt. He sorted through the money and handed her a large stack of hundreds. "This should take care of you for quite a while here, groceries, clothing, movies. But if you have to get away or move fast here are two credit cards that you can use to get cash and Philippe will help you do so. I'm going to wire Philippe some more money to give you in about a week."

"Ed, you know I don't like to ask questions, but is Philippe someone you are sure you can trust with your life?"

"I'm trusting him with your life, Darling, that's a lot more precious than mine. But I need help. He's the only one I know in the world, that has the connections and the knowledge. I have to rely on him. There is no one else."

"It's just that..."

"You've never met him before. True. I didn't want him in the States. I didn't want anyone to know him. Just in case. I was protecting him. Now he's protecting you and me."

"All right. Then I guess I'll have to trust him as well."

"That's my Eve. I have to go meet Philippe now. I don't think I'll be coming back here until this is over. However long it takes. Philippe will get messages to you from me now and again." Ed Gately held his wife in his arms trying to memorize every inch of her as he had last night as they'd made love. He knew and now she knew as well, he might never return. He kissed her as she raised her arms to hug him around the neck. Then he reached up and took each of her hands in his and kissed their palms. "You know I love you, always." He whispered against her hands as he looked into her eyes.

Her eyes had filled with tears, she blinked as she drew away from him. "You'll be late. I love you, dearest. Come back to me."

Colonel Ed Gately took a last look at his beloved wife then walked through the door. The balconies didn't overlook the front door so she couldn't watch him walk up the street. But she wouldn't have as she was lying across the bed crying.

Forty-five minutes later, he and Philippe were sitting on a bench watching the colorful boats in the fishing village of Marsaxlokk. "We'll be walking over to that building over there. Looks like an old mansion, but its apartments now. Everything is ready. Which is why we're meeting here. You'll be leaving in a couple of hours. Broad daylight I know, but by tomorrow morning you'll be further and safer."

"Something's happened?

"You're double was spotted last night in St. John. He was only changing planes. But they didn't know that. He'd just gotten off a Virgin Atlantic, so he had his one small piece of luggage and was walking to the flight for Belize. Somebody looked at him, was startled then walked off in a hurry. He hung back a little to see what would happen. Guy went straight to a pay phone. He had first tried to use his cell. Guess it wouldn't work."

"Good man."

"Yep. Glad he was around. He loves doing this kind of stuff. He's done doubles before. He can look like anybody. Anyway, he didn't stay in Belize, got a ticket right out since he'd been tracked already. He knew they'd be too close if he stayed so he took the next flight to Peru."

"Great! They can chase him for a while. Another day or so should be enough I think."

"I think you're right there. They'll be on his tail in no time. He's sharp though. Now let's go get you set up."

Two hours later, Philippe and an older man walked across the bazaar. Philippe waved goodbye to him as the older man limped onto a large fishing trawler. The mate, and the man then took off the mooring lines and raised hands in farewell as the boat got underway.

Philippe stood on the stone dock, "Be safe, my old friend," he whispered to himself. He knew before he went home he had one more task to do. He drove to the other side of the island and parked outside of Mdina. He walked into the town, went up to Evelyn's apartment and knocked.

When she opened the door, he stood there, silent for a moment before he said, "He's on his way. He asked me to come and let you know so that you wouldn't be waiting up for him."

"Thank you. Thank you for telling me."

"If you'd like, tomorrow I'll bring my wife around to meet you. She can show you the real Malta, take you to Sliema to the department stores. It's not far from Valletta."

"I'd like that. I do need to know how to get around here on my own."

"Very good. I'll have her over here around 10:30. Then you two can go where you like on your own. All right?"

"Thank you so much, Philippe."

"I had mentioned it to Ed, so he knows about your excursions. I'll see you in the morning then. Good night."

"Good night, Philippe."

As she closed the door, she felt gratitude that she wouldn't be completely alone. But worries about her husband and how much she could trust this man and his wife still nagged.

Senator Barry Danner left the Senate floor well after nine o'clock at night. But he felt it was time well spent, as the bill to increase spending to NASA had finally passed. All hurdles had been overcome and he knew he would be praised by the Leader for a job well done. This meant that any needs NASA had over the next five years would be met without the usual haggling. They had virtually opened the pocketbook. Granted it wasn't as much as they had originally wanted, but there were many small pockets of money that could be moved into the NASA spending package if needed.

He smiled to himself, small indeed. Those hidden pockets were worth over one hundred million each. This meant not only could they welcome visitors, but they could now build their own ship, to return the visit. He nodded to others as he walked confidently down the hall, accepting congratulations from several who had backed his proposals from the beginning.

He finally felt free of the weight he'd been carrying for almost four years. The bimbo was out of his life. Thank heaven Melissa had never found out about her. There were no loose ends. Granted Mary had disappeared, but she knew nothing that could affect him. He wondered idly, as the elevator took him down to the garage, if burning the house had been a mistake. Well, she hadn't been in it after all. Smart woman, that Mary. A real shame she didn't show off her better qualities, but she was too old for him back twenty years ago when he first met her and he was still a bachelor, a junior senator and they were the same age. He wondered if she remembered his father introducing them.

The elevator door opened and he walked down the line of cars to his limousine. A much younger man was standing there.

"Where's Jim?" He asked as he got in.

"Got the flu and went home sick a couple of hours ago. They called me to come and fill in for him. I'm Michael."

"Oh. Well Jim is getting up there in age. Hope he's not too sick. Anyway, I'm going straight home tonight."

"Yes, Sir."

Without another thought to the driver, Senator Danner began pulling papers from his briefcase. He hated being idle during the forty-five minute drive to his home. Which was why he never drove himself as many of the others did.

His cell phone rang, "Lissa, I'm on my way home now. Just got out of there. Break out the champagne, the bill passed." He listened for a moment then laughed. "Okay, see you in a bit, hon."

He looked at his watch then out of the window, expecting to see the lights of the Beltway.

"Michael did you find a new way to get me home? What happened to the Beltway?"

"Sorry sir, your presence is needed elsewhere right now."

"What do you mean by that?"

"Sir, I've been asked to bring you to a specific place as soon as you left. That is what I'm doing."

"Damn. I'll have to call my wife and tell her something came up and I'm going to be late." Sometimes he hated the high-handed way the Leader just walked in and took control of his life.

Michael pressed a button on the dash, looked in the mirror at the handsome dark haired senator who now looked annoyed.

"Your cell phone will no longer work, Sir."

"What? I just used it."

"Sorry, Sir. But you can no longer receive or send calls."

"What is this, some kind of weird kidnapping? I thought you worked for the Leader."

Michael answered truthfully, "No, Sir. I don't. I can tell you that I work for someone who works with him. I cannot say anymore, Sir." He pressed another button and thick plastic rolled up forming a barrier.

Senator Danner decided to sit back and enjoy the ride. There was little he could do at this point. The Leader must have already found out that the bill passed and wanted to congratulate him. Why couldn't that man ever do anything in the light of day? Every damn meeting was in the middle of the night. Who was he anyway? This man that everyone referred to as the Leader.

His father, John Danner, had told his son that the new Leader of the group ruled with an iron hand. He had talked to him of firm decisions that had come before in the early 1900's, in his own father's time. The time when the Federal Reserve Bank was set up. The history of the world and the United States rested its very basis on the strong leadership and progressive decisions of their group for almost two hundred years. Then came a leader who was soft on pressing the decisions of the group on the world leaders. The immediate result was World War Two. Unlike the planning and need for the First World War, they had lost their grip on many of the key people that were needed to feed continuity to the world.

As soon as the present leader came to power, changes in focus were quick, and the President and other heads of state knew immediately that they were again returning to the forward march of progress toward world unity. It was taking a long time to root out those who had a different vision of the world. But it was happening.

The limousine stopped at a set of iron gates, on one side was an old gatehouse. The driver leaned out and pressed buttons on a black box recessed into the wall of the little house. The gates opened slowly and the limousine drove slowly for another five minutes around twisting curves that finally ended in a paved circular drive.

"Please wait here, Sir."

The driver left the limousine and walked up the flat steps to the massive front door. He didn't wait to be let in, as Senator Danner expected, he simply walked in the door. Danner kept his eyes on the front door, waiting for it to open and the driver to return. He was startled when the drivers' door opened and a large muscular man with a bald head, and an earring in his ear got in. This was no chauffeur.

"Who are you?"

The man looked at the Senator in the rearview mirror and laughed as he started the car and headed back down the drive much faster than the ride in. The gates were still open and as soon as the car shot through they swung closed.

"Where are you taking me? What's going on here? Who are you?"

The new driver ignored his frightened passenger. He watched as the Senator tried to use his cell phone. But as Michael had told him earlier, it was useless. He tried the handles of the doors and windows but nothing happened.

The driver was roaring with laughter now. He hated politicians and when he was told about this job he couldn't have been happier. Lying sons of bitches is how he thought of all of them. For the next hour, he followed the route that he'd been shown earlier on the map. All the while, Mr. Big Shot was yelling orders or just yelling. He couldn't be sure since he'd turned off the speaker.

Then there it was, as shown on the map, the turn off next to the abandoned gas station. He swung the big car down the road and pulled in behind the derelict building. He went into the trunk and took out the tied up, gagged, elderly chauffeur, Jim, who immediately began to struggle against his bonds.

"Sorry, old man. If you didn't work for that piece of shit in the back seat you wouldn't have to go through this." He hit Jim hard on the head with a weapon that looked like it had been made out of a sock. The man went limp.

The driver untied the unconscious man and shoved him into the front seat beside him, then started the car up and turned back onto the narrow main road. The bridge was only a mile away now. He drove into the middle of the intersection and looked to the left where he saw the lights of a construction truck blink twice. He left the car in drive, jumped out as he pulled the limp body of the chauffeur over into the driver's seat and slammed the door.

The car moved slowly down the slight incline toward the bridge. The large dump truck was bearing down on it at top speed. As planned it smashed into the side of the limousine, effectively shoving it off the road beside the entrance to the bridge and into the river. The truck driver switched gears into reverse, went back and picked up the phony chauffeur.

The big truck turned down the road that the limousine had just left.

"Everything go okay?"

"Yeah. Guy was screaming and yelling in the back seat like a crazy man. When do I get my money?"

"Right now." The driver reached in his heavy vest, pulled out a .32 and shot the phony chauffeur in the head. He had barely taken his eyes off the road, he didn't want to miss the turn at the gas station. He pulled in behind it as his now dead passenger had only minutes before, and shut off the lights and the engine. He went around the front, checked the damage to the truck, then yanked the body out of the passenger side and dragged it through the broken door, into the derelict building. He propped the door back into its place, got back into the truck and left. He didn't turn on the headlights as he drove down the narrow gravel road that led to an old farm. He pulled the truck into the back of the farmhouse, next to a nondescript dark blue Ford. As he walked over to a well he shrugged out of the vest, wrapped it around the gun and dropped the package. He waited until he heard the splash.

The clean-up of the truck was going to be another matter, but he had several hours before he had to be back at Sir James' home. Michael carefully took the entire passenger door off the truck and replaced it with another one he'd left there when he'd worked out the plan. Then the passenger seat, and the cloth covering of the top of the cab.

When he had finished, it was getting light and he drove the truck back up the road, parked it well away from the derelict gas station and covered it quickly with dead branches and brush. They wanted this truck found.

He walked through the woods back to the farmhouse. He had to clean up his work area. He was glad it was getting light. That way he would be able to see that nothing had been left. He had spread out drop cloths to wrap the bloody parts from the truck. He had replaced every piece of the truck that might have had blood on it including the boost step, where some blood had pooled when he'd pulled the body from the truck. He then dumped everything down the well, replaced the wood cover he had removed the day before and threw branches and dirt over it.

Michael then left the area. He'd come back tonight with yet another car and really mess up the tracks. With so many tracks already, he'd been out here with three other cars and a different truck over the last two days, the police wouldn't be looking for just one car. They'd simply assume it was used by teenagers or druggies.

Michael went through the back gates of the mansion at 10:00 that morning and was greeted by Sir James as he came into the dining room from the kitchen.

"What is this world coming to, Michael. It seems as if a United States Senator is missing. I think I'd like to return to England for a while. Why don't we leave this afternoon? Do call the airport and have the plane readied, Michael."

"Sounds fine to me, sir. I had planned on doing a little extra work around the place tonight, but it should be all right."

"Very good. Get packed."

At two thirty that afternoon the two were headed toward the airport, when the music they were listening to was interrupted by a newscaster screaming about late breaking news.

"Senator Barry Danner's limousine has been found in Virginia. Apparently the car was hit broadside by a large vehicle and the force of the crash pushed the car into the Little Palm River. The limousine has to be pulled from the river before the bodies can be removed. The trunk of the vehicle was seen sticking up out of the water, by a youth on a bicycle earlier this afternoon. He immediately reported it to the police.

"Senator Danner disappeared last night after leaving the Senate floor. He was last seen getting in the elevator for the garage. His wife..."

Sir James leaned over and turned it off. "You know, Michael, I've been thinking of giving you a raise. Your job is very hazardous and the hours are certainly terrible."

"Well, there are times I could use more sleep, Sir."

"Today being one of them, right?"

"I can sleep on the plane, Sir.

"Speaking of the plane, Michael, there's something I'd like you to put your mind to. Once we get on the plane, we can discuss it."

Michael pulled the Mercedes into the garage at the airport next to their private hanger. He went around to the trunk and pulled out their two bags. His sunglasses hid his bloodshot eyes. He was truly tired. Driving that damn truck was bad enough, but hauling the truck doors back and forth had been a real workout. Sometimes he wished he had someone he could give part of his duties to, but so far hadn't found anyone. He'd been on the lookout for the past year.

The two walked into the office and checked in with the customs and TSA officers there who verified the comings and goings of private craft.

"Headed back home, Sir James?"

"Yes. Have to keep things going over there. My family will open the house up for tours if I'm gone too long."

"It would put a few dollars into the bank for a rainy day if you did that."

"Not to mention the muddy feet tracking through the house on a rainy day." Sir James said quickly.

"Heheheheh. You're right about that. Must be a mess to clean up. Well, you two are all cleared. When do you think you'll be coming back?"

"Oh, probably next month. Right now it depends on how I find things at home. We'll see."

"Good trip, Sir."

Michael followed his boss onto the plane. By the time the tow truck was pulling the limousine from the river and the coroner's people were taking the bodies out, Michael and Sir James were well out over the Atlantic.

The captain of the trawler, Olexaakk, left the old deck hand pretty much alone. He knew he was just getting passage to get home to Greece. He looked pale, sick and was probably just going home to die. The man had offered to help if needed, but Captain Abela was accustomed to just working with his mate. The old man would probably get in the way trying to be helpful.

The two-day trip was uneventful and the old man shuffled and limped up the dock and into the shack to show his papers. A minute later he was out again, shuffling and limping into Piraeus. People were lined up waiting for the bus that would take them into center of Athens. He shuffled into line with them, got his ticket at the small booth, followed the others onto the bus, dropped his ticket into the open palm of the driver and limped to the back. His clothes reeked of long days of saltwater and sweat.

Blue eyes looked out over the half glasses that were planted over the heavily jowled face. They peered carefully at the other passengers from under the unruly thatch of gray hair sticking out under a stained cap. The equally stained duffle bag seemed ready to fall apart at any second, with loose threads hanging from the dark piping.

He had to change before he got to the airport, and needed one of the easily accessible rest rooms. The one good thing about Europe, you didn't have to look for a building and then hunt for a public restroom. Here, with all the tourists, and the enormous population they were built into the basements of five hundred year old buildings or the backs of restaurants on a side street and actually offered a small measure of privacy.

He waited for a stop where several people left the bus and placed himself strategically in the middle of the group. There it was. He went in, looked around at the men moving through and headed for an empty stall at the end. As he expected no one gave him a second look. He took his time making the transition to a cleaner, younger man. He was now well tanned, standing straighter, wearing sunglasses, and no more jowls. He got rid of the stained duffle bag and clothing in the trash and shook it down into the bottom of the bin. He would swear he still smelled of fish. But there wasn't much he could do about that. His sweater and slacks were European in cut, marking him as a countryman. His Greek had always been excellent, which was why he'd wanted to use the country as a way to enter the country to which he was headed.

He left the public restroom half an hour after going in, walked towards the Syntagma Square bus stop, stopped in a store and bought a small back pack. Then a few stores down he picked up some odds and ends to fill the pack. He walked slowly back to the bus stop and picked up a ticket for the E95 bus to the airport.

His wife wouldn't have recognized the young Greek man who entered the airport, and informed the uninterested customs agent that he was just going to Switzerland for a couple of days. He received the needed stamp and was passed through. He looked at the ticket for SwissAir that Philippe had purchased for him. He had forty-five minutes to spare before the plane left. Just enough time to get to the gate, check in and grab something to eat.

Once he was in Switzerland he'd be safe for quite a while, but he had a lot to do. How well he got it done would depend on his ability to keep his wits about him.

As soon as the Lear jet had landed at Heathrow, Michael left the plane, went inside and booked a flight for St. Thomas in the Caribbean. The plane was leaving in two hours. He returned to Sir James who was waiting for him in the Private Club area to let him know that he had to leave almost immediately.

"That's fine, Michael. Follow that trail and see if you can find Colonel Gately's wife. Once we have her we have the leverage to bring him in. The doldts that are down there now can't find their own mothers."

"You're sure you'll be okay?"

"Home soil, Michael. Home soil. Now get going."

As soon as Michael left to catch his flight, Sir James went over to the desk and asked that his plane be serviced. He had to take off immediately. He beeped his pilot who was in the hanger area and gave him the destination. The lanky, dark haired pilot was accustomed to changes and began filing a new flight plan.

An hour later, Sir James Galston was on his way to Switzerland. He paid the pilot well and after fifteen years had had no reason to doubt him, he had always kept his mouth shut. He stayed with the plane, and slept in the back of it unless they were home.

He had a momentary wave of sadness that he could not let Michael know what was happening. But he had a firm timetable and Michael was not a part of it. Michael had been at a loss when he left the service. Bored with civilian life he had heard that Sir James was looking for a body guard. With his background in surveillance, covert operations, and knowledge of several types of martial arts, Michael had been an invaluable assistant to him.

Galston smiled as he lifted the crystal snifter to his lips for a sip. The brandy was old, French and expensive. He only drank it when he was alone. The FBI was going to go crazy trying to figure out the connection between the Senator, and when they found him, the patsy. They'd know they had a conspiracy on their hands, but there were no threads, no leads, and the only person who was guilty was miles away.

The Leader would also be able to help them. But to help them would mean to give away the whole plan. This was a short flight thank heaven, but still he hoped he'd timed it correctly.

When they landed at Zurich airport. He was greeted as an old friend. The Swiss were always the most hospitable people when you had to travel. Still, they remembered him from other times that he'd come here.

"Ach. Sir James so good to have you with us. Will you be staying long here this time?"

"Unfortunately no. Just a few days, Gustav." He told the rental agent from whom he always rented a Mercedes.

"Well, enjoy your time. Will you ski this time?"

"Not this time. Just have a couple of meetings. Always business you know."

"Ja. Never getting the chance to relax. Not good, Sir James.

"No, Gustav, it's not a good thing. Maybe soon, I'll come, bring the family and go skiing."

"That would be a good thing, Sir James."

He finished signing the papers and left the warmth of the office. The weather had turned frigid, the roads were getting icy, but he only had a little way to go to reach the Intercontinental.

Colonel Ed Gately, or Spiros Knossos, the name on his passport, rented a car at the airport and drove the few miles to the Intercontinental. He checked in quickly and went up to his room. The first decent bed he'd seen since he'd left his wife, three days ago. Hard to believe three days had gone by. Uneventful so far, which meant he'd given them the slip. With them chasing around South America for a few days, it gave him a chance to take care of the situation his disappearance had placed in motion.

It was five pm. He had an hour to rest and shower. The timetable had been set up so many years ago, he was shocked he could still remember it with all the other garbage he had to hang onto. Perhaps, it was because this was his lifeline, his only lifeline. He had to remember it.

One hour later saw him being shown to a table for one in the elegant dining room of the hotel. He ordered. He looked around at the other diners. Only one face that he recognized. Good. But now they had to watch each other to ensure there was no one else watching.

To all outward appearances he was totally engrossed in his meal, and then ordered his dessert and coffee. The older man that he'd recognized completed his meal and left. It was a good ten minutes later before a young couple left their table and left the restaurant. Ed followed them a scant minute later after signing his bill. He strolled through the lobby to the entrance and looked out to see the snow had started falling. It had been predicted.

The person he was supposed to meet was sitting in the lobby, he passed him and went into the bar. It resembled a study in a professor's home with its rich dark paneling and green shaded lights. Niches here and there held old books, small paintings, and in one a delicate tea set.

Twenty minutes later, the older man entered the bar took a seat in a dark corner, alone. After he had ordered, he lit his pipe. That was the signal. So far everything looked clear. Tomorrow, at one p.m.

Gately finished his lager and went up to his room. Despite his anxiety and fears of the coming day, he slept soundly.

He awoke with the sunrise and looked out of the windows to be greeted by the crisp new snow glistening under a bright sun. He had time to eat and head out for the one o'clock meeting. At last. He'd been worried that the older man wouldn't remember. But he should have known better. After all he'd designed the way the meeting was going to be handled should it ever be needed.

One o'clock found him entering a small tavern in Winterthur, not far from Zurich. He was shown to a booth in the back. Ed was shrugging out of his coat when the older man entered.

He walked straight back to the booth, slid in across from him and grabbed his hand.

"Hello, son."

"Hello, Dad. I realize now why you planned everything the way you did. You knew what he was getting us into didn't you?"

"I had my worries. Remember I'd grown up with him. We were

actually good friends. He thinks we still are. I make sure that anything he asks me to get done is done. That's it. I still make my own plans and arrangements."

"So he thinks Clothilde is going to be taking over from you?"

"Yes. Poor dear hasn't a clue about his games or that we even exist. She's a wonderful girl, your sister. She does help me at times with a few things, but she believes it to be work I do for the environment. But she could never handle the Leader. However, so far I'm still in fairly good shape. He's not going to be happy about having been duped."

"So, can you call off the dogs?"

"I'm not sure. I don't think so."

"Great. Now what do I do, Dad?"

"I knew if you needed to run, that it would have to be here. You're going to get some work done. Then we'll get your wife and have her get a little work done as well. I knew if you could get here, I could keep you alive until you have to take over."

"Take over? It sounds as if you want me to be the Leader."

"Actually? Yes. I've already set things in motion. But remember the premise and the goals are still and always will remain the same. We just can't continue this non-stop murder and mayhem. His plan for unity needn't rest on massacre and murder to bring people together. He's no better than a Hitler, or a Genghis Khan. You realize that your DNA is the only way that they'll accept you. Mine is on file. When you walk in as the heir yours will be as well."

"Dad, this group. It's your whole life, and everyone who is in it, it's their whole life. Nothing else matters but the goals of the group. That makes no sense."

"Son, we had this talk, years ago. The groups' premise and goals make sense. What ruins it is the person at the helm. They usually wind up in that spot for about forty years. Long enough to really damage things."

"Now when we finish lunch we have a few things to take care of so that you can make it back to your beautiful wife."

"Dad, there is another problem. You know Evelyn couldn't have children. So I will have no heir."

"Well then, you will have to see who Clothilde marries. A niece or nephew is perfectly acceptable."

Their order was brought and Sir James said "Enough talk now, let's eat."

They left the restaurant and began walking past the small shops, huddled against the frigid cold. They stopped on a bridge, overlooking a frozen river.

"There is something that is vital for you to know, Son. You may not know that NASA has made contact with extra terrestrials. They are going to be visiting here in less than two years. The Leader is rushing toward unity before they arrive."

"Contact? Aliens? How? Unity? By killing half the planet? God, how can the others put up with this?" His questions ran one after the other in his shock.

"Family. They are our family as much as we are a family."

"So, if I hadn't run when I did you wouldn't have realized what he was doing?"

"Oh. I realized it all right. But as long as we were committed to moving forward toward unity, with as little upheaval as possible, I was willing to let him continue. Then came word from NASA. Well, anyway NASA got their budget passed before Danner was killed."

"Senator Danner? Wasn't he one of the group?"

"Yes. But he had done quite a few things recently, which ultimately could expose the group. Not only expose, but ruin whatever good we've done over the years."

"What was so bad that he had to be killed?"

"You don't need to know that story. When we have more time. Right now, we don't. We'll take my car."

They drove out of the little village and onto the road headed toward Lucerne. An hour later they turned off the main road onto what appeared to be private property.

"This is a small clinic. When my father was alive one of his best friends had been injured in a camping accident. We came here. They do excellent work. I'll stay with you until it's complete. I don't want you in any danger while you are vulnerable."

"Dad, plastic surgery takes forever to heal. You can't stay out of sight that long."

"What they are doing for you won't take that long. Plus it heals quickly. I've seen how it works. We'll be out of here before you know it."

The massive oak door opened as they walked up to it, "Sir James, so good to see you. When you called this morning, I was so very surprised. Now what can we do for you?"

"Dr. Spregg, My friend here needs to have certain areas on his face slightly altered. You know what I mean. Also, you know what you did for the hands of my other friend?"

"Ja."

"Do that as well. How long?"

"Let us see. Today is Saturday. We can have him set to go anywhere by Friday."

"Let's try for Wednesday. Now. We are going to leave here, and we will both be back to stay for a few days, if that is all right with you? It is just after four thirty we should be back here about eight o'clock tonight. You can start then. He'll get plenty of rest while he's healing. Oh, no one else is here this week?"

"No. I was just beginning my vacation. When you called I was just leaving to go to Italy. But I'll go next week and only stay the week."

"Doctor, I'll pay you for the vacation you missed as well as the cost of the work. That way you will have compensation."

"Sir James. You are truly a man of honor. I will have everything prepared for you when you return. There is plenty of food here. I shall see you back here tonight. But do be careful the roads are very treacherous at night."

"Hmm. Yes, I remember." Sir James answered nodding. "We shall see you later, Dr. Spregg.

They left the Clinic. When they returned several hours later, they parked their cars in the shelter of a lee, well off the road just a half-mile from the Clinic. Walking over land they checked out the Clinic. Circling the entire sprawling complex alone and then together. Satisfied they returned to their cars and drove in.

"Welcome back. Welcome back. I thought you had gotten lost or something. It was getting late."

"Just took us a little longer than we had planned. Is there somewhere we can park the cars, Doctor?"

"Of course, of course. Drive them around the back there is a garage there. You can put them in there."

"Thanks, Doctor."

Ed took the keys for the Mercedes from Sir James and was back within minutes. He was clapping his gloved hands together. "It's starting to snow yet again. I think I'm already tired of it."

"I'll take you to your rooms. They are actually suites. Since no one else is here I gave you the best ones."

They followed the thin, slightly hunched back of the elderly doctor down the hallway. "Here we are, number 9 and number 10. Across the hall from each other and right near the dining room. Now, do you still want to start tonight?

Sir James and Colonel Gately exchanged looks. "Yes. The sooner the better."

"All right, then meet me in the dining room in fifteen minutes. I'll take you down to get ready. Sir James, since I have no nurse here you might like to help out."

"I had already planned to."

"Excellent." The doctor went back down the hall humming to himself.

10

Mary Fleming drove the last few miles down the dark road. Vivaldi's Spring wafted through the car. She'd kept music on during the entire ride north. Each time she'd stopped for gas and to use a rest room, she'd kept a blue turban like wrap around her head, with oversize glasses she'd purchased at an all-night pharmacy several months ago.

Finally, she was home. Her real home. Mary pulled her car directly into the garage, closed the doors and went into the dark house. It was chilly and she turned up the heat. Walking through the house as she did each time she returned, she turned on the lights. She wouldn't have to leave again.

If nothing else, dear Senator Danner had provided her with a nice home and a way out of the rat race she'd long ago begun to hate. Mary put on a pair of sweats and walked into the kitchen to make some hot chocolate. The large cape was perfect for someone alone, her great aunt had lived there for years by herself. Over the past few years of receiving extra funds for keeping Sarah at Denton Group, she'd repaired it, furnished it and slowly moved all her belongings there. Over the past six months, all she'd needed to do was jump in the car with just a small overnight bag.

Several days later Mary walked into the living room, sat in the recliner and turned on the television. The last few days of peace and quiet had given her a chance to relax. Particularly after she'd heard the news of the suspicious fire at her home the afternoon she left. She knew she hadn't left anything on in the house that would cause a fire. Danner must have come after her. She'd left the car that she used for commuting into Washington there, CNN had showed pictures of the singed car in her driveway sitting in front of the ashes of the house.

She had been sure years ago she was playing with fire, but Danner had dangled the deal in front of her. He knew someone who needed a job and hadn't much experience. Give her a job and he'd make it worth her while. Sarah had been that someone. She certainly didn't have any skills, just a liberal arts degree with a major in History. When Mary had replied that she had nothing for her to do, Danner had told her she would be working on special research for him.

Mary had kept copies of the subject matter that he wanted Sarah to research for him, as well as copies of Sarah's reports. A strange group of subjects they were. Dealing with everything from UFO's and space travel to geological oil surveys in Antarctica and Egypt.

She sat there as the eleven o'clock news came on. Seconds later her wine glass crashed to the wood floor as the reporter intoned the tragic news of the deaths of Senator Danner and his long time driver in a motor vehicle crash. Mary listened fascinated to the story. The details of the search for what police described as some sort of large truck. There were scrapes of bright yellow paint imbedded in the wreckage of the limousine.

She continued to watch the television well into the wee hours of the morning. But when she finally lay down to go to sleep she was too nervous. She got up and padded barefoot to the front door, set the house alarms and turned on the special security fence she'd had set up by a firm from Canada. She walked through the house wondering how long it would be before the Senator's backers found her. She'd been stupid to think he was acting on his own. She'd worked long enough in Washington to know better.

She no longer felt safe. How long could she remain here? She looked out the window, imagining shadows, figures running in the darkness between the trees. Would they be looking for her? Did they know about her? Who were his faceless backers?

Mary Fleming would not have been recognized by her former co-workers, they called her the iron maiden behind her back. This nervousness was something new for her as well, she'd always been self-assured. Every plan made well in advance and thought out in the finest detail, she never moved unless she knew where she was going. Now she was thrust into a situation that left her feeling lost.

The Leader watched the flat screen in front of him. Sir James had completed the task quickly and well as always. Now he would have to see how General Anders was faring. His time was almost up. His own men had been keeping an eye on him since he'd left the gates. The man seemed to be chasing his tail. A pity his dear friend had been killed. But one must make some sacrifices to achieve success. He was sure Anders would not fail.

A soft knock sounded at the door and then it opened, Edgar, the butler, stood there.

"Yes, Edgar. What is it?"

"General Anders to see you, Sir. I told him you were busy."

"Never too busy to see the General, Edgar. Give me two minutes then bring him in."

"Very good, Sir."

The door was shut quietly. The Leader turned off the television, walked over to his desk, calmly lit a cigar and sat down to look out the window at the wet snow covering the deep green laurel that hid the room from the lawns.

In exactly two minutes, a soft knock was again heard and General Anders entered the study. He stood just inside the door, hesitating. Unsure, whether he should walk forward or remain where he was, standing at attention, his cap under his arm, his eyes darting around the room.

The leather chair spun around and the Leader stood up to greet him.

"Well, what are you waiting for, General? Come. Sit down. You have more information for me?"

"I'm not sure. I've checked everything, everywhere that I could."

"On your own, General?"

"Yes. There was no one who could help me."

"Pity." The Leader said as he carefully laid the cigar in the molded ashtray on his desk and leaned back in his chair.

"According to what I could find, Colonel Gately must have been an orphan. There is no record of his mother having given birth anywhere they lived."

"Really." The Leader's expression never changed as his gray eyes watched the general's every move.

"Uh. Colonel Gately was enrolled in school, in first grade, not kindergarten. That's the first time there is a record of him."

"So who were, or are his parents, General?"

"They are both dead. His mother died about six years ago, myocardial infarction. His father died about five years before that, complications from diabetes."

"Friends?"

"I couldn't find any alive. His only two close friends died a long time ago. Other than his wife, there was no one, even at the pentagon, who really knew him. I did talk to them."

"What about his teachers?"

"I haven't had a chance to check on them in person, but at least three of them are alive still."

"All right, General. Suppose we give you till next week this time. Do you think you could get me the whole story?"

"Ah... Sir, if I could speculate?"

"Speculate? Of course, go right ahead." The Leader picked up his cigar, checked its light, and carefully relit it while he listened to the General's thoughts. A bemused smile hid behind his hand.

"I believe Ed Gately was placed with the Gatelys for a reason. I don't know why, you understand. But he has no family, no adoption papers, there are no papers to show that he was placed by any agency. Because he went to school that's why we know who he is. He went in the army so we know who he is. But where he came from we don't know, Sir. I really think someone's running him."

"Really, General. That all sounds pretty sinister, don't you think? This little child, is adopted or taken care of by a family of strangers. Then grows up to be run by some, some, let us say a clandestine spy group. Oh, I doubt that, General. I really doubt that."

"Yes, Sir." The General physically backed up a step, he moistened his lips constantly.

"I do welcome your thoughts, however, General. But you should realize that many families raise the child of another family member who might be in unfortunate circumstances. I hope you checked that before you began to look at bizarre theories.

"Anyway. As I said you have until next week, to complete the task. You might want to also attend the funeral of Senator Danner. It's such a shame about his unfortunate accident. He and his family have done so much for us over the years. A great loss. I'm pleased to see that you put your own family first, General. Always make sure they're safe."

The General couldn't suppress a gasp. His ruddy face went white with fear.

The Leader continued to watch Anders fidget for a moment through the filmy smoke of the cigar.

"Well," he said as he rose, tall, regal, white hair brushed long against his collar, "I will see you next week at this time, General. Enjoy." With that he turned and walked over to the wall lined with books.

Dismissed, General Anders stumbled out of the room in his shock, not even closing the door behind him. He had been under such stress the past two days, and now the Leader lets him know that the one thing he felt he had done successfully, put his family out of harm's way, has also been a failure.

He got into the back of the sedan, unaware of his surroundings. The driver turned around and looked at him. "Where to, Sir."

"My home. My home," he said again, his voice a whisper."

The Leader watched the car leave, pleased with how things were going, but there was much yet to complete. Gately's disappearance had done nothing to disrupt the major plan, and the secondary plan was well underway. Without Sir James he had a much freer hand to complete the second plan. He turned away from the window and pressed a hidden button on the desk. A drawer slid open and he picked up the phone, dialed a few numbers and depressed a small switch on the receiver.

"Hello, Omar. We need to….."

Michael had been scouring the Caribbean for Gately's wife for three days, island hopping by small plane. When he couldn't rent one quickly enough, he would resort to renting a pleasure boat to investigate some of the more private resort islands. Despite the speed of his search, he knew he had been thorough and decided to go north to Bermuda.

He chartered a plane to take him the few hundred miles to the small pink sand island. As the plane circled overhead he noticed the large number of cruise ships docked at both St. Georges and Hamilton. Maybe it was not unusual, but Sir James had advised him to keep a sharp eye out for freighters and cruise ships as well.

The other islands he'd searched had only one or two cruise ships to check out. There were six already docked and it looked like another was just being moored at the far end of the line in Hamilton alone. Despite the small size of the island this was going to be tough going. Once landed, as a British citizen he was easily passed through customs. He rented a Vespa, and pulled out onto the roundabout behind a bus loaded with tourists and locals headed toward St. George.

He parked in a back street behind the historic cemetery and walked over to the local harbor master's office. He presented himself to the receptionist as a reporter for the London Times.

"Michael Brown, London Times," He said as he shook her tanned hand. "They've asked me to do a bit on your Harbor while I'm here on holiday. But it looks like I caught you at a busy time. A lot of tourist traffic this week. Last time I was here there were only three or four ships on the whole island."

"So nice to meet you. I'm Mindy Forrest. Oh, you're so right. Three of the ships have had some sort of engine problems and couldn't leave on time. So now we're completely backed up. But, that's okay they're all scheduled to be gone tomorrow."

"All on the same day, you mean?"

"Yes. That was a little tough in the scheduling. We have to bring in our back up men to help. We have back up just for vacations and illnesses, you know."

"Sure, that would make sense," Michael said as he relaxed his stance from his normal military bearing and smiled at the pretty young woman. If he hadn't been working he would have enjoyed spending some time getting to know her, despite the large diamond on her left hand.

"But, I'm sure you want to meet Captain Wallace. He's in a meeting right now, but I can set something up for later, if you'd like to speak with him."

"Well, I must admit I'm enjoying talking to you, but if I could get a few minutes with Captain Wallace, that would help to get me paid."

"If you can come back this afternoon about three o'clock, I'll put you on his calendar."

"Perfect, I'll be here. So how many ships can the island handle with all the tourists?"

"We're at full capacity right now. The Captain was saying this morning, he hoped no one else had engine trouble, because we can't squeeze another ship in here."

He looked at his watch then and said, "I better get going. Another appointment. But I'll be back at three and thanks, Mindy, for setting that up."

"Nice meeting you, Mr. Brown."

He walked out of the small white building and across the paving stones of the square. Ballast stones of the old sailing ships now smoothed from the centuries of weather. They made good use of everything in those days, he thought to himself as he headed to a tiny bookstore, tucked into the basement of a house down a side street.

The owner of the store was the widow of a friend of his. Whenever he was in Bermuda he stopped in to see her. He ducked under the low granite transom and squinted in the gloom after the bright sunlight. There was only one other customer in the shop and he could hear Sally humming to herself in the back room.

"Could I get some help out here?" he asked, pitching his voice higher than normal.

"Coming," the hummer replied.

She walked out, just as the lone customer ducked back out onto the street.

"Michael, I can't believe it. You always show up out of the blue. Last time it was, what, three or four years ago. Now here you are back again."

"Just for a day or so, Sally."

"Look at you. I think you must be doing something with the gangs, Michael," she said as she walked to the door closed it and reversed the 'open for business' sign. "You're always wearing the best clothes."

"These? Just some casual stuff for the tropics."

"I see the clothes they sell to the tourists on this island. Yours are the best of the best quality so don't try to fool Sally now." She tossed her long grey hair back over a round shoulder as she talked.

"Well, I don't work the gangs. I just work for someone with enough money to pay me what I'm really worth. Or I should say what they think I'm worth."

"Good for you. Come on in back, I was just making a pot of tea. Made these fresh this morning," she said as she offered him some scones.

"You're trying to fatten me up as usual, Sally. Even when Ethan was around you were dragging out food for me."

Michael laughed as he said it and the two settled into catching up for the next couple of hours.

As Michael left, Sally turned the sign back to open the shop again for customers. He waved to her just before he turned the corner to head back to the harbormasters office. The smile was gone now from his face. Sally never knew what a wealth of information she was. As usual she'd given him the most recent news and gossip of the island. But as always some of what she said was what he was looking for.

Her little book shop was a quiet place for the locals, ship crews, and tourists alike. They would often chat about books, travels and unusual things that happened that they should write about one day, with the comfortable, intelligent bookstore owner. This time it had been an engineer of a ship docked at St. George, had told her he couldn't imagine what had happened to one of the turbines. One minute it was running as smooth as glass, he'd gone out for supplies, came back and it had stopped, dead.

Michael hadn't thought much of it when Sally mentioned it, but a little bit later she said that the First Mate from the Rising Star, docked in Hamilton, had come in the day before. Hadn't expected to have the extra time in port, but the turbine had gone dead and they were stuck here for repairs.

That fit what the secretary had told him. Something was wrong, very wrong. He could feel it. He returned to the little Vespa, and started up the laptop he'd put in the carry space with his change of clothes. Quickly he e-mailed a message to Sir James using the code that they always used when separated. Then headed for his meeting with the harbormaster. He was running a little later than planned, but he would still be on time.

He opened the door expecting to see Mindy. Instead there were four men standing near her empty desk. The shorter of them broke free and came over hand outstretched.

"You must be Michael Brown from the London Times. I'm Galen Wallace, Harbor Master."

"Yes, Sir, I am. I didn't know I'd be interrupting your meeting. Your secretary..."

"It's fine. We're all finished. Just ironing out some last minute timing issues." Captain Wallace turned toward the other men. "I'll talk to all of you and the others again tomorrow morning, in case anything happens in the meantime, keep me posted."

The men nodded and murmured their assent and left the building. Not one of them gave Michael a second look.

"Come on in my office. Pretty tiny by London standards, I'm sure. But my main office is in Hamilton. Not much bigger though. Now, how can I help you?" Wallace said as he sat down behind the desk.

"My paper wanted a small column on how you handle all the cruise ships, tourists, and crews in and out of here on a daily basis. Looking at the two harbors today I'd say you're pretty backed up."

"Backed up is putting it mildly. Plus we've got four ships expected in here day after tomorrow. They're staying at sea an extra day to give us time to free up."

"Is this an unusual situation?"

"Truth be told, I'd say there was some tampering going on myself, never seen anything like it. Maybe in a year two ships have a problem, get delayed. But this? No. If there was a storm coming in we'd have to get all the cruise ships out of here as quickly as possible. But usually it's never more than two from St. George and four from Hamilton. The passengers are told they have a certain amount of time here and they want every minute of it. So no one can leave ahead of time. No complaints from them for leaving late though." He chuckled.

"Do you think you'll be able to get them all out on schedule?"

"It'll be tight, but we can do it."

"I heard the reason this happened was two or was it three ships had broken down almost simultaneously?"

"Three. That is what is really strange. The Captains and their engineers are at a loss as to what could have happened. Parts needed, repairs are still being made. These ships are always kept in top condition. What's worse the parts had to be flown in, nothing that could be found here on the island."

"How many passengers on those ships that broke down?"

"Between the three," he rifled through a stack of papers and chose one, "eighty-five hundred passengers. But once you add the crews, you're looking at over twelve thousand people."

"So right now you have almost twenty-five thousand passengers and at least thirteen thousand crew members roaming through the island."

"You're about right. It brings in plenty of money for the stores, restaurants and night life. It's hell on us though, and the island administration, particularly when we're used to only six ships total on the island at once."

"Well, sir, I think I have enough to put something together for a column. I don't want to take up any more of your time. Thanks for seeing me on such short notice."

"No problem. Always happy to keep the island in the news, keeps my paycheck coming in on a regular basis."

Michael left the office and returned to his Vespa. He drove straight back to the airport, all thoughts of finding Mrs. Gately were gone. He was sure something was going to happen on this island or just off of it in less than forty-eight hours and he didn't want to be anywhere near it. He was able to book a flight for early the next morning to England. He checked for messages from Sir James, but nothing yet. He planned to stay in the airport until his plane left. But then he remembered Sally.

It wasn't too late, so he took a bus back to St. Georges and walked quickly to the bookstore. The door was still open.

"Sally? Sally?"

She bustled out of the back room as soon as she heard his voice. "Michael, what's wrong?"

"Sally, something is going on here on the island. Do you have any way to go visit someone off the island in England, the states? I don't think this is a safe place to be for the next few days."

"Michael, what are you talking about?" Her once cheerful round face frowned up at him.

"There are things that are going on here in Bermuda that shouldn't be happening. I'm just worried about you. Perhaps you have a relative somewhere?"

"Michael, this is my home. Ethan was all I had. Now this store is it. I'll be careful, Michael. Thank you so much for thinking about me."

"Okay, Sally. But remember what I said. Please." He gave her a hug and left her for the second time that day. He got on the next bus back to the airport. Not wanting to sleep anywhere on the island this trip.

Once he landed at Heathrow, he took a taxi to his own apartment. The woman who cleaned his apartment every week would pick up his mail and lay it on the entrance table. He hadn't been home in over two months and she had actually put a small box on the table to hold the mail. He decided to leave everything where it was and walked through the bedroom into the bathroom stripping his clothes off as he went. He was worried that he hadn't heard from Sir James since he'd sent that message from Bermuda yesterday afternoon. But he was tired and needed rest. Minutes later he emerged from the bathroom vigorously rubbing his wet head. His muscular body bore several healed scars, but none recent. He threw the towel on the floor, slid into bed and was immediately asleep.

The beeping awoke him several hours later. Michael leaned over, unlocked the night table drawer, picked up the receiver and listened in silence for a few moments.

"Got in at nine this morning." He listened then said, "Yes, I'll be sure to take care of it. Its," he paused and looked at his watch next to him, "three thirty now. I can be there by then without a problem." He hung up, locked the drawer and got ready to leave home again.

Sir James slid the phone in the pocket of his heavy parka. He had understood Michael's frantic message from Bermuda all too clearly. He wanted him in plain sight in the presence of others when that massacre took place. But it had meant not talking to him until now. Michael's resourcefulness and sense of loyalty might have caused him to stay there and try to thwart the plan. His expertise might place him in the sights of the authorities afterwards.

But the Leader's plan had to go through. He hated it as much as his son, but the American people, the Swiss, Canadians, the citizens of the world were so very complacent with their little lives, the humdrum of living day to day. Everything was happening to others. Nothing touched them. They would throw in a few charitable dollars, or sigh audibly about the chaos in the world and go on about their ordinary day. But he had already made an effort to stop the upcoming carnage with an alternative plan without any bloodshed and the Leader had laughed at him for being soft. Come three o'clock today that would all change, life as people knew it would change forever. The September 11th human total would be nothing in comparison to this. The thought of it chilled him. How the Leader could sleep at night, he would never know.

He had been walking down the path back to the low buildings of the clinic when he saw a movement out of the corner of his eye. He turned to see his son coming toward him.

"Hi, dad. I figured you had calls to make and wanted to give you some time. But I need to talk to you. I'd rather leave Evelyn right where she is now. I'll forward money on to her and she'll be safer there. If I try to get to her it might cause her to be noticed."

"Ummm. You're probably right. I'd had some concerns myself. So when we leave here tomorrow, we head directly home."

"Do you really think that's wise?"

"The act you feared will occur today. Your passport will identify you as my son. Everyone will want to be home."

"Evelyn should be with us then."

"Edward, think and think clearly. Your instincts are correct not to move her now. To all around her, she is a woman alone. Your reticence to move her is correct. Those she has met will help her through this. Plus the money you send will let her know you are safe. Your sacrifice at this time will mean both your lives later. Understand that."

"This is what it's like then. Sacrifice everything for the group and the cause."

"Yes. That is exactly what it is like. But you and I have to oust the Leader before the 'others' arrive."

They entered the clinic through a rear door. The sounds of shouting followed by gun shots stopped them where they were. The two were unarmed and from the tumult, decided they were outnumbered. Without a word, Ed slipped the latch so the door would lock, and they stepped outside into the cold again. There were so many tracks in the snow it would be difficult for trackers to tell one from the other. But they couldn't use their cars. As soon as an engine turned over, it would be heard by the intruders.

They retraced their steps and angled through the frozen undergrowth, around toward the front of the compound. Both were eager to see who had come calling on Dr. Spregg.

As they made the circuit, Ed put his hand on Sir James sleeve. They halted. Up ahead on a rise, which met the end of the parking lot, stood a tall figure holding a rifle, its scope and size betrayed its Russian manufacture. The two men crouched down, blending into the winter landscape.

Ed calmly pulled the string from the hood of his parka, and as his father watched, quickly fashioned a small strong garrote. He made his way up the rise, and smelled the acrid cigarette smoke from the man. The guard's balaklava Ed knew would hinder some of his peripheral vision, but it would also make it more difficult to use the garrote. Surprise would have to be complete.

In one swift movement he rose, slipped the garrote over the man's head and pulled sharply downward. The move effectively slid them both back down the hill, out of sight of the clinic. Sir James grabbed the gun as it clattered over the jutting rocks, rendering it useless for them to use except as a club.

Gately patted the body down for other weapons and was rewarded with a Glock and a knife sheathed in his boot. Sir James pulled the balaklava from the head which was now facing at an impossible direction from his body. The intake of breath caught the Colonel's attention.

"Muhammed DalAhmed," he whispered and then signaled frantically to move away.

They did just that dragging the body with them and leaving it behind a large out cropping well away from the scene. Armed only minimally, they proceeded to move as quickly as they could toward the nearest town.

They kept close to the road despite the dips and crevasses, hoping to find at least one of the interloper's cars that they could grab and drive to safety. They came upon a small rental car parked well over two miles from the Clinic. No one was in it, but the keys were in the ignition.

They jumped in, turned the car back down the mountain and headed toward freedom.

Both cautious men, they never left personal items or money lying about, even when going out for only a short time. Thus they were prepared now as always for an immediate flight from Switzerland. They left the car in a tow away zone in Zurich and took a taxi to a hotel. They walked into the hotel together, one went toward the elevator and the other into the bar.

Five minutes later, Sir James came out and the doorman got him a cab. Minutes later Ed Gately left the bar and went outside. He strolled along the sidewalk, looking in shop windows before turning into another hotel. This time when he came out he got in one of the cabs lined up outside.

Both men left the cabs at the airport. One took the first Lufthansa flight toward Germany, the other headed to Heathrow and home. Sir James knew that above all he had to get home and begin the process of purging the Leader from the group. Obviously the terrorist faction was now being used to reach him or his son. They had to be stopped first.

Gary Stebbins, chief engineer for the Rising Star had just finished a late lunch. They'd finally gotten her underway, and he was hoping for an uneventful trip back to England. The passengers had put up with the four day delay pretty well, but only because there was plenty to do in Bermuda. But many were now beginning to grumble about work concerns.

He went into the crew quarters, grabbed a fresh pack of gum and a new paperback from the locker above his bunk, and headed to the engine room. He went down the steps at the end of the hallway, stepped through the steel door and closed it behind him. In deference to the crew, the door had been painted the soft color of the hallway on that side, but on the other it was all engine room gray. He stopped and listened to the healthy thrum of the engines.

Stebbins walked along the metal catwalk between two of the turbines. He heard an odd sound, pitched higher than the deep steady sound of the engines. He stopped, began to look around at the turbines and saw a stranger moving toward him from the intersecting walk that ended in the depths of the room. The sound of the engines began to slow and the thrum was giving way to a scraping sound.

"Sir, no passengers allowed down here."

"I am not an ordinary passenger," said the well-tanned man as he came closer. Dressed in khaki shorts and shirt, one hand rested casually in a pocket, but the right came forward from behind his back holding a gun. Gary Stebbins immediately began backing up toward the stairway, his hands out in front of him.

"Mister, you don't want to shoot that gun down here. Just go back to the passenger section." Stebbins heard the engines clatter to a halt, with a sound almost like a loud cough. "I have to fix the engines. You really have to go topside."

"I am going to return to the passenger section, but they will not be pleased to see me and my friends," his heavily accented words distracted Stebbins in his backward travel toward the steps.

Without warning the man fired catching Stebbins squarely in the center of the forehead. The engineer fell backward from the force of the bullet, his ruined head striking the steps of the steel staircase. The man stared at his handiwork momentarily, then pulled Stebbins body down the rest of the stair, leaving a grisly trail of blood and brains to stain the metal.

The Rising Star had been the third ship to leave Bermuda that day. But now it was ten miles out and stalled yet again. The captain called for the chief engineer as soon as the engines began to slow and when he failed to raise him, sent the first mate and two others to look for him. Radar informed him that they were not alone out on the ocean. There were three other ships near his and four more headed toward him from St. Georges and Hamilton.

The Captain ordered the other ships hailed. Except for those just heading out from Bermuda, his calls were met with silence. Then one by one those four ships went silent as well and radar showed all eight ships as dead in the water as they were. Suddenly the bridge door opened and the first mate entered slowly followed closely by two men, who shoved him so hard in the back, that the man fell forward, landing at the feet of the Captain.

"What are you doing on the bridge?" the Captain demanded.

"You are no longer in command of this vessel. Your ship's security men will not be coming to your rescue. You will sit over there with the rest of your people," the bearded, heavier one of the two said as he coldly shot the prone first mate.

The Captain jumped back against the controls, and then warily moved over to where the rest of the crew huddled in fear. Three other men whom he vaguely remembered seeing around the ship entered and silently took over the radar and other posts on the bridge. The chattering of printouts that had been requested earlier for soundings and weather was the only sound on the bridge.

"Ah, so good of you to have these prepared for us. We only need the soundings, however. We are not concerned with weather," the murderer who was in charge said as he sat down in the Captain's chair and began to go over the papers. The man at the radar station spoke to him in a language which none of the bridge crew recognized.

"Yafid, you may speak English. These men will be most interested in this experiment. Westerners are always so curious about new scientific achievements. Just think, Captain," he said as he turned to the man, "you, and the crew and passengers of all these ships are going to participate in a spectacular scientific test. History will be made and you will all be part of it.

"Unfortunately, people might think you had tempted the Bermuda Triangle once too often," the man chuckled. "But no. We are going to test a scientific theory. Yafid has informed me that all the ships are in place and ready to begin."

The Rising Star's Captain had been watching the leader of the group and hadn't noticed a small metal control box that had been placed on the panel adjacent to the shining forward lever. Now the leader went over to the control box.

Captain Galen Wallace stood in front of the harbormaster's office trying to understand why the small pilot boats that transported the harbor pilots had not returned. There had been no answers to his calls to them. It had been over twenty minutes since he had last heard from the pilot boat Santee. Then silence. He had no choice but to inform the authorities that something had gone very wrong.

He punched in the emergency number that normally was used only when hurricanes were approaching. A pleasant voice almost sang in his ear. "Bermuda Emergency Control."

"Bea, this is Captain Wallace, I need Henry."

"Yes, Captain."

He waited only seconds before Henry Kilcorn answered.

"Galen, Bea said you sounded upset."

"Henry, those eight ships and the pilot boats are not responding. I think we have a serious situation on our hands."

"Galen, wait a minute. Slow down. What do you mean they are not responding?"

"I mean that I spoke with Porter on the Santee almost a half hour ago. He should be within sight of the port, but he isn't. I can't raise him, the Martine or the Cybele, or any of the cruise ships on the radio. My office radar shows them sitting out there in a circle. Just sitting there. A couple of those ships left over two hours ago."

"Okay, I'm calling out the island guard. Keep trying to raise them. I'll inform the governor as well."

At least something was getting done, but what on earth was happening out there. He looked again at his radar and he couldn't believe his eyes. Each of the ships seemed to be moving up and down. The movement stopped, only to begin again even more erratically for a few seconds than each one winked off the screen. Captain Wallace stared at the blank screen as if willing them to reappear only they didn't.

He hit redial and shouted into the phone, "Henry, they're gone! They've disappeared. All eight of them and the pilot boats! One second they were there, then gone. Gone!"

"Galen, cruise ships don't just disappear."

"They did. They're all gone. I'm taking my boat out. If anything happens to me, read the records from the radar."

With that he jammed his cap on his head and left on the run. The hurricane warning sirens began to scream just as he left the steps of the office. The weather station was next door and he made a quick detour into the office.

"Blake, what's happening?"

"Tidal wave!" The weatherman shouted back at him. "No storm, nothing, but according to the instruments there was some sort of earthquake off shore and it's set off a tidal wave. Let's go! We're lucky if we've got a minute or two." The men took off by the back door and ran up the street joined by people running from shops and homes. All were trying to reach high ground before it hit.

Galen grabbed onto an elderly woman who was trying to run as she held on for dear life to her cane and cat. But they were already too late as the water slammed into their backs, washed over them, and roared on to claim more victims. Only minutes later, it receded leaving the tiny island completely devastated.

The automated beep sounded in the silence of the room. The Leader reached over and pressed the button to silence the annoying sound. It was over. Done. The first part of the plan had been executed. Now the second part must be completed without a hitch. His people knew where all the perpetrators were, now it would be a simple matter to eliminate them.

By the time the CIA, FBI and Homeland Security found out that the problem in Bermuda had been a terrorist act, the terrorists would be dead. All except for the three that needed to be left for them to find. Yes. The agencies must have a capture to wave to the countries of the world to show that they had done their work. The three men were only go-betweens of the two radical groups and had no idea who the groups worked with.

The Leader's slim hand pressed the control panel near his chair and the bookcase in front of him opened to reveal a large television. CNN came on automatically, as one of their many human mannequins voiced horror at 'what appears to be an earthquake of enormous proportions has inundated several cruise ships. It caused a tidal wave that has nearly obliterated the island of Bermuda."

So the idiots assume it to be an earthquake. Yes. Yes. Let them ponder over their charts, graphs and machines. Part two will be over, and part three will be almost completed before they figure out what happened. He turned off the television and made a phone call.

"Begin phase out now," he said when the phone was answered, and promptly hung up.

Michael had reached Sir James Galstons' home, Badgely Manor, just before five o'clock and was surprised not to find him there. He had assumed his boss had been there for days taking it easy. The sprawling home was originally constructed in the early fifteenth century with four turrets. During a later restoration and renovation two more turrets and several more rooms had been added. At the end of the nineteenth century, Sir James' grandfather, Sir Charles Clayton Galston added the central grand staircase.

Sir James' daughter, Clothilde, found him staring out a window in Sir James' study that overlooked the long drive. His own small car sat where he had left it near the garages.

"My father should be home shortly, Michael. He asked me to have you take your regular room and wait for him." Auburn hair, stylishly cut framed a round face with dark eyes that stared up at him.

"Well, I hadn't expected to stay this time."

"You know my father. He expects you to stay when he says to take your room." She smiled as she walked toward the front door.

"Right." Michael always felt uncomfortable talking to Sir James' daughter. He couldn't understand why she didn't seem to be more in command than she was. Being his heir to the group she should be more aware of who he was. He had wanted to talk to Sir James about the situation, but stopped himself, thinking it was not his place.

Clothilde intruded on his thoughts. "I have to go. I'm due in London for dinner, otherwise I'd stay and keep you company." She laid a delicate hand on his arm. "You know where everything is, Michael. See you later."

"Yes. Thank you, Clothilde."

She was an attractive enough woman, good figure, but not his type, even if she hadn't been Sir James daughter. He left the study and went upstairs to his room in the east wing of the manor. The west wing was the family wing. He'd been told, when he was hired by Sir James years before, that the west wing was off limits to all except those who cleaned it. The doorway off the center staircase was kept locked by a combination lock and a device that read the eye of the allowed occupants. There was no back stairwell that he'd ever been able to find and not for want of trying.

Michael stretched out on the bed and turned on the television and began flipping channels. Nothing to do now, but wait for his boss. He wasn't accustomed to being idle. Maybe try to look around the manor again, hadn't done that in some time.

Shouting on the television caused him to pay attention. He was shocked by what he was seeing. The newscaster was pointing to what was left of several buildings, 'I'm standing next to what was the harbor masters' offices and the weather center on this once beautiful island of Bermuda. There are conflicting reports of either an explosion or earthquake approximately ten miles off the coast, which caused a tidal wave of epic proportions to hit this island several hours ago.'

It had happened. He hadn't known exactly what it was going to be, but he hadn't expected it to be this horrible. But the newscaster was still talking. 'Eight cruise ships that were sitting off the coast were sunk at the time of this cataclysm. The number of people lost on the ships alone is thought to be well over thirty thousand. There are no known survivors from the ships. On the island, while there are survivors, there are believed to be thousands dead or missing.

'This is considered to be one of the worst single disasters in the history of the western world.'

Oh, my God, Michael thought, how could they have allowed this to happen? This couldn't have been what they had planned. They just couldn't have. What have I been helping them with? The newscaster droned on, 'There are reports from seismologists that this was not an earthquake but an explosion. If this was an explosion, so far no one has claimed responsibility for this catastrophe. Experts are conferring with officials from the NTSB, FBI, CIA, Homeland Security and their counterparts from Great Britain MI6 and the Home Office. We will keep you up to date on this horrendous tragedy as reports come in.'

There was a knock on the door, and Michael sat up, startled from his concentration on the news. "Come in."

"Well, he's done it," Sir James said as he entered the room and glanced toward the television. "He'll probably get away with it."

"He planned this? Did he have any idea how many people? How much devastation?" Michael asked. His tone of voice hid the fact that he was actually waiting for his employer to tell him he definitely had no part in this.

Sir James looked drawn and haggard. The fast trip from the clinic to his home had taken its toll.

"Oh, yes. His agenda, our agenda, he said, demanded this. Much of the work you have done is for him, Michael. But now you are going to be working completely for me." Sir James gave a signal to someone just outside the door and a younger man entered.

"Michael, I'd like you to meet my son, Edward."

"I didn't know you had a son, sir." Michael was standing now, staring at this man who was just a little older than he, but looked slightly familiar.

"You're frowning, Michael. Most likely he is quite familiar to you." Sir James was smiling at Michael's confusion. "You've never met. But you've heard of him, as he has heard of you. He just flew in from Germany.

"All right. We don't have a lot of time and I need some sleep. Let's get down to the planning room."

The three men left Michael's second floor bedroom and in deference to Sir James, walked slowly down the steps, through the main hall and into the formal dining room. The large table had already been set for dinner, but that would be a long time coming tonight. The older man pressed a panel beside the highboy, and it slid away revealing a narrow stone staircase.

As soon as they started down the steps the panel returned to its normal place in the wall. The planning room had originally been a dungeon two levels beneath the house, which left room for a basement above to be used for wine cellars and household storage. Michael had been down to the planning room frequently in the past few years, but Edward was amazed by the high level of equipment that was now being activated.

Four enormous screens fed in either television or internet information. Phones, faxes, computers, and through a set of old rotting iron bars, was what looked to be a machine room and laboratory. The other side held several small rooms with cots and a bathroom at the end.

"Good lord, Dad," Colonel Gately exclaimed, "no wonder you wanted to get back here."

"Yes. Well let's just hope the Leader doesn't figure out that I am back here. I have one more thing to do before we get down to business." With that he picked up a phone that hung on the wall.

"Gerald, kindly have the staff begin their two week holiday. They are to be out of the house within an hour. Don't worry about the usual dust covers. Just pack and leave. Dial the number 4160 when you are twenty miles from the house and let it ring once. Thank you, Gerald and tell the staff to enjoy themselves."

Sir James held up a finger as both Michael and his son started to speak. This time he picked up a desk phone and dialed another number. "Clothilde, my dear, I know you are headed toward London right now, but when were you planning to return home? I see. Well, why don't you go get yourself some special funding when you reach London and stay with one of your girl friends for the next few weeks, I've given the staff a holiday."

He waited, listening for a moment, then, "Yes, dear. That's right. I don't have time to talk now. So enjoy yourself."

He hung up. "Good, now whatever happens we're ready for it."

Michael sat apparently relaxed in one of the chairs, but Colonel Gately was walking around inspecting what amounted to his father's 'war room'. But as soon as Sir James spoke the other men reacted and pulled chairs up to a wooden table in the center of the room.

Sir James looked at the large clock and then at his watch, "We really don't have much time, Michael, but I have to bring you up to date. I met Edward in Switzerland after I left you at Heathrow. Sorry I had to send you on a wild goose chase, but I couldn't let you know where I was. I took him to a clinic for a few things. But last night, or should I say very early this morning, a group invaded the clinic. He and I barely escaped. We made it here and we are only hours ahead of them, if we are lucky.'

"So that's why you don't want anyone here. But won't they find us down here?" Michael asked.

"The spring on the panel is designed so that if anyone has touched it and entered it won't open again except from our side to leave. The panel looks like the wood of the rest but it covers lead.

"Now, any other questions?"

"Yes, sir. Edward," Michael tilted his head toward Colonel Gately, "he wouldn't be the man we've been looking for, now would he?"

"Yes. He would be."

"I don't understand any of this, Sir James."

"You will. Now let's get down to business."

With that, the older man pulled a folded piece of paper from his inside jacket pocket and opened it onto the table.

"This is a list of people who will be killed within the next hours. They fulfilled the Leader's plan and are now to be, as he put it 'deleted'. These men are also some of the civilized world's worst enemies and eliminating them will not be mourned by most. However, there is one, who has been acting the part of a terrorist and must be pulled out if he cannot escape. He is working for me as well. If you noticed everything down here is set up for four people. He is the fourth." Sir James planted a finger on a name near the middle of the list, Ahmed Moustaph Sahlem.

"So you've planned this for a long time, Dad?"

"Too long. Now that it is time to work, I'm not sure whether it will or not."

"Where is this fourth man? Does he know how to get here?" Michael asked.

"Yes, but time is short. The signal was the destruction of the ships. But all of these men have been under surveillance. They are all to be eliminated within twenty-four hours following the loss of the ships. Half that time has already gone by. The Leader has picked these three to be arrested." The names were placed separately on the sheet from the rest.

"Do you want us to go and rescue him?" Michael had been fidgeting for some time and was ready for some action.

"No. That would draw us out and place attention on him. I had planned that he would have placed himself in such a position as to be here by this time. However, that has not happened. I am open to contingency suggestions as to how we can maintain security here and assist him.

"As with you, Edward, you had to get to the designated place on your own. However, with you it was easier as I had access at that time. In order to gain access now I would have to call the Leader. I believe that he is the one that had us hunted down and I don't want him to know where I am. If he isn't, I still don't want him to know where I am."

"Sir, are you breaking off with the group?"

"No, Michael, I'm taking over the group and leaving that maniac to the wolves," Sir James left the younger men sitting at the table and walked down the short hall to the last room, pulled two blankets from a shelf and laid down on the narrow cot.

The two men stared at each other for a moment, each feeling awkward, as they realized that the older man was not only taking a nap, but, giving them time to get acquainted.

Edward spoke first, "I take it you never heard about me, Michael. My father wanted it that way. Planned it that way. The people who raised me, my, uh, foster parents, took over when I was an infant."

"Why would they take on someone else's child?"

"People do things for different reasons. They wanted a child. Couldn't have one. My father was looking for someone with a need."

"How do you know?" Michael said as he eyed the other man. His mind was gauging the strength, size, and intelligence of Sir James' son.

"He told me, they told me. When I got older, he showed me. No one and I mean no one ever lied to me about who I was. I always knew." Ed said as he got up from the table and walked over to a monitor staring at a picture of what was left Bermuda. He didn't need any sound. The devastation spoke for itself. He had almost taken Evelyn there instead of Malta. But had decided it was too close to the Leader. He'd been right.

Michael was still speaking, "Why would they tell a child about that, Edward. That makes no sense. You might have told someone else. A policeman, a teacher, another child."

"You think I'm lying. I don't lie. My father doesn't lie. The Gately's didn't lie." His voice a growl, Edward turned toward Michael. His face was calm, but Michael realized Edward's eyes had gone from blue to a pale gray.

"I didn't say you were lying. I asked you why they told you when you were still so young."

"Could be they trusted me," Edward said as he turned his back on the other man and sat down at a computer.

Michael stayed where he was. He'd messed this one up. One minute Sir James' son was talking, the next he'd shut down like a vise. He'd underestimated him. He shouldn't have. Just because the man had grown up in America, with money, he thought he'd be soft. He wasn't.

They sat in silence. Soft snoring came in waves from the small bedroom, accompanied by Colonel Gately tapping away on the computer keyboard. The printer spewed forth sheets of paper sporadically, breaking into Michael's thoughts about what their next move was, how they would have to make it and what kind of weaponry he might have to get.

The buzzing sound slipped into the room like a mosquito. Sir James was instantly awake. He came out of the room and stopped next to the phone and pushed a button just below it.

"Where?" Sir James said.

"20 yards", came the whispered answer.

"Ready." Sir James walked over to the stairs and pressed a lever hidden in the darkness of the staircase.

Scarce minutes later the back wall of the last bedroom opened up and a short dark-haired bearded man entered.

Michael was stunned. He'd had no idea there was an entrance from this basement. He'd always thought he'd known everything there was to know about Sir James. This day had shown him he'd been very wrong. Despite Sir James age, the man seemed like a magician.

"Gentlemen," Sir James said as he walked over to the computer area and sat down, "This is the fourth man, Richard Caslen. We are now together. We may begin."

The media was at full throttle. Every newspaper headline was screaming terrorism. Every television newscaster spoke of the unspeakable horror that had been perpetrated under the guise of a natural disaster.

The Leader sat in his study. The day's papers beside him, television screens spouting forth conjecture, hearsay, rumors and scientific facts. That was the only part they had finally figured out. Thanks to the geologists and their seismographs. It had taken them much less time than he had expected. Barely a day later, authorities placed blame squarely on terrorists. They didn't know which group, but the worldwide intelligence agencies were wildly hunting down anyone who had ever said a bad word against democracy.

He was almost laughing at their antics. Every agency was trying to outdo the other in claims of arrests and knowledge of the perpetrators. But while phase two had been completed and phase three was well on its way, there were still loose ends. One of the terrorists in Scotland, who was supposed to have been terminated, had disappeared. He wished he had Sir James' trained puppy dog, Michael, available to do the job. The man had never made a misstep, had never been caught, and was completely loyal to Sir James.

He'd given him several offers to come to work for him and the man refused. He knew he had offered the man more than Sir James could have been paying him, but to no avail. Michael would never have let anyone get away from him. He hadn't heard from either one of them in days. That was unusual. At least Sir James would have called. Perhaps he was ill. He had looked tired at their last meeting.

The Leader picked up the phone and dialed a number. "Frank. This is Anthony Vanderlin. I was wondering if my friend's plane had come in yet. No? I had been expecting him." He paused listening to the Supervisor of Private Air Operations. "Well, I guess he decided to stay home for a while. Thank you, Frank." The Leader's frown belied his pleasant voice.

He pressed a button and left the study, as the screens rolled themselves away with a quiet hum. The study door closed with the metallic snick of its secured lock. The Leader seldom left the study in the middle of the day and when his butler saw him mounting the stairs, knew to keep himself and the rest of the staff downstairs.

The television in the lounge had been blaring the news for the last hour. The two teachers who shared the house with the girls, and acted as housemothers, were sitting there in the midst of their charges. Ilena quietly slipped past the open door, her backpack over one shoulder and left the sprawling mansion that had served as her home for the last five years.

She hadn't seen her father since she had come here from the boarding school in Boston after eighth grade. Now he was calling for her to return to the United States as quickly as possible. She worked her way down to a side gate knowing her boots were leaving prints in the snow.

Just outside the gate there was a limousine. Ilena put her gloved hand on one of the iron gates and looked back at the peaked roofs of the school rising above the trees behind her. Then she turned, went through the gate and shut it firmly behind her. A uniformed chauffeur stood beside the open rear door and she slid into the warm interior. The man closed the door and returned to the driver's seat.

"It will take at least two hours to reach the airport, Miss."

Ilena nodded as she pulled off her gloves and hat, and settled back against the leather. Her long, dark hair framed a pretty face, her cheeks and nose red from the cold. She never wore makeup and her lips retained a natural pink. But she had her father's eyes. The deep brown, became black, unfathomable, when angry. Those at the schools she'd attended had learned to stay away from her when something hadn't gone her way, or she felt someone had done something to her.

But now she relaxed, glad to be on her way home. Finally, her father had called her home. The last year had been an absolute bore and she'd been asking why she had to stay in this godforsaken place another two years. 'Finishing school' they called it. Finish off any sense of individuality was more like it, she had thought many times. As a result she had been in trouble frequently for doing things that the elderly spinsters who ran the school considered 'unseemly'. The only thing that kept her from being expelled was her father's position and the fact that he had built the science building, which had been named for his late wife, her mother.

She dozed off and came awake only when the chauffeur called out to her that they were at the airport. The car drove up to a Lear jet parked on a side runway. The driver got out and opened the door, just as a man dressed in khaki strode up to the limousine.

"Hello, Ms. Ilena. I'll be your pilot today. We're flying to Heathrow first, Miss."

"Why?" she retorted. "My father said as soon as possible. I shouldn't think flying to Heathrow is the quickest way."

"This route was specified. I don't ask the reason, Miss," the pilot answered.

"Oh, well, if it's what he wants." She was upset, but then decided she might be able to stop and get in a little shopping in the airport. She ran up the stairs into the plane and settled herself in for the second leg of her journey.

The plane took off less than ten minutes later. She hoped she'd never have to see these mountains again, she thought as she idly picked up a magazine from the table in front of her seat.

When the plane landed, and the door opened, Ilena went down the steps and was greeted by a tall middle aged man, with a decidedly military bearing, standing in front of a Rolls Royce. "If you'll come with me, miss? The plan is for you to begin your work from here. That is the message I was to give you."

Ilena recognized the message immediately as coming from her father. That would be how she would know she was still in safe hands and whatever he had for her to do was starting.

This time Ilena didn't get upset and got in the back of the Rolls with the man.

"My name is Michael, miss. I often do work for your father."

"Nice to meet you, Michael. I'll admit I was surprised to come to England instead of going directly home to Washington."

"Well, things are a little difficult right now in the United States."

Ilena quietly accepted the explanation and looked out of the window at the passing scenery. They had been driving for over two hours when the car stopped at a large wood double gate, slowly it swung open. The car drove through and the gates shut behind them. The driveway was long. The Rolls wended around a large silent house and drove directly into a garage.

When they got out, Ilena was surprised to see that the driver of the Rolls and the pilot of the jet were the same man. When she mentioned it the man spoke up, his speech definitely American, unlike Michael's clipped British accent.

"I should have introduced myself earlier, I'm Edward."

"Nice to meet you Edward. Now where do we begin?"

"This way, please, Miss." Michael said quietly as he directed her to a door at the back of the garage that she hadn't noticed before.

He went down the dimly lit stairway in front of her. Edward bringing up the rear, closed the door to the garage and followed them. At the bottom of the stairs, they were greeted by a much older man.

"Ilena, I'm glad you made it here safely."

"Uncle James, I should have known my father would have you pick me up. He refuses to leave home for much of anything. Definitely not for me."

"Um, yes. Well, Ilena, we have to talk. I'm the one that sent for you. Your father still thinks you are in school." Sir James put his arm around the young woman and drew her over to the table as he spoke.

"I don't understand." Ilena sat down and looked around at the four men. One she hadn't met was standing in the shadows at the rear of the dungeon room that housed the computers.

"I very much doubt your father would be worried about you at this time, but you are his designated heir to the group, and things are not going well. As I'm sure you noticed from the news."

"What does he have to do with that?" she asked distractedly as she squinted at the man in the shadows.

"Everything, Ilena." Sir James sat down across the table and began telling her the story of the destruction of Bermuda. He paused only to ask if she was hungry then continued while one of the men put something together for all of them. When Sir James was done, over two hours had passed and the strain around the young woman's eyes was noticeable.

"Uncle James, you're making it sound as if my father is completely responsible for the deaths of all those people. You work with him, why didn't you try to stop this? The reasons you've given me make no sense at all. There is nothing that would cause my father to do this." Ilena's eyes flashed with temper as she spoke, looking around the room at each of the men.

"Your father feels that the unity of the world when we meet the visitors is of enough importance to do anything required to obtain that unity. He has said that and he means that."

"Does he plan any new adventures?" She asked sarcastically.

"I have been out of touch with your father for several days now. Once the terrorists groups that he had used were decimated he said he would bring the world leaders together for a dialogue. I have not seen that begin."

"Well maybe he is still getting rid of the terrorists." Ilena countered.

A voice spoke that she hadn't heard before, deep with a slight accent.

"The terrorists were all hunted down and killed within forty-eight hours of the incident. Only three or four were arrested and placed in United States prisons."

"How does he know this, Uncle James."

"He had infiltrated them for me and just barely escaped with his own life."

"Why didn't you stop them from killing all those people? Those people were simply on vacation, or living their lives and they are all gone. Thousands!"

"All those lost were westerners and according to jihad, expendable. The terrorists groups do not like, nor do they understand the constant desire of westerners to go on trips and be away from home. They believe their religion is their work and their home. They only leave their home to do their work if they are told to do so. Otherwise they remain." The man came over, and sat down at the table with the group.

"The Rolls was not followed. The plane has been refueled and is on the side runway according to plan."

"Thank you, Richard. Now that we have you safely out of harm's way, Ilena, we can continue our mission. Michael, it is time to send this information to the designated papers and the offices."

Michael took the sheet of paper from his boss, brought up the original document on the computer and routed it to all the designated fax machines. The internal fax had been set up to bounce across at least five separate sites, so anything faxed could not immediately be traced back to the home computer. It took several minutes longer than an ordinary fax but Sir James had been adamant about the precaution. As he stood over the machine waiting for confirmation Michael wondered what they were going to do next. A glance at the words on the page told him he had just done it.

President Stapleton had just completed a Cabinet meeting when his secretary knocked and entered the Oval Office.

"Marge, don't tell me they haven't left yet."

"They've gone, sir, but this just came in. I was faxing out and happened to see it come in along with a bunch of other things. I think this is different."

"Somebody wants us to keep someone out of jail?" he said as he took the paper. He began reading and the color left his face. Stapleton knew that here was the ammunition he needed to get out from under the thumb of the group. But the newspapers were getting it at the same time. So he couldn't even keep it under his hat for a minute.

"Marge, get every intelligence head in here and their seconds. I want them now, as well as Defense and the Joint Chiefs. Then get me the Post. The owner."

"Right." Despite her bulk, the woman scurried from the room. She knew what that message said and if it were true, not only the United States, but, the world, was in for more major shocks than the destruction in Bermuda.

Marge Clark had worked in the intelligence community for almost twenty years before seeking something else and when President Stapleton was looking for a confidential secretary she was the perfect match. As a result her own loyalties to her boss and her country would not allow her to even speculate on what would be the outcome of that message.

Once back at her desk, she placed the priority calls. One call remained unanswered. She called all back up numbers for General Anders. Nothing, not even an annoying answering machine responded. Marge felt a quiver up the back of her spine. Something was wrong. Very wrong. She had no authority to order anyone to go to his home.

She returned to the Oval Office. When the president looked at her face, he knew things had gotten even worse.

"What is it, Marge."

"General Anders, Sir. I can't raise him anywhere. Even his home answering machine doesn't come on."

Stapleton knew Marge didn't get worried easily. He pressed a button on his desk that connected him with the head of the Secret Service stationed at the White House. "Saunders, I need you."

Within two minutes the man was coming in the door. "What is it, Sir?"

"I've been trying to reach General Anders on an urgent matter. He cannot be reached by his cell, his office phone, his answering machine at his home, is not picking up. Send someone to his home and begin an immediate silent search. I mean silent. As soon as he is found I want to be notified immediately."

"Uh, Yes, Sir. He, uh might be...."

"Immediately, Saunders."

The man turned on his heel and left the room. He'd never seen Stapleton in such a state. He was headed down the hall and almost bumped into the Secretary of Defense and the Head of the FBI, rushing towards the Oval Office. Something more had happened. He decided to head to the General's house himself.

Saunders returned to his office, grabbed a coat and called out to his usual sidekick, Foster that they had a quick job to do for the 'Big Guy'.

Foster caught up to him in the hall, "What's up."

"Damned if I know. He's in an uproar. The suits are running into his office as if the devil himself was after them."

"You think those terrorists have hit something else?"

"Who knows where those crazies are concerned," Saunders answered.

Foster reached out to put the portable light on top of the car as they got in.

"No lights. This is a quiet look."

"Right."

They went down the drive, through the gates and headed into the Virginia countryside toward General Bud Anders home. Forty-five minutes later they pulled into the driveway of a large white colonial home. It could have been built during any decade or century. But it was only twenty-five years old. The garage door was closed. It was getting close to twilight but no lights were on in the house.

The two men walked up to the front door and rang the bell. They waited a few moments then knocked. Saunders tried the door and it opened. No sirens went off to alert an alarm company. Foster closed the door behind them. The house was all shadows and flickers of light from draped windows. The smell however was unmistakable.

The two men stood in the foyer as they pulled on latex gloves and turned on penlights. They moved around to different rooms on the first floor, before following the distinctive odor to its source in an upstairs back room that looked like a storage room.

They looked at the body of the General, lying on the floor near a window. They carefully moved around the room, observing, noting the gun in his right hand, the hole in his right temple. A piece of paper lay in his left hand. A single cryptic sentence, addressed to no one, gave no explanation, but opened up many questions.

The two men left everything as it was, backed out of the room, gloved hands closed the door and they quickly left the house. They drove to a gas station that they knew still had an old telephone outside. Saunders got out and went to the telephone. He dialed a number that would place him directly in touch with the President.

"Saunders here, Sir. The subject is dead. Suicide. The note said, and I quote, 'I was left no alternative'."

Thank you." The line went dead.

Saunders got back in the car, Foster placed a call to the local police for a wellbeing check on the general's home. The two men returned to the White House in silence, as each man tried to figure out the meaning of the General's suicide note.

President Stapleton sat at his desk, grateful for the space between himself and the people he was sharing his office with.

"Thank you all for your patience. We were waiting for someone, but as I just found out from that call he will not be coming. He is unable to join us."

"Aren't we waiting for General Anders?"

"Why isn't he coming?"

"You called all of us here, for what?"

"What's going on that's so important that we all got pulled away from our families, our duties."

The men and women were speaking at once. They were unaccustomed to being pulled to the White House at a moment's notice and then being made to cool their heels waiting for one person.

The President stood up, turned his back on the group and glared out at the darkness for a moment. The last few days had held greater upheavals to this country then the last several years since September 11, and it wasn't over yet. Well, he decided, it was time he took the reins and rode this damn horse that was threatening to ruin not only the country, but the world.

He turned around and silently stared at each of them in turn. "General Anders will not be joining us today, he is dead."

"What?" "How?" "When did this happen?" Again the group broke out into loud exclamations and questions.

Stapleton sat down and waited until they had quieted again. He couldn't believe he'd had to spend the last two years listening to their excuses, explanations and poor advice.

"Now that you've decided to listen, I'm going to pass out copies of a fax that arrived here a short time ago. But please pay attention to the others addresses at the top." He passed out the single sheets to each of the twenty people in attendance.

Gasps from some and silence from others gave him some measure of who knew and who didn't know the information on the paper.

"I can see some of you are totally shocked by what you have read." Stapleton turned his gaze onto those who had reacted to reading the message in silence. "I see a few of you already were aware of these situations. I wonder how."

Secretary of Defense, Steven Loomis, FBI chief, Ted Garvey and the CIA head Michael Ferguson, continued to keep their silence, but they couldn't keep their eyes from looking at each other.

The Leader had returned to his study after a light supper. He was comfortable in the knowledge that plans were going forward. In the morning the call would go out for the World Leaders to meet and plan action against acts of terrorism such as had just been perpetrated. He would lead them into the Unity beginning tomorrow. All had fallen into place.

One television screen came down in front of him. CNN as usual was on, "We have late breaking news, an anonymous source has given the Washington Post, The New York Times and others information that the world is going to be contacted in less than two years by extra-terrestrials who have been in constant contact with NASA. I repeat constant contact. While one would think that this might be a hoax, there is more to this news. The death of Senator Danner, just following passage of his bill for more funding for NASA has been connected to this arrival. There is evidence that apparently the deaths of all those in the recent tragedy of Bermuda was not only connected to Senator Danner, but part of some bizarre plot to prepare for the arrival of these visitors from outer space.

"We will keep you informed of developments on this story as it unfolds."

The Leader jumped from his chair. Who could have tied these things together? There was no way. Unless that damned General Anders decided to use his knowledge for some leverage. He hadn't called with a report recently.

The Leader jabbed his finger on the buttons to dial the number for the General and was met only with constant ringing on the other end. As he waited he could feel his heart pounding in his chest. Frustrated, he slammed the receiver onto its cradle. Why hadn't Sir James called him? Where was he? No word on Gately either. For the first time in his life he felt out of control of the events around him.

The television was flashing the words breaking news on its screen, but the Leader wasn't looking at it. He was rifling through papers on his desk as if searching for something. He threw a paperweight across the room where it struck a book shelf with a solid thunk. A picture frame crashed onto the floor and the computer keyboard dangled near the floor from its wire.

'The body of General 'Bud' Anders was discovered this evening at his home in the small Virginia town of Scollay. Investigators are saying it looks like suicide and a note was left. General Anders had been on the Joint Chief's staff at the Pentagon for the past several years after an illustrious career in army intelligence. General Anders was fifty-nine years of age. We will be giving you details of this and our other top stories as they become available. Now back to......'

The Leader had snapped off the television. 'Weakling' he thought to himself as he stormed from the study, 'crumpled under a little pressure'. He walked up the stairs to his room, in the quiet all he could hear was the pounding of his heart. 'Too much excitement in one day' he thought, as the first sharp pain went down his left arm. He tried to take a deep breath and his chest suddenly weighed too much do so. Barely able to move from the door to his bedside table his finger pressed the button to ring for Edgar, as he lost consciousness.

The man came immediately and found the Leader slumped on the floor. Edgar called an ambulance and then dialed the number for the Leader's doctor.

Almost a thousand miles north of the Leader's outrage and sudden illness, Mary Fleming decided that she had waited long enough, threw two slim, pre-stamped, padded envelopes on the passenger seat of her car and drove to the interstate. It was nearly midnight, almost an hour later, she drove into the parking lot of the Bangor, Maine post office and slipped the flat packages into the mailbox. A third, thicker one she kept with her at all times. If someone decided to kill her now at least most of the story would be known.

She jumped back into her car and headed northeast up the coast. She could stay at a bed and breakfast there until she was sure the CD's had arrived at their destinations. She glanced in her rearview mirror, noting the cars that had settled in behind her for the trip. Only one looked familiar, but she knew she was probably paranoid by now. She drove up the Interstate for a few miles, then switched over to Route 1 to find a place to stay.

When she stopped at the first set of lights, she again checked the cars in her mirror. The first one behind her looked like the one she'd seen just after she'd left the post office. Making a sudden decision when the light turned green she didn't turn left onto Route 1 she made a fast U turn and returned to the interstate. Since she had been the first car in line, any car behind her was trapped by the oncoming traffic and unable to follow her if they had wanted to.

As she drove down the ramp onto the interstate she again looked in her mirror and was gratified to see three tractor trailers and an RV following her. Mary knew then that she could lose herself between them if she was careful. Hopefully, the trucks would be traveling at a decent speed.

Several hours later, just after seven in the morning, Mary pulled into a small bed and breakfast with parking in the rear, away from the street. She registered and carried her small suitcase up to a cheerful room at the back of the house, overlooking her car. The floral patterns and ruffled curtains normally would have been a restful welcome, but today she was just glad she was off the road and out of sight.

She dozed off in fits and starts as she sat on a window seat where she could watch her car. When she'd stopped for gas just off the interstate she had checked under the car with her flashlight to make sure they hadn't put a tracking device on it. So while she felt fairly safe she didn't slide into bed until it was almost noon.

Although Mary didn't know it, with the Leader's illness, many of his personal team, not only backed off, but stopped tracking their quarries completely. Only those whose targets were considered to be actual terrorists continued to trail them and they reported through a blind number to Michael and through him to Sir James. Soon after Mary had made her decision to turn back to the interstate, her designated surveillance and terminator had been pulled off.

Sir James decided to wait two or three more days in their dungeon hideout before returning to the states and picking up the pieces of the Leader's debacle. The fallout from the exposé had wreaked havoc on the Cabinet, Senate and Congress as well as in the Pentagon, Homeland Security, FBI and CIA. The people of the United States were not just demanding answers they were demanding that those responsible be brought to justice, and tried immediately. The 'man in the street' had turned into an angry mob.

Sir James read through the communiques that came through Michael's network and realized that the terrorist threat to the United States as well as to other countries had been decimated by the Leaders tactics. They were in most cases without money, running for their lives, and hiding in disarray without leadership.

"This is good news. This is what we originally hoped for, getting rid of the terrorist threat. But now we are left with the clean-up. We will be ready to leave and take up the reins of leadership. The Leader is in a private hospital and once we are in the States I will make contact with him."

Michael who had kept his earphones on so he could keep track of the television in case any unusual news came on, now pulled them off and called out to the group.

"Someone else has leaked information to the press. Get this." He turned up the volume.

"CNN has received information from a source who claims to be in hiding that they have information that Senator Danner definitely was responsible for the disappearance of Sarah Martin. The source also claims that attempts had been made on their own life. An arsonist, thinking our source was inside, burned their house to the ground because they knew too much. This source is being treated as genuine because of information they have given us regarding the research and background of the communications with the extra-terrestrials who are supposed to be visiting us soon. The wealth of information received from this source has been as one editor put it 'phenomenal'.

"Well, well, so Senator Danner's part in all this has truly come to light along with his blunders. Come. Let's get ready to go now, close, lock, secure and password everything. If we are able to return we don't want a reception committee."

Methodically Michael, Richard and Edward closed down generators, televisions, and all of the computer equipment. Then they joined Sir James and Ilena at the entrance. As they did, Sir James punched in a secure code, which would slide inner doors over the entrances, exits and air intakes, effectively blocking any trace of the dungeons existence. He then slipped a small piece of paper to his son, Edward, which contained the code to get back into the dungeon if needed.

Because they never knew what they would face outside, they each had small packs of food and water along with weapons strapped to their bodies. They slipped from the underground passage and moved from tree to bush until they reached the hidden door to the garage. To be safe they were taking two cars to the airport by separate routes. The cars left the drive and turned in opposite directions. Two hours later the Lear jet left Heathrow with the five safely aboard and Edward at the controls.

Upon arrival at Dulles Airport, Sir James and Michael drove immediately to the private hospital where the Leader was convalescing from his heart attack. The other three remained on board the plane, which was parked at its permanent berth away from the main airport.

"Ah. You have finally come to visit me, Sir James. You have been keeping a very low profile during all of this hubbub."

"Would you expect I would do anything less? How did you let your health get to this point? I should think you of all people would have taken better care of yourself. Did you really have a heart attack?"

"Unfortunately yes. The heart attack was real. When I heard the news of General Anders. He must have sent information to Stapleton and the others before he died. Such a good friend. A good man, Sir James. A good man." The leader said carefully watching for a reaction from Sir James. "His conscience must have gained the upper hand. What do you think?"

"Yes. Well, who knows why people do things like that. Suicide. Well, I didn't know him that well," Sir James responded vaguely, well aware of the fact that this room might be bugged. "So, how are you coming along?"

"Oh, I'll probably be going home in a couple of days. I've hired a nurse to take care of me for a couple of weeks so I can go home sooner. That's the only way they'll let me out of this place."

Sir James sat quietly in one of two chairs beside the bed staring at the man he called Leader and chewed his unlit pipe. Finally, he spoke, "Why don't you stay here a few days longer. Make sure you're ready to hit the ground running when you get home. You might wish you had in light of everything that's going on."

"All the more reason for me to get back in the thick of things now. This action depends on a strong leader and with Stapleton running amuck on his own, I have to get out of here now. This couldn't have happened at a more crucial time."

"I understand how much you want to get back to business as usual, but don't you think a few more days of rest here are in order?"

"I'm not sure whether you're being kind, or whether you want to take over from me," the Leader said his voice low almost menacing. "My brain hasn't changed. My heart might have decided to do a dance, but my brain is in control. I'm going home. We should have a formal meeting two weeks from now. As soon as I get home I'm sending out the word. That man has got to be reined in or else."

Sir James stood up, looked at the Leader, "As long as you are prepared to take on all obstacles, the job is still yours." He stared at the Leader as if memorizing him lying there, vulnerable, a tube draining medicine into his arm, a monitor ticking away in rhythm. Without saying another word, Sir James, back straight and defiant, turned on his heel and left the room.

He stopped for a second beside Michael who was standing at the nurse's station. Not a flicker of recognition passed between them, as Sir James spoke with the nurse, he gestured toward the Leader's room, "He says he's leaving in a day or so, is that correct? I want to make sure I have everything ready for him when he gets home."

"Well, he's getting one of the best nurses around to care for him at home, so he should be out of here day after tomorrow,"

"Wonderful. We'll all be ready to take care of him. Thank you."

Sir James went to the elevator, left the hospital and got in their car. Michael, who had faded away from the nurse's desk during the exchange, came out to the car only minutes behind him.

They drove back to the airport and boarded the plane. With a flight plan filed for Colorado, they taxied down the runway and flew west. On the way, Sir James told them of the next steps in his plan. As they neared Colorado, Sir James gave his son the coordinates of the runway. As they neared the cleft in the mountains well over a hundred miles northwest of Boulder, Colonel Gately circled the area twice and then fought the updrafts to land the Lear safely. As the plane touched down and moved down the narrow snow covered runway they could see the fortress Sir James had begun forty years earlier. Now would be the first time he would need it.

Nestled into the side of a mountain, unnoticeable from the air, and at least fifty miles from the nearest town, it was totally self-sufficient. Michael had known Sir James had such a place in the United States, but this was the first time he'd been here.

As the five of them left the plane, Sir James, introduced them to their new home. "This will be our new base of operations. There are three smaller planes and a helicopter here, so we don't have to use the jet unless we need to get somewhere quickly. We have plenty of fuel and there is a couple that has cared for this place for years. I contacted them just before we left Washington some weeks ago and told them to prepare for winter for thirty people. Thus ensuring plenty for all of us."

Ed looked around at the palatial mountain home and said to his father, "Only one person missing, Dad."

"I know, Edward. It's still too risky to move her from where she is. I know it seems like a long time, but Evelyn is safer there, in case we have to move quickly."

The others had missed the quiet exchange between father and son, as they moved away to explore the home. Michael went through the dining room toward the back of the house and walked around in circles in the kitchen before realizing that there wasn't one window in the kitchen or even a back door. He opened a narrow door tucked unobtrusively in a corner between the light wood cabinets thinking it was a pantry and found himself facing a solid rock wall. Not as he expected, a staircase to a basement.

He heard footsteps behind him. "Ah, you found my joke, Michael." Sir James chuckled.

"Joke is right, Sir James. I thought it might be a bathroom or pantry."

"Exactly. Let us go through the rest of the house, I want everyone to be fully acclimated to their surroundings, then I'll show you the house secrets. This house was started many, many years ago, but everything in it, all the electronics are the most up to date within the last few months."

A half hour later they gathered in the wood paneled study. Ilena who had said little on their long journey now began to express her misgivings, which had been festering for quite awhile.

"I don't understand why we are sitting here in this house, Uncle James. This is not helping my father, or you. I have been waiting for some fantastic revelations as to what we are going to do." The young woman had walked over to where Sir James was standing beside the fireplace, and glared up at him, hands on hips, her face flushed. "I want some answers and I want them now, I've grown tired of your little games."

"You will all have answers soon enough, my dear. Indulge me for just a few moments longer, all of you. We've been out of touch too long. I like to keep up with what your father is doing."

"You said yourself my father is ill. You wouldn't even let me see him."

"He believes you to be in school, Ilena. You don't want to further shock him by suddenly showing up at his bedside, now do you? He has had a heart attack." Sir James stared at the defiant young woman. "We have work to do, and while your father is recuperating this is the best place for you to be. Too many people know you were in that school. You are safer here as well."

With that he turned, signaling them to follow him and returned to the kitchen. Ilena reluctantly brought up the rear of the group. Just as she entered the kitchen she saw Sir James disappear into a corner between the cabinets. The men stood looking at the rock face of the mountainside, then at each other. Edward was the first to place his hand upon the rock and he immediately slid sideways behind the cabinets.

"What the….!" Michael exclaimed and then, "What the hell…" He then put his hand on the rock as well and disappeared.

Richard turned to Ilena, "Miss?"

She tossed her dark hair and moved forward to take her place in front of the rock wall. She was followed immediately by Richard.

"That was a real trip, Sir James. Where are we?"

"We are in the mountain now. The house was built to cover an entire cave dwelling that had been here. That was only one of five hidden entrances and exits from the house into this area. That was the most spectacular though. I had it added on about five years ago. The other entrances are more normal. I'll show them to you later. Now we have to get to work."

The rooms in the cave had been set up similarly to the Badgely Manor dungeon. But here there was a lot more room. Switches were thrown and lights, air filtration system and monitors immediately came on.

"If we need to leave here in a hurry we have access to cars, planes and even a helicopter without going through the house. But hopefully that won't be necessary. Now." Sir James had turned on one of several computers while he was speaking. Fax machines came to life, television monitors began spouting the latest news.

"Now, the next originally planned phase of the operation was a large meeting of all the world's leaders for the purpose of unification, but that unification would have been organized through threats of more terror. We will be meeting with them but not in person."

With that Sir James began punching codes into a small box in front of a monitor that took up half of one of the large walls. Within seconds, President Stapleton, Prime Ministers Fairwell of Britain, Saulnier of France, Nihoto of Japan and other leaders of various nations were demanding what was happening.

"Good Evening, Gentlemen, Ladies." Sir James was speaking but the clipped British accent was gone, transformed by the digital chip within the microphone. "As you know certain terrorist acts have been perpetrated against the world, one of which is the disaster in Bermuda. I am not responsible for that act. I did know that a terrorist act was going to be committed. The magnitude of that act is a mere hint of what the group can do.

"I am here to state that we wish to unify our entire world under a cohesive world governing body. We already exist throughout the world in or behind each of the seats of government. We are now ready to announce ourselves to the people of your countries.

"The devastating terrorist act, which was perpetrated upon so many innocents, was misguided, wrong in the belief that people would be unable to work and govern with others throughout the world without fear, being the sole guiding force. Those who perpetrated that act and their leaders have been dealt with and some are in your custody as we speak.

"I and others within our group believe that there is no reason to force you to govern together through terror and fear. There will be no more acts of terrorism and bloodshed. We offer instead reason, guidance, and our group as the binding that ties the countries of the world together to meet the outsiders. Our future as a planet, the planet earth, is around the corner with the coming of these aliens to our skies.

"We will assist you all in putting differences aside, molding the separate to become the one and placing the future of the world in the hands of everyone. A global government, not one country here or there is the goal. Many of you know us, you fear us because of what we have wrought and sanctioned in the recent and even distant past. The greater good, health and welfare of all the people of earth, however, is our most basic goal and desire. Not destruction, greed, decimation, fear, and terror."

Sir James paused, keyed some numbers into the small box in front of the monitor. "You will see a number at the bottom of your screen. When you have convened, discussed, and assessed this situation one of your number will call that number and we will begin to work with you all to prepare this most auspicious beginning of the new era of the earth. However, there is a deadline. We must have this government in place and working, by the time planned for the meeting with those who come to earth to meet with that global governing body."

The screen went dark immediately. Michael, Ilena and Richard all spoke at once.

"What does this mean?" What are you planning?" "Is this what my father was going to do?" "Are we coming out into the open? Why won't the UN simply take over the meeting?"

"Ilena, your father planned this meeting but to present a different message. His plan was to offer more threats, more terror, until they all knelt to his desire with him as the head of a new government, as well as the leader of our group. He would then be the only leader to negotiate with the aliens. He would be the sole representative for the Earth. His goals would be put forth, not those of mankind.

"I have offered the people of the earth continued rule of themselves as a united earth, they would come to us only for assistance, arbitration with problems. A benign overseer."

Michael spoke quietly for the first time, "Sir, I would think that they would have traced your transmission and be able to hunt us down."

"No, Michael. I know the technology for tracing is quick, but I was on a minimal amount of time using various satellites to transmit. The next time I need to speak with them will be different yet. The phone number is also a blind line going nowhere. It simply triggers a previously set response in Eastern Europe."

Michael nodded, his worries about his employer's safety, for the moment, put to rest.

"Now, I think we should all get some rest. We have a lot of work ahead of us and we need to be working at optimum efficiency." Sir James strode out of the room as he gestured to his son to follow him.

The others stayed where they were looking at each other and then at the door. Richard was the first to move, "I think I'll take him up on that suggestion and find myself a bedroom. I'll probably sleep for a week, so one of you wake me up if something happens."

Ilena glared at his departing back, thinking how easily they were all drawn to Sir James path. With her father so ill, in a hospital and unable to complete his work, she did not want to be drawn in as well. But then she thought of the work he had completed, the annihilation of thousands of people to make a point. She didn't want to follow either one of the men, one was as bad as the other she felt. She turned toward the one person left in the room, Michael, but he was lounging in a chair apparently asleep already.

Obviously nothing was going to happen at this moment, so she decided to find a room for herself as well.

But Ilena had misjudged Michael, he was wide awake and watching her. Sir James did not trust her nor did he. He would not be leaving her alone for a minute, but as usual, Ilena would be unaware that he was watching her every move. He listened to her steps rising up the stairs and left the room to stand at the bottom of the staircase, peering upwards, waiting to see which room she chose.

Once the door was closed, he silently mounted the stairs two at a time, slipped past closed doors and chose a hallway chair just around the corner from Ilena's room. From that location he could watch her door in the mirror strategically placed diagonally across the hall. He'd completed many such watches in his lifetime and probably would complete many more, as long as he worked for Sir James.

Morning came quickly for all of them. Michael as usual appeared to be the first up, but the lines under his eyes belied his statement of having a good nights' sleep. Sir James looked at him sharply, then said, "Were there any problems?"

"None at all, Sir."

"Good. We have a lot to do today and I need you and Richard to do a few things."

"Richard?"

"Yes, I want him to begin to act as your back-up, and assistant. You both do very well on your own, but things have heated up and you need to have help. I know I can trust you both, you have both been tested in ways you can't begin to know and passed.

"Michael, don't think I don't know that you haven't wished for help. I've put a lot on your plate and you've never complained, however, without sleep, even you can make mistakes. I want you to give Richard some of the background of what you do, particularly the clean-up."

Richard came around the corner of the kitchen at that moment, "I heard my name mentioned and the words clean-up. I hope I didn't make a mess somewhere."

Michael looked at him in shock. Richard was no longer the swarthy, dark haired middle eastern. His hair was light brown, his skin tanned but without the thick beard hiding a square jaw and sideburns he simply looked like he'd been on vacation.

Richard laughed at the expression on Michael's face. "I think the drains will need a good cleaning after all that hair."

"Michael, I think that is the first time I've ever seen you surprised." Sir James said. "You assumed that I had recruited a genuine middle eastern for the undercover task. Actually no, poor Richard was one of Clothilde's old boyfriends who just happened to have been raised in the Middle East. I'd had several long meetings with him and recruited him a few years ago. Clothilde had thrown him aside long before he started working for me.

Sir James looked at both men for a moment, then said, "Well, if you two are going to be working together, you need to know more about each other and what your capabilities are. I suggest you both head downstairs and work things out." With that he gestured to a set of spiral stairs fit into a closet door that he had just opened.

Evelyn was sitting on a bench in Sliema watching the boats slide up and down the coastline, distractedly picking at a small thread at the hem of her blouse. She was tired of the stores, the museums, the intimate little restaurants, they all lacked the one thing she needed most, her husband. She'd been left alone before when he'd been off on assignments, but this time was different. It had been different from the beginning when he awakened her at dawn to leave on an unexplained, unplanned trip. His face had been grim, set, so unlike the man she'd known for over twenty-five years.

When she'd been trailing around behind him as an officer's wife she'd expected to be worried constantly when he was away, whether for a day, a week, a month, or even more than a year. But now? No, not now, when he was assigned the nice quiet job as a military liason to the White House. There were nights, she remembered as she thought back, he had come in late, early in the morning really. The next day he had always seemed distant, his eyes concerned. Obviously there was a lot more to that comfortable job than she had thought.

"Evelyn? Evelyn?"

A pleasant accented voice broke in on her thoughts and she looked up to see Philippe's wife Celine standing in front of her.

"Oh, I'm sorry, Celine. I was just thinking about my husband. You know with so much going on these days."

"You don't have to apologize. I'm the one who should apologize for being late. I had to pick up some dry cleaning and there was an accident on the way back to my house."

"Celine, it's all right. You have put so much of your life on hold to spend these past weeks with me."

Evelyn got up and the two women began walking away from the water and toward the shops lining the street.

"No, I'm happy to be with you. Philippe has always spoken of your husband as being the person who had made our life possible. I don't understand all of it, but apparently at some point when they were in the Gulf War, Philippe was almost killed or captured, I don't know. Your husband risked his own safety and life for him. They were both nearly killed I think. Philippe has a terrible scar along his back, long, jagged. I can't imagine what kind of weapon could have caused that, certainly not a gun." Celine shuddered as she spoke.

"When he came home after meeting you and your husband in Valleta that day, he just said, the man I owe my life to, our life to, needs help and he asked me to meet you the next day." Tears trickled from her gentle brown eyes, "I'm so glad he did."

The women hugged each other for a second, and Evelyn said, "We need to get some coffee and think happier thoughts." Even as she spoke her thoughts were still on her husband, but she didn't want her younger companion to share any more of her own sadness. She wasn't accustomed to talking to friends. Her life was totally entwined with her husband. She had never felt the need other women had for going places with groups of girlfriends, gossiping, comparing clothing. She had never found a need for that kind of friendship, even now. She glanced sideways at Celine, she looked like a model, tall and blonde, still in her early thirties, much younger than Philippe. She probably didn't even really understand why her husband had forced this friendship on her.

The Leader sat propped up on pillows in his canopied bed. The somber ornate black walnut with the dark green hanging seemed to match his sour mood. The fully vetted nurse had been hovering around him for the last three days and he hated her and her smiling ruddy round face. Why the hell this woman had to be around him every minute, even when he decided to just go into the bathroom, she was standing guard outside, asking if he was all right, if he needed help. Then making sure his sheets were pulled up to his neck when he returned to his bed. Damn he knew he was weak. But did she have to make sure he felt like an invalid? He wondered who had hired her. He had been assured by his private secretary, Seth, that she had passed all tests with flying colors. Maybe passed too well, the Leader grumbled to himself. He wasn't sure he even trusted Seth.

He had hired Seth eight years ago when he had been unable to hire Michael away from Sir James. But Seth was definitely not a Michael. A former Navy seal, Seth was slim, quiet and deadly with a knife or gun, but had none of the creativity or the intelligence of the formidable Michael. He still did not trust Seth to any of the inner workings of his life. The Leader knew Seth had to know there was more that needed to be done than just handle the day to day business of running his household, doing background checks on people and personally protecting him outside of his home.

The phone rang interrupting his thoughts. He picked it up and when he heard the voice on the other end, said "one moment" put his hand over the mouthpiece and told his nurse to leave the room immediately. She heard the tone of command and left. She crossed the hallway and went into the combination bedroom and sitting room she had been given. Once the door was closed she pressed the lapel pin on her uniform. The Leader's voice was immediately at her ear, too soft to be heard by anyone else, should they be in the room.

"You can't mean that. Who would have called that meeting? I certainly did not. I'm not up to even walking outside my house, let alone fly up to Canada for a meeting. I'm lucky to be alive. It's been less than a week, and I'm home. I should be able to in another week."

There was a small pause then the Leader began to yell. Why are you doing this? I've followed all of your orders. No! No! None of that was my doing. That stupid fool Anders. This is his fault! If he wasn't dead already…. I, I…

His voiced became almost a hiss. "I strengthened this group to be an iron fist. We are not to be reckoned with by anyone. You should be aware of my…." His voice stopped. The nurse heard him yell again, "No! You can't! You wouldn't!" Then silence. It was apparent whoever had been on the other end had hung up.

She could hear his labored breathing, as a nurse she wanted to go to him. But she knew she had to wait for him to call her. Otherwise he would think she had been listening outside the door. It was another ten minutes before the buzzer in her room went off.

She calmly went in to the Leader's room. He was still in his bed, but drenched in sweat. She began her customary fussing, called the maid to change the sheets, and got him into the bathroom to change his pajamas. She knew whoever had been on the other end of the line and what it meant, another job would be ending shortly. She had her instructions.

It was Wednesday, it had been arranged for her to only take Sunday off. Based on the phone call, most likely she would be out of a job on Monday. Oh well, this one paid better than most, so she could wait at least a month before the next job. Besides, she didn't care for this arrogant man. To her, he failed as a human being.

The Leader came out of the bathroom to see her standing beside his bed, placing his pills in a small paper cup. He was walking slowly, but his back was straight, black eyes glaring at her. It seemed that was how he looked at most people, the nurse thought to herself.

"I want you out of my house, now. I will decide who will take care of me. Pack your things." He paused as if for emphasis as he stood looking down at her. "Now!"

"Of course, sir. I'll have the agency send someone else."

"No you will not 'have the agency send someone else'. I will get my own person."

She left the medicine on the table and left the room, pretending to fuss with her collar, she again activated the listening device she had planted in the room on her first night. As expected he was using the phone.

"Seth, I want you here immediately. I don't like that nurse you found for me, she is just too cheerful. I don't think she is competent. Get me someone else." There was silence for a moment then, "I don't give a damn if she has a better security clearance then the President, I want someone else, now. Or better yet, why don't you come over here. You can be making your calls and checking my medicine. Yes, why don't you do that now." The leader slammed the phone down.

The nurse jumped as the sound blasted her ear. Then she heard the phone ringing, and the leader answered it. "What now?" There was a momentary silence and she heard his gasp.

"I'm so sorry. I just had a call from those damn fool telemarketers. I....I." The man was silent for several moments then the nurse heard him say, "Yes, yes, I understand. I have no idea who called that meeting. I haven't talked to anyone, not even him in days."

The nurse sat down on her bed still listening attentively to the sound next to her ear. All she could hear was the leader's raspy breath. Then he was whispering, "You can't do this. You can't. I've followed every order. Who else would you, could you trust? Hello? Hello?"

The connection had been broken. The nurse threw her clothes in her suitcase and went back across the hall to tell the Leader she was leaving. He was pale, sweating, his breathing was shallow. Forgetting his previous orders, she grabbed her stethoscope and touched his now clammy skin. She looked down at his night table and realized that he had not taken the medicine she had put out for him. She forced the pill under his tongue and said, "Sir, I'm calling an ambulance you need to return to the hospital." Matching deeds to words she picked up his phone and dialed. Once she hung up, she notified the household staff to be on the alert for the ambulance.

The nurse noted the difference in time she gave him the medicine in her small case notebook, his blood pressure and the fact that his health had taken a turn for the worse. She always had to be prepared for questions in these high profile cases. But she knew that this particular case was going to really become a problem very soon.

"What are you writing? What are you doing, keeping a diary?" The Leaders' raspy voice questioned, even his whisper was in an imperious tone. "Give me that now!"

"I'm sorry, sir, I can't give a copy to you until it has been transcribed. Just like your hospital record. It can be made available to you in a couple of days. Right now, these are just notations about your medication." The nurse returned the notebook to her pocket.

His momentary strength left him and the Leader leaned weakly against the pillows. The nurse helped him into his robe so that he would be ready when the ambulance came. But just as she finished pulling his robe onto his arms the door opened.

Two men dressed in black, hoods over their faces, rushed through the door. They did not speak, and pushed the nurse away from the bed so roughly that she fell to the floor hitting her head against the wall. She was dazed. Fearing for her life she feigned that she was unconscious.

The men wrapped the frail spluttering Leader in his bedclothes and hustled him from the room. The nurse heard their feet, thudding down the hall toward the stairs. She picked up the phone and dialed a number that she had memorized long ago.

"The subject has been taken." She whispered when the receiver was picked up. She didn't expect a response and didn't hear one. She hung up the phone and dialed 911 again. She told the operator that someone else in the household hadn't realized that she as the nurse was taking care of him and thought the gentleman was in distress. The ambulance canceled she went back across the hall and completed her packing. Her head was hurting, but she had to leave the premises as quickly as possible.

Scant minutes later, her large tote over her shoulder, and her medical bag in hand she ran down the steps to see the butler lying bleeding across her path to the door. She knelt and felt for a pulse without success. She didn't want to search deeper into the house, her window of opportunity was fleeting and she had less than five minutes now to be out of the house.

Her car as always, was off to one side of the driveway, she threw her bags in and started the motor. The blast blew out most of the windows in the mansion and those of the surrounding homes. Little could be seen of the small frame that had been the nurse's car. Nothing could be seen of the nurse.

The two had been pondering their loose ends for quite a while. There were several and any one of them could lead some intrepid investigator or stupid reporter to their door eventually. They had maintained their distance for years. Operating through the Leader whose personal wealth and magnetism had made him the perfect foil for all of their work. But now, he had gone too far.

The late afternoon sun shone down on the balcony as they sat under the tiled roof, shaded from the strong rays. Their languid movements belied their concerns. Only the tense set of the man's jaw and mouth gave any hint of problems.

"We've come too far not to complete this. We're so close, darling." The woman moved over to him, sat down on the arm of the chair and began rubbing his neck. He raised and turned his head, enjoying the feeling of her long fingers.

"I know, I know. But right now, without Sir James, we don't have the continuity we need to continue to operate. I don't believe Vanderlin ever told Sir James about us. That he was not the final authority. If Sir James is operating as I think he is, we are going to have a bigger problem. His man, Michael, can without a doubt, bring us down."

"What about Sir James son, Edward?"

"If he begins to work in concert with Michael, Sir James doesn't need anyone else, and definitely not us. We have to locate him and get him, get them all under control. Once he left his pilot standing in Switzerland, we lost him completely."

"Maybe he's back in England?"

"No, the plane turned up in the states. But was found too late, the plane left without filing a complete flight plan. That means it had probably been on the ground at the most three or four hours. They could be anywhere by now. I think it's time for us to send the emergency signal to Sir James. We'll see where his answer comes from."

The two walked into the villa, soft leather couches beckoned from quiet corners near bookcases. Two wine glasses sat on an old carved wooden desk tucked into the curve of a staircase. They went through the door behind the desk, their bare feet not making a sound on the tiled floor. The ceiling of the room curved under the stairs and then arched out into the middle of the house. It was apparent now that the entire home had been built around this hidden center room.

"Philippe, are you sure you want to make contact now?"

He put his arm around her, "Celine, we've known ever since Vanderlin began planning that fiasco off Bermuda we could eventually come to this. He is completely out of the picture now, Sir James is obviously taking over the original plan. He has to know, and be brought fully into the picture of what is really at stake here."

"Yes. Much as I hate to admit it, it is the only way. Time is growing short."

Philippe brought the laptop to life and tapped in a few codes, picked up his cell phone and dialed. He then sat back and waited. Celine wasn't as calm and kept moving around the room.

Thousands of miles away, Sir James and the rest were eating lunch, when he felt his cell phone vibrate in his pocket. He reached inside his jacket and pulled it out. There was a text message on the tiny screen, and when he read it, he gasped. The others in the room immediately turned toward him.

"It has begun. All of you, now! Turn off the stove, everything. We have to get to the room. Now!" He swiftly began clearing the table, throwing the disposable dishes into a garbage can.

Ilena, Michael, Edward and Richard moved without question, and sanitized the kitchen. Although Ilena's face showed her dislike for what she was doing, she'd already gone head to head with Sir James in private, and knew better than to question him now.

They wordlessly followed Sir James through the secret passage at the back of the kitchen. As soon as they were all through, he immediately pressed another button, which made the door open to an innocuous pantry.

"All right, everyone," he began as they rushed down the steps and into the hollowed mountain. "As you know I have started to continue the plans as they were originally. But, as I often suspected there was someone above the Leader, Ilena's father. He was not in charge. I have just been contacted with a code that means that your father is dead. I have to respond to this person, whoever, and wherever they are. But this also means they don't know where I am. So, Edward, Michael kindly bring up the monitors and the scramblers.

"Be assured, I am not going to give away anything to this person until we find out more about them. Richard, let's get our news channels on and see what's been happening while we rested."

Five minutes later Sir James sat down and responded to the message with one of his own. It bounced off multiple satellites, routed through Australia, the Pacific Ocean and the Bering Sea before landing in the Mediterranean villa of Philippe and Celine Camillieri on the island of Malta.

"We have our answer. Judging from the length of time of the response, he has been very clever and has gone to ground somewhere. It's going to take quite a while to unscramble the trail, time we just don't have."

"Why don't we have him fly here? It's safe enough."

"Actually, no, I think I have another way of getting to him. We can use Evelyn."

"But then Edward will know who we are and tell Sir James."

"Exactly, Celine. That way the problem of their trusting us and taking the time to build that trust will be eliminated. I'll send Evelyn as our courier to meet with Edward and Sir James. The problem is now where can they meet that will be completely safe."

Philippe began punching in codes on his laptop as Celine leaned over him. First the pictures of Edward Gately came up "I'm pulling all of the alerts for the two of them from the police, customs, and international security systems." He overtyped 'cleared, alert canceled' then 'allow all entry, VIP status'. He then brought up Evelyn and did the same.

"Unfortunately, it's going to take a few days for that to get through to all of the agencies. But while we are waiting, we can plan our next move with Sir James." He pulled his wife around to him and kissed her. "Good job. Now let's get busy."

It was hours later before the two emerged from the inner room. The villa was lit by soft lighting from lamps placed here and there. The lights came on automatically whether they were home or not. They allowed no one to know when they were or were not in residence.

"When are you supposed to meet Evelyn next?"

"Tomorrow for lunch. She said she wanted to go exploring on her own for a while, she had some thinking to do."

"Sounds like she's getting tired of sitting around doing nothing. Let her know when you see her that she'll probably be seeing her husband soon. That should cure her. Make sure she has a suitcase and things to travel on short notice. I don't think she'll mind doing that, do you?"

Celine smiled, "Not in the least. That is one woman who truly is in love with her husband. Just the mention of his name and she glows. Amazing! Particularly for an American."

"All Americans are not as they are depicted on the television. Ed is an amazing man. He found and chose an amazing, loyal wife. But, remember, Ed is really British. He sounds like an American, fought with the Americans. But he has a deeply British core. So, my dear, we can't lump him with the rest." Philippe opened the double doors leading from the kitchen to their balcony as he spoke.

Celine took out a chilled bottle of wine and glasses and followed him out. A half-moon was reflected in the gently stirring Mediterranean as they took their first sip of wine. The silence held for just a moment before she spoke. "So. What do we do about the group? I mean really, they have been following Vanderlin for decades now. Sir James has always been the number two man to everyone. When we sent out that call just now to the members, when we meet them next week in Canada, what do we do?"

"We are not meeting them. They don't know us. They do know Sir James. He will meet with them and we will meet with him and Edward there. Things will settle down, we can pull the rest of the countries together and begin final preparations."

"They are confused. The Prime Minister in England wanted to know why they had all received a statement demanding their unification. I believe right now the countries of the world are in chaos and far away from unity, as a result of these actions."

Evelyn took a deep breath when she stepped out of the hot sun and into the cool of the church. She had needed to return to this place, this church with the odd name. Celine never brought her to Valleta and instead took her to Sliema and shopping, forever shopping. How could she buy? Celine always seemed to need a new jacket or scarf. But then she was so very young. There were some days she looked younger than others, as if she'd had Botox or collagen treatment or something. Philippe was obviously much younger than Ed. It amazed her that he and Ed had known each other in the Gulf War. He must have enlisted right out of high school.

Her thoughts rambled as she walked aimlessly between the pillars, past the beautiful statue of the Virgin Mary and the graves beneath her feet to find herself at a small side chapel set off to the left of the main altar. It was cooler and very little light filtered in from the grimy stained glass windows. She was surprised to see steep stone stairs leading down to a crypt on the inner wall between the pews.

Curious, she went carefully down the steps to an iron gate and peered through into a room lit by one bulb. The room contained sarcophagi of knights. The gate moved under her weight, as if inviting her in, but she felt uncomfortable and instead sat on the bottom step contemplating where she was. Somehow, she knew this was where Ed had come when he had left her alone while he met with Philippe. Too late now, she wished she had asked more questions of Ed before he left her. But it wasn't her way. He had always been so strong. Leading her, loving her, yet needing her, reaching out to her and talking about things he probably shouldn't have spoken of, just to get her thoughts on them. Her life had revolved around his for more years than she wanted to remember, but now, it seemed she needed to find her own place and become more than she had been.

She reached in her handbag and took out the small folded piece of paper he had given her when they were still in college. That worn paper had been her talisman, traveling with her everywhere. He had told her only that she would know when to open it. Sitting on these steps, alone in this church, more than twenty-five years later she knew it was time to open it.

She heard footsteps and quickly slid the paper into her pocket. She looked up and was startled to see Celine staring at her with a thoughtful look on her face.

"Celine! I didn't expect to see you today. I was just sitting here thinking about those knights from so long ago, buried here, where hardly anyone cares or even knows their resting place or who they are."

Celine nodded and then said, "We have to go. Your husband has sent a message that it's safe for you to meet him. Do you want to get packed or just leave your things in the apartment? The rent is paid through the end of next month. You can always return later and pick up your things."

"I should pack a few things, if only for a couple of days. The rest can stay there." Evelyn noticed the strange tone in Celine's voice immediately. The friendly, naïve, girlish quality was gone. This was someone she suddenly didn't feel comfortable being around. Yet, she really had no reason to doubt that she was actually going to finally go home or at least rejoin her husband. It had been all she had thought about since he walked out of the apartment in Mdina over six weeks before. So many unspeakable things had happened in the world since then. But her life had been serene, thanks to Philippe and Celine. No, she had to be wrong.

They left the church together. Celine was walking so quickly that Evelyn was feeling breathless trying to keep up with the younger woman. They finally reached Celine's BMW, sitting under the trees beyond the wall of the city.

Normally Evelyn felt comfortable with Celine's driving, but today that changed. The young woman usually drove leisurely through the tiny towns, chatting and pointing out the island's oddities. The pumpkins drying on roofs, the rose bushes at the ends of the grape vine rows, the quarries for digging the blocks of limestone for the island's homes. But now it was all business and speed, her blue eyes focused intently on the road.

Evelyn barely covered her intake of breath. Celine's eyes were brown. She didn't wear glasses and usually a person wearing contacts of different colors did so rather frequently. In the six weeks she had been with Celine she had always had brown eyes.

Evelyn didn't want to draw attention to the fact that she was staring at Celine's eyes trying to see if in fact there was a tell-tale line of dark around a blue lens, but no. It appeared her eyes were without any lens at all. When she had cried a couple of times in talking about her husband, her eyes had been teary, but didn't show any fogginess from contacts. What was happening here?

Twenty minutes later Celine brought the car to a stop near the fountain just inside of the walls of Mdina. Evelyn got out saying, "I'll just be a few minutes." She didn't wait for a response from Celine and just walked as quickly as she could into the little street next to her building. On her way up the steps to her apartment, she moved the folded slip of paper from her pocket, and tucked it firmly into her bra. She was sure Celine had seen her with it and felt much safer with it near her heart.

Ten minutes later she opened the door to Celine's car and threw her soft overnight bag into the back seat. "There that wasn't so long now was it?" She was careful to speak casually, she certainly didn't want Celine to think that she had grown suspicious.

Celine nodded and said "Not long at all, we're right on schedule."

"We're keeping to a schedule? Oh, you mean for flight times?"

"No, Evelyn. We have to meet with Philippe in less than an hour at our home, to go over some things before you meet with Edward. There are some things you need to know. It could still be a couple of days before you are actually with him. We want to make sure it's safe for you to travel again. There was an alert for both of you."

"What! An alert? What kind of alert? Safe to travel? Celine, what's got into you? What is this all about?"

"I'm sorry. I've really said too much. I'm so accustomed to just talking to you normally, that I've said more than I should have. Philippe will explain all of it to you."

"I should certainly hope so. You've both been so kind and easy going, I can't even begin to understand what this sudden change is all about."

"You will soon. Yes, you will soon." Celine became silent for the rest of the drive.

"Whoever they are, they want to meet with us, son. It appears they already know that we have started to step into the breach as it were."

"How soon do they want to meet?" Michael said as he turned away from the computer he had been working on.

"They are not giving a time. That's the strange thing, they said a known courier will present us with their final information."

"So what do we do about the heads of state we've put in an uproar. If we leave them hanging about they'll start hunting us down. The U. S. attorney general is already turning over every rock in the world looking for supposed assassins and murderers like him. The news is full of his wild statements. He sounds like he is going to battle the devil himself on the White House lawn, and he doesn't care who the devil is, or whether he has the right one."

"You're absolutely right, Michael, I had almost forgotten about him. He is a deadly force to be reckoned with. He and a few more of his hired help need to be dealt with though. I think we can leave a few clues in the President's and the Post's fax machine to effectively take care of him without exposing ourselves. He's already committed murder, so it shouldn't be too difficult to leak the actual facts about a certain gyroscope being tampered with to a few sources. You have the file. Make sure you use the total blind alley."

"Yes, Sir James. It will be out within the next half hour."

"Now that should remove one of our biggest problems. I'm glad you remembered him, Michael, before we moved along any further. I had mentioned him many times to your father Ilena, but he refused to eliminate him. I believe they had some history, which I never could quite understand. The man was obviously a killer when the previous president chose him, and the present one was left with his legacy. What a mess the Americans make of their democratic process."

"Dad, the people don't know about all of that. They never would have allowed a murderer to be an attorney general. Besides it's not an elected office."

"We don't have time to dwell on that now. It's over and done with, anyway. Damn!!"

"What, Sir James?"

"Sir?"

"Dad?"

Everyone spoke at once as they watched Sir James take his cell phone from his pocket. Normally, they never knew when he received messages because he took them in privacy, but this was different, they were all here together and this was about as private as it was going to be for some time.

"It's them again. Ed, read this."

Ed walked over to his father, from where he had been sitting under a framed world map. He looked down and read the text message on his father's phone. He gasped.

"I can't believe that. I won't believe that. The words were correct. It can't be." His voice was a whisper as he slumped to the seat beside his father. Neither Michael nor his Father had ever heard such emotion from him.

Ilena and the others surrounded them, "What is happening?"

"We no longer have the luxury of time. They are forcing our hand to act faster than we wish to. Granted it is only a matter of a week or so, but we needed that week. We do have at least three days. We will put them to good use."

"Michael, Richard," Sir James said as he walked over to them and led them to the rear of the room, between two natural outcroppings of the mountain, talking quietly and quickly. They stood there together, listening to the older man, nodding now and then. He pointed them in the direction of a presently unused computer, and returned to the others.

"Ilena, we need you to put together some documents for us that look official but mean nothing. Over here I have the perfect machine, and letterhead from everywhere and everyone and will show you how to use it. Come, my dear." He walked past his son, who was still sitting on the small steel framed couch.

The large manor house had been sitting dark for years, waiting to be noticed. Hand- picked crews came weekly, cleaning floors, washing windows, mowing lawns, trimming formal gardens, checking fountains, plumbing, electricity. Today, however, there were food suppliers and linen rental trucks. The regular staff was supplemented by other heavily vetted staff, from all over the world, to serve the elite arriving guests.

They had very little time to prepare bedrooms, bathrooms, and set up the small cottages for the lesser VIP's, who would have to walk from there to the meetings held in the ballrooms and salons of the manor. Security guards were everywhere and the only rooms without a camera were the en-suite bathrooms. The public bathrooms were not that lucky. There were three security guard sites on the property, including the one in the secured basement area. There were ten German shepherds who were gentle with children, their handlers, and anyone they were told was just fine. All others were considered a walking meal.

Michael and Richard sauntered through the manor house together watching the preparations, having flown over night from their secret location in Colorado.

"I think we are going to be ready on time."

"Still looks pretty chaotic to me, M."

"Always, does. I've done many of these kinds of things, over the years. The worst part is the security of the people coming in with the food. It seems the baddies always try to get someone in during the last hours with the catering or valet staff. It's assumed due to the rush, security breaks down and people get through easier. I always push our people in the opposite direction. The security staff here has been used by us for years. They are paid very well. If they spot something or someone, it's a bonus in their pocket and a generous one, so they are careful. They also know that they are constantly vetted, so should someone try and compromise their situation they better come to us before we come to them. The consequences are not something anyone knowingly wishes upon themselves."

"Has anyone ever sold out?"

"Just once, well, it wasn't really a sellout. It was more like stupidity. They didn't know enough to keep their mouths shut."

Richard nodded and they continued their tour outside of the seventy-five room house. The sky was clear blue with very few clouds, and the same weather had been forecast for the next day. But it was very cold here in the Laurentians. There had already been some snow and those who lived in the nearby towns were getting prepared for heavy snow storms at any time. But Richard and Michael had only needed to prepare for these two days and almost all of the dignitaries had arrived and were getting settled in for the conference.

He was glad he was working with Michael and not against him. Just the workouts the man put himself through had been difficult enough. But when he saw the concealed weaponry Michael carried on a daily basis he knew he was deadly. He was a man who was prepared for anything, at any time and who relied only on himself. In addition to his Glock, Richard carried a knife concealed in his boot and a couple of throwing tools and felt perfectly comfortable. But then his proficiency was only with those types of weapons so perhaps for him that was best.

They were passing one of the linen trucks while the rear gate was slowly coming down with an enormous bin of linen. A man was holding onto the bin, he had on a weight belt to ease his back with the constant lifting. Richard looked up into his face, recognized the number two man of EL Jazehra and kept walking. He knew with his light coloring and dark glasses the man most likely would not recognize him. But he knew better than take a chance.

Richard walked away from Michael and asked loudly in his British accent about a tree growing away from others in the area. He thus effectively placed the man between the two of them. Michael realized what was happening and took three steps toward the deliveryman, apparently assisting him with the bin, while Richard seemed to be tipping it toward him.

"Oh, they should have given you help, my friend." Michael said, as he surreptitiously patted the man down and found him bulging with weapons. "We will help you with that. It's too much for one person."

Michael took the man's upraised arm, pulled it down behind his back so sharply that it snapped and he cried out. "Oh, are you all right? That bin must have rolled over your foot." Michael said just as Richard rolled it off the lift and over the man's foot.

"We will get you some help." Michael continued speaking in the same easy manner in case there were any eavesdroppers as he signaled two of the regular guards to place the man in the secured basement area. They hustled him there using the door through the garden shed.

"Michael, if he's here, there are others as well. Plus there might be larger weapons in the trucks."

"Now, I know why Sir James wanted you, I don't know these people. He could have walked right by me. This is a whole different set of game pieces. Well, that was the second bin of linen off the truck which means there is someone already inside with another one."

While Richard secured the truck and drove it to an area some distance away from the house, Michael mobilized the guards to look for the first bin of linen with an unknown number of deliverymen. Michael reported the situation to Sir James realizing this could be unexpected and his boss might want to deal with it differently.

He and Richard met up again in the basement of the manor house and walked in on the once proud Mohammad Alifah. The man was on the floor in the corner of the small concrete room in his underwear, feet bound, writhing in pain, and his broken arm flopping. He looked up at them. "I know you. Yes. I know you. Are you traitor to us? Or traitor to them?" His pain seemed forgotten as he tried to bargain and bully.

Richard spoke then, his voice soft, menacing. "I am a traitor to no one. You, Mohammad, have nothing to sell today. This man with me? He knows who I am. He knows where I came from, who my family is. I know who your family is Mohammad and where you came from. We have your truck. You, Mohammad, have nothing to sell us today." He turned his back on the man.

A table in the corner held the varied weapons he had been carrying. Even the inside of the movers' weight belt held small sharp knives and weapons. But the most interesting item on the table was a small silver tube. Richard picked it up and handed it to Michael. They put the rest of the weapons into a small bag. They took the bag and the table with them, leaving the injured terrorist alone.

As they closed the door, he shouted, 'I need a doctor.'

"I thought you called a doctor, Richard."

"I got so busy."

"I'll check on him in a little while. I have some skills with those kinds of injuries," Michael said coldly, "besides we have to check on who and where his friends might be."

They left the secured basement area by a concealed door to the outside. Once they reached the gravel path, they split up and Michael headed indoors, while Richard continued walking the perimeter of the grounds.

Michael turned a corner and headed down the main gallery toward the conference room when he heard a commotion from the top of the staircase. There, two guards were manhandling a man in coveralls, with the same logo as the linen truck. Michael ran up the stairs two at a time to help them with the struggling suspect.

"We found him snooping around in the study."

"Sorry fella, I don't think delivery of linen allows you entrance to the upstairs and definitely not the study, so whoever you are, I think you need to join your buddy."

The three hustled the man out of the house and into the small room, stripped him down to his underwear and left him with his injured comrade. There were no windows in the room. The only light was turned on from a switch outside the door, effectively blinding any occupant in the room for a few seconds.

The door slammed shut and the solid thud informed the prisoners of the fact that the door would not be an option for escape. They started yelling for a doctor immediately but through the thick concrete walls little could be heard or understood.

Richard came up to the group at that moment. "Do you know the other one we just found?" Michael asked.

Richard looked in through the slit in the door and blinked. "Yes. Oh, yes. He is the man that plans all of the operations, Hasan al Naif. He wouldn't be here unless he felt that it was critical to get the job done. He has only gone on one other job. He usually remains in a safe place far from the work to be done. Did he have weapons on him?"

"Not many. But he did have two more of those silver tubes and a couple of very nasty garrotes." Michael answered as they walked away from the now pitch black room. "We'll let them enjoy themselves before we talk to them.

The two men walked toward the front of the mansion just as a white limousine pulled up in front. "I thought everyone had arrived." Richard said as they watched the slim, tanned chauffeur race around to open the rear door.

A tall, very blonde, young woman, dressed in a pale gray suit slid in one fluid movement from the car and stood with her hand out to assist the next passenger. An older woman, with short dark hair got out of the limousine and looked around as if surprised at her surroundings. The younger woman led the way to the door of the house as if she belonged there.

Michael and Richard rushed forward to meet them at the door. "May we help you ladies?" Michael asked and then his breath hitched as he recognized Edward's wife. He covered it quickly with a cough, but Richard gave him a strange glance.

The older woman started to speak, but the blonde woman put

her hand on her arm and said, "We are here for the conference and to meet someone." Her voice was like a crystal bell yet with a sing-song quality to it. The shorter woman looked at her, startled. Clearly, there was something strange about this entire encounter and Richard was watching Michael and the two women, when out of the corner of his eye he noticed a movement.

He looked toward the limousine and was surprised to see that it had left the driveway and was parked. He had neither heard nor seen it move. When he looked back at the two women the chauffeur was standing behind them. It was then that he could see a clear resemblance between the man they had taken to be the chauffeur and the blonde woman.

Michael also seemed to be startled by the appearance of the chauffeur in front of them and Richard heard another slight intake of breath from his companion. The chauffeur nodded toward the two of them, and reached out his hand to open the door for the women. His shoulder momentarily brushed up against the taller woman and Richard was sure his eyes betrayed him. A golden shimmer played around the two figures for barely an instant, then was gone as the trio walked inside the dim foyer and the door closed behind them.

Michael and Richard looked at each other, with Michael the first to recover. "What was going on there? How did that limo get from point A to point B without a sound? Did you see what I saw?"

Richard, glad that his assessment of what had just happened was validated, answered him. "I don't have any idea how that limo got parked, the chauffeur got to those women, and I certainly don't have any idea about the rest of it. Michael, I've seen and heard a lot, but I think we need to get inside and find out just what the bloody hell is happening here."

"I agree. After those terrorists, then seeing those people with Edward's wife, I didn't suspect anything until things got weird."

"That was Edward's wife?"

"Right, you weren't in the States at the beginning of this mess. Edward and his wife had disappeared, and there was a black order out on both of them. We knew it was lifted a few days ago, but we didn't know who lifted it. The Leader is dead, so he didn't lift it. We are now looking for someone else and we may have just found them.

"Before we go in there I need to let Sir James know that Edward's wife is here. This is an unexpected development that he needs to know." He pressed the key on his cell phone that secured the connection and quickly sent a coded message the thousands of miles where it was picked up less than twenty seconds later. Once that was done, the two men followed the trio into the manor house.

Sir James slipped the cell phone from the inside pocket of his jacket and read the message. He had known that Evelyn was going to be used as the courier and had let Ed know. But neither had expected her to be at the manor house for the meeting. Did they expect Edward to be there? Did they expect him to be there? Is that why they sent her so soon? But Michael had said she wasn't alone and there was something happening that Michael obviously didn't like.

"Ilena, Edward, there are things happening at the manor house that we did not expect. Evelyn has shown up there with two others. Do you know who that might be, Edward?"

"I left her in the care of my friend Philippe and his wife. I don't understand. Something must have happened to them for Evelyn to be at the manor house. I just don't understand."

"What does this Philippe look like?"

"Blonde, my height, but very slim, I'd say he's pretty Nordic looking except that he usually tans easily."

"You trust him?"

"Of course. I certainly wouldn't have left Evelyn with them. He helped me disappear when the Leader decided I was a threat and kept her safe, at least until now. He is someone I would trust with my life and I have."

"All right then. Let's assume the worst. That Evelyn has been kidnapped and is being used as a pawn to draw us out. I'll see if we can get a picture of this pair. It takes a lot to shake Michael and apparently he's shaken."

"Dad, why don't we get up there, help to get this sorted out? You said we can leave here unobserved."

"No, definitely not yet, Edward. I have what we need here. I'm going to have Michael and Richard get Evelyn out of there and bring her back here. If anyone can do it they can.

"But we cannot forget the weapons those terrorists were carrying and whatever has distracted Michael and Richard, I think they need to find out what is in those silver tubes and ensure there weren't any planted before the terrorists were caught."

Sir James mouth tightened to a thin line as he began sending a return code to Michael and Richard with their new orders. Edward and Ilena stared at him a moment before something on one of the television screens caught their eyes. The Attorney General of the United States was being led out of the White House in handcuffs, surrounded by Secret Service. Ilena turned up the sound.

The newscaster seemed out of breath as he yelled into his microphone, 'Incredible developments here, ladies and gentlemen. There you see the United States Attorney General apparently under arrest by the Secret Service being placed in a car. Last night the President's Cabinet was called in on an emergency basis and has remained there all day today.

"We have seen a large contingent of National Guard surrounding the White House and many Secret Service Agents entering the building. No one, and I repeat no one has been able to find out what is going on inside the Oval Office where it is assumed this lengthy meeting is still continuing. No day to day staff has left the White House. However, this morning's shift has entered as usual.

"It was noticed by this reporter that as each of today's staff came up to the gate, not only were the staff passes checked at least three times but handbags and brief cases, were confiscated and each member of the staff was escorted into the building by Secret Service or one of the armed Military. To all appearances, the White House has been locked down. No one from the White House press office has come out to speak with us. Several of the senior journalists here have requested a briefing on developments, but so far those requests have been ignored."

Sir James pressed the remote to lower the sound on the television again. "Well, it looks as if the President is taking control and purging the bad fruit. That should keep the Attorney General busy for the next twenty years or more since high treason is punishable by death. The murder and conspiracy charges alone should be enough to hold him until they have completed all of their investigations.

"I wonder how many others he will send off in disgrace. I doubt he will get them all, but the others will be sure to be more careful.

"Now, Edward, I have certain things that you and Ilena will have to do. There is a frightened woman running for her life that we have to help out. She has helped us immensely without even being aware of it. Here is where she is staying. Ilena you will have to make first contact, I am sure that by now she is frightened of her own shadow. We have to get her back here and totally out of sight, before some of those with the President realize where half of that information that he is using came from."

"Dad, I thought you wanted to bring Evelyn back here, shouldn't I be helping with that? She'll want to see me so she knows she's safe."

"I can't send you there, Edward. It will compromise some things that Michael and Richard are doing for me. Also, your mind would be on Evelyn and I need you at your optimum for this. Being that close to her would not be in her best interests to rescue her.

"Edward, you and Ilena will go to Maine immediately. I am giving you the area where Ms. Fleming was last seen to find her, convince her as quickly as possible that no harm is meant to her and her safety is of the utmost importance and you are all that stands between her and her continued safety. Once you locate her you will have at best, ten minutes with her. If she does not wish to leave with Ilena within that time, you must leave her and return here.

"I don't want to lead anyone to her, but if I found her the others can as well. They were closely on her trail when the Leader died and she was no longer considered a threat. But with this new information, others of the Leader's group will return to her as a possible link.

"I will remain here in contact with all of you. I want to know everything that is happening at all times. You know how to contact me. Ilena this is your first mission and it is vital. Remember, she does not know your father or of the group. She is simply a carrier of vital information. If she offers you the information but does not want to leave with you, take the information from her in whatever form it may be, but leave within ten minutes with or without her."

Ilena looked at the man she had known all of her life and at that point made a decision, "Uncle James, this is what I was waiting for and you're trust in me will not be disappointed. Thank you." She hugged him, tears welling up in her eyes. "My father never trusted me to even drive by myself less than a year ago. I won't disappoint you."

Sir James returned the young woman's hug and sent them out to the Lear jet. He knew it was going to be a tough trip. It was snowing hard in Bangor right now, but he knew his son was an experienced pilot and would land on a beach if he had to, to get the job done.

Michael had read the text message to get pictures of the pair with Evelyn and asked Richard if he had taken any while they were at the entrance.

"Of course. I always like to know who my next enemy might be so it's become pretty automatic by now. I'm pretty sure I took two of the women and at least one when the man joined them."

"Great! Send those to Sir James. He wants to find out if Edward can recognize the two of them."

He watched as Richard brought up the pictures he'd taken with his cell phone, scrolled through them and found he had taken five in all, despite being rattled.

"Good job! Even more than you expected. Hopefully, they'll come through clear on the other end."

They sent the pictures through to the Colorado safe house where Sir James was waiting anxiously for developments to continue to unfold. He watched as the pictures came up on his cell phone. The man fit the description of Philippe, slim, tanned, and blonde. But this man appeared much younger than he should be for being in the Gulf War.

Sir James immediately forwarded the pictures to Edward's cell phone. When Edward had boarded the plane he had placed his phone between himself and Ilena on the cockpit's console so any information that came from Sir James they would both be able to see or hear immediately.

He was flying east over Nebraska when the pictures came through, the weather was turbulent and he needed to give his complete attention to keeping the plane in the air.

He glanced quickly at the phone, "Ilena, text back to my father that Philippe is definitely the man in the picture and I would imagine that is his wife beside Evelyn. Let him know I've never met Celine, but I'm sure, knowing Philippe's taste in women, that is Celine."

Ilene sent the message back to Sir James. When Michael and Richard heard that the two were the people taking care of Evelyn they realized they had to find out where they were in the house, why they were there and if at all possible get them out of there. But Sir James also wanted them to search the house and ensure it was clear. The silver tubes were an unknown and neither he nor Michael and Richard liked unknowns. Worse there was no laboratory where they could be opened or safe place to detonate them.

The linen truck that had been used to transport the terrorists and the weapons had been placed well away from the house in thick woods over a mile away. But the tubes that they had confiscated from the terrorists were now stored within a led lined box until it could be determined what they were. They were both worried that it wasn't safe enough yet.

They each took a complement of five men, informed them that they were looking for more terrorists, more silver tubes, and a tall young blonde couple with an older woman. They then split up to search. Michael's group took the first floor, while Richard's took the second.

The plan was that as they entered each unoccupied room, one stood blocking the door to the room, while the rest methodically scoured the room for the tubes. It was a painstaking, slow search, made slower by the effort to keep the rooms as neat as possible.

Richard's team on the second floor went immediately to the study where the terrorist had been found. The largest of the men stood guard at the study door while the others began searching seat cushions, drawers, books and shelves of books. Richard took the oversize desk for himself. He started opening the drawers, then ran his hand lightly under the ornate edge and was rewarded half way around the desk by feeling the cylindrical tube that he didn't want to find.

He bent down and stared up under the desk at the ominous silver tube. It was held in place by a small clip wedged into the sliver of space where the top of the desk met the base. It was tight against the wood and the silver tube glowed red and was much warmer to the touch than the others had been. Richard backed away from the desk, his eyes darting around as he gestured to the others in the study to leave, and gently closed the study door.

In the hallway, he signaled the others as agreed for immediate evacuation of the building. With that, the rush began to move all of the delegates to the conference as far away from the building as possible. Each of the men unceremoniously opened every door they came upon and in quiet voices ordered any occupants to leave the building.

Richard ran down the stairs, all the while looking to see if he could see the strange pair that had entered the building with Edward's wife. Delegates and staff were rushing from the building, bumping into one another in doorways as the quick tapping of high heels accompanied the thudding of heavy soles as over two hundred people fled the building. Michael's well trained men were guiding them into any available limousines, vans, or SUVs and driving them twenty miles to an out of the way hotel that had been reserved for just such an emergency.

While some of them registered panic, most of the delegates seemed to take it in stride. Many were from countries long accustomed to terrorism in all forms and were always prepared to flee for their lives. But still, neither Richard nor Michael could find any sign of Edward's wife, Evelyn. They scoured the meeting rooms where papers, briefcases, water glasses and pitchers were strewn in every direction as people fled.

They had just met at the front door when they felt a vibration that seemed to come from all around them. They raced from the building, not running for a car, but for the brick fence surrounding the manor some fifty yards away. They were barely five yards away from the fence when they heard the glass break and had just reached the gates and thrown themselves on the grass behind the wall as their ears seemed to explode and searing heat washed over them.

"Gentlemen, I believe you need a ride." Michael and Richard looked toward the voice at the same time. A rear door of the white limousine opened and the blonde woman held out her hand. They followed each other into the car, only then realizing that their clothes were in shreds, their faces and hands cut, burnt and bleeding.

"We know you stayed behind looking for us or most likely Evelyn." The woman said quietly. "We regret we could not have reached you sooner, but there were certain elements that we had to be sure of before we could speak with you.

"May I introduce you to Evelyn Gately. My husband, Philippe, is Edward Gately's friend. I believe that it is now time to see Sir James?"

Evelyn nodded slightly when introduced to the two men and then reached into the console in the limousine to get napkins and water to try to clean them up.

"Celine, these men are badly injured. We should take them to a hospital before going anywhere else."

"It's all right, Evelyn, they'll be fine shortly. We need to move quickly."

The two men watched the woman called Celine move up behind the driver. They had tried to listen to what was being said but they were having trouble hearing after the concussion of the explosion. Both of them were slumped against the leather of the rear seat barely moving until Michael took the wet napkin from Evelyn and began to check on the damage to his hands. Richard used another napkin, wiped his face gingerly as he looked at himself in the mirrored door of the console.

The limousine was moving quickly through the hills, away from the mansion, and away from the interrupted conference. Richard pushed himself straighter and looked through the window at the smoke rising from the ruined estate and whispered, "I think that is the end of Hasan and Mohammed. A shame we didn't have a chance to chat with them more."

Michael chuckled weakly, "At least they won't have to wait around for a doctor. But sometimes with rooms like they were in they might just use up one of their nine lives. Anyway, we better check in." He flicked a glance and raised an eyebrow at their hosts.

Evelyn had been watching the two men warily, when she did speak it was almost a whisper. "Why were you looking for me?"

Neither man answered immediately. They looked at each other, then at the couple up front. Michael imperceptibly shook his head as he looked directly at Evelyn. Based on his many discussions with Edward over the past days, he felt Evelyn would understand. She moved away from the two men and sat by herself in the middle of the limousine.

She understood then that these men also did not trust Philippe and Celine, she was certainly in agreement with that. She had not understood why they were continuously traveling since they had left Malta. Celine just kept saying they were on their way to meet Edward. She had thought Edward would have been here, in Canada. But no, these men, obviously British, were there.

Then she remembered the little piece of paper she had finally had a minute to read in a bathroom. The little piece of paper she knew she had to read before she left the place that her husband had told her was safe. It had been a shock and a revelation. But these two men she felt were very close to her Edward. With that thought, she relaxed more than she had in days.

Mary Fleming noticed the girl as soon as she left the coffee shop. Unsmiling, not even wearing make-up, but she was still very attractive. The young woman came up beside her, and whispered, "Mary, your safety is of paramount and immediate importance to the United States."

Mary's mouth opened as she gasped, "Who? What?"

"Your country needs you, Mary." Ilene whispered. Then she said, urgently, "I am here to get you to safety, now."

Despite the obvious youth of the girl, Mary believed what she was saying and nodded. "Please, let's go."

Ilene hugged her and as she did, moved her gently and quickly into the waiting dark gray sedan. They sped away from the curb, before Mary's followers even realized that someone was with her.

Edward left Bangor by a back route he had memorized to reach the second car that he had placed just off the interstate. Ilena kept holding Mary, who no longer looked anything like the graying, sharp tongued, hard-nosed director of research at the Washington think tank. Mary was obviously afraid, but although tears were at the corners of her eyes, it seemed as if through sheer force of will they didn't stream down her face.

They pulled up to the second car, were in and on their way within seconds. The dark green SUV merged into the traffic on the interstate until they reached the next exit and quickly took it, slid through a Walmart parking lot and emerged out of the back and entered the Bangor Airport grounds through a back freight gate.

They had already filed their flight plan to leave only a half hour before and their plane was taxiing down the runway in the snow, before Mary's terminators even finished filling in their bosses on their failed mission.

Once they were well on their way, Edward had Ilene open some brandy for the frightened woman, who was still afraid to speak to them or even ask a question. "Ma'm, I'm sorry for how we had to get you off the street, but there were people..."

"I know. I know. I didn't know what to do anymore. For a while they didn't follow, then it started up again yesterday. I've been staying with people in public, in front of others since then. I haven't slept in over twenty-four hours."

"You're safe now, Ms. Fleming." Edward said softly as he turned the plane west, "We're going to be flying for a few hours so you might want to take a nap."

Ilene brought the woman blankets and pillows. Mary Fleming thanked her and then grabbed her arm and said, "I mean I really thank you. I don't know who you people are, or what's even going to happen to me, but I feel safe with you. Thank you."

With that she pulled the blankets over her, turned toward the window and was soon asleep.

Edward checked the weather ahead, calculated their cruising speed and keyed in the arrival time to the Colorado house. Seconds later, Sir James Galston read it on his monitor and smiled. Ilene was a natural. Excellent. He had barely three hours to prepare for a meeting that he wished wouldn't be for another three weeks. Once Mary Fleming arrived he would have to give her his full attention, so anything else he had to do before Philippe and his wife arrived had to be done now.

There were many things that he could not share with his son or Michael, and certainly not Richard. True he trusted them all, but what they didn't know could actually save their lives. The worst part of that was that they needed to know things in order to act intelligently in case something happened to him. He had given a lot of information to Edward, but it would not be enough, when there was so much he didn't know.

Still he couldn't take a chance. He went through the house and down to the lowest level, the one place that he hadn't taken the others. Thick carpeting muffled his footsteps that traced a path to a set of steel doors set into the side of the mountain. He pressed his right ring finger in the center of the handle of one of the doors and they automatically opened. He stepped through and they hissed close behind him.

It always amazed him how much wealth could be hidden in a country that prided itself upon tracking everyone's earnings. He knew better than keep his wealth and source of power in the country of his birth. Here, the topography of the country was made for hiding anyone and anything. He sat down at his own computer. It was not networked to anyone of his group or his family but it was integrally linked to this house and certain aspects of its security.

His fingers were flying over the keys, transferring power sources, updating codes, laying in the information for his son to access all files from any source. He began powering up the hidden cameras in the surrounding territory. All the security mechanisms that he'd had built in over the years, he now turned on. The only possible access from now on would be either with one of his own aircraft, or if he personally gave access to another aircraft. Any other aircraft making an attempt to land without that access would be deflected from the area.

He stood up from the chair, stretched and walked to the rear wall and slid open a panel set into the wall. Thick glass was bolted to the steel frame of the window. He stared at one of the items behind the glass, stroking his salt and pepper mustache and beard as he thought, 'I wonder'. He shook his head, looked at the other items which only momentarily held the elderly man's interest, before he slid the thin wood closed, to again become flush with the wall.

He checked and rechecked everything he had done to make sure there would be no errors. Yes, he wanted the united front upon which his group had been founded, but he knew that those opposed would seek to stop it at all costs. The Leader, Vanderlin had been able to get rid of most of the worst terrorists, but there was and always would be someone to take their place. Those in Canada must have been there in retaliation for the Leader's termination strike. Plus Vanderlin's henchmen were loyal only to him. They also had to be eliminated, but that could not be done now. They were scattered and dangerous. He was lucky to have infiltrated them when Vanderlin first began to gather them. It had been most fortunate for Ms. Fleming, as they had kept him aware when the orders had gone out to eliminate her.

He looked around at the innocuously small simple room, he wondered if his son would figure it out. He probably would. He looked at his watch. He had just about a half hour before Mary Fleming arrived. He really wanted to talk to this amazing woman. She had succeeded where so many had failed. But he had to keep her away from the Vanderlin tribe, or whoever was still trying to run them. His plants in the organization were still unaware who was directing them since the death of the Leader.

His cell vibrated. He checked it. Ah, Edward. He must have had a strong tailwind. He was early. He closed and locked the room and took the elevator back to the living area of his home.

Twenty minutes later, Edward and Ilene came into the house with Mary Fleming. She was looking around, her mouth open in awe at the size of the soaring ceilings, and the soft coloring of the house.

Sir Galston, always the gentleman, stepped forward and kissed her hand. "My dear lady, I am so very, very pleased to meet you. Please come into our little kitchen and we will get you something to eat. My son often forgets that people need to eat more than once a day." He walked beside her, gesturing grandly as if he were in his manor house in the British Isles, not in a clandestine mountain hideaway.

"I'm sorry, sir, I don't know your name or anyone's name. Apparently, you are behind my rescue."

"That is true. I sent my son, Edward and my other associate, Ilena to 'rescue' you, Ms. Fleming. My name is Galston, Sir James Galston. I know you have a lot of other questions, but right now our primary plan is to get you fed and comfortable. I will be sitting down with you for a while going over how you came by your information. But for now, tell us what you would like to eat."

Mary Fleming sat down at the large marble topped table in the kitchen, taking in everything. "Well, I think, I'd love to have a fresh salad and fruit. I've had so much coffee just trying to keep awake and alert."

Edward went over to the fridge, "No problem, I can get that done for you, Mary. I'm sorry, we didn't speak much on the way here, but we had bad weather and I didn't want to get distracted."

"I hope you don't mind, sir, I do appreciate your hospitality, but I mean, I still know nothing about why you came after me, or really who you are. You gave me names, but, I mean, let's face it you could be anyone and tell me anything. How do I know you are not going to kill me later? You don't seem like killers but……"

"I understand your misgivings, Ms. Fleming. We will answer your questions. Now have your salad. Ilena, will you find our guest some changes of clothing, and place them in the closet of the blue room? Thank you, dear.

"I'm sorry I can't offer you the option of either going shopping or wearing some of what generic clothing is available. We couldn't take the time or chance a visit to your home to collect your things."

"Sir Galston, I have my life. I never thought I would ever say that. My life has changed so much that I don't even know who I am anymore."

"Ms. Fleming we do have to talk. Based on the information you sent to various people you know quite a bit about many things. That is what placed your life in danger."

"Oh, I realize the information is valuable, I really don't know anything about or even understand much about the information. I had to save it first on diskettes rather than CD's only because of the way I had to record the information. I didn't have a CD burner available to me in my office at the beginning. Only certain projects that were highly funded obtained the best equipment. I may have been the director, but my function didn't require such capability. Basic back up and hold to the operating budget that was the key to holding on to my job. When I reached my house in Maine, I was able to convert diskettes to CD, but these are the original diskettes. I mailed out the CD's."

"Well, Ms. Fleming we are not worrying about budgets here. We are worried about the future of this earth and all the people on it at this time. We are also concerned about certain visitors that we are expecting within the next two years. Would you have knowledge of that?"

"What visitors? What do you mean you are worried about the earth's future? Is that what all of that research was about, global warming? Are you Green Peace?"

"When you are finished eating, we will go to my office and go over what we can learn from your information."

"I should explain, though. I only converted the earlier diskettes to CDs, those were only the diskettes from the beginning of Sarah's research. I have the last of her work with me as well."

"Who is Sarah? Do you mean she made conclusions from this research? The diskettes you have contain her conclusions?"

"Oh, no, nothing like that. It was still research but it was focusing. Whereas, at the beginning, the work was scattered, I was told to direct her research into certain areas. At the start, she was told to look at mining, glaciers, geological surveys, the Arctic and Antarctic Circles, the countries around the equator, the heat indices. With the research over the last year or so, she was given specific things to do based on certain areas of the previous work she'd done."

"Ms. Fleming, you said you were told what Sarah was supposed to work on. Who told you? Who was requesting this research?"

"Senator Danner. Barry Danner."

Sir James eyes glittered and he was nearly rubbing his hands with glee upon hearing there was new information that as yet no one had or no one except the now deceased Senator who had directed the research. "Did the Senator only speak to you about the research?"

"No, no. Once Sarah was working, and had produced her first research papers, I began to get anonymous phone calls, short e-mails, even postcards. As her research continued and she continued to send out papers on her work, the requests increased from one or two a month to a different one every week. She was working hard and she was good, thorough, with a good mind and a lot of capability to keep up with her deadlines and the needs of the job."

"So why was she let go?"

"I received a phone call from Senator Danner. I was told to let her go, immediately. I was very surprised because I had just received an e-mail on Friday with more work for her. But on Monday when I arrived at work I had a phone call from the senator. A messenger came over with an envelope with a severance check and a plane ticket to Seattle, ah, her home. I was directed to place everything in a corporate envelope with a good reference. I did so. He also told me that if anyone came sniffing around I was to call him to let him know who and what they wanted to know.

"Not even three weeks later her mom called. I did as I was told and called the Senator on his private line. I recorded that as well as all of the calls. I have that with me also. I left after that call. I knew," Mary stopped speaking, she looked at her hands, they were trembling, her once manicured nails, chipped. "I knew, she, Sarah was dead. I was the link to the Senator and I knew I would be next. I left the office. I guess you know the rest." She sat slumped against the chair, relieved to have let out some of what she had been holding for weeks.

"You were prepared for an escape, why?"

"I knew enough about Barry Danner. There was always a woman, young women, each one was younger than the one before. He used them up and spit them out. He had never asked me, or anyone in the Denton Group to work for him before this. He asked me to meet him for dinner at the Ritz. He said that he and his group needed some topnotch research done and he knew someone who was bright and was looking for work. Could I hire her and have her do the research?

"I knew someone else he had help him out like that about ten years ago. A very dear friend, he also worked in research, for a think tank. He disappeared when the job was done. His body washed up down in Virginia. It was the same kind of situation. Hire someone to work as a researcher. It was always the same. But I needed the money. I told myself that my friend just had an accident and this would be all right. I wanted to retire with a nice house and a nest egg. I wonder if my home is still there."

"We know the house in Maine is still there unlike your place in Maryland." Sir James put out his hand, "If you are finished eating, let's go to the office and play those diskettes of yours, Mary. We'll have tea or coffee there or something stronger if you prefer."

"No. No, I'm fine, just a glass of water."

"I'm sure you need to rest, but things are moving rather quickly and I need to talk with you before finalizing our plans and strategies." As he spoke, Sir Galston led the woman down the hall followed by his son and Ilene and turned into his study. It was similar to his study in England, soft leather chairs, rich wood paneling, an ornate desk and soft lighting. A desktop computer monitor glowed in one corner and a well-stocked bar stood in a corner opposite.

Mary had kept her large black handbag either over her shoulder or in her lap during her entire trip from Bangor and even while eating in the kitchen. Now she reached in and pulled out several cardboard diskette mailers. She stared at them momentarily before handing them reluctantly to Sir James. "Sorry. I've held onto these so desperately for so long that they've become part of me. They were all originally in one larger mailer, but that was paper and gradually broke down in my handbag, so I just left them in their little cardboards."

"I understand, Mary. Thank you for trusting us with them. I promise you anything that we find will only be used to help mankind or help us to help mankind. At some point you might even think that we have a private agenda, but our agenda is simply to help bring our world together in peace."

"Ms. Fletcher, when you converted these diskettes did you make sure they didn't get damaged in any way?" Edward asked her as he took them from his father and slid one into the slot in the hard drive.

"No. No I didn't. I had already read what was on there. I know what was there. I scanned in Sarah's reports each time she sent them to me to pass on."

"Sent them?" Ilena queried.

"Interoffice mail, I never met with her until the day I let her go."

"Oh. Um, so how did you direct her as to what was needed?"

"I would send her an e-mail memo. One thing I did do when I left the building that day, I ran a delete program on the hard drive. I realize that with work they could recreate it, but these people are more interested in immediate results. I knew that the time needed to retrieve what was on my hard drive they might not want to spend."

"Smart lady," Sir James said. He was thinking that this woman might actually be an asset to their team if she wanted to join them.

Edward was reading the results coming up on the computer when he suddenly shouted, "Oh, No, they couldn't have been looking at this."

"What, Edward?"

"Look at what they had her working on the last few months. The glaciers in the Arctic and Antarctic, their present level of melting, the possible introduction of an unnatural heat source to melt them and the temperature needed to increase the melting by twenty percent."

"Go back to a previous diskette and see if we can find out what they originally asked her to check into, Edward, that would have led them to focus their efforts in the poles."

"Will do, it may take a few minutes to scroll through all of the data on each one of these. I don't want to skip around too much, we might miss something crucial."

"Ilene, use the lap top beside the desk and help him. Mary, is there anything that you can tell us that will make the search of the material proceed more quickly?"

"I'm sorry I'm not really sure what you are searching for, I did label the diskettes, but only so that I could jog my memory." Mary got up from the couch and walked over to the scattered little pile.

"All right, we need to know if there is anything on extra-terrestrials, and why they are seeking to melt the glacier fields at the Poles."

"Here, the one marked 51. This probably has everything you need on it. I almost didn't scan it, because it seemed so weird. I was actually laughing as I was putting it together."

"I should have caught that one myself, Dad. Area 51. I didn't even think, I thought it might have been a disk number or something." He slid the diskette in and started looking at the files. "Here's Roswell, Brazil, New Hampshire, France, abductions, landings, Illinois, discussions."

"Check the document 'discussions', Edward."

Cool air had been blowing throughout the white limousine as it streaked silently through the darkening landscape. Michael hadn't noticed earlier, but there was the slightest fragrance hovering in the car, not unlike the smell of ozone after a storm, mixed with a light floral smell. His hands and face weren't hurting as much. In fact, he had almost forgotten the severe pain of the burns on his skin.

He turned to speak to Richard and noticed in the dim light of the liquor cabinet console that the burns and cuts on his companion's face were nearly invisible. He looked quickly at his own hands and they looked normal. There were no burns, no scars.

Michael touched Richard lightly on the arm and pointed to his hand. Richard gasped and looked at him and then at Evelyn, who was staring out a window. The blonde pair in the front of the car continued to stare out the windshield of the car.

Richard looked outside of the car and realized that he could see the sky but couldn't see the trees, or other cars. Then he realized while he could hear the engine he couldn't hear the hum of the tires on the road. He wanted to shout, "What the hell?" Instead he tilted his head in the direction of the window as he stared at Michael.

Michael followed his gaze and realized what was upsetting Richard. He was upset as well. 'Where the hell, were they and where were they being taken?' He thought. He got up from the seat, realizing that the extreme pain and shock of his injuries and the surprise of his rescue had made him lose his normal cautious awareness. Michael immediately moved forward in the car, passing the silent Evelyn, who barely acknowledged his movement. He tapped the driver on the shoulder.

"I believe your name is Philippe. I want to thank you for rescuing us and apparently, for healing our wounds as well. However, we want to know where we are, where we are going and how are we getting there. It feels like this limousine is flying."

Philippe glanced at his wife. "I can tell you, Michael, we are on our way to Sir James in Colorado. Yes, we know where he is. I will say that it took us quite some time to figure out where he was. He is a very cautious man.

"Now that you are feeling better, I would appreciate your contacting Sir James to let us through his defenses. His base is impregnable and without his codes or his help, everyone in this vehicle will die as soon as we come within a certain radius of the site."

Michael turned around and bumped into Richard who had moved up behind him. "You heard?"

Richard nodded. They both doubted that their equipment had survived the blast. It would be impossible to get through to them.

"I can get you through." Evelyn said quietly. She opened her small cell phone and keyed in a number she knew by heart.

In the Colorado study Edward's phone rang with a peculiar sound. He immediately answered, "Evelyn?"

Sir James Galston was on his feet in an instant. "How far away are they? I must know immediately!" He scribbled some numbers quickly on a piece of paper and shoved them in front of his son's eyes.

"They're coming in over….over Kansas right now."

"Good give them these coordinates, 38° 82' N, 104° 101'W, and tell them to stay right on them and do not waver."

Edward relayed the coordinates to his wife. He could hear the strain in her voice and knew he would owe her more than anything for what he had put her through. He heard her repeat them to the pilot along with the caution not to waver. He turned to speak to his father who had his back to them standing at another computer hidden in what had looked like the bar. The screen was barely visible. He wrote something down, stared at the screen again, and made another notation. He hit a button and the screen and keyboard disappeared from sight and again the bar counter was back.

"Tell Evelyn the pilot must be on the ground within forty-two minutes. He cannot land before thirty-five minutes. If he misses that time frame there will not be another opening for twenty-four hours. When he lands, if there is another vehicle, and I do mean any other vehicle behind him it will not be able to land." With that statement he turned and left the study. He looked like he had aged thirty years.

Edward stared at his father only seconds before relaying the message. He heard Evelyn hesitate when she said twenty-four hours.

Michael couldn't believe what he was hearing. He knew a lot about defense mechanisms and what he was hearing about the defenses of the Colorado hideout meant that Sir James had gone to extreme lengths to defend that place and without him. But then he realized that the Colorado house had been started long before he had even met his boss. Incredible sums of money had to have been spent on an ongoing basis for decades. Plus, he had apparently kept up with the most cutting edge technology.

Inwardly, Michael shook his head to realize that at Sir James' age, he couldn't keep going like he was and still keep on top of this intricate situation. But they were all relying on him to pull the United States and the world out of the plot that the group had started. He looked up at the blonde couple, they had listened to Evelyn's coordinates and directions without even showing surprise, but Richard had obviously been shocked by the request for the time limitation for landing.

Richard kept his eyes glued to the clock in the vehicle. Watching the minutes moving away until they would be out of this insane plane, car, whatever it was supposed to be. He could feel the descent begin just after the half hour was up. Then as soon as they had passed thirty-five minutes it felt like they were almost in a nose-dive down toward the earth. He was gripping the arms of the seat and noticed that Evelyn's face had gone pale with fear as it seemed they must have dropped through the earth.

Then there was the sound of the ground under them. Richard looked at the clock, they were down and taxiing with two minutes to spare until the forty-two minute deadline. The engine was slowing and then finally stopped, within an instant, the vehicle was surrounded by a blinding white light.

A mechanical female voice spoke, "Kindly exit your vehicle one at a time with your hands up. If your hands are not above your head we cannot guarantee you will continue to live. You may believe that you are known to us, but we will decide that. You will follow the lit path that you will see when you exit your vehicle. This is the order of exit. Do not try to change the order of exit or everyone will be suspect. First to exit will be the pilot."

Philippe stood up, glanced at his wife and immediately left the vehicle raising his hands up as he exited the door. A minute later the metallic voice spoke again, "The next to exit will be the man known as Michael." Michael edged forward and placing his hands over his head exited the vehicle. Evelyn was called next followed by Richard and then finally Celine.

As each left the plane, they had no way of knowing that they were each following a different lighted path, with nothing but total blackness on each side. They went into a room and were told to place their hands on a plate for fingerprint identification. Then they were told to look into a small eyepiece that checked and photographed their eye identification.

Within minutes Michael and Richard were instructed to leave their respective rooms and follow the lit path. They found themselves coming through opposite doors of the kitchen. "That had to be the strangest thing that I've ever been through." Richard said.

Michael nodded, "But at least we know now why he came here for safety. I can't believe the capabilities that this place has. One thing we know he has made every effort to make sure we are all safe."

"Where do you think they are now?"

"We could try the study. But do you think we should leave here? I think we should wait for them to come to us. Once they know what's going on with the couple, they'll probably come here. Besides, I'm not so sure that this place isn't booby-trapped until everyone that came off of that plane, car, whatever, has been vetted.

"Well, at least we can get something to eat while we're waiting for those two to get through what Sir James has in store for them. I wonder how much Evelyn will have to go through before she is allowed to enter here?" Michael pulled sandwich meats and sodas from the refrigerator.

Richard grabbed the bread and some plates, "Might as well get rid of the hunger while we're waiting.'"

"I can't remember the last time I ate. Where were we?"

"I actually think it was just before we left here."

"You're right! I can't believe it's been that long." Michael finished piling things into his sandwich and sat down at the counter. He fingers touched his face and he realized that not only had it been a long time since he had eaten, but since he had showered and shaved.

"I hope we can leave this kitchen pretty soon, I really need to get out of these clothes. Say, Richard, did you notice even the clothes aren't shredded any longer? If we told anyone what happened, that you and I were burnt and cut everywhere, no one, and I mean, no one would believe us."

"I had thought about that when I was walking down the lit path. My face feels fine, my hands are fine and I could swear that I lost my shoes in the blast. But here I am no scars, none of the tightness and itching of healing and no stitches. I saw one of the deep gashes on my hand, Michael. I should have gone to a hospital for several stitches. It looked like the bone was exposed."

"Wait and see how things go for Philippe and his wife, if they aren't going well, we can at least put in a good word about the healings.

"But actually, Richard, I don't think that would really help them at this point, in fact it might make things a whole lot worse. Philippe is supposed to be Edward's best friend. So is this Philippe or someone or something made up to pose as Philippe?

"I think we'll know pretty soon. We landed over a half hour ago and Sir James is on a timeline. He doesn't have time to waste, so those people had better have very good explanations. I don't think he'll be playing around with them."

"If they hadn't landed at the correct time and place, I don't think we would be alive now."

"I agree. I..."

He stopped as a loud noise erupted from somewhere within the depths of the house or the mountain. It was impossible to tell where. The sound climbed in decibels and the two men covered their ears. Glasses shattered, objects around the kitchen started to tremble and move towards the ends of counters and tables. Then suddenly the noise stopped.

Richard started toward the door. Michael caught his arm. "We don't know if this kitchen is booby-trapped, we have no idea what plans Sir James has. He hasn't told us, he can't communicate with us."

"Michael there has to be a computer in here. We can't just sit here. We have to let him know that our phones and ear phones are gone."

"You're right, I should have remembered he would never have a room without access. Maybe we should try the hidden room. We know there are computers pretty much everywhere you need to be in this place." As soon he said it, they heard footsteps outside of the doorway that led to the front of the home. The two men stepped quietly to each side of the door, ready in case it was someone they didn't know.

The handle turned and they heard a voice they both knew. "Michael, Richard, sorry it took me so long to come to you. Evelyn has told me what happened to both of you and why you couldn't let me know you were staying in here. Your caution has saved you. If you left this room you would not have enjoyed your welcome. Just consider it a failsafe. So let us join the others. We are in the study."

For the second time Sir James guided the two men to the warm study. When they entered, Edward who was holding his wife, looked up at them, and mouthed the words "thank you". Mary Fletcher, turned toward them and visibly shrank back against the couch.

"Ms. Fletcher, I would like you to meet two more of our group. They helped to reunite Edward and Evelyn. They are also part of your protection against those who would harm you. Now, with Ilene," he gestured toward the dark-haired young woman who was curled up, seemingly half asleep in a wing chair, "you have met us all.

"As you can see, we are a small but quite formidable group. Now that we are together, we can properly plan our moves from here on. Edward, I want you to complete going through all of the information that Ms. Fletcher was kind enough to bring us. I realize that much of it has been printed, but this is much too slow. We have to speed up this process, we now have very little time and we have been out of touch with the powers for several hours.

"Ilene, if you would show Evelyn, Ms...."

"Please call me Mary, all of you."

"Very well, Ilene, if you would show Evelyn and Mary upstairs to the blue room and Edward's room they should be fine. As soon as you do, please return here so that we can continue." Sir James had walked over to her and whispered the last in her ear as she left her chair.

The rooms and halls of the White House looked more like a building under siege. Armed troops and Secret Service Agents roamed from room to room throughout the entire building. The staff that came on the morning before had been relieved by the evening staff only to find they were unable to leave and instead escorted to a large bare room in the upper basement fitted with rows of cots with folding screens between each for privacy.

The president was sitting alone in the room known to the public as the war room. He stared at the empty seats around him and wondered idly what had Colonel Gately known all those many weeks ago that had sent him running? He had been the liason with that odd, all powerful group, yet he felt the man himself could be trusted. He should have known when he disappeared something was definitely amiss.

He got up and began pacing around the room, trying to decide and plan like he used to, before that group decided he had to follow their agenda or die, was their alternative. An 'accident' so regrettable the country would be easily led toward their agenda. Always an agenda, while it hadn't changed, had instead changed to a more benign way of achieving it. He was sick of hearing the word.

He looked up at the pictures of the world, lights flashing, made small by the vastness of the dark around them. He looked again at the empty seats and reached for one of the phones near him and called his private secretary and asked her to join him.

She was there in minutes. The enforced isolation had not fazed her and she seemed as fresh as when she had come to work two days before.

"Sir?"

"Marge, tell me something and I want your honest answer. Whatever your first response is to the question I am going to ask you."

"Of course, Sir." Marge could sense the tension in her boss and was actually frightened of any question he might ask in light of the events over the past thirty-six hours.

"Marge, if you were in a position to bring peace to the world, the entire world, bringing all the people of the world together, to govern together, without threat of arms, or retaliation, no matter race, religion, by simply answering yes or signing your name to a document, what would you do?"

The secretary's mouth opened in shock about halfway through the question and by the end she sat down. "They mean without any fighting or loss of life?"

"I believe so."

"Then there would be no question only a yes or signing your name would be the only answer. But, sir?"

"Yes, Marge. It seems too good to be true."

"Right, that is exactly what's wrong with the whole premise. Yet, we have been so schooled to mistrust, by those who have cheated, lied, and killed to achieve their goals that now that possibly, just possibly this is the one time that we could truly have what was offered, we fear it as the greatest lie of all."

Marge moved to sit in one of the cushioned leather chairs. For the first time since this crisis had begun, she felt overwhelmed. She trusted this man whose back was now turned to her, as he stared at the images of the earth. He knew he wasn't alone. He knew that in Britain, France, Russia, China, Germany, all had found traitors in their midst. China and Russia had shot them once they had left the building. In Egypt and Israel and around the globe the story was the same.

Either the traitors were killed immediately or placed in such extreme detention so quickly that no phone call, video, picture, or gossip gave away their location. Now the other leaders, like himself, were alone. Fearing to trust those left on their staff, or each other. The others probably had someone like Marge. Someone the power brokers had overlooked in their quest to take over.

He turned and looked over his shoulder at the woman who looked more motherly than his own perfectly coiffed mother. This woman might hold the key, she might, without knowing, be aware of the information he needed to make a decision. To help him talk to the others before the allotted time was up. He looked at the clock. Twelve hours left. Not much time to save or destroy the world.

"Marge, you've talked to a lot of people that have walked into and out of my office and many of those before me. In one capacity or another over the years, you may have heard something, seen something, that may help me, help America, help the world.

"I need to know other than those we've unmasked, who you wouldn't trust in your house at night while you sleep."

Marge smiled at that. She looked the president square in the eye, and said "Truth be told, sir, you are the only one of that group I would trust. The smart ones would steal everything that was valuable and the dumber ones would steal everything that was left.

"But, I think there are a few others you need to look at, or perhaps talk to, who would tell you something close to the truth. I'm not saying they're truthful or honest, sir, they are not weak, but they do have some knowledge of what is perhaps really going on and the intelligence to keep a low profile and their mouths shut."

"But you yourself haven't heard anything? Marge, I realize that you live your life keeping confidences, but I'm asking what you may know, think, speculate, have overheard. Even if you think it might be silly, or even if you have to, in this case break a confidence, the safety of the country, hell, Marge, the earth, is at stake."

Marge stared at him. She remembered all of the rumors, and

overheard whispers she had heard over the years before she began working for Michael Stapleton, the strange and not so strange things she had seen on Capitol Hill. Plus some of the late night goings and comings of Edward Gately before his disappearance, the odd faxes that had come in on her secure fax and she had taken them herself to the quiet military man who could be found alone in his basement room working on his laptop.

With her photographic memory and ability to speed read as well as read upside down she had learned many things that for the first time in her life she felt that she had to divulge. "Sir, could you please sit down? I'll be as precise as I can. I won't say how I come by this knowledge, but I will say I learned it either by accident, through other's carelessness or through the course of my day to day work both here and before I came to work for you."

Stapleton had been watching her face as she fought with herself to break years of silence for the first time in her life. It was then he knew his instincts had been right on when he tapped her for his confidential secretary and when he had asked her to talk to him. He pulled a chair closer to the one she was in so that anything she said he could hear.

"Sir there is a man, or was a man that people referred to as the 'Leader'. He apparently has been running many people in the pentagon, CIA, FBI and many of the members of your cabinet, Congress and the Senate for many years. As the names changed he would either bring them in or bring in someone else who would listen to him. Your predecessor was one of their trusted confidants."

The president nodded as he remembered the strange trip he, himself, was required to take not long after taking over as president. Marge knew these people or at least where they had infiltrated. Marge continued quietly filling him in on how the government had been operated for decades from behind the scenes. How people disappeared, committed 'suicide', suffered strange unexplained car accidents, fires, private plane and helicopter crashes. How bills were really passed in Congress and the Senate, and how the President decided what he would veto or if he would pass it as written, everything was done to give the illusion to the American people that their elected officials were working for them.

"Then Colonel Gately began working here. Someone was faxing him very strange memos. But for the first few weeks they came up here instead of going to the fax in his office."

"What do you mean strange memos?"

"Things like 'meeting tonight at 2'. That would be all that there was on the paper addressed to him. At least four of those came to him that I know of, but then they stopped. I didn't give it much thought until he disappeared.

"If you remember I stayed here for a few days because my kitchen was being remodeled and my room was just down the hall from his office. Because I didn't have to worry about getting to work on time I had the luxury of staying up late. I remember I had seen a page, who worked for Senator Danner, down there, while I was going to breakfast one of those mornings. I knew this girl because the Senator used her to run all of his errands, bringing things here for you.

"She actually knocked on the Colonel's door. She waited then walked in and came right out immediately. I saw Colonel Gately arriving about ten minutes later, so I know he wasn't in the room. That night while I was reading I heard a door slam and footsteps rushing down the hall. It was just past midnight. Then later I heard footsteps returning, I looked at the clock it was nearly five o'clock in the morning. Not forty-five minutes later, I almost bumped into Colonel Gately as he ran down the hall. I was just opening my door when he went rushing by."

"So that was the day he disappeared. Did the page have anything in her hands, a briefcase, papers?"

"Just a folder, a red folder."

"So he was also a traitor."

"No. No, Sir, I don't think so. I think that's why he left. I think he found out what the Leader and his group were planning. Or he was told and he couldn't tell you. Perhaps, he thought that if he ran he could stop it."

President Stapleton listened for the next two hours as Marge, like a dam unleashed told him the secrets of Senator Danner, General Anders and others including the now disgraced Attorney General.

When she finished, the president thanked her. Then he asked her if she would stay in the room for the next hour. He showed her where there was a little kitchen for those late night meetings. "Marge, I'm going to lock you in here. I don't want anything, I mean anything to happen to you and I don't think anyone even knows you are in here. There is a couch over there and some blankets if you want to take a nap. I will personally return to get you. If anyone knocks don't open the door, Even if they say I sent for you. I am locking off the access to this room myself."

"What? Why?"

"Because you are a wealth of information, just like that director of the Denton Group you spoke about. She was probably the person who sent us those files. It is truly amazing the bravery of some people under the most frightening of circumstances."

With that statement the President left the room, turned to the door, blocked the keypad from the Marine Guards with his body, and changed the code on the door to one that he knew he would never forget.

"Gentlemen. No one and I mean no one gets in that room. I have changed the code and the one you knew is now invalid. I will return. No one gets in until I return and personally open that room. Is that understood?"

"Yes, Sir!" The four Marine Guards who were already standing at attention seemed to raise their bodies even taller. As the President turned and left, two of them crossed their rifles across the door, while the other two stood back to back facing opposite ends of the hall.

The Leader's old home had been taken over by his secretary. Those who had not been murdered along with the nurse and butler, had originally been locked in the basement, until the Leader's secretary decided they had become a liability. The blast from the car bomb had caused them to have over twenty windows replaced. He decided he did not need to replace the staff.

Neighbors down the road were told that the old swimming pool was being destroyed and had been blasted away. No police were called and the bodies of the Leader's butler and what was left of the nurse and her car were buried or hidden on the property.

Seth Thorson had been tired of his boss constantly comparing him to Michael, who worked for Sir James. Why couldn't he do this or that? Michael could do it. Well, Michael hadn't finally killed the old man. He had Anthony Vanderlin pulled right out of his plush bed and now he was running the group. No one even knew whether the Leader was dead or not. With the use of all of the same equipment and addresses and codes, no one outside of those in the house knew that the Leader was finally gone.

Seth had put out a call to various members of the group from all over the world. But few had responded. He kept trying to reach the South African and Chinese leaders. He needed them to put forth the next terrorist act that the Leader had planned. But they hadn't responded. He figured that as usual he was being impatient. He would give them another hour or two and try again. Meanwhile, he would see what Sir James was up to.

This should give the old man a start. He keyed in the overseas codes for the Englishman's cell phone. When he heard his voice, he started, not expecting to hear the strength in the voice of such an elderly man.

"Yes?"

"Sir James, This is Seth. Seth Thorson. I worked for the Leader."

"If you worked for the Leader, why are you using the Leader's personal phone to call me?"

"The Leader is dead. He died a little while ago. I just wanted you to know that I'm in charge of the group now."

"Oh? Yes, I knew the Leader had passed away. It is a shame that you had to execute the butler and the nurse. I think that was, shall we say overkill, Seth?"

"What? How do you know that?"

"I know many things, Seth. I'm sure you have tried to reach many of the group already. Not many answers?"

"No. No one has called me back. Did you tell them the Leader is dead? Is that why they won't answer me?"

"No Seth. They can't answer you, because they are either dead or in a dungeon somewhere. Everything is over. Good bye, Seth."

Sir James folded up the silver phone and placed it in his jacket pocket. Just as he suspected Seth thought he was in charge. So apparently he had been sending orders to what was left of the Leader's henchmen. He wondered how long it would take them to return to the Leader's house and eliminate Seth.

He had just entered his own bedroom to get a nap and change when the call came through. Sir James had Michael place cameras and bugs all over the Leader's house years ago. When they visited the Leader in the hospital, Michael had activated the entire system and had engineered the hiring of the nurse, replacing the one that Thorsen had vetted. She had known that it was dangerous, but then all of her jobs had been dangerous. Seth must have booby-trapped her car the same day he killed the Leader and the butler.

Her death had been a loss. It was always difficult to locate a registered nurse who would be interested in undercover work. She had worked for him for almost thirty years. He had suffered many losses during the course of his work for the Group. But now even the group had been decimated. It had grown bloated, and inbred upon its own power. But now the coming of the extraterrestrials had allowed him to excise some of the bad fruit of the group. The Leader had played into his hands, believing he was invincible. Seth had been a natural patsy. He had acted as Sir James had expected when he had placed him in the Leader's sights when he had been trying to bribe Michael to leave his employ.

He finished his shower and slid under the covers for a much needed nap. He knew he would wake up in an hour.

While Sir James was resting, Michael and Richard sat at opposite ends of the hallway. They still didn't know where the strange couple was being kept in the house, nor were they sure about Edward's wife. To them she acted strangely, or perhaps it was just being around those two people for so long. So to be safe, they kept Sir James under a more careful watch than usual.

Edward and Ilena were watching the monitors while the others were upstairs. Ilena was watching Edward more than she was watching the monitors. He didn't turn away from the monitors when he asked her, "What do you want to ask me, Ilena?"

"Sir James. Is he really your father?"

"Yes, he is."

"How could he just leave you here? I mean those people were strangers and they agreed to take care of you?"

"He did it for my safety, Ilena. Your father sent you to all of those schools here and in Europe for your safety and to help with your upbringing. My father felt a family was more important to my safety and upbringing."

Ilena curled up in the leather swivel chair had turned her back to several of the monitors showing the mountainous terrain around the hideaway. She stared at the man. "My father was not a very nice person. Is yours?"

"Ilena, do you mean that he was not nice to you or others?"

"He wasn't nice to anyone."

"My father is a very nice person. He is not nice, however, to those who are evil or wish ill to others."

"So that is why you trust him?"

"Yes. That is also why Michael and Richard trust him."

"They do trust him. But there is something more. I know they work for him, but I mean something different."

"Oh. Yes." Edward turned around and looked at her quietly for a moment before speaking further. "Ilena, they respect him. They believe in him. They believe in his efforts for a better world."

"I'll have to think about that, respect and belief. That might be what it is. I'm not sure yet. Sir James did allow me to go with you. I could have refused, but I was so surprised about him giving me something to do, that I just had to do it."

"Ilena, he trusted you."

"You're right, but I think it was also a test."

"Yes, it was a test. A test that you passed, but I'm sure there will be more tests that will be even more difficult. You will have to trust him in order to believe in what you do. From here it is up to you." With that Edward turned around to his bank of monitors.

One of the faxes rang and started churning out paper. Edward went over to it and began to read. He looked at his watch. Sir James had been upstairs almost an hour. They had approximately six hours left before the various countries began to get in touch with them or if they decided to contact them at all. They may be deciding to hunt them down and kill them rather than join together.

Seconds later, Sir James strode through the door, looking as if he had been on vacation. Richard was immediately behind him. "Well, has anything occurred while I rested?" His look included Ilena as well as Edward.

Edward handed him the fax. "This just came in. The monitors are quiet. The White House, 10 Downing, as well as the rest of the other country's seats of power have continued to be silent and surrounded with loyal troops. I've been monitoring some chatter, but nothing that shows a decision or them working in conjunction with each other."

"After centuries of them working against each other, twenty-four hours is much too short a time for them to decide to work together. Edward, Richard, we are going to bring our guests to the study. Ilena, would you meet us there?"

As the three men left the room together, Ilena transferred the feeds from several of the monitors to the study so nothing would be missed. She then left the room as well. Michael slid through a rear wall between the monitor panels as soon as she left. He checked on what she had done and nodded silently to himself.

He turned off the lights and went back out the way he had come in ran down some steps, went down a long hallway turned a corner and met up with Sir James, Edward and Richard just as they were ready to open up the locked titanium doors. Sir James had already explained to them that he'd had a large concrete room built with steel rebar doubled throughout, lined with six inches of lead and two inches of titanium surrounding it. Inside, the room had been made to feel like a five star hotel, but without balconies and windows.

Sir James spun the vault like wheel then placed his thumb on the scanner. He stood silently in place for barely fifteen seconds before turning the handle. He walked into the beautiful room through its mirrored foyer. "Thank you so much for being so patient with my security precautions. I'm sure you can understand that your capabilities are for us somewhat, ah, shall we say unusual."

"We are here, Sir James. This is where we had planned to be. I must say that your own capabilities, particularly in keeping this place hidden are formidable. There were two planes on our tail when we came in. We were quite unsure of whether or not they would follow us through."

"If you remember I had said that any vehicle behind you would not get through. They did not. There was an opening for one vehicle only on those coordinates. Now, we are going to have a meeting and find out what this is all about."

Sir James turned and left the room with Celine and Philippe following. Edward spoke to Philippe as they walked down the hall. "Thank you for taking care of Evelyn, Philippe. But what the hell is going on? Evelyn is barely speaking, it's' like she's in a permanent state of shock. What happened?"

Philippe turned to him, "She should be all right soon. She saw some things, she has not asked for explanation. Edward, she noticed things that we did not expect her to notice. We underestimated your wife. Because she seemed so pliant, so quiet, and so willing to just go shopping and restaurants, we thought she was like other American wives who stayed home to wait for their husbands. Shopping and dining fill their days. But she was always noticing, thinking, and constantly waiting for you."

"I guess you did underestimate her. She doesn't like shopping and dining out that much. She only goes out shopping if she has to, for groceries, something special to wear to a party, or a wedding. Even in college, she spent most of her time in her dorm room studying, reading, writing poetry or short stories. I met her once at an evening lecture. I remember she even brought a book with her to read in case the lecturer was boring."

Richard was walking behind them, listening carefully to Edward talk about his wife. Apparently, what he and Michael had thought was odd behavior was normal for Evelyn. So she was just that quiet. Still. Richard mentally shook his head in wonder about this woman.

They reached the study and found that Ilena had arranged many of the chairs in a circle around the desk. There was a large coffee urn and cups with some pastries on a tray. Sir James looked at Ilena, "Did you hire a catering service?"

"No, Sir James. I was starving and went rummaging in the kitchen a while ago and found all of this. I assumed others would need at least something to eat so I just threw this together. They taught it at that finishing school. I guess this means I got finished." She laughed a little at her joke and the others laughed with her.

"Excellent, Ilena, excellent. Sit down, everyone. We have very little time now to prepare." He looked at Philippe and Celine. "The two of you obviously have quite a bit to do with what has been happening in the world, the expectations of the arrival of our 'outside' visitors, and last but not least some unusual powers of your own.

"We are asking you at this time to tell us who you are, what are you manipulating, what are your goals, and why you came here instead of allowing Edward to return to Malta for his wife? You must be precise. We do not have time here for long drawn out stories. But I will expect honesty. I do not respect subterfuge."

Everyone turned toward Philippe and Celine who sat next to each other at the side of the ornate mahogany desk. Philippe for the first time in Edward's memory seemed unsure or at least unprepared for the urgent demanding questions of Sir James.

"The answers to all of your questions are simple, Sir James. We are not from here. We are not from earth. I came here many, many years ago, trying to understand people of this world. I have observed many of the major undertakings, wars, rescues, disasters, both manmade and natural. I was there observing the Gulf War, when I was for the first time injured. Because I was visible to many and as you see me now, I was unable to do more than keep myself alive until someone rescued me. That was you, Edward."

"I promised you then that I owed you my life, for in fact I did. You got me into a place where I could be healed and heal myself as well and you stayed with me. I would have died, because I was weak and unprepared for injury. But it taught me not to make that mistake again.

Once I healed, you and I met just a few more times. You were the only person on this planet, at this time that asked me no questions, and, did not expect anything from me. You were and you are a truly unique person. Now that I have met Sir James, your father, I understand you.

"Celine is my mate. I had her come with me to live in Malta as the look that I chose, this look, is safest with a mate, a wife. As we evolve in age, we evolve in power. We were guiding the Leader as you called him, by phone calls, and clandestine meetings that rivaled even those he had with the group. Before Celine joined me I had guided the group and stood behind certain other groups in each of the countries, before they joined the group and after.

"I won't explain, I will demonstrate." With that statement, Philippe stood up and immediately shrank from a slim, six foot three blond, tanned well-muscled man to a five foot six round face Japanese, then before they could recover, he stood as a tall, powerful black man that Edward remembered seeing at one of the meetings. He had been introduced as an envoy from a South African nation. The shifting continued, as he became a small Chinese woman, who spoke, in a lilting voice, that memory made Edward gasp.

"You were there, at that meeting, before we left." Edward was on his feet.

"Yes, Edward. This was how I have been able to infiltrate, observe and work to help this world achieve solidarity. The situation is very serious. Those who are coming, mean to take over this world, the earth and use it for their own purpose. You might feel or believe that what I am saying is like one of the old movies of fifty years ago."

"Philippe, what proof do you have that the extraterrestrials mean the earth harm? Others will ask, we must know, we must answer these questions now."

"Celine, will you give them our proofs? We have not just one proof, but several."

Celine reached into the bag that she had been carrying with her since the couple had left Malta. Evelyn had noted weeks before that with all the shopping Celine did, she always used the same large handbag.

"The technology used to sink the ships off of the coast of Bermuda was brought to the terrorists on earth by those who wish to land here." She brought out a small notebook, which she opened on the desk. "This is the original design for that technology. Please look not at what is on the paper, but what is used to make the marks on the paper. Please feel free to test that. It is not any type of pen or pencil that you have available here on earth.

"Here is our second proof. The silver cylinder that was used at the mansion." Celine pulled one from her bag, but it was encased in a clear gel inside of what appeared to be a Lucite case. "You have seen the power of one of these. The fools that were using this only knew to keep it cool. As long as it is cool it can be bounced around, thrown around. This technology is also not from earth it is from them."

"Celine, Philippe, do you have more of those silver tubes?" Sir James asked quietly.

"Yes, but in Malta, not here. We brought samples of things. Our home in Malta is impregnable, much as yours is here. We have made every possible effort to pull together whatever might be necessary for you and the world to understand what you face." Celine looked at each of them as she spoke.

Sir James cleared his throat as he stood up, walked over to the coffee urn and picked up a cup. No one spoke as they watched him fill his cup. When he turned around and faced the group, his eyes had narrowed under the grey eyebrows. "Not enough, my girl. Not enough. Who is to say this is not your technology?"

Celine looked at Philippe. "This might change your mind, Sir James." Celine reached into her handbag again, only this time she turned it inside out and folded out the lining. "These are the messages that were actually relayed to NASA. These are the messages that were sent to the terrorists who have the technology."

"Edward check what we have on the messages to NASA."

Edward immediately pulled over one of the laptops lying on the desk and keyed up what they had for information. He worked at it for several minutes before he said, "Okay, here is what NASA has said the messages were. I'm printing them out now."

Marge sat in a shadowed corner of the 'war room' wondering what on earth she knew that was really so vital to the president. It was a good thing the President had no family who might distract him. She knew she had obtained a lot of knowledge over the years, but she had refused to make judgments, gossip or conclusions. Apparently something she had told the president had given him information he needed. She would much rather have him draw conclusions.

She got up and walked slowly into the little kitchenette. There were a couple of tables and chairs near the wall in the back of the room. She opened up the refrigerator and took out some bottled water, sat down at one of the tables and checked her watch. It had been almost an hour since the president had locked her in here.

She wasn't used to inactivity. If she turned on a desktop she'd have to use her sign-on, which would immediately let anyone know who might be watching that she was in here and that she was accessing information. She got up and went into the 'war room' when she heard a hissing noise coming from an air vent. She looked over toward the noise at the far end of the large conference room. These air vents shouldn't break down and they shouldn't make noise.

Marge started to walk toward it to shut the open vent, when another vent began hissing, and she smelled a faint odor. But she couldn't identify it. She hurried back into the kitchenette, and closed the sliding door. She grabbed paper towels soaked them in water and jammed them around the edges of the door.

There was no other exit out of the kitchenette. She was in the lower basement of the White House and there was definitely something being pumped into the separate air vents of the 'war room'. She took her cell phone from the pocket of her blazer and used the president's private number. She knew he would have it on vibrate, but she quickly texted him, 'poisoned air into room'. She hoped he would have a chance to read it and get to her.

The President was in the private study off of his bedroom when he felt his phone vibrate. Just as he read the message and stood up the klaxons in the hallways began to sound. He went outside and started down the hallway at a run with several Secret Service agents beside him. He ran down the several flights of stairs as instructions were announced over the loud speaker. He remembered hearing the shouts and yells of the others on his conference call as he read the message on his cell.

This was a concerted attack. He rushed up to the Marines still at attention in front of the War Room door. He punched in the new code and the red alarm light over the door came on and a metallic voice announce that the air inside was unsafe. But he already knew that. "Do you men have oxygen masks, fire apparatus, anything? Someone is in there and they are alive."

The Marines and Secret Service swung into action. One of the on-site engineers had heard the overhead announcement about air quality and had seen the group rushing down the stairs. "Sir, I followed you down here, I can see if I can flush the air by reversing the vents," He ran down the hallway to the utility room with the President on his heels, turned on the lights and jumped back and shouted, "Oh, my God!"

The controls that operated the vents had been covered in cement, which meant that it would take hours to break through to flush clean air into the vent system for the War Room.

The President turned back to the Marines who had donned portable air packs and were opening the door to the room. They spread out throughout the room, looked under chairs, the tables and shook their heads. They had found no one.

The President shouted, "Check the kitchen, she might be in there, all the way in the back, on the right." He directed them and began coughing as the poisonous air filtered out into the hallway. The Secret Service agents pulled him back.

"Come, sir. They'll find whoever it is." They fast marched him up the steps to the relative safety of the floor above. They had scarcely arrived two floors above when they heard the heels of the Marines running toward them.

"Found her in the kitchen. She'd blocked the door with wet paper towels. Gave her the few extra minutes we needed to find her." One of the Marines said as they carried her up the stairs. As soon as they were all on that level, they closed the stairwell door, then started up to the next level.

"Marge, Marge! Can you hear me?"

"Yes, Sir." Marge pulled the oxygen mask from her nose and mouth. "Thank you so much, all of you. I can walk, really."

They kept moving upwards, quickly the entire basement of the White House was evacuated and all levels were sealed off. The President spoke quietly to the nearest Secret Service Agent, looking at his name badge. "Maitlin, I want to find out who in this building in the last twenty-four hours had access to that basement utility room, and the knowledge to tamper with those air vents. I want those answers within the next hour. I have an extremely important phone call coming in, in about two hours and I need that answer and I want that person or people in front of me in the oval office."

"Yes, Sir."

"Come, Marge we are going back to my office." With that he took her arm and escorted her back to his upstairs office. "Have a seat, and rest. I'm going to finish that conference call I was on if the others are available."

"All right, everyone. We have reached the time when we must place the call to the heads of states. But I am going to delay for approximately one hour." Sir James walked around the study, looked at each one in turn. This time Evelyn and Mary Fletcher had been included.

"While I was upstairs I received some communications that there have been attempts made upon the lives of each of the heads of states. Worse yet their very buildings in each case were infiltrated to make these attempts. Therefore, when we make the call, we will let them all know that we are giving them extra time based on these new developments. Also, it will give us time to find out who is trying to undermine our plans."

Michael asked the question which had been on Sir James mind for days. "Could it possibly be someone from the Leader's staff that believes this will work toward achieving the same goal?"

"I believe so, Michael." He looked at Evelyn who seemed so silent, sitting next to her husband. For some reason her demeanor bothered him. Edward had his arm behind her on the back of the couch but not touching her. Something was wrong. There was tenseness in the study, but that could easily be explained by the upcoming call.

Edward got up from the couch, "Dad, do we have maybe five minutes? I need to talk to you." He walked out of the study and Sir James followed him without even asking what was wrong.

They walked in silence down the long hallway toward the kitchen, Edward put his hand on his father's sleeve and they stopped in the center where they could see if anyone came looking for them. "Dad, something is wrong with Evelyn. I've felt it ever since she returned. She was always quiet. But now the sweetness, interest, loving warmth that I've always felt just being with her is gone. She seems cold and distant now. I went to hold her and it was like I had touched a piece of cement."

"Has she talked to you about what went on in Malta at all?"

"No. I've asked her. What she and Celine did during the day and if they got along together? Just tried to make conversation. But she said nothing, absolutely nothing. She stared at me like I was some sort of experiment."

"How does Philippe seem to you? Does he act the same way?"

"Not really. There is a lot here that we don't understand, Dad. I believe that whatever we say during our conversations with the President, Prime Ministers, whoever may be left, they shouldn't be in the same room. You and I both trust Michael, I would like him to look more into who Philippe is in Malta, who Celine is. What has happened to my wife?"

"This is a tall order, Edward, Even for Michael. All right. I do agree with your assessment of the situation. I'm going to keep Mary Fletcher with us. She is vulnerable and I want her nearby. We send Celine and Evelyn off with Michael. Richard knows the technology even better than Michael so with your assistance and Ilena nearby we should be able to work this out quickly. Philippe will stay with us."

Plans made, they continued talking very quietly as they returned to the study. Celine and Philippe were standing very close to each other in a corner. Edward and Sir James looked at the two of them and they each raised an eyebrow at the other. The golden glow that Michael and Richard had reported from Canada, surrounded them. They parted and the glow disappeared.

Sir James walked over to Michael, stood close to him for barely a second, and moved away. "It is time now. Let us move forward."

He led the group from the room and headed toward the kitchen again. Michael put his arms around the shoulders of Celine and Evelyn. "Ladies, I've been told to give you the designers' tour of this beautiful mountain home of our host." He gently guided the two women in the direction of the large plush living room and the other rooms on the main floor and effectively in the opposite direction of the kitchen.

The President had been able to make contact again with the other leaders. In each case, because they had all been occupied elsewhere they were all safe. But over thirty people had died in total throughout the various homes or seats of power due to the concerted attack.

He was sitting next to the phone staring at his secretary when the so-called red phone rang. He looked at his watch. Right on time. His palms were sweaty. He hadn't been this nervous in years. But he, no they all had questions to ask and they wanted straight answers.

He put the phone on speaker, because he wanted his secretary to hear what the countries of the world were up against. He trusted her, and her ability to assess information quickly.

"Yes, this is the President."

The distorted voice stated, "We are giving you an extension due to the recent actions that have taken place in many of your homes and offices. We had no prior knowledge of the concerted effort to disrupt your seats of power. However, we are making every effort at this time to place those responsible in your custody. If we fail to be able to take them alive for world justice, we will make you aware of their demise. We will make contact again in six hours. This should help you all assess your situations, eliminate the problem staff that you may have and we might come to an agreement at that time."

The call ended abruptly with a click. Marge looked at him. "How could they possibly know what happened here, inside the White House?"

"They know it was a concerted attack and that means that they have some way of knowing what happens in each of our buildings all over the world. Yet, they claim they didn't know what was going to happen ahead of time. If that's true it means that we are in a vise. Are we going to be able to find out who did this?"

"They said they are trying to find out who did it as well. But what does he mean give you six hours for an agreement?"

"They want an agreement for a worldwide government. They wish to act only as a 'benign' overseer, to assist with any disputes. This has to do with the upcoming visit by these supposed extraterrestrials."

"Can you trust them? Who are they? But, how do they know what has happened here…and… and in the other countries as well?" Marge was obviously shaken by the phone call.

"That's the problem, we don't know if we can trust them. All of the countries together, it sounds like a wonderful idea, a utopian world without war. A united world, working together on hunger, global warming, conservation, without passports, just personal information cards to move from place to place."

"Sir, it does sound like utopia, a place that everyone in the world would love."

"Well, this speculation is not getting us closer to who tried to kill everyone they believed would be in the War Room. But they have given us six hours to give them a decision, which should be enough time to find out who is behind these attacks."

Just as Marge stood up to pour some coffee, there was a knock on the door and the lead Secret Service agent Saunders came in the room. "Mr. President, we just found one of the maintenance men dead in a crawl space, his uniform had been taken. We still have someone on the loose in the building. The marine guards will be outside the door and follow you if you leave, Sir."

Marge's face had gone white and she gasped at the news. The president nodded as he listened to the man, "Make sure you get my deepest condolences to the man's family. I don't care who you interrupt or disturb, turn the place upside down."

"Yes, sir. It's being done right now."

"I want everyone in the place vetted again, badges matched to job." The president's voice was rising and he stopped himself. Sorry, I don't have to tell you your job, Saunders. Thank you for letting us know.

They had just entered the hidden control and planning room. Mary Fletcher was looking around in awe. She expressed surprise as she went through the secret door in the kitchen. When she entered the control room she turned to Sir James, "I cannot believe half of what I have seen today. I feel like I have entered the world of science fiction."

Sir James chuckled, "not science fiction, Mary. Just well-placed and well-designed up to date technology. For the right price anyone can have everything you have seen in this home."

"Yes. For the right price, that is the key."

She made herself comfortable on a small loveseat while the others began to check into what was happening while they had been listening to Philippe and Celine.

Sir James was sitting with his back toward the others when he felt his cell phone. He pulled it out and looked at it for a second before answering.

"Clothilde? Are you all right?" There was a short pause before he said, "Of course, I'm fine, has something happened?" "When?" "Hold on." He turned quickly to Edward, "Turn to the BBC."

The picture that came on showed his manor house smoking, the roof, a portion of the walls and all of the windows were gone. It was surrounded by fire engines, people running with hoses playing water into the ruins. The newscaster was breathless, "This is a devastating loss. This mansion was built by the family of Sir James Galston more than six hundred years ago. The nearby town of Letherbridge also suffered from the blast that nearly leveled this ancient home. Auto and house alarms were set off all over the countryside for at least fifteen kilometers around the area. Letherbridge residents sustained broken shop and home windows. We understand that no one was at home at the time of the blast. Sir James we believe is in Australia and his daughter was staying with friends north of London, where we were able to speak with her quickly by phone. She was going to contact her father.

"We understand that the queen herself is going to issue a statement and has requested that the British Secret Service investigate the situation to make sure that this was not a terrorist act. Sir James is well known to be politically active for those who are oppressed all over the world and has often been the subject of controversy and has even been called a dilettante by his detractors.

"We have spoken with investigators who have said a helicopter had been flying low over the village and the rest of the area only minutes prior to the blast."

Sir James was speaking quickly and quietly to his daughter as reflections of his home played out in front of him. "Now, Clothilde. We've spoken of this before. Act now and be careful. You know what to do. Use the other numbers when you reach the appointed place."

He cut the connection. "Richard, I."

"Sir James," Philippe interrupted, "I believe that someone thought you were there. Judging from what the news is reporting, it might be possible that the blast was caused by a silver tube, but I wonder if there was a helicopter crash nearby. I don't believe that they could have left the area quickly enough."

As if on cue, the news report was continuing. "As if there is not enough happening in the Cheshire area, there has been a report of a helicopter crash, about ten kilometers from the site of the blast that leveled Sir James Galston's house. Investigators are on site at that scene at this time as well. The Prime Minister has stated that because a helicopter was seen and heard minutes before the blast that they be investigated as one case until they know otherwise. We have been told that no other information will be available on either of these situations until they have more information later today or tomorrow. To quote the local DCI, "it's early hours. It could be several days of investigation before we can begin to know what happened here."

"It sounds as if you are correct, Philippe." Sir James voice sounded weary. His home gone. "Richard, you know Seth Thorsen. I want you to tell Edward and Michael everything you know about him. I believe he perpetrated this as well as the planned termination of Mary and a few other things as well. He is running the group, those that are left. We have to eliminate them and eliminate them now.

"Michael does have a few well-placed operatives, I would rather he use them than leave here right now."

"I have a few myself, Sir. Most of them are in Britain and I can reach them immediately if needed."

"Good, do so. Use the scrambler to reach them so they think you are in Iraq or Russia. Tell them to hunt, infiltrate and finalize."

Mary gasped at the coldness of Sir James words. He heard her and turned. "I'm sorry, but this is war. This man was the one that came after you. Others had stopped seeking you. Do you remember when you had a few days without being followed?"

"Yes, yes it was over a week. All of a sudden there were no cars behind me, no people staring when I looked in a shop window, then it started it up again."

"Exactly. Seth began to run the network. We'll have to slide along it to stop it from working for him and turn them, or eliminate them.

In fact I think I know how to do it." He stopped for a moment and reached in the pocket of his jacket and withdrew a small sheet of paper. "Richard when you reach your people, have them contact all of the people on this list in Britain and travel to this address. Explain to them that the person at that address is responsible for the deaths of people at number ten Downing Street, as well as attacks throughout the world. There are people that are hostages in that house who must be rescued as well. They have no part in his doings."

Richard stared at him for a moment then returned to the work of contacting his small network. He knew they kept their passports and traveling money ready and would be happy to have some action. It took him well over two hours to contact and instruct everyone. In the meantime, Sir James had been working on his personal laptop in the small alcove.

Michael had finished his tour and asked if the ladies would like some refreshment. Evelyn said she was very tired and just wished to lie down, so Michael escorted her to her room.

"Would you like to go to your room as well, Celine or would you prefer to join your husband?"

She stared for a moment at the door that Evelyn had just closed. "Let us find my husband." Michael nodded and they started down the hall to the front stairs.

"Michael, Evelyn is not the same as she was in Malta. Not the same as when I met her. I think that being around Philippe and me for such a long time has made some serious change in her."

Michael listened to her musical voice with its strong unusual accent. He wondered at the accent as Philippe did not have one, and he had met several Maltese in his travels and knew this was not their accent. The two were still an enigma to him. "Well, I think once she is able to spend more alone time with her husband and he isn't rushing around she'll be fine."

"You are probably correct." They were walking toward the kitchen when they met Edward.

"I was just coming to find you. Where is Evelyn?"

"She was feeling tired and went to your room."

"All right, I'll go check on her. My father wants to see you in the planning room." He gestured with his head toward the rear kitchen wall. He left them and rushed up the stairs to his wife. He opened the door and saw her lying across the bed.

"Evelyn," he reached out and touched her shoulder as he sat down on the bed beside her. "Evelyn, this has been too much for you. But we're together now. I shouldn't have left you, but I couldn't go where I needed to go with you. It wasn't safe for you."

She moved away from him and kept her face averted as she answered, "You never told me the truth. I always trusted you, and now, we've been married over twenty years, I find out you're not even an American. You're British. All our lives together it's been a sham. No truth. You don't even look the same. What happened to your face?"

"I am still the man you married. Dad had me get some work done on my face, slight changes. But, I'm still me. My allegiance is to the United States, but as well to my father and in what he believes. He is an honorable man. I gave you that paper all those years ago, so that you would know and understand that I wanted to tell you all of those years ago, but I couldn't. How long ago did I give you that paper?"

"In college, when you asked me to marry you."

"What did I say to you when I gave it to you?"

"You said 'this will tell you when you need to know, who I am. But always believe that I love you now and forever.' She turned to him and began to sob. He put his arms around her, "I love you, Evelyn. More than I did then and I loved you so much then that my heart felt like it would burst when I saw you. Please, darling, don't lock yourself away from me, talk to me again. I can't take away the last months and what we've both been through, but now we're back together."

"All the secrets, Edward. All the strangeness, like Philippe and Celine, her eyes were always brown in Malta, then, just before we left they were blue. The strange shimmering golden glow every time they get within inches of each other. Then worst of all, that mansion in Canada. It blew up and your friends, Edward, your friends, they should have gone to a hospital. They were burned, cut, bleeding. Their faces were in slivers. They looked barely alive, I thought they were dying in front of me! But in minutes within the car, just sitting in the car they began to heal." Her soft voice had risen sharply as she described the condition of Michael and Richard.

"Evelyn, calm down. I need to know more about that, and Michael and Richard have absolutely no memory of how they healed."

"I don't know how they healed. Celine opened the rear door as we pulled up beside them. They had jumped over the brick fence just as everything blew up. They were lying in their own blood. I thought they were dead. We came up beside them and she called to them, they started moving and she pulled them both into the car. I don't even know how she managed that. They weren't walking. By herself, Edward, she pulled them both into the car.

"They were sitting across from me, no, not really. They couldn't even sit up, Edward. They were lying on the seat. I told Philippe and Celine to get them to a hospital and he said there was no time. But there was this smell. It was a good smell. You know, after a summer thunderstorm and you go outside. I could see the bleeding stop and then their faces started to look like faces again. They began to sit up straighter and began talking."

"Good, good. How did the car become a plane, Evelyn?"

"I don't know. Philippe was at the wheel the entire time. Then when we were given the coordinates to fly here, that was when I realized that we weren't in a car any longer that we were flying. It was the second time that had happened. We were leaving Malta. I thought we were going to the airport. I was looking out of the window at scenery then, suddenly we were over the Mediterranean. We flew straight on to Canada.

"Edward, please explain all of this. Who are Philippe and Celine? I mean who are they really? What is going on here?"

"I thought I knew Philippe when I left you with them. Now I believe Philippe and Celine are from another planet, sent here to observe. The powers they have shown would bear that out. Now they are telling us that others, other extraterrestrials, who want to come here in less than two years are not benevolent, not helpful, but have instead helped to fuel terrorism all over the world, before they take it over."

"I don't understand. I've been with Celine for weeks and I believed she was just a young woman, who was part of the idle rich. Not working and shopping was her hobby.

"She couldn't understand why you never purchased anything. She thought all American wives shopped constantly."

"Well then, what they are observing isn't helping them understand the differences in people."

"I don't believe that they really observe single individuals that much. Much of what they learn is from the media. That is why I need to explain to you what is happening right now. We are trying to help the governments of the world combine to finally form a unified world government. When our visitors from outer space come here, they will be faced with a united world instead of the petty piecemeal bickering bureaucrats we've had all of these years. I don't know why it's so important, but, my Father, Philippe and Celine truly believe that it is extremely important. It is the only thing that they have agreed upon."

Edward's phone buzzed in his pocket, he took it out and looked at the screen. Sir James wanted him urgently. "Evelyn, I have to return to the group. Perhaps this time you should come with me, share with me, with us and perhaps find answers to your questions." He took her hand as he got up from the bed.

Evelyn grabbed a sweater as they left the room. She put it around her shoulders, as she moved closer to her husband as they walked down the stairs. She walked slightly behind him, a frown, almost a scowl on her face. It was a look that Edward had never seen. They reached the bottom of the stairs and turned toward the kitchen just as Michael and Richard came out of the door.

Michael gave Evelyn an odd look and Richard came up to Edward and said, "Edward, do you mind if I steal your lovely wife? You father needs you to take care of a couple of things." Before Edward could respond, Richard took Evelyn's arm and steered her toward the game room that was at the far end of the hallway.

Michael put his arm around Edward's shoulders, "Sorry to tear you away from her again, but your father needs to get some information from you. Alone."

They went into the hidden room. Sir James looked up from a

computer screen. "Good you're here." He got up and said "Edward we have to talk. I want to know what you know about Evelyn. Where she is from, how you met, her parents, everything."

"Why, this sudden interest in Evelyn?"

"Because, we can't find her," Michael said. "Oh yeah, we know where she went to college and that she met you, but, once you began to leave her for long periods of time her life is a little strange."

"Dad, Michael, what are you talking about her life is strange. We went back to her hometown while we were still in college. She showed me her parent's graves and introduced me to her elderly grandparents who had raised her."

"Surely, son you know how easy that is."

"Of course, but she had pictures of her family, memories you know."

"Did you ever meet any of her childhood friends, or a best friend?"

"No. She said she had been one of those awkward kids in school, everyone chose her last for games, or didn't choose her at all. When I met her she was waiting tables in the cafeteria to help defray some of her college costs. She used a small inheritance from her parents and some help from her grandparents to pay for school and wanted it to go as far as possible.

"I know she has been acting weird but in part it's my fault. I had always wanted to tell her who I was. So, when I asked her to marry me, after she said yes I gave her a piece of paper telling her who I was. She opened it up on the way to Canada.

"Look, Dad, Michael, we've been cooped up in here for weeks now. We're not looking at things right. We can barely see the sky, or tell if it's day or night. We're suspecting each other of God only knows what. I know my wife. I think we need to move out of here and find out who is responsible for destroying your home and attacking the seats of power."

"You are absolutely correct, Edward. We are, or perhaps, I am chasing shadows. I'm not accustomed to this much inactivity. However, I think it is best if I stay here. I have given this a lot of thought.

"Originally, I had planned to come here as a final place to direct the last aspects of any plan that was in motion. I believe I underestimated our adversary. Someone, or some group is still directing situations that I expected would not be possible with the death of the Leader.

"At this point I don't believe that all of it is Seth. He didn't have the expertise or knowledge to contract a concerted attack like this. No, we are dealing with someone else. So, yes, I agree with Edward. We will include Philippe in our plans. What do you think, Michael? Could you team with Philippe?"

"Sir James, I believe I work better alone, and I have worked with Richard already, I think that would make more sense."

"Ordinarily, I would agree, but I believe that Philippe has talents that might serve our investigation."

The others had remained silent during the exchange between the men. But now Philippe spoke up. "Sir James, Edward, Michael, you are correct I do, we do have talents that will help you. But we can help you more if Celine and I are together with you. We can move more quickly and with less observance than your plane or helicopter.

"I know you have seen something when the two of us are close together. That is our protection screen. Your science calls it a force field."

"Philippe why didn't you use the field before you were injured?"

"Yes, you would think I would have done this, but Celine was not with me then. It works only in concert. I had always been cautious and had been able to move, slide away sideways, you know the 'lucky one' they would call me. But that hit, that day, I couldn't move away from it in time. It was not expected, and I don't believe the person who threw it was an adult. I know there was a confusion of the mind and then I was hit.

"Usually, confusion of the mind is from children around the age of twelve or thirteen. Before then children are in a playful mind. After that they begin to become more settled, still confused but nothing like ages twelve to thirteen."

"All right, Philippe. Your vehicle is very unusual, but should something happen others would need to know how to operate it."

"I agree. Michael, you and Edward, should both learn how to operate our vehicle. Also, learn as many of the capabilities it has that we have time to teach you. Sir James, I have here the plans to the vehicle. I know the capability exists here on earth to replicate it, but it should be kept a close secret from the military."

Sir James nodded. "I wonder how Lloyds of London would list your vehicle to insure it." He stopped speaking, walked quickly over to the closest laptop. His hands ran over the keys. "Insurance. Insurance." He spoke quietly but the others heard him.

"What about insurance, Dad?"

"I forgot. I cannot believe I forgot something that the Leader had put in place. There is another group that will continue his plans, in fact I believe they were behind some of his ideas that he claimed as his own."

"You know who they are?"

"Oh, yes. They have infiltrated every single area of the world. We cannot have or do anything without their having it analyzed as to the costs. They actually own everything, banks are insured. Even this place is insured. Every piece of land on earth is insured and Vanderlin? It was well over thirty years ago he told me."

Sir James stopped speaking and stared straight at the monitor. His mouth had formed a thin straight line under his neat moustache, his normally straight back had sagged back against the chair.

Edward rushed to his father. "Dad! Dad!"

"I'm all right, son." The older man raised his hand, dismissing his son's concern. "I have wasted so much time not remembering that one conversation. He was feeling very satisfied with himself that night. He had found the woman he planned to marry. He had looked for quite a while. He had actually bought an engagement ring twice before and then something happened and he broke off the relationship before even giving the woman the ring.

"Strange. He said that should something happen to him before he was ready he had insurance that everything he planned would always be carried out no matter what. He had something in place as he called it, his insurance against someone trying to usurp his power. No matter when it happened the steps would be followed."

"So that means when he died, whoever his insurance was, is now in charge of his network." Michael said thoughtfully.

"Exactly. I would say that whoever this person is, is much younger than he was, well educated and has great wealth and the power to move quietly without anyone noticing him."

Philippe looked at the monitor over Sir James shoulder. "Who is this person, Sir James?"

"One of the women Vanderlin went out with before he married. I kept a running list, each time he changed. I had to. I wanted to keep track of his children, who they were. I lost track of four women after he broke up with them. When I was finally able to track them all down, three of them had died and one was in a mental institution."

"Dad, were any of these women engaged to him? Or did he buy a ring for one of them?"

"Yes." He pointed to a name on the screen. "That one. MaryBeth Hodges. I never understood why he did not marry her. The family and connections were perfect. She died five years later. She had moved to Mexico and was living there. Her father died in a car accident and she returned for the funeral. Her hotel room was broken into and she was killed by the robber."

Michael made a derisive noise. "No one investigated this?"

"No. They caught the man, he was a short term employee of the hotel. Apparently he thought the room was empty. She came out of the shower and startled him."

"That whole story stinks. It stinks of the Leaders' games."

"You're right, Michael. That's why I brought this list up. I recalled the entire conversation and my own tracking of each of those ladies. The only reason Vanessa Morrison is alive, I believe, was that she was sent to a mental institution because she believed she was being stalked. It started about a month after she broke up with Vanderlin and continued for at least two years, until the poor girl broke down completely.

"The other two were killed in car accidents. I felt they were obviously staged to look like one car accidents. But at the time I was busy in England and I had no way of bringing pressure to bear upon small town police in America."

"Sir James, is it possible the Leader had another older child by one of these women?" Michael asked as he read the information on the screen.

"Of course it is. That is exactly what I was thinking. Speculate for a moment. If Vanderlin had a child forty to forty-five years ago, he would have educated that child and raised that child apart from himself. He would have the child schooled to be the leader, ruthless, opinionated. What if that child then turned on Vanderlin and killed him? His nurse imparted enough information to me before she died to let me know that someone else had pulled the strings."

"Dad, he might not have known it was his child that was behind it."

"True. If he didn't, then we will have the devil's own time trying to find that child, because I'm sure all of the trails have been cleansed. But perhaps, just perhaps, there may have been a mistake somewhere. That, Michael, is where you come in."

"My candidate for mother is MaryBeth. When she was in Mexico, she might have been raising his child. I'm sure when she came here for the funeral she was alone, so that child was left in Mexico. I believe she was living in Guadalajara. See what you can find out before you leave here."

"Right, Sir James. I'll call up a couple of favors. It shouldn't take too long." He walked over to another one of the computers, sat down and his thick fingers began flying over keys.

"Philippe, I would like to know if you and Celine can use your unusual vehicle as a mobile headquarters. That is, set up a network to my computers, voice scrambler, and keep food aboard as well, so that Michael, Richard and Ilena all have a place to return for immediate movement?"

"That is very easily done, Sir James. If I can load one of your computers into our ship and a, uh, scrambler machine, we do have a small refrigerator unit on board for food."

"Good." Sir James motioned to one of the laptops sitting on a far table. "Take that one, and you'll find the spare scrambler equipment in the center drawer of the desk next to you. Take whatever food you need. I would suggest things that are easily made into sandwiches or energy snacks."

Michael looked over at Sir James from where he was working and asked, "By the way, Sir James, where is Ilena?"

"She is working on something special for me. She should be finished in about a half hour or so."

Michael frowned at the answer. Concerned that Sir James was keeping secrets, but, knowing that everything that his boss had done so far had been well thought out and at times had amazed him. However, he didn't trust Ilena, Philippe, Celine or Evelyn. To be honest with himself, he didn't even trust Richard, even after having come through their brush with death.

His e-mail signal flashed in front of him. He clicked on it and realized it was from Tino. Just the person he was hoping would answer. He had a lot of faith in Tino and his capabilities. He was hoping his belief wasn't misplaced. He finished his reply in seconds and sent it on its way. He would have to play a waiting game now.

Although he had sent out a dozen fast e-queries, if he didn't receive any more answers within the next hour, Tino would be on his own. The team needed to be on its way, but they needed a direction.

Two hours later, the team was ready to leave. Sir James had contacted the leaders once more and reassured them that because of the concerted precise attacks upon their seats of power the request for an answer to whether they would act together to form a world government would be deferred again until the investigation was complete and the criminal or criminal placed within the custody of the world's powers.

Each one of the group noticed that the prime ministers and presidents seem relieved. Whether it was because the answer was further delayed or whether they were thinking the entire idea sounded very good to them.

But none of them had a chance to give the change more than a passing thought as the newly aligned team prepared to leave the hidden mountain retreat. Edward was torn between wanting to leave with the group and staying with his wife. But a short chat with his father convinced him that he was definitely needed to assist his father with channeling and processing any incoming information.

It was six in the morning, three weeks after they had arrived, when Philippe piloted the vehicle out of the upper Colorado Rockies. The weather was cold, and any normal plane would have needed to be de-iced before heading up into the snowstorm that was blowing down from Canada.

The group was warm and comfortable. All of them glad to finally be active again. Philippe asked Michael for the coordinates of his friend in Mexico. Barely one hour later, they landed on a tiny abandoned looking airstrip well outside of the city of Guadalajara.

Michael walked down the steps of the plane and walked toward the aluminum hangar that kept the few planes undercover and its office. He strode into the building and took off his sunglasses and hooked the earpiece into the neck of his sweater.

"Hey, Michael. Good to see you." Tino's round frame came barreling out of the office. He was barely five feet seven inches tall, and looked to be just as wide.

"Como esta, Tino?"

"Bueno!" He put his arm around Michael's shoulders and drew him back into the small office. Fans blew the heat around, cracked windows with tape over them would give any passerby the sense the place was abandoned and derelict. An old army cot was tucked away in a far corner away from the door, a pillow and a thin blanket showed that it was still being used.

Tino saw Michael look at the two bare scarred desks. "Don't worry, man. This is where I do immediate business. I knew you wanted privacy. This is the place for privacy." He pulled a briefcase out from behind one of the desks and opened it on a desktop. "Here you go. I think this will give you the answers you wanted."

Michael looked down the page, at about the middle of the page he stopped and looked at Tino. "You can verify this information?"

"Oh, yeah. Here is the documentation to back it up. I knew you'd want to see it." A thick finger tapped another sheet of paper.

"Right." He looked at the second sheet, a birth certificate with a fancy stamp in the corner. "Was there any other information, where the child went? Who adopted after the mother was killed?"

"Saving the best for last, Michael."

Michael's face had become tighter with each revelation shown to him. He stayed completely silent for moment. "Tino, what are you up to these days? Are you working full time or just doing odd jobs?"

"You know me. I go where the job and the work might take me. But, to tell you the truth, Amigo, I haven't had anything to keep me busy for a long time."

"So you would be free to help us out with some work?"

"I haven't worked with you for a bunch of years, Michael. I might be rusty."

"You, rusty? I doubt that. But you pulled this off and I'd like you to come along with us. I take it you are still working alone?"

"You know me. More than me I have a crowd. But I still haven't settled down."

"Great. What do you need to get to leave with us right now?"

"One moment, Michael." Tino turned around and opened up a small door in the bottom part of the wall. He pulled out a worn duffle bag, opened up some of the desk drawers and threw in rumpled clothes, toiletries and zipped up the duffle bag. He looked up, a big grin on his face. "I'm all yours."

"I think you beat your time from the last time we worked together. I think you took five minutes that time."

The two men left the building and walked toward the plane. Tino went up the steps first and as soon as Michael had closed the door, the steps slid in under the vehicle and it took off. There wasn't even a lurch or sound of the wheels on the tarmac to alert Tino that he was almost airborne, so when he looked out of the window not even a minute after entering, he gasped at seeing the sky.

He fell into the nearest seat. "Madre de Dios! What kind of jet is this?"

"A very special one, Tino. A very special one." Michael said as he smiled at his old friend. "You'll get used to it pretty soon."

"Where are the seat belts?"

"Not all of the seats have them." Michael pointed to a seat further toward the rear of the plane. "Try that one, Tino. It will make you feel more comfortable."

Tino got up, thick arms outstretched for balance, walked slowly to the other seat and buckled the seatbelt with a loud click. "Michael, I may live in an airport hangar, but I'm not really a great flier."

"No problem, Tino." Michael clapped him on the shoulder. "We have a lot of traveling to do and I've invited you along for the ride. Let me introduce you to the others. Richard, Ilena, and up front Celine and Philippe, husband and wife, you make the sixth person in our little party."

"Where are we going now?"

"Well, apparently we have some pressing business in London right now. We will be landing well outside of the city. A couple of us will be going into the city. The others will remain here on the plane."

Sir James pondered over the information that Michael had faxed him from the plane. This was not good. Nothing about it was good. Michael made sure that he had taken Tino with him. Good thinking. Not leaving a loose end to perhaps innocently chatter about the most recent strange job. Michael knew Tino, and had let Sir James know that Tino was an asset in a tight spot. So at least he wasn't extra baggage.

Sir James texted Michael with the name of a person he was to contact and also the manner in which the contact had to be made. Lloyds of London was strict in their protocol and strict in the manner in which their personnel handled the business of their wealthiest clients. With the recent loss of his home, the insurance company would be expecting his getting in touch with them. Sir James was sure that Michael and Ilena together would be able to manage this very strategic move. Michael had met the contact at least twice on errands for Sir James so this should not be the cause of any surprise. Ilena on Michael's arm throughout their travel to and from the meeting should keep anyone watching off guard.

The plane landed shortly after ten in the morning on an old airstrip abandoned by the RAF over two dozen years earlier. The plane was moved inside the rickety hangar to be out of the prying eyes of any local busybodies. Ilena and Michael had changed into clothes more befitting the British gentry. They walked down the lane outside of the old airbase and continued on to the small train stop at the village of Billson. Ilena had memorized the schedule and knew they had about a ten-minute wait before the arrival of the train. This was a local spur and would connect up with the London special after about a half hour.

When they arrived at their destination two hours later, the pub was crowded with the usual noisy lunch crowd. They walked in and slowly made their way to the rear where there were two small rooms, the door to the one on their left was slightly ajar. Michael pushed it open further and saw the man he needed to meet. As planned, Ilena remained just outside and ordered fish and chips. When it arrived she paid the server, but she stayed at the end of the scarred wood counter and ate. Because she was unsure of how long the meeting would take she took her time eating and had not quite finished when Michael reappeared and brushed her arm casually as he passed by. She turned and walked out of the pub just behind him.

"Time to catch the train." He said quietly as they returned to the noisy street, headed back toward the station and took the early train back to Billson. There were only two trains into London in the morning and two in the afternoon. They had expected to take the later one, but to be able to make the early one was good for their timeline.

The two walked down the road, disappeared into the old barn and entered the plane.

"How soon can we leave?" Michael asked as soon as he was aboard.

"We can leave now. Did you finish so quickly?" Philippe asked.

"Yes. We need to get as close as we can to the crash site of the helicopter. You have those coordinates?"

"Oh, yes. We can be there in a matter of minutes."

"Good. Since it is still daylight, we should be able to finish everything today, instead of having to wait until tomorrow." Michael pulled coveralls out of a large duffle bag that had been stowed under a rear seat.

Tino watched him for a minute, then said, "Looks like you're going to do some dirty work, need some help?"

"Sure, Tino. I'll show you what I'm looking for, but you'll need some of these as well. Don't want to get those fancy boots of yours messed up."

"Right, Amigo. Those stitched up shoes of yours can't take much mud either."

Michael threw his friend booties and a coverall just as Richard came back from the front of the plane. He was already dressed for their next job. "We'll be landing next to the crash site. Celine checked ahead and all of the officials have left the site. Apparently, tomorrow morning, they'll be towing the wreckage out of there, so we got here just in time."

"I would not count on the site being unoccupied. Usually a guard or two is left on site, so before we get off, we can check with heat sensors." Michael responded.

"You're right. I'll let Philippe know so just in case, we don't have a UFO search on in the area before we're done."

"Why would you have a UFO search here?" Tino asked.

"Well, Tino, this plane is not your usual plane. So many people would get a little upset if they saw it."

"It looked ordinary to me, but it didn't take off ordinary." Tino answered.

All of a sudden they heard the whap-whap sound of helicopter rotors. Michael looked at Ilena, "Philippe's answer to possible guards. Good choice."

Michael, Richard and Ilena had all begun to learn how to operate Philippe and Celine's unusual vehicle. They had poured over copies of the plans, made from the original left with Sir James. They had each spent time with Philippe and Celine before they had boarded the vehicle, as well as while they were in flight. Sir James had been adamant about them all learning how to fly and use the vehicle to its ultimate degree.

Michael, who was accustomed to operating vehicles of every type found it easy. Ilena whose greatest hobby growing up had been video games also quickly adapted to the strangeness of the vehicle. Only Richard, had a difficult time as he tried to analyze each move or adaptation the vehicle made. He constantly referred to the plans to match the maneuver to the specifications.

Michael realized that Richard would actually be the more valuable pilot of the vehicle in a tight spot as he would be able to tell whether or not something was right. He had informed Sir James of that fact. As a result, Sir James decided that each and every time the plane flew he wanted Richard on the flight. He had known that Richard was mechanically inclined but his working knowledge and understanding of the plans would definitely be invaluable.

They landed and two young men in the uniforms of the local police came up to them from a small tent that had been thrown up for shelter near the crash site in case of bad weather.

Michael, Tino, Philippe and Celine left the helicopter and greeted the men.

"We didn't expect any more people here today. Are you getting things ready for them to be carried away tomorrow?" The younger one asked.

"Yes. It was thought that there might be more scattered debris and they wanted to make sure we didn't leave any sharp pieces of the craft around for any of the young locals."

"I'm glad somebody finally thought about that. I caught a young lad here last night, said he'd been dared to get through the tape. I guess they didn't know we were on guard." The older one said, "Oh, I'm Constable Bolton and this is Constable Neely."

"I'm glad to see such sharp eyed men on duty here." Michael said. His demeanor and tone were stiff and military. "We won't be here very long, just a quick tidy up."

Tino and Philippe had moved off to the edge of the thin tree line. Celine stayed behind waiting for Michael to calm the two young officers, before they moved off in the opposite direction. They moved in and around the heavier debris field. Both Celine and Philippe had small instruments with them. They explained they had devised them to look for the presence of the small silver tubes or the resultant explosion. They had also left the plans for the little gauge with Sir James as well as one working example. He had asked his son, Edward to try and build one or more as quickly as possible.

Celine's instrument began buzzing in her hand and Michael looked at the direction gauge with her. "This way, it shows there might be a live one here, not an exploded one." She said as she began walking north in the direction of the little village.

The buzzing increased in tone and sharpness until they were immediately over it. They could both see the glint of the tube through the dirt and leaves that had built up from the crash and general foot traffic in the area. Celine put on thick gloves, pulled out a small hollowed Lucite tube, placed the silver tube in it and wrapped it in a soft instant ice pack. She then reset the tiny gauge and the two continued on their search.

Forty-five minutes later the four felt that they had completed a good search of the area and there were no more alerts from either instrument. They returned to the helicopter just as it was getting dark, said good night to the two officers and flew off.

"I can tell you I am not comfortable with that little device on this plane." Richard said after the others told him of the find. "I've seen, never mind, I have felt what that little thing can do."

"We're going back to Colorado and leave it off. We have too many places to go, too quickly and under some possibly turbulent conditions. Sir James can keep this stable." Michael said, "Remember, I was with you, I am not happy having it this close either. But if it is kept cold and stable it is not a problem. The only thing that saved those people working that area is that it has been fairly chilly and cloudy. Once they had a strong sun and warmth, it probably would have exploded."

"I agree with Michael," Celine said, "those investigators and rescuers were extremely fortunate. It was cool, early evening when the helicopter crashed. But I believe, based on where we found it, and its relationship to the debris field, it must have been thrown by someone on the helicopter at the last minute. They did it in the belief that even if they survived the crash the cylinder would kill them."

"Well, one thing we have learned is that if thrown about it won't blow up." Michael said as he sat down near Ilena who was reading a book near the rear of the plane. "But there has to be some sort of trigger on the cylinder itself. We really need to be able to study this weapon."

"I agree. The cylinder I saw in Canada was tucked under a desk and it was warm and glowing, it was no longer a cool silver little cylinder."

"Philippe and I have studied these as well as we could without triggering them, which was how we were able to make the gauge. Richard was the first to see that it glows red. Could you say how long it was from the time you saw the glow to the actual blast?"

"I would say no more than five minutes. But perhaps thirty seconds prior to the explosion, there was a shudder of some sort, as if....as if the building felt the blast coming, I would say. Michael may have had a different experience. We were not together when I found the cylinder." He looked toward the back of the plane where Michael seemed to have drifted off to sleep. "Thinking back on it, I would say that there is a possibility that just before the explosion there is some sort of inaudible vibration, like a shock wave that actually precedes the blast.

"Well, perhaps you can ask him later. But whatever that cylinder has inside is more powerful than any other item I know. The size makes it easy to conceal, and I would wager that whatever it is constructed of would not set off a metal detector."

"You are correct, Richard. Philippe tested it already. He has carried one we have at home at various times through various airports without raising alarm."

"I understand, anytime someone upgrades the security system they could become more sensitive."

"I wonder if our adversaries are aware of that fact."

"Many people believe if it looks like metal, it must be metal, so they won't take the chance. I have found while observing with Philippe that people may be quite brilliant, very cautious, and still forget to check something so simple as to learn the type of metal covering their weapon."

Just then Philippe let them know that they would be landing in less than ten minutes and that Sir James had been alerted. Celine told Michael that they would not need to leave the vehicle, she was going to meet Edward as soon as they landed, and they would leave immediately in order to keep to the plan that Sir James had set.

Michael nodded, "Good, I did not want to lose time but I knew we had to get that off of this plane. You'll explain to Edward how to take care of our little specimen?"

"I certainly will. Knowing how carefully Sir James organizes, I would suspect he has the perfect place for this."

Michael looked at her for a minute, over the last half hour he had begun to think of Celine as he would any colleague, instead of someone whose origins were not of this world.

As Philippe had said they landed barely ten minutes later and Celine hurried from the plane. Five minutes later she re-entered the vehicle and they took off.

Tino finally stopped snoring and awoke just as they left the hideaway's secured airspace. He snorted and rubbed the heavy growth on his face. "I thought we had stopped." He looked around and then out the window at the bright blue sky. "When do we get to a hotel, Michael? You usually travel first class."

"We're on an extremely tight schedule, Tino. There's a bathroom in the back, but this is our hotel for the next forty-eight hours. I know you didn't exactly volunteer for duty, but you know how it is."

"Hey, amigo. One thing I can say about you is life is never dull around you. So where do we go next?"

"I'll let you know in a little bit, Tino, I have to check a few things."

Richard, Ilena and Michael had all received a text page from Sir James. They moved to the middle of the plane to discuss the next problem they would encounter. The situation was escalating as another concerted attack had been made upon Parliament in London and Congress in Washington. Sir James was still getting information but it seemed as if there were attacks on the governing groups in other countries.

Michael walked up to the front of the plane and let Philippe know where they were headed. A half an hour later a white limousine moved slowly down the quiet street and turned in at the gates of the Leaders' estate. The gates opened within seconds, the car went through and drove up the narrow tree lined drive and stopped in front of the enormous Tudor like mansion.

Michael, Richard, Tino and Philippe all left the car but only Michael and Philippe went up the three steps to the front door. Richard and Tino both slipped away around the sides of the house. Michael rang the doorbell and remembered the last time he had rung the bell and awaited the Leader's decision to see him. 'The more things change' he thought.

But then the door opened, "Yeah?" A tall beefy man, stretching the seams of a security guard's uniform stood in front of them.

"We are here to see Seth Thorsen."

"Really, and who's we?"

"We are here as representatives of Sir James Galston." Michael spoke just as Seth came up behind the guard.

"Peter, Peter. It's fine. These men are friends." Seth Thorsen's blonde hair was long and pulled back. His square face and blue eyes were not smiling, Even though his voice sounded quite jovial. "Come in, come in." The back of his hand as he gestured showed the curved end of a tattoo that continued up under the left sleeve of his black turtleneck.

"Please excuse the place, I've been doing some demolition in preparation for remodeling."

"Ummm, so you inherited the Leader's estate?"

"Yes, of course. He had no family, poor man, except for the people around him. Like me, he paid us all quite well. But I think he had a special place in his heart for me, treated me like the son he never had."

They walked into the Leader's old study. The dark paneling, books, television screens and moldings were gone. Wiring hung from the ceiling and cabling snaked out of the studded walls.

"Are you going to pull up some of the floors and rugs as well?" Michael asked. "With all the work you're doing I'm sure you don't want to leave stained carpeting in the foyer."

"Oh, I had a party a couple of nights ago, a whole bottle of red wine broke out there. Some people get so drunk. You know how it goes. But yeah, I'm definitely going to be having all of the floors done. So I really didn't care.

"Anyway, to what do I owe the privilege of a visit from Sir Galston's, uh, right arm?"

"Well, Sir James wants to know if you are continuing on where you thought the Leader had left off, or if you were moving ahead on the actual plan?

"What do you mean? The actual plan?"

Michael didn't answer immediately. He walked around the room, listening to the echo of his steps, looked out of the windows at what was left of burned rhododendrons. "Well some of the things that have occurred recently were not part of the final plan and to continue might actually cause the plan of cohesion to fracture. That of course would result in the opposite situation, which could be war between countries instead of global government.

"If you are not responsible then Sir Galston sends you his regards and wishes you well."

"Well, since I'm not aware of any recent occurrences that you might be talking about I guess that means you are leaving?"

"I guess that means just that, Seth. I can't wait to see how your remodeling project turns out." Michael and Philippe walked toward the door of the study, one on each side of Seth. Just as they reached the door they could see a prone body lying in the foyer.

"Peter?" Seth turned on Michael fist raised, but Philippe had anticipated him and grabbed Seth's upper arm and threw him against the nearest wall. The force with which he landed knocked him unconscious.

Michael nudged the bulky form of Peter and could tell the way the man's neck moved that it was broken. Tino still knew his job. He had gone through the house so silently that the bodyguard dropped where he waited outside of the study.

Richard came down the stairs from the second floor and Tino came around from the rear of the house.

"Hey, Amigo. I hope you didn't mind me taking care of this one for you. I found the bodies of two women in the basement. They were shackled to the walls. You do not need to go down to look."

"Really," Michael looked down at Seth, "he might know a few things about that as well."

"I'd much rather see the rest of this tattoo." Richard said as he grabbed Thorsen's left arm and cut the knit sweater from cuff, up the arm and down the back. "Uh. Just as I suspected, the coiling snake."

The thick end of the tail of the snake which had shown at Seth's wrist, coiled up around his arm over his shoulder with the open mouth ending in the small of his back. The colors were deep and vibrant throughout the tattoo, with the dominant color being the red that coursed through the body of the snake and gleamed forth from its eyes.

"What is the meaning of the coiling snake, Richard?" Michael asked as he looked at the multicolored tattoo.

"Not so much the meaning as the level of depth, color and size. Our friend here is apparently quite high on the totem pole of 'Hadi Skupina'. They are found worldwide but usually in Eastern Europe. The more color they have on the snakes, the thicker the snake, the longer the snake, the higher the level in the group. I would say Mr. Thorsen is at the very least the number three man."

Tino pulled up the sleeve of the bodyguard and found only a thin snake coiled to just above the elbow. "It figures. A nobody."

Richard's heel suddenly came down on Thorsen's wrist. "Were you looking for something, my friend, perhaps this little item?" Richard slipped a slim dagger from the hidden holster under Thorsen's right sleeve.

The man grunted and tried to raise himself, then realized his wrist was broken. "You coward! You broke my arm, I can't move my fingers."

"Oh, that's a real shame, Seth. What about those bodies in the basement? They'll never move again." Richard said to him.

Michael signaled to Philippe and they started up the steps to the second floor. "Richard, why don't you and Tino have a chat with Thorsen while we check upstairs."

As the two reached the upstairs hall, Michael said, "Philippe, we need to find a secret compartment in the Leader's bedroom. I doubt if Thorsen even knows it exists."

"He was certainly not aware that the Leader had a child. So it is quite probable that the Leader did not trust him."

"I agree. He had only been with the Leader a few years. He assumed much, but knew very little."

"The group that Richard is talking about, are you aware of them, Philippe?"

Philippe looked at him, his thin face never showed any emotion, but his eyes always looked directly at you when he spoke to you. He had never shown any of the duplicity that Michael had grown so accustomed to when dealing with people.

"That group is known to me, to us. Celine and I have encountered those butchers before. We believe that they were either on the ships in Bermuda or directed the people that were on the ships. They work to kill and maim in Africa, they instigate and infiltrate with the snake hidden under designer suits in China and Iran. Yes, I know them. Their group sells protection and terror to the highest bidder. But we have never known who their chief was. Each time we drew close there was the dead end as the Americans say. They fly in and out of Malta at will, one of the reasons we made our home there. We could keep an eye on them. We caught one, but he committed suicide."

The two were searching the Leader's bedroom carefully as they talked. They each took one side of the large ornate fireplace mantle, looking for anything that might open to reveal a secret. Michael's fingers moved over intricate woodcarvings, when a leaf depressed under his touch and a long dark panel between the front of the mantle and the wall popped open.

A large metal file box, a rifle, a box containing a small handgun, as well as several bundles of cash, and a large elegant jewel case were stashed in the hidden space. The two men grabbed everything including the guns and left the room.

They ran down the stairs and Michael said, "Time to leave." Tino hung back to say goodbye to Thorsen in his own way and caught up to the other three just as they were entering the car. Twenty minutes away the vehicle rounded a corner into an alley behind a factory became a blur and was airborne.

"Before we go anywhere else we must again return to Sir James. I do not feel comfortable opening any of this. Ilena, this money is yours. It was hidden in your father's room. This jewelry box I would say is also yours. I don't know how much you know of what your father had, but at least you have this."

Ilena raised her dark eyes to Michael's blue ones. "I'd like to say I don't want anything from him, Michael, but right now, I realize that I don't have anything either. So I'll take them and thank you both for getting them for me. I certainly didn't expect anything."

"Well, we don't know what is in the file box, and that is why we have to return to Colorado. We don't want to make any wrong moves."

They were silent for the rest of the flight. As soon as they felt the sudden sharp descent they knew they were close.

This time upon landing, they all left the plane. Tino, who was seeing the mountain home for the first time made an exclamation as he rounded every corner. When he went through the hidden doorway in the kitchen, he yelled, "Madre de Dios! What is this place? Like a carnival ride."

Sir James came forward, holding out his hand, "You must be Tino. You have been a great help to Michael and our group. Welcome to my home."

"You are Sir James? Oh, Sir. I never thought I would ever get to meet you. Michael always said he worked for a very great man. Señor, you are amazing."

Sir James smiled at the man's unabashed candor, then turned to Michael, "You said you had something that you wanted me to open?"

Michael handed him the large metal file box. "We found this behind a hidden panel in the Leader's bedroom. We gave the cash and jewelry box to Ilena. I felt we should come back here and have you see this before we went to the next destination."

"Excellent. You checked for other places. Including the study?"

"The study was gutted down to the studs, wires were hanging out everywhere. If anything was there, Seth had already found it. We completely checked the bedroom, we only found one spot."

"Good. You can open it and see what we have."

Michael pulled a small device from his pocket and inserted it into the lock. Only seconds passed before it clicked. When the lid was pushed back, colored file folders were jammed into the box, but no color was repeated and nothing was written on any of the tabs.

"Well, everyone, I think we are going to be doing a lot of reading."

Sir James said as he pulled out a thick red folder. "Each of you take a folder and we will see if we can find out the Leader's important secrets."

Even though they had each taken a folder there were still many left, Michael grimaced inwardly, reading was not something he enjoyed, he would much prefer to act. But he knew this was necessary if they were to move forward and not have to look over their shoulders.

For the next few minutes except for the sounds of pages being turned the room was silent. Then Sir James spoke, his voice barely above a whisper. "According to what I have read in this folder, the Leader, Vanderlin was definitely under the guidance of someone else for at least the last twelve years. This file is more like a diary of how much he hated this person. Whoever it was would call him and make demands and force the issue of outer space interaction. He did not even believe in the existence of these extraterrestrials. He felt that the person pulling the strings was also lying to him for some reason."

Richard who had been nodding while Sir James was talking said, "Sir James, this folder," he held up a white one, "seems to be his investigation into the person who was leading him. It shows that he had a tracer on his phones to try and trace where the calls were emanating from. Unfortunately, he concluded that the calls were continuously rerouted, much like what we do here. He has drawings here showing the points he was able to follow the calls through." Richard passed the drawings around to everyone.

Ilena said, "Each of these calls ends with the same Washington DC exchange and then routes to California, or Toronto, but they all end in Washington. So that has to be some sort of common denominator."

"It would be, my dear, except that exchange is for the Senate Offices of the United States. It would be extremely easy to place an extra clip on the phone wiring for those offices and no one would find it until there was a problem with the service."

"Oh." Ilena looked downcast momentarily, then brightened as she said "Why don't we see whose offices they belong to and perhaps there was someone there who is suspect."

"That is the phone number for Senator Danner's offices who was murdered not too long ago. He was also a member of the group, so for the exchange to come through those offices would have been a major blow to the Leader." Michael said.

"Oh, my goodness so my father never did trace the person."

"No, but he did have many people working on it. Michael, hand me that pink file."

Michael reached into the box and took out the file Sir James requested. Sir James began reading, then got up, folder in hand and left the room. "I will return shortly. Everyone please stay here and continue."

The elderly man walked through his kitchen, through the darkened dining room and turned to head up the stairs when he saw the person he was looking for sitting in a window seat in the living room staring out at the mountains.

He tucked the pink folder inside of his suit jacket and walked over to Edward's wife. "Good afternoon, Evelyn. Admiring our beautiful scenery?"

She turned startled. The thick rugs muffled footsteps and she had been sure everyone was occupied elsewhere. "Oh, yes, Sir James. The mountains are very lovely in the sunset. I thought everyone was in a meeting, so I came downstairs to sit and get something to eat."

"We are in a meeting, I came out to talk to you. I have had so little time to talk and get to know you. I mean as my son's wife I should be more attentive to you."

"Oh, Sir James. Please don't feel that you have to hover over me. I'm fine. I'm accustomed to spending time alone. I used to do needlepoint, or other crafts, but I got bored with those. Now I read, and sometimes browse the computer. I must admit I love the computer games." She smiled up at him.

Sir James sat down opposite her on the window seat. "So tell me about yourself, Evelyn. Edward said you were an only child? That must have been lonely growing up."

Sir James noticed the change in his daughter-in-law's demeanor immediately.

"I don't usually talk about my past, Sir James. It is relatively boring. I grew up, went to college, met your wonderful son, got married and here I am."

"So if you needed to work that would definitely be a short resume, my dear."

"I suppose so. I did start to work in advertising right after college. But then Edward was transferred and it seemed too much to be constantly changing jobs every time he moved. So I stayed at home. We tried to have children, but, nothing ever happened. The intensity with which you have to work to have them with all of the doctor's visits, doing everything by a time table was impossible, because Edward wasn't able to be on that schedule."

"I understand." He patted her hand as he looked at her face and could see what his son could see, the dark eyes, heart shaped face, a real beauty, now beginning to age. "How did you meet Edward, Evelyn? He never tells me such things."

"Oh, I was working in the dining hall at college. It helped to defray expenses. He would sit there at his table after he'd finished eating. We would chat while I was putting chairs up for the night, you know cleaning up."

"Ah, he was lying in wait for you then." Sir James smiled at her, trying to lessen the tension he could feel coming from her in waves.

"You might say that. He asked me out and that was it. I never went out with anyone else after that."

"Did your parents like him?"

"My parents had died. My grandparents who had raised me died soon after Edward and I got engaged. I was considered a hardship case. My parents did leave me a little money, so with that and the scholarships and stipends I was able to finish."

"What would you have liked to do for a career if you hadn't met Edward?"

"Well, as I said, I did start at that small advertising agency. It has grown. I probably would have stayed with them. There was some creativity in the work and the pay was good and would have increased. I hadn't thought much beyond getting my degree and getting my first job."

"Hmmm.... So you would have just stayed with the one firm instead of moving about from one place to another?"

"Yes. Probably, I don't know, it's hard to say. I enjoy stability. Possibly because I was alone so much of the time growing up that having the same group of people around gives me a sense of being grounded. But, Sir James, what is going on, why all of these questions?"

"Nothing at all, my dear, as I said, I just wanted to get to know you a bit better. I had better get back to the meeting before they forget who I am. Relax and feel free to get yourself anything you want to eat, anytime, Evelyn."

He stood up and walked back through the kitchen into the meeting. "Did anyone find out anything new while I was gone?"

Edward began for the group as they explained what they had discovered and what it might mean in terms of who had been guiding the Leader and where they might take the next step of their own plans to unify the world and save the present global leaders.'

"Good, excellent. You all have a grasp of the situation and these files have certainly given us the insight we needed. Here is what we will be doing as a result. However, since we now know that Vanderlin did not trust Seth and was aware of his allegiance to the 'Hadi Skupina' we know we are looking for someone else. My friends, we do not have a lot of time."

Sir James felt more certain than ever that he knew who had been behind the Leader and who had been leading Seth Thorsen to continue to execute the Leader's previous plans. But he had no proof, and did not share his suspicions with the others. Instead he spent the next hour outlining a plan he had been going over in his mind for quite a while, but, the information found in the Leaders file box still did not make him decide that he was correct.

The group pulled their chairs closer to the table as Sir James mapped out the next phase of their operations. It would be tricky and would not be possible without the capability of Philippe, Celine and their vehicle. They had less than twenty-four hours before they had to again speak with the world leaders. Although there had been no more concerted attacks upon governments, Sir James knew he had to be able to give answers, concrete information, and a plausible plan for the future.

The President of the United State greeted the British and French Prime Ministers at ten o'clock in the morning, the Chinese, Russian, Israeli, and Spanish Prime Ministers at noon and the rest throughout the afternoon.

The city of Washington, D.C. was teeming with National Guard troops on every corner. Police were patrolling streets that were too narrow for the National Guard tanks to comfortably ride down. All traffic into and out of the city had been halted. Helicopters were landing just inside the perimeter of the city and limousines would pick up the dignitaries and shuttle them to the White House.

It had been deemed easier for each of them to come to Washington, then for the President of the United States to leave Washington and go to them. All of the countries wanted to be part of this unprecedented meeting. The diplomats knew that the next day they would all be contacted by someone who claimed to be able to assist them, but they were still uncertain. Worse they were concerned that if they did not comply with this voice they would be killed or worse their countries obliterated. Every country had traced the transmissions, but each trace of the same transmission ended in a different country.

Britain's MI6 had traced them to Egypt and not further. The Secret Service had traced them to Australia, while China had traced them to Croatia, and France had traced them to Washington.

At seven p.m. all the diplomats were gathered in the small sitting room just outside the president's bedroom. The rooms had been searched every four hours over the last twenty-four hours. The heating and air ducts had been lined with miniature cameras, every extra chair and table brought into the room had been checked for listening devices and the room sealed until everyone was ready to file into the makeshift conference room.

Everyone understood the need for secrecy and the cramped conditions, and there was little comment from anyone as they struggled to find comfortable positions on the temporary seats. Sealed bottled waters and juices were made available for all of the delegates. Dinner would be held in the traditional family dining room after the meeting.

Conversation was muted, but constant. Those who wanted to have a more private conversation moved away from the crowd into corners and turned their backs. The president moved around the room greeting everyone. His face showed the strain of the past several weeks. His secretary could have told anyone who was interested that he would only nap for an hour at a time, and his intake of coffee had sharply increased.

But Marge was downstairs, at her post, monitoring faxes, e-mails and researching information that her boss wanted as quickly as possible on the computer. The president had the resident tech install two more computers and had increased her security clearance to equal his own. That unprecedented move had allowed her to get information for him that he never would have had time to access.

She beeped him now and he responded on the receiver at his ear. She fed him the information she had just found. Stapleton thanked her, walked over and stood beside the British Prime Minister.

"Could you come with me into the next room, Miles?"

Miles Fairwell nodded and the two went out of the crowded sitting room into a small study. The lean, gray haired Prime Minister stared at the President, from behind rimless glasses, wondering what was happening.

"Sorry to drag you away, but I didn't want anyone to hear me ask you about Sir James Galston. What do you know about his house being blown up?"

"Ah, I thought you might want to know if that was part of this. MI6 is not sure what happened. They are sure that the helicopter that crashed was the same one that had been flying overhead at the same time. They have been unable to identify the type of explosive. However, you might be interested to know that they are sure it was the same type of explosive that was used in Canada some weeks ago during a worldwide business conference. Everyone was warned just minutes before that an explosive device had been found and to leave. The radius of damage from both explosions was in their words 'exact'."

"So, the conspiracy grows. Why would his home be targeted?"

"Well, we have been unable to speak with him. He was reportedly relaxing at a resort in Australia at the time of the explosion. We spoke to his daughter about an hour after it occurred and then she also dropped out of sight."

"What does Sir Galston do for work? Is he a playboy, financier? I've never heard of him before on the global scene."

"He is considered a philanthropist and worker for the needy. When he has voiced political concerns it was regarding worldwide issues of peace and health only. However, he is extremely wealthy and has always valued his privacy. His daughter was well known in her late teens and early twenties as a party girl, but she's become much more private as she's grown up and is rarely seen in public."

"No wonder I haven't heard of him then, a very low profile kind of guy. So tell me, what would he be doing involved with our problems?"

"That, Mr. President, I wish I knew."

The two men walked back into the other room and it was obvious from the attention they received, their absence had been noticed. The President decided that the best thing to do was to be up front with the group.

"Ladies and Gentlemen, I'm sure you're thinking we were just having a clandestine meeting, but to be truthful and honest, I needed to ask the Prime Minister a question and I wanted to be certain I could hear the answer. I have heard the answer and now, I'm going to share with all of you.

"Some or all of you may have heard about the explosion of a manor house in Britain." Stapleton looked around and noticed many nods. "Well, it is my belief that the owner of that house is on our side and whoever has caused the infiltration of our governments, has tried to kill us and our people, as well as the loss of life in Bermuda, also tried to kill the owner of that house.

"He has gone into hiding for his own safety, but I'm hoping and I think, he might be trying to help us as well. Sometimes one person can make a difference. I wanted to verify the cause of that explosion and the Prime Minister gave me the answer I needed.

"With that information I believe it is time for us to go into dinner." The President turned and led the way down the hall to the dining room. Behind him, everyone was speaking at once, trying to understand and make sense of what he had just said.

Once they were all seated, many tried to ask more questions. He just responded that right now, he knew very little, but he was hoping to learn more as quickly as possible.

The team flew in over Auckland, New Zealand. They again had left Sir James, Edward and Evelyn back in Colorado. They needed to check out the information found in the research work that young Sarah Martin had completed. They had brought Mary Fleming this time because she was familiar with how the research had been prepared and might have other information that might help.

Mary and Michael left the vehicle that had driven down the main street and parked in an open parking lot behind an older office building. The building had to have been well over a hundred years old, but the entrance and lobby had been tastefully updated to include the expectations of modern customers. The lobby held an internet café, a couple of boutiques, and the entrance to a spa that took over much of the rear of the area. They took the elevator up to the fourth floor and entered the offices of Turner Global Geology.

An older woman was seated behind a desk and looked up as they came through the door.

"Hello there, might I help you?"

"Ah yes. I'm Michael Clark. My mom and I were trying to see if we could get some information about Antarctica, the glaciers. She's a little worried about going there, you know with all the talk about the melting of the glaciers and such. I told her there's really nothing to worry about. So before we book or don't book the trip, someone suggested we talk with your firm."

"Well, I think I can help you there. I'm Imogene Turner, owner of the company." She laughed at their reaction. "Yeah, I know. You thought I was the secretary. I can't stand formality, never could. Office receptionists, or secretaries, require you to pay them to sit at a desk, answer a phone, talk to people for you, and in the end they usually aggravate the hell out of you."

Michael looked at Mary and then at the tall raw boned, gray haired woman who stood up, came around the desk and shook their hands. "I'll tell you this, a couple of people more or less, certainly won't change the rate of the melt. It's too damn late for that."

"See mom, I told you we could go. She'd heard that the melting had sped up recently and was worried that it might, uh…. calve, while we were out there on it taking pictures."

"Yes, Michael Clark, that is the right word. When people are exploring, or touring the glaciers there are always experienced guides who like me are trained to be sure of the stability of each glacier. If they notice signs that a glacier is starting to calve, they'll not only keep everyone off, they make sure no one is within a mile. You can never be sure how much or how deep the break will be.

"I know, Mrs. Clark, you've probably heard the rumors about the instability of the glaciers brought on by the greenhouse effect. That is true, and yes, they are melting faster than they were even three years ago. If you want to see them, get there within the next five years. The Pacific and the Atlantic are both rising already."

"You have got to be kidding, the oceans are rising? Only five years? What is going to happen?" Mary spoke for the first time. She had been afraid to speak earlier, but the information she was hearing stunned her.

"Why don't you two come into the other room, it's where I keep the equipment to make sure I make a living. If you don't mind, I'm just going to put out my 'out to lunch' sign and lock that door. I do that when I come back here. It's the only part I dislike about not having a secretary. I can't hear people come in if the machines are running." As she walked she pushed back long straggling gray strands that had escaped a woven barrette, behind her ears.

They followed her into the other room. It looked like they had left Auckland and were standing on the glacier. Michael looked around, studying, making sure he remembered what he was seeing in case it was needed later. "This looks like the glacier, but you get to stay warm."

"Yes. Yes. I can no longer go out to the glaciers. I had some health problems. So I work from here, my team is in contact with me from Antarctica. I had this built and I change or break off the pieces based on their input."

"This is incredible, Ms. Turner." Mary was walking around, inspecting, touching, her eyes filled with awe at the depth of detail.

"Well, the only thing missing is the sun. With the sun shining down on a glacier, you can….. Ah, yes. Anyway, what I wanted to show you is over here. We cannot understand why or how, but about six months ago, the glaciers over here on the southern end, began to calve more quickly, melt more quickly than they have in hundreds of years. We have taken thousands of core samples over many decades and, we have studied those from fifty years ago up to five months ago. There is no doubt. We were losing an inch of land a month, then two inches, now it is up to four inches of land a month. At this rate earth will be a water planet.

"We have worked every model, looked at the element of pollution, yes, global warming as well, the old 'greenhouse effect'. It is as if a volcano from the center of the earth had suddenly broken through and was warming and melting the glaciers." Imogene Turner wiped away a tear. "Sorry, I get a bit emotional about Mother Earth.

"But like I said if you want to go see a glacier, go now. There won't be any of the grand glaciers we are accustomed to in fifteen years." She led them out of the room, and opened up the door to the hallway. "It's been nice meeting you Mrs. Clark, Michael Clark. Stop by if you like after your trip to the glaciers. I'll be here." Her crumpled rolled up jeans, over worn earth shoes seemed to reflect her saddened thoughts.

They thanked her and left. When they returned to the car they called Sir James to discuss what Imogene Turner had told them.

"Michael, were you able to get pictures of the glaciers? How they were arranged?" Sir James seemed to be unusually enthusiastic about the recent information.

"Yes, Sir James. I've been uploading them. They are just about done. Luckily Mary was walking around with her, so she didn't notice. Here we go, I'm transmitting them to you now, sir."

The group on the plane crowded around the laptop. Edward and Sir James were watching the same images. The gauges, wind speeds, the simulated ocean at the edges of the glacier, the markers showing date and increase of the encroaching water, all were shown in the slightly grainy color pictures.

"Excellent, Michael. Mary, you did well, drawing her out. I had heard about her illness but I didn't realize that she could never return to the glacier. To have met her and talked with her is a definite achievement. You recorded her words. We might need that later to help us work through this.

"With all of her work, she does not know what is happening, which means it most likely is something our extraterrestrial friends might be instigating. Philippe? Celine?"

"We agree with your assessment, Sir James. The problem is locating their agent here on the earth. The extraterrestrials and whoever that person might be, is behind the increase of the glacier melting, the attacks that the Leader perpetrated, as well as the concerted attacks on the governments. I believe Sir James that you now have your proof that the extraterrestrials are coming with less than earth's well-being as their plan."

"We have the proof we need, but it is not concrete as yet. These governments will need very concrete proof in order to work together against this threat. They need to see it as a definite threat.

"All right. Ladies and Gentlemen you are headed to NASA. We need to know the exact time and content of the contact. Who was there then and is not there now. Michael, Richard, Philippe, I believe you will work better at interacting with these people. I will see to it that your entry is facilitated. Ilena, you know what to do. Good work, everyone."

Sir James leaned back in the leather chair. "Where is Evelyn?"

"I think she's in the living room reading a book, Dad. Why?"

"Just wondering, Edward. I'm going into the planning room. After you are sure Evelyn will be comfortable for at least the next couple of hours, I would like you to meet me there." He left the study and walked down the hall to the kitchen.

He didn't like what he was thinking, suspecting. But with each hour, each new revelation he felt certain that he knew the identity of earth's traitor. He stepped through the door into the now silent computer room. The lights were dim, the way he liked them when no one was working. He stared at the large black screen on the wall. It was time to hand over the secrets to Edward, but would he be handing them over to the enemy at the same time?

Who was Evelyn? The question was beginning to bother him. He felt fairly sure he knew, but there were so many doubts. If he was wrong, and he could so easily be wrong. It was a mistake he, not only did not want to make, he could not afford to make.

No, he was sure Edward would not have made an error, definitely not a lifetime error. So, he could not take the easy way out. Just because the facts seemed to match Evelyn's background, was no reason to believe that she in fact was the one behind the Leader. But, with all of the security in place, unless she knew certain codes on how to circumvent the blocks, neither she, nor anyone else, could send signals to outside of this house. He had been checking constantly and no signal, other than theirs, had left the hideout. 'Hideout', that was what it used to be, but after seeing the incredible devastation of his home in Britain, this was now his home.

He looked up as Edward came into the room. "How is she?"

"Slowly, she is becoming more like herself. I think that witnessing the sudden change in Philippe and Celine, plus I had that work done in Switzerland, that had to have caused her to become so withdrawn. I had told her she could trust them, well Philippe, then all of the mystery about reaching me. Reading the information I had given her so long ago at the same time?" Edward was shaking his head, the movement shaking his hair which had grown much longer and the gray was now obvious. "It all left her not really trusting anyone, Dad."

"I understand, Son. You are absolutely certain she will be fine?"

"Yes. Right now, she is getting herself some lunch. I've filled her in a little bit on what was happening, why we are here and that your home was destroyed. However, she is still trying to figure out Philippe and Celine.

"To be truthful, Dad, so am I. I know how Philippe looked years ago in the Gulf War. Hell, I was barely twenty-three myself. He still looks twenty-three years old. Evelyn swears that Celine had brown eyes not blue. The golden shimmering when they come close together."

"I know. However, he has already said they are not from earth. Where they are from, how many more there are, and what is their true intent? We do not know, Edward. I am very unsure as to how far we can trust them. With Richard and Michael there, I feel that we can keep an eye on them. But, we do not know the extent of their powers.

"If you remember, Edward, Philippe seemed to be saying that if Celine had been with him he would not have been injured. So they definitely have powers together that they do not have separately. What are those powers?"

"I don't know. Yes, I knew him. I rescued him, I visited him several times and we talked a lot during my visits. But for some reason he only mentioned my seeing him apparently in the hospital during and after his recovery. I overlooked it as possibly amnesia. But knowing who they are, I don't think so. We were friends, before he was injured. I considered him my friend. That is how I knew the type of women he liked. Why

I kept him away from me while I was in Washington. He would have attracted many of those women and he was happy living in Malta. I didn't know he was married or 'had a mate' until I saw him in Valletta."

"Do you think that with their way of thinking they run all of the days together? Do they perhaps form a different kind of day memory?"

"I really don't know. There are so many questions that have to be answered. I don't think we have any answers, Dad. This is very frustrating to me. I'm usually able to understand, figure things out, get things straight."

"We do have some answers, Son, we just need to find the right players. So as usual we are looking for a certain person or people who have been working with the incoming extraterrestrials. For some reason I believe that the date of their arrival is sooner rather than later.

"I believe that is why your friend began to move forward."

"I agree with that, Dad."

"All right. We have work to do. We still have files to go over, Edward. We may still have answers. The Leader was kind enough to leave us plenty of material. We just have to use it to find the answers."

That said, the two began pulling apart the balance of the Leaders file box and even going over those files that had already been searched through by the whole group.

The plane was streaking north and west from Florida. The NASA visit had been more productive then they could have hoped. As Michael, Richard and Philippe watched the reruns of the original transmissions from the extraterrestrials they noted that each time they came in over the Arctic Circle.

They were probably going to be too late to find anything or anyone, if someone had even been there at the time of the transmissions. They hovered over the area of the coordinates watching and waiting before landing. They mapped the area thoroughly, looking for areas of residual heat, or any other anomaly with thermal imaging.

It was painstaking work and neither Michael nor Richard had the stomach for it. But Mary, Ilena and Philippe watched each grid carefully as they went over it. They were rewarded when Ilena yelled, "Yes!"

"Look, everyone, that is more than just a trace."

"She is correct." Philippe said. "That is a fairly vibrant color. We are apparently not too far behind them. Do you wish to trail them?"

"You can follow their signature?"

"Yes. As you say follow the breadcrumbs."

Michael texted Sir James to let him know what was happening.

Then at the older man's request they were listening to him through the speakers. "All right. You have trailed them to this place. However, is there anything here that will let them know that you have found the site? Check for an electronic signature, immediately. You have been there for some time, is that correct? Have you checked the spot before or is that definitely a new part of the grid? Is the color enhancing? Answers quickly, please!" Sir James sounded worried.

Philippe answered, "You are correct on everything, Sir James." He answered calmly as he placed two fingers against the left side of his head. They did not feel the vehicle move but, they did notice that they were suddenly over a large city and according to the directional readout moving south at an incredible speed.

"Thank you, Philippe." Sir Galston was still with them.

"I should have been more alert to the danger, Sir James."

"But you were there early enough to track their signature, is that right, Philippe?"

"Yes, we are on their trail, but not that close. Has there been an explosion yet?"

"Nothing reported yet. I'll let you know."

Half an hour later Sir James called them back. "It's been listed as an earthquake in the Arctic. They tracked the epicenter directly to the coordinates you were hovering over. I believe they used one of their favorite weapons and may actually have an unlimited supply."

The others had listened to the exchange and were looking worriedly at each other. That had been a close call. This meant that possibly someone knew they were on the hunt.

Michael was the first to speak. "Sir James, I think that when we spoke with Drake Oliver down at NASA, his secretary might have been well aware of our discussions. He is of course in a position to keep anyone aware of all the comings and goings of Mr. Oliver and update a contact on any situation with the upcoming visit."

"Did you get his name, Michael? We may just have to have a little chat with him."

"Yes, Sir James, Jerry Smullins."

"Good. Now, do you know where you are trailing this adversary?"

Philippe answered, "As of now, we really do not have any idea. We are presently passing over the Midwest. I am concerned that we are heading into a trap. I would like to stop trailing until we can find out where we are headed."

Michael and Richard spoke almost as one. "Yes." "I agree."

Richard spoke up, "Philippe, is there any way you can simply track the signature without actually following it?"

"I believe this is a possibility." Philippe said as he went up and sat down beside Celine who had been piloting the vehicle since they had left Florida. Within minutes they had slowed and the vehicle was driving down a quiet two-lane blacktop road. "We are in the Texas Panhandle. The trail is continuing on but drifting westward."

Sir James spoke then, "I am going to contact Drake Oliver at NASA and some others I know. I think we have finally made some progress. If they are sure we are on their trail, and they are running, then we can catch them. Michael, Richard, Tino, all of you, keep Mary safe. There is no time to bring her back here. Let me know the destination as soon as you have it." Sir James signed off.

Sir James picked his cell phone up from the desk in front of him and keyed in a number. He waited a moment, before he punched in a few more numbers. "Hello, I was trying to reach Drake Oliver, I'm a friend of his." Edward watched his father's face and knew immediately that there was trouble.

"When did this happen? I just spoke with him two hours ago, and he seemed fine at that time."

"Yes, well, thank you for the information. No, no one else will be able to assist me." Sir James ended the call and sat back in his chair. "Now I know what it feels like when you lose control of things."

"Dad, what has happened?"

"Drake Oliver has died suddenly. His secretary was with him when he passed away."

"Well, that really seems to connect the secretary to whoever is pulling the strings."

"Yes it does, doesn't it?

"Edward, please have your wife join us." His voice had changed and there was a brittle almost cruel undertone in it that Edward had never heard before.

He said nothing and left the room in search of Evelyn. He found her sitting in the living room window seat.

"Hello, Dear. I was just enjoying the view. It makes me wonder why some of the mountains are filled with trees and others right next to them are bare and rocky."

"I never thought about that, interesting. Leave it to you to think of such things." He kissed the top of her head as he wrapped his arms around her and stared out at the mountains. Edward wondered idly how far his father's property actually extended. Probably everything he could see. It would make sense for his security. It was probably pretty cheap when he purchased the land.

"Come on, Evelyn, Dad wants you to join us. I think he misses having a crowd around him."

"I don't want to get underfoot. I'm perfectly fine right here. I know where you are, you are near me, which makes my life much easier."

"I understand, but he really wants you to come into the computer room. Probably, he wants to share more about what we do."

"Well, all right, if I must." Reluctantly, she stood up as Edward took her hand and led her toward the secret doorway in the kitchen. As he expected she was startled as she stepped through into the computer/planning room.

"Thank you for joining us, Evelyn. I'm sure you have been wondering what we are doing when we disappear from view. Usually we are here. Right now the others are out riding around."

"Oh, I was wondering where everyone had gone. It seemed as if either Richard or Michael was hovering over me, as if I would break."

"Ah! That was my fault, my dear. You had been through such an ordeal, I was truly worried about you."

"Oh, thank you, Sir James. I appreciate your worrying about me.

I guess when I arrived I was feeling extremely overwhelmed. My life is normally pretty uneventful. So with all that has happened, I just couldn't seem to cope."

"That is perfectly understandable, my dear. Well, I asked Edward to get you because I think it is time that you start learning much more about what your husband and I have been doing." Sir James watched her face as she looked at her husband and then back at him.

"Please don't feel that you have to include me in your work, Sir James. I'm quite content being kept in the dark. It is enough that I have my husband nearby."

"Well, ordinarily that might work well. However, there are some things going on that will require us to leave you alone for very long periods of time. We may be here, but you will be unable to reach us, call us, or speak to your husband. Up until now, Mary has also been here with you, but she is also away right now.

"Edward has explained to me that you are accustomed to being alone for long periods of time and don't really crave the constant gadabout existence which others need. However, sitting in the living room window seat, certainly doesn't seem to me to be a very healthy existence."

Edward started and his head turned to look at his father. "She enjoys the peace and tranquility afforded by that view, Dad."

"That may be true, son, but you certainly cannot expect her to remain there for twelve to twenty-four hours at a time."

"I'm sorry, Sir James, I thought you meant maybe five or six hours. I do like interacting with people, it's just that I don't like running in and out of malls and stores. You know the clubs and groups of women, who are supposed to be volunteering for charity projects and wind up tearing each other apart about husbands and clothing. It is a waste of everyone's time."

"Ah. Yes. Well, I realize that normally when you were alone, while Edward was away you could drive to the country, so that even though you were alone, you had many different choices every day. Here, there are no choices.

"You cannot leave here until we all leave. You cannot drive out of here safely unless you know the route. There are security safeguards, not only around the house, but around the mountains that you see. Those mountains are all connected to this house, both as part of my property and as part of the security systems. The security system is presently in place. If you remember the difficulty Philippe and Celine had in landing here? That was with my allowing them to land."

"This is scaring me." Evelyn turned to Edward. "Does this mean I can't even open a window or a door to the outside?"

"My dear, the windows do not open and any door that looks like it might lead to the outside, does not. Worse yet, you might set off an alarm."

"So basically I'm a prisoner here?"

"No, you are not. You, we, are living here only until we can complete our work. We do not want anything to happen to you. Not only would it distract Edward. It might very well be fatal to you."

"So this is why you need to let me know more about what is happening?"

"Yes, it is, Evelyn." Sir James watched her carefully as she was obviously pondering the situation. However, he did not like the calm that she projected. She professed to being scared, but is seemed to him as if she wanted to challenge him. He looked at Edward, who had his arm around his wife. But she seemed unaware of him. She was definitely hiding something. Now he was sure of it.

"Evelyn, you have a problem. Please, tell me what it is. What is really troubling you, Evelyn? This is the only time I will ask and it is best that you tell us now."

"Evelyn, what is it? What is going on?" Edward put both his hands on her shoulders and turned her to face him.

Evelyn violently twisted herself free of Edwards grip, walked over to the entrance of the room and turned to face them. Her face was flushed and her voice dropped into a cold hiss, "Sir James you don't fool me. You think, no, you believe, that I have something to do with the problems your precious group is having. You have no idea what you are dealing with. You have had me here under your thumb for days, with all of your security, and you still couldn't prevent anything from happening. Your stuffy, old, family manor house is all gone."

Edward's face first registered shock, then anger. "You can't be Evelyn. What have you done with her?"

"Oh, Edward, you were never home so I never had to worry about you catching on to what was happening. But your father, he is a smart old man. You should pay more attention to him."

"Edward, I knew you would never believe me if I told you. She is the Leader's oldest child. This is why Ilena was always kept away in school. Evelyn was in charge."

Edward dropped into the closest chair and stared silently at the woman he had loved since the day he saw her wiping down the tables in the cafeteria. Had that been a set up? Had her life with him been a total sham?

"You have an implant, don't you, my dear? It took me awhile to find the mini signal that had laid itself over the signals that were ours. But it is why you had to be at that window. It was the closest you could get to the outdoors. That window seat bulges out from the rest of the house like a bump. It is actually there for another reason, which helped when I was looking for a signal.

"Evelyn, I believe that you will have to go into one of our special rooms, if you don't mind."

"It will stop nothing, Sir James. Everything is in place. The glaciers are now melting Even more quickly now and the seas are rising. The extraterrestrials need more of a water world to be more inviting for them. So I set that up for them."

"Who are your operatives, Evelyn? Where are they? Do you know the devastating effect of those little cylinders that your people are using?" Sir James had moved much closer to her.

"Of course I know what they do. The idiots, I told them not to hold onto them too long after they were set to go, but of course they wanted to make sure, so they were too close when they blew up your home. The result was they incinerated themselves.

"It's a real shame your people killed Seth. He was definitely a good man. Not a lot of creativity, but an excellent lover, Edward."

"Evelyn!"

"Edward, she's just trying to get to you. So, your father set up everything, including your marriage to Edward?

"Yes, he had discovered your shabby little plan and decided that would be the ultimate way to make sure you couldn't overthrow him. But he kept on trying to run things instead of listening to me. Even when he was flat on his back, I had to put a stop to that."

"Come Edward, it's time to have Evelyn enjoy some of our other hospitality."

The two men grasped her by the upper arms and marched her over to one of the doors in the computer room as she struggled against them. They went through into a very dark hall. There were several turns, then a light came on in a straight line on the floor, which directed their steps downward and around a curve, before it went off, another light came on momentarily further down the hall, then darkness, but they continued walking. They turned several more times and a light came on in front of a door.

"Ah. Here we are, Evelyn, your new home. I know you enjoy solitude so this should suit you just fine." He pushed her into the room and slammed the door. It had looked like wood, the clanging thud belied its metal content.

"Edward, that room is three feet of reinforced concrete, lined in six inches of lead then another three feet of reinforced concrete, inside a mountain that is separate from the main house and mountain. That is why we had to walk so long. The light and dark constant transition is very useful in disorienting whoever is coming down here."

"I couldn't believe how you found your way down here, Dad. I mean without lights."

"This was built by me for my use. It was to be expected that I would be bringing someone down here. So I had to be on the right and there is a tiny glimmer of red forming an arrow as you walk along. It lights up right beside you so the person on your left will not see it. Luckily, my peripheral vision is still quite adequate.

"Now, son, let us get to work. Unfortunately, I'm sure she has put things in place that will take us quite a while to discover. But I need to tell you, Edward, I truly regret having had to expose her, to hurt you in this way. I have obsessed over this for days. I suspected her quite some time ago. But it wasn't until the team returned from Mexico with the information they had from Tino and then the hidden files from the Leader's home."

"I'm speechless, Dad. I didn't know. I never suspected anything. Then Seth? What on earth was she thinking?"

"Oh, she was thinking all right, Edward. Your wife is a brilliant woman. She was thrilled that you were in the White House, she had complete access to you, the Leader and everyone. She had a position of strength. Utter power. According to what I can figure out, the Leader had worked with her when she was alone, while you were away. While you were away in the Gulf, is when she let the Leader know she was taking over. I found a diary of sorts in that pink file. She had refused to meet with him and told him what his next steps were to be.

"She manipulated you to work in the White House. That was very easy. The Leader didn't have a problem with most of her requests since it gave him the same powers, he thought."

"So she recruited Seth to work for him?"

"Yes, she did. Although I knew Seth and steered him as well toward working for the Leader, I had no idea that anyone was behind him. She was also running the Hadi' Skupina in Eastern Europe. Vanderlin knew about it, but he didn't know that Seth was part of it at the beginning."

"I can't believe I never knew. I can't believe I never suspected. That's probably why we never had any children. She probably manipulated me there as well."

"Sorry, Edward. That was real. She cannot have children, that fact really upset her father. He was looking for a dynasty. Imagine Vanderlin and me, your children's grandfathers."

"That would have been very interesting on Christmas. So what do we do now, Dad? I mean, we know who is behind everything now. My own wife. God!!! Just thinking it, is gut wrenching."

"Well, we have to get back in touch with Michael and Richard and see where they are now. They should have the trail down by now. We have to learn everything ourselves, we cannot look to her for information. Oh, and say nothing to them of Evelyn."

They stepped back into the computer room and Sir James punched in the numbers to raise the team. They had an immediate response.

"Sir James, we were just trying to reach you." Michael sounded a little relieved. "The trail headed directly toward the Galapagos Islands then doubled back onto itself. They might be looking for us, realized that we were no longer following them. Because we are parked in a parking lot and they are looking for a flying vehicle we may be able to trick them into showing themselves."

Sir James looked worried, "Michael, they know more about that vehicle you are in than you are aware. Is Philippe nearby?"

"Yes, he's right here."

"Hello, Sir James, how can I be of help?"

"Philippe, right now your safety and the safety of the rest of the team needs your expertise with your vehicle. The fact that your vehicle can change from car to plane has been leaked. Please do not ask me how I know this. You need to camouflage your vehicle in a completely different fashion from anything that has been done so far.

"The fact that they have turned around means that not only are they going to look for you but they plan on getting rid of you. You have very little time."

"Thank you, Sir James"

"What is going on?" Michael had picked up the phone.

"Help Philippe with anything he needs right now. He is trying to save the lives of all of you. I am going to hang up now, we don't know the capability of those that are now tracking you."

"Dad, what on earth is happening?"

"When I thought she was thinking, she must have been sending out new orders. The people they were trailing have turned around to locate them. We don't know if they are extraterrestrials or the Hadi' Skupina. I am hoping for the Hadi' Skupina. They have little in the way of brains. They never think for themselves."

"How will we know what happens?"

"I have faith in the team, but a lot is trust in Philippe and Celine. I am not sure what their vehicle can do besides what we already know.

They cannot return here until they have either eliminated the quarry or captured them. I do not expect them to capture them.

"While we are waiting I am going to contact the meeting in Washington. It is ahead of time, but I think we need to prove to them that work is in progress."

"Right. I wonder if they will be glad to hear from us, Dad. We really have led them a merry chase."

"True. Well, here we go."

"Mr. President. Mr. President." Marge came bustling into the dining room.

"What is it, Marge?"

"They are asking for all of you, stating that they have an update for you."

Marge went over to the rear of the room and set up the feed to pick up the call. The room had gone silent the minute Marge came in. All eyes watched her as she set up the phone and placed it on speaker.

"This is the President of the United States, there are representatives from countries throughout the world here to listen to what you have to say."

"Thank you, Mr. President for taking our call. I would like to tell you the head of the snake has been cut off."

The statement was met with an immediate gasp from one of the delegates.

"Ah, as I thought. The person who gasped understands what I just said. Would you all look at the left wrist and arm of that person?"

The delegate from Romania jumped up and started out of the door. The Secret Service blocked his escape and in the process rolled up his sleeve to display a large thick and multicolored tail of a snake. The man was bald and his round face was dripping in sweat.

"You don't understand. We are a charitable society. We help children. We don't do horrible things."

The person on the phone audibly cleared their throat. "Your group supplied the personnel to take over the ships in Bermuda. Your group supplied the personnel and weapons to orchestrate the concerted attack upon the various seats of government only days ago. You came to this White House meeting. My question to you, Sir, is why?"

The question was shouted by the occupants of the dining room in their native languages, in the hope of an answer. The rotund man, now stripped to the waist, was nearly hysterical, the snake incongruous against the flab of his back.

The President could not believe his eyes and ears. Marge was now standing behind his chair. Miles Fairwell tapped his spoon against his water glass. The noise died down, but the whimpering of the Romanian could still be heard.

The voice from the phone spoke again. "We told you that we were working on this for you, for all of you. It is true. We have captured and are holding the head of the perpetrators. We are still fighting to complete and stop all activity that was set up by this person. The network is not only large and deadly, but they have been given weapons by the extraterrestrials, who plan on visiting us very soon.

"Please be advised that the visit is not in two years as you were given to believe, but in a matter of months and possibly even sooner. The concerted attacks upon you, was to keep you separated and at each other's throats. Further, these people are also responsible for the speed of the glacier melting on both poles. We are making every effort to stop this even as we speak.

"The gentleman you have with you now, I am sure will be able to assist you with details. Thank you all for your attention."

Again, there was bedlam as each person in the room was either speaking or shouting. The Secret Service had already removed the crumpled Romanian from the room. This time President Stapleton tapped his glass for order.

"Gentlemen, Ladies. I believe this phone call was extremely revealing to say the least. These people have not only been able to reach into our midst, but reveal a traitor to the rest of us in our midst. I don't know about all of you, but I am amazed by not only their level of intelligence, but, their ability to operate and achieve results.

"As usual they have hung up without awaiting our questions. I'm sure all of you have as many questions as I. Perhaps, they are correct we should be asking our Romanian friend. Apparently, the information was a great shock to him. Otherwise he never would have revealed himself."

The President beeped Saunders, the only Secret Service man he trusted. In less than a minute the man was at his elbow. "Were you waiting outside, Saunders?"

"I was just getting the prisoner ready to go to the lockup for immediate questioning, Mr. President."

"Good. The group has several questions we would appreciate your asking of our guest. I also have a question, who is the person that poisoned our vent system and are they still here?" They were both speaking quietly and with all the noise around no one could hear them other than Marge.

The President tapped again on the glass, hoping silently that it wouldn't break and embarrass him. "Ladies, Gentlemen. This is the head of the White House Secret Service he will be passing among you to get the questions you would like asked of the prisoner. If any of you have someone traveling with you that you would prefer to ask your questions, please have them accompany Mr. Saunders."

Ten men and four women walked into the room within minutes of each other and attached themselves to Saunders, who threw his boss a look that said 'why me'. It took over a half hour before they collected the questions and then Saunders led the group from the dining room.

"I think that we have had a very busy evening and we could all do with a good night's rest. I realize that the accommodations will not be those of a five star hotel, but hopefully that will not be for long. Apparently, we do have someone in our corner."

"Dad, I really need to ask you a question. You called NASA. You couldn't get through to Drake Oliver. He had died just since you last spoke with him. Why did that send you to Evelyn?"

"Son, his secretary may have been a link to the head, but he would not have permission to kill him without orders. Those orders were given almost immediately after the team left him. She has been trying to cut off all those knowledgeable about what is really happening with the two poles and the extraterrestrials."

"Did she get to the Turner woman in New Zealand?"

"I don't know. She was able to listen in on some things and not to others. The implant that she has is extremely powerful. Son, when was the last time you were away from her for at least three months before you went to Malta?"

"I'd say it had to be when I went to Alaska. The President wanted me to give him an update on the entire Alaskan pipeline, from the perspective of a land attack on it and the situation of allowed deterioration. I was basically gathering intelligence for the President."

"The orders, did they come from him directly?"

"Yes, I was in his office, he spoke to me personally."

"Did you do other jobs like that for him?"

"Yes, of course. Usually they didn't last that long. But, this particular job was way out in godforsaken country. I had to learn the lingo of the workers, learn what to look for, build trust to get people to open up. I was on my own. Went top to bottom of that line, I found a lot of allowed deterioration. The problem wasn't the guys who were there, it was the fact that the owners wouldn't give them the money for replacement parts to keep the thing in good working order. If a guy retired, he wasn't replaced. They are working with a bare bones crew and they are all getting old."

"Did you tell Evelyn anything about that job?"

"No, No. I just told her that the president had sent me on a fact finding job, and I'd be gone for two or three months. I'd call her when I got there."

"How soon was that after he took office?"

"I'd say it was only a month or so. When I returned with the information he wanted to go after everybody to get the House and Senate to appropriate money to upgrade the pipeline and force the owners to hire enough personnel."

"Ah. I remember that was when the Leader had him called in for a meeting."

"Yes. He looked like a broken man when he returned. For a couple of days his secretary cancelled his schedules saying he had the flu."

"I wonder if she was calling the shots then?"

The two men stayed in the computer room, leaving only to get sandwiches and more water. Edward asked his father about what Evelyn would do about food and was surprised to be told that her three hundred square foot cell was self-contained with all of the comforts of home.

Philippe and Celine were in the front of the vehicle with Michael and Richard hovering behind them. Tino was in the back with Mary and Ilena. They all understood that they were in for a fight, but perhaps if Philippe and Celine could work something out they might avoid it all together.

"Celine, have you put in the jump coordinates?"

"Yes, all of them are in, the sequence is my name followed by yours. All right, everyone, please sit up here as close as possible to us. You are all probably going to experience some extreme nausea, maybe not right away, but during the course of our sequencing of changes. Try and have something close to you for that."

"Philippe they're almost here. I'd say five minutes away. It looks like a regular Lear jet. I'm scanning it. At least ten people on it."

"All right, let me know when they pass over us, see if they turn around. If they do that it means they can read the present signal we are emitting."

The group sat waiting, nervous, in a tight group in the front of the white limousine at the back of a parking lot. The silver jet flew low over the mall. People looked up and remarked about the loser buzzing the parking lot.

Two minutes later the plane turned around just as a green Cadillac left the rear of the parking lot and drove on to the closest entrance ramp to the interstate. They sped west doing the speed limit of seventy miles per hour until they had left the mall almost twenty miles behind. The Lear meanwhile had buzzed the mall three more times. Customers and staff called the local police who responded and called on the Rangers to get a helicopter in the air.

The Lear circled one last time then flew away east. It hadn't gone far when it turned and headed west. In the Cadillac, Celine said, "They picked it up again, here they come."

They drove around the back of a Walmart this time and pulled in by an enormous trash bin and then drove away in a black Expedition. This time instead of getting on the interstate they drove down a county highway that held an array of fast food restaurants, strip malls, big box and home improvements stores.

Philippe had begun the cycling process, which changed not only the type of car, but the signal the vehicle emitted which was what the Lear was tracking. The difficulty of changing vehicles was that they had to go to a hidden place in order for the car to change, Even though it only took seconds for the change, he knew that he could not cycle too frequently.

A Suburban drove out from behind a large Chinese restaurant and this time sped onto the first ramp onto Interstate seventy headed north. The speed limit was seventy-five miles per hour and Celine pushed it to eighty. This time the readout showed that the Lear was still on the Cadillac's signal and was staying near the Walmart store.

Richard laughed when Philippe mentioned it. "Just a little trickery on my part, it will only give us about a half an hour. It is just a toy, but it does work. I picked up the signal and fed it into a memory stick and threw it out of the window just as we pulled away from the dumpster. I hope they enjoy looking for us in there. When we reached the Chinese restaurant I did the same thing."

The others laughed, releasing some of the tension they had been under for the last hour. Michael said, "I'm glad you are on our side. They'll have to land somewhere and go back to the Walmart to verify the signal. Good man."

"If we begin flying too quickly they will pick up the signal, so we are going to be on the road for quite some time." Celine sounded worried.

"Why would there be a problem driving back to Colorado like this?" Ilena asked.

"The vehicle is not set up to be driving on a road at such slow speeds. We usually begin flying within ten miles or so after we start. We have now been driving for over thirty miles, and we are not far enough away." Philippe answered.

Celine spoke up, "They are landing. They have slowed and dropped to under one hundred feet. I'll give it ten minutes before flying back to Colorado."

"Good." Philippe looked at Michael who was frowning. "What is wrong, Michael?"

"We haven't completed our tasks. Worse yet, these people, whoever they might be, could follow us back to Sir James."

"Michael, why don't you get in touch with Sir James and let him know, perhaps he will have some direction for you." Mary suggested.

"Thanks, you're probably correct. I just hate to tell him that we still don't know who our adversary is at this time."

"Amigo, right now, we are still alive. Let him know we're still alive."

"You're both right." Michael immediately called Sir James and let him know their predicament."

"Michael, have Philippe and Celine fly in as usual. How soon can they be here?"

"Tell him if we start flying now, we should be there within forty-five minutes."

Michael relayed the information. "Fine, we will be ready for you. When you are preparing to land, keep in touch with me with your range and altitude. This is crucial. I will call you back in about a half hour." Sir James hung up.

"He sounded preoccupied. I hope everything is all right." Ilena remarked.

"He is trying to keep so much going at once, dear. I can't believe that one man has done what he has." Mary said to her.

"I just worry. He was always like a part of my family."

"I understand." Mary reached over and gave the young woman a hug. "From what I have seen he thinks of you in the same way."

Ilena nodded and returned the hug. "Thank you, Mary."

Philippe said. "We're pulling into that rest area ahead. It is time to fly."

Everyone waited expectantly. The big SUV drove off the interstate along with a couple of other cars. But they took the service road to the rear of the building holding the snack bar and rest rooms. There was another service road that went off into the wilderness and they used that road to finally leave the land behind and speed toward their destination.

Michael moved to the back of the vehicle angry that he hadn't been able to face their quarry and find out who they were. Richard followed him. "Michael, we were headed into a trap. It wouldn't be of any help if we were dropped out of the skies and killed."

"Yes, I know. I just hate to leave an assignment incomplete. That has never happened. I have always worked alone. Now, well, let's just say I have difficulty working as a team."

"I understand you there. Sir James had me working alone as well for so long, infiltrating the various Middle Eastern terrorists groups. Usually anyone I was working with was someone I was probably going to kill. I was certainly not a true team member."

"I guess not. I forget that you were working behind the scenes while I was more visible. That's probably why he wanted you to begin to work with me. Some of the assignments certainly required more time for cleanup when you worked alone. Two people could have completed it much more effectively." He was thinking about the dump truck door and the area that he felt he had never completely cleaned up properly.

His phone vibrated against his chest and he responded immediately. Yes, Sir James, we are airborne. I'll check with them." He moved forward and asked, "How soon before we are ready to land?"

Celine answered, "It will be about twelve minutes."

"Twelve minutes, Sir." He listened for a few seconds, "Celine what is your present altitude?"

"We are at thirty-six thousand feet."

Michael repeated that into the phone. "Celine, Philippe, prepare to start dropping altitude," he paused, waiting for the signal from Sir James, "Now!"

"Sir James says that you have a stalking Lear, out about seven hundred and fifty miles and closing."

"Yes. Tell him we know."

"He says do not drop your present speed, just your altitude. He wants you to land like a helicopter if you can do that."

"We should be able to." Philippe's hands were flying over controls.

Everyone was holding on, feeling the speedy descent to the hideout, thousands of feet in mere seconds. Michael was watching the scan showing the following Lear, which had increased its speed. Perhaps the pilot realized that they were preparing to land and was making a strong effort to catch up to them.

Then a loud bump as they finally touched down. Sir James voice came through over the loud speaker in the landing area. "Don't leave the vehicle. You will feel movement. I'm just moving the landing pad."

They were moving into the side of the mountain. Ilena looked out of the window and she yelled,

"Oh, my, gosh! There is absolutely nothing down there at all!"

They all looked out of the windows and were shocked to realize that there seemed to be no ground below them. Then they heard metal on metal clanging and a sliding sound and the early evening twilight was gone.

"All right everyone, please hurry from the vehicle and follow the lit path." This time it was Edward's voice.

They rushed out of the two doors and followed the white lights on the dark concrete path. Doors slid closed behind them as they moved forward for at least the next five minutes.

They all came through one of the doors into the large kitchen and were shocked when they felt a soaring vibration as if the entire mountain was under attack. The group stood still, staring at each other as the vibration increased in intensity. Glass was heard to break in a cabinet, items sitting on the counters slid toward the edge.

"It's all right, everyone. I think this means the Lear hit the mountain's defenses." Richard said.

"I know I heard this before. Is that what this sound means?" They were nearly shouting over the din.

Then it stopped. Everyone let out a deep breath. Ilena started to open the door to the hallway leading to the living room. Michael stopped her. "No, wait here until you see Edward or Sir James. When the defenses are up, walking around might be a problem."

Minutes later, Sir James came into the kitchen. "Welcome back, I am sure you are all tired and hungry. I would prefer that you all rest and have something to eat before we move forward. It is highly important that you are all are at your best.

None of them had even realized that with all that had been going on over the past several hours that they hadn't eaten. They thanked Sir James as he left them and went upstairs to his own room.

Michael followed him, understanding, just from seeing the strained and tired face of his employer that he was headed for a much needed rest. As usual Michael took up guard duty just around the corner from the door to Sir James' room. He knew he should have Richard begin to take up some of these duties. But he felt that guard duty over Sir James would probably be the last thing he would give to Richard.

By being around the corner, he was unseen by those coming up the stairs to their rooms, but he could see each person in the strategically placed mirror. Mary Fletcher was the first to head for her room. From the weariness of her steps he knew she would be sleeping for quite a while. Tino and Ilena came up the staircase a few minutes later talking quietly. He smiled as he saw Tino pat Ilena gently on her arm with his big ham of a hand.

He realized that he had never seen either Celine or Philippe come upstairs to take a rest. Nor did they ever seem to tire. They looked as fresh standing in the kitchen as they had when they had left days ago for Mexico or later for NASA.

He heard footsteps coming up the stairs. It was Edward. He looked terrible. What on earth had happened here, while they were gone, Michael wondered? He hadn't seen Evelyn, but then he hadn't been looking for her either. He really didn't care for her. He couldn't understand what Edward had seen in this woman who did practically nothing with her life. She sat around and waited for Edward to come home, from where ever he had been. What kind of life had that been for the last twenty-five years?

Edward walked down the hallway to the end, "Hello, Michael. I know you sit here guarding my father. Did I ever thank you? No, probably not. But I am grateful to you for your loyalty to him. He deserves it." He turned, back straight and walked away not waiting for any response from Michael.

A door closed quietly at the far end near the top of the stairs. That meant everyone was up here except for Richard, who was probably staying in the kitchen with Philippe and Celine. No one told him he had to, he knew his duty, Michael thought. Good. Richard was proving his mettle every day, a man very much like himself with strong loyalties.

Three hours later, Sir James' door opened and he emerged looking rested. Michael immediately stood up and went to him. "Michael, you need rest as well. You should have been sleeping."

"I'll sleep later, Sir. It is important that everything goes well, and it can only go well if you are safe."

"Thank you, Michael. Have you seen Edward and Richard?"

"Edward is in his room. Richard is downstairs with Philippe and Celine."

"Ah, yes. Philippe and Celine. Would you invite them into my study please, Michael, and then I would appreciate it if you would have Edward meet us there, along with Richard? We have a serious problem."

At the bottom of the steps, Michael turned right toward the kitchen and Sir James turned left down the hall, past the living room with its now empty window seat, and went into his study. He walked over to the sideboard and poured a small amount of aged scotch into a crystal glass. It reminded him of a statement he had heard more than a few times, of finding 'courage in a bottle'. He needed more courage than a dram of whiskey could bring. He had even stopped smoking his pipe here. The smell would float through the ductwork giving others a clue to his whereabouts.

He left the empty glass on the sideboard and turned to sit at the deep mahogany desk. It was a copy of the one back in England. The one he was sure had been destroyed by the attack of that…that person. He couldn't even say her name. Right here under his nose. He should have had her investigated long before Edward married her. He could have. But he trusted his son. Besides it never occurred to him that his son's wife could be the perpetrator of such madness. But then again it might have been Thorsen. Perhaps he had underestimated the man.

The door opened and Philippe and Celine walked into the room. "Apparently you two don't require much sleep."

"Actually, we don't sleep at all. Over the years, I have had to feign sleep, but no, not real sleep, as you require. We do take rest periods in between times of extensive physical activity. But simply sitting still, as we are now usually fulfills our needs." Philippe was speaking in a matter of fact manner as if the information he was sharing was as ordinary as telling the time.

"That is a good thing for searching a human quarry who must take the time to sleep for at least a few hours. But what about the occupants of the Lear, who or what were they, Philippe? Were you able to scan them when they were close?"

Philippe and Celine exchanged glances just as Edward, Michael and Richard came into the study. "Ah, excellent, Gentlemen, I just asked Philippe if they were able at any time to scan the occupants of the Lear jet. I am awaiting an answer."

"We did scan them, Sir James."

"Good. However, you seem very reticent about sharing that information. It makes me wonder why and then I wonder why you did not share the information with Michael and Richard when you were trying to get away from the jet."

"We hesitated then and we hesitate now, Sir James. There are many things of which we are aware. However, we are very unsure about your level of acceptance."

"All right, let me be the judge of what you are aware of and should tell me, such as who or what was on that plane?

"There were members of Hadi' Skupina, Seth Thorsen's group."

"How do you know that? You never saw them get on the plane."

"True, but each human has an electrical signal. We learned long ago to identify people by their signal or as some call it an aura. It is as unique as a fingerprint. This way even if someone is disguised or undergoes plastic surgery, we will not be fooled as to their identity. Our scanner searches and matches those auras much as your science matches fingerprints, or eyes. Two of those on the plane had signals that matched auras we had captured several years ago."

"Very good, this is plausible. So I ask again, why are you so hesitant to discuss this?"

"There were others on the plane as well. They were perhaps a delegation."

"The extraterrestrials I take it."

"Yes, Sir James."

"They must have picked them up in the Arctic at the place you were getting ready to inspect. Yes, that would make sense.

"Well, the Lear no longer exists, which means its occupants no longer exist. So I would assume Thorsen's friends will be looking for them."

"I would suspect that would happen, Sir James."

"Well, I have another question for you, Philippe and Celine. Edward's wife, during the time that she was with you in Malta, did either of you notice anything unusual about her?"

"Other than she seemed to be totally enamored of her husband. She never bought anything other than a sweater during the whole time she was there. She would often cry, I mean just tears when speaking of her husband. Not loud sobbing or anything. She was always very sweet and quiet. I couldn't believe she was American. She was so unlike any other American woman I have met. But then I really haven't met too many." Celine said.

"I never saw her except the couple of times when Edward was with her. She seemed very quiet, intelligent. One of the things that I distinctly remember was that unlike most wives I have met she was not at all inquisitive." Philippe added.

Celine nodded in agreement. "That is true, she never asked questions when we were together, what did our house look like, how many children we had, what I did, or what Philippe did for work. Didn't I have friends for her to meet? She did, however, seem very preoccupied. I assumed it was about her husband. In fact I was the one who asked her if she was ill a few times. She would look at me somewhat startled and say no she was just worried about her husband."

Philippe looked at Edward and then at Sir James. "What happened here? What happened to Evelyn, Edward?"

"We are not sure, Philippe. I do not know whether she is an unwilling participant or whether she is the instigator of the global acts of terrorism and the voice behind Vanderlin, or even part of Thorsen's little group."

Edward was watching his friend carefully as he responded to the news. "I realized that she was not herself when we arrived here, Sir James, but I would strongly consider what she has been through. Many of your troops return from war situations with Post Traumatic Stress.

It reacts differently in different people. What you believe to be her showing signs of being a traitor could easily be that."

"Philippe, we are considering that. But I have other proofs that she is someone other than we have all thought, including Edward. As you all know, we collected papers from the secret panel in Vanderlin's bedroom. According to the information there, as well as the information that Tino gave to Michael, Evelyn is his eldest daughter. She was born and raised in Mexico. She was his insurance of a dynasty as Leader of the group.

"I have her birth certificate listing Vanderlin as her father. I have tested her DNA. She is definitely his daughter and Ilena's sister. There is no doubt."

"So what do we do? Was she behind the group all of this time, the Bermuda tragedy?"

"She has not given us any information. I am wondering if someone is using her, knowing who she is and has given her some sort of implant. I have been unable to locate it, but I suspect it based on the fact that she has been able to give orders and information without leaving much of a trace on my security. I believe that she might be the cause behind the trap all of you were heading toward. Possibly even the reason my friend Drake Oliver was murdered."

"When did that happen, Sir James?" Michael asked.

"Soon after you left him, his secretary murdered him. Security picked him up as he was leaving NASA. Unfortunately for their side, he was a very weak link. He gave information right away, stating that he had his orders to eliminate Oliver immediately. There would be no way for him to receive those orders except from someone who knew that we were going to him for verifications and exact content of the contact messages from the extraterrestrials. Fortunately, we already had the information we needed before the orders were given. I think their timing was off. They had planned to get rid of him prior to your visit. But the secretary didn't get the message in time. Possibly that was due to the time difference.

"All of you were together and all of you were in an extremely vulnerable position. I had to take her out of the picture and see whether or not that made any change to what was occurring." Sir James stopped speaking, picked up his cold pipe, toyed with it for a moment before laying it back down on the desk.

"Philippe, Celine, you have certain capabilities together that you do not have alone, I think that you should share those with us." Edward sounded tired when he spoke, "You may be able to check for an implant, or even remove it. Evelyn was herself when I left her in Malta. The person I met when she arrived here was not the person I've known and shared my life with for the past twenty-five years."

All eyes were on the pair. They looked even more ethereal if that were possible. Then Edward spoke again. "I mean, look at you Philippe. The Gulf War was well over twenty years ago. Look at you and look at me. I take care of myself. I realize that you say you are not from earth, but now, we need, I, definitely need more answers from you."

"So you are asking the same information as your father. Yes, we understand. Even though we have given you plans for our vehicle and assisted you with finding the people or information you wanted. But you want to understand us, who we really are, where we are from. It is the need to trust that you are lacking. This is inherent in the human race, the need to trust and so far, despite the help we have given you, you are unable to trust. Do we understand you both?"

Sir James and his son both nodded. But this time Michael spoke up. "You're correct, Philippe, I have watched you and Celine work together and there are times that you work almost as if you were only one person. I would like to know if this is something that is part of your race or part of the fact that you have been together for quite a while. It seemed at one point, Philippe, that you performed an initial task and Celine amplified or expounded upon that task. Am I correct in that assessment?"

"You are absolutely correct, Michael. It works in reverse as well. If she begins something I can push it to the next level. As we told you before, that golden glow is a force field with which the two of us can shield ourselves. But it is even more. As the field flows between us and around us it helps us communicate without speaking, share ideas and immediately move them forward. Also, if we are operating our vehicle and have to enhance its' capability it also becomes an extension of our thoughts."

Sir James had risen from his chair and was now walking around the room listening to the discussion. "Philippe, can you and Celine embrace others within the force field?"

"We have never tried, but I'm sure that if someone were to stand between us, as long as Celine and I are in contact, yes, possibly even two people."

"Well, it might also happen that those who have the ability to make a force field might also have weapons that could penetrate others force fields. Is that something you and Celine have?" Sir James had stopped circling the room to stand in front of the two.

"You two have come to us. You have offered your assistance to us. You claim to be from some other world. Well, what other world? You have given assistance to us, kept us whole and helped us to get places faster than any other plane or vehicle I know of on this earth. However, what are you doing about FAA flight plans, visual sightings? Do you have some sort of cloaking device along with the force field?

"Do you understand me, Philippe, Celine? Without answers that can be verified I do not believe we can continue as we have. Yes, you presented the information on the extraterrestrials, but then you yourselves are extraterrestrials. The information you gave us about the first messages that were received by NASA was verified by Drake Oliver, but now he is dead." Sir James voice, normally cultured and quiet had risen in anger.

"Dad, Dad!" Edward jumped up from his chair and put his arm around his father. "Give them a chance to talk. They haven't done anything to harm us. They kept everyone alive. They have tried to help us."

"We do not try to be secretive. But we are unaccustomed to talking to humans about ourselves. I realize that this reticence can be misunderstood." Philippe was looking at his hands, long fingers, perfectly manicured, a slight tan. "We only meant to help, if perhaps we could show you our place in Malta. It is our base...

"No, Philippe, it will not be possible. The team, all of us will remain here, work through the information we have, before we do any more. Here, where we can access the information we need on Thorsen's group.

We are not working for ourselves. We are working for the future of the world.

"Now is the time for the cards to be on the table, Philippe, all of the cards. No more secrets, nor more hidden agendas. I have had quite enough of hidden agendas with Vanderlin. I cannot wait to tell Ilena she has an older sister. I am sure that will be very pleasant." Sir James was obviously still upset. He returned to his chair and stared at the two, who still showed no emotion.

Philippe began speaking, but while he was speaking his hands gestured toward one of the walls, that became opaque covering the paintings and sconces. Pictures flowed depicting what he was telling them of his and Celine's world. Also, it showed pictures of what their species looked like in their normal habitat. They were not too dissimilar to how they looked now, except they had all had long yellow hair and their skin seemed nearly transparent with soft golden overtones.

He continued to show the history of his planet as he spoke. Then he spoke about the surprise discovery his people made of Earth and their government's decision to send someone to make observations. He was the first volunteer and he had come here early in the earth's known history, well prior to the rule of the Egyptian pharaohs, and the building of the pyramids.

Michael and Richard looked at each other shocked, then at Celine, as Philippe continued. He explained that at times he would give hints or assistance to certain specific individuals as he moved through time. Often his mode of travel, or how he looked was written about or drawn or depicted in different ways. But, he had never had problems with others trusting him until now.

"I can say to you, Sir James that you must have heard at some point that Nazi Germany had outside help in their great surge of technology. Their agenda was global unity, so was ours. Then I found out about the truth of their policy toward the Jewish population. Assistance was immediately stopped. At the end, some of their people used devices to leave Germany. Devices that were meant to help them in the war effort, but the machines were not complete and their getaway became a permanent disappearance."

Sir James nodded slightly as he listened to his son's friend.

Philippe continued talking, after he was injured, although he had healed, he needed to return to his home because for the first time since he had come to earth he knew he needed help. The world had changed so much and in so many unexpected ways that he felt he had to find a fellow observer. Philippe told them that he remained on his planet for a year of earth time. He had spent most of that time seeking the correct companion to accompany him.

But while he was home he learned that there was an inhabited planet four hundred million light years beyond our Milky Way galaxy. The planet was primarily a water planet. The inhabitants were considered to be warriors who had taken over that planet and continually moved throughout various galaxies conquering, settling and where his people increased land space, these warriors increased the water on every planet they conquered. These warriors had made excursions onto their planet but were met with such unified defense that they left. This is why we are trying to unify this world as quickly as possible. The only defense is unity."

"So these warriors are coming here, worse, some are already here and have already begun to overwhelm the earth in preparation for the rest." Michael sounded annoyed. "Why didn't you let us know earlier? Why didn't you tell us this at the beginning? You have nothing concrete here, Philippe."

"I understand you, Michael. You need something to show everyone. Talk to the geologists. Talk to them quickly. The explosion in the Arctic they believed to be an earthquake, by now they should have learned that it is not.

"You have asked me to be 'up front'. You all have to understand that there is not just one problem, there are several. Because, several people, people that you know, Sir James, have their own agendas to make use of the resulting chaos to make the earth over for their own use.

"I believe you all know that there is a thread that has run through the history of earth. Perhaps I should not say a thread, but an understanding that apparently in every generation you have geniuses, that through their creativity, brilliance and inventiveness, have moved Earth's civilization forward. Unfortunately, in many cases their inventions have pushed capabilities far ahead of the human ability to cope.

"As I gave you the plans for our vehicle, so have I given others the ideas that have helped your earth to become what it is today. However, now it is true that others are coming and when they do, they will not be bringing help and assistance. They are disrupting the poles, which will shift the earth on its axis to increase the oceans and decrease the land. A polar shift is and has been expected over time, but not yet, not yet. They are pushing everything years forward. The earth has its own pace. These warriors are pushing that pace well beyond expectation"

"So those on the Lear jet, that is probably what they were doing?" Edward asked.

"Yes. The preparations have already begun. They would only need a few of their number with the assistance of some misguided people here on earth."

"Well, we always have an abundance of misguided people." Michael said. "I'm sure they didn't have to look far to get a group of them together."

Sir James had been noticeably quiet for the several minutes. His head down, chin resting upon the upright tent of his hands. "We need to know what they look like, Philippe. Or perhaps they look like you?" He looked up, his face flushed as he stared at the golden man.

For the first time that anyone could remember, Philippe showed emotion as he recoiled from the veiled accusation.

"I feel like we have been watching a magician. Pictures at will on a wall, tales of a warrior group coming to earth to wreak havoc and death upon an unsuspecting public. Very pretty tales, Philippe, very pretty tales."

"Michael, you and Richard will be using the vehicle, take Tino with you. Let us get this geological proof. You spoke with Imogene Turner, Michael, she will remember you, unless she has also been eliminated." He stared at Philippe as he said it.

"I believe you came to us because you felt that we would forward your cause. You had the silver tubes. You have tried to lure us to your base in Malta. Why?"

Edward, and the rest appeared confused by the turn of events and Sir James continued in anger and mistrust. They had asked Philippe to tell them more and he had, but they also agreed with Sir James about the implausible story they had heard.

Richard quietly spoke up, "I think we should take Philippe's suggestion. We have been out of touch of recent developments. I think we should find out the latest information about the so-called earthquake. Also, since we have the capability to view pictures taken by satellites and telescopes, such as the Hubble, we need to check these out and see if we can view this planet or even Philippe's planet. Possibly find out where Thorsen's people are based. We may have a major fight on our hands and there aren't many of us."

"Thank you, Richard. You are certainly correct. I agree with you. Let us adjourn to our planning room. We have been out of touch. I am weary of this talk. Let us seek and verify and move forward." Sir James rose from the desk as he spoke and headed toward the door.

The group followed him down the hall to the kitchen and through the door into the planning room. Celine and Philippe sat down near the rear of the large circular room and watched as the monitors were activated and desktop computers were booted up. The two sat close enough that the golden glow of their force field could clearly be seen.

Edward, who had been quiet during most of the discussions and explanations, stared at his friend. Something had been bothering him for weeks and seeing the pale glow surrounding them jogged his memory about what he had seen nearly a year before, but he had been tired, no exhausted back then, and did not trust his eyes.

He walked over to Michael and Richard, "Do you think you fellows could help me over here? I'd like to get these two desks closer together to get a better dual visual."

The three were huddled together bent over the wood tables that were laden with computer equipment. "I needed to speak with both of you." He was whispering, his voice no higher than the muffled squeak as they dragged the table around. "I think we have a bigger problem here. There are more people on earth like Philippe and Celine. I just don't know where they are now. But I remember seeing that glow when I was still at the White House."

Edward stood up, and backed away from the other two and the tables, "That looks about right. I should be able to get plenty of work done this way. Thanks."

The other two men gave Edward a strange look, as he walked over and asked Philippe, "Are you certain, Philippe, you didn't bring others back, beside yourself and Celine?

"Why do you ask that, Edward?"

"Just a thought," He responded, "Just a thought."

Michael spoke up, "Sir James, I think we need to get moving again. While we are sitting here others are making physical efforts to undermine all of the work we have already completed."

"Yes, Michael, you will be leaving here very shortly. You three get some rest. I want you sharp and ready for anything. We are going to bring the fight to the enemy." Sir James had turned to face all of them. You have three hours. I suggest you use it wisely."

Just over three hours later, Michael, Tino, Edward, Ilena and Richard were meeting with Sir James in a room near Philippe and Celine's vehicle. They were going over Sir James plan making sure that they all knew what they needed to do.

Richard was skeptical of their abilities with the vehicle. "Look, I've gone over the schematics and worked with both of them on exactly what that machine can do, and frankly I'm worried that we don't even know half of its capabilities. I am sure that Philippe has some ability to interact with it on a thought level, in fact I'm positive of it."

"Then do you want Philippe to go with you?" Sir James looked at each of them in turn. "Do you trust him?"

"I trust him with us. I do not trust him with Celine with us." Michael answered.

"Very well. Tino could you ask Philippe to join us?"

"Sure, Señor James."

The man rushed from the room and ten minutes later returned with Philippe.

Sir James, still dubious, told Philippe that he would be going with the group. He would follow the orders of Michael or Richard. The older man made sure that Philippe was fully aware that his presence on this mission was not his idea.

The now six-member team filed out of the room. They had slept and eaten and for the most part felt much better than they had in some time. The group settled into their seats knowing this time they had to succeed and find out who was truly behind the attacks. They also understood that they might not make it out of this alive, but none of them even hesitated. Everything up until now had only been a rehearsal.

The vehicle flew up and out of the Colorado Rockies into a clear, cold February sky. But this time they did not leave unseen. Ten miles east beyond the range of Sir James security field a helicopter had landed in a derelict mining town, watching the western horizon for any plane apparently rising out of the mountains.

The two watchers were freezing despite having been fully outfitted for the weather. They hadn't expected to be here so long and had failed to bring any food or more than a couple of bottles of water. As soon as they saw the quarry they reported it and were told to return to their base. They were not to travel any further west.

The two men fired up the helicopter and rose up over the town. The wind was a great deal stronger than it had been when they had landed and they were immediately fighting down drafts. Before they realized it the wind had pushed them closer to the hidden base. They heard the alarm as first the gyro, then the altimeter needle began to go crazy. Then the helicopter began to vibrate, at a rate of speed beyond anything they could control, the windows blew in, shards cutting their faces. But the men didn't notice because they were screaming, from the shrieking sounds assailing their ears. Within forty-five seconds the entire machine had disappeared from the sky, along with its' occupants.

Sir James notified the airborne team that he would be unable to assist them from the base for a while since he would have to increase his security. Apparently, someone had noticed their takeoff, which meant that he would be cutting himself off immediately. As soon as he received Michael's answer that they understood, he pushed two switches that armed the various paths around the mountains. Anyone rappelling, hiking or using any kind of vehicle in the area surrounding his home for several miles would have an unwelcome greeting.

He left the planning room and went upstairs to awaken Mary. He knocked on her door and she opened it immediately. "We have to go to a secure area, Mary. People are trying to reach us. The team has left, only you and Celine are here. Of course Evelyn is here as well, but she is already in a secured area."

The two started down the hall and Celine came out of the end room. "I heard you knocking on the other door. The vibration, was it another jet?" She asked.

"No. Someone was waiting at a distance. They were watching for us to leave. They probably think everyone has left here. We need to go downstairs to the safest area of this home. It is impregnable and we can also escape if the need arises."

The three of them went quickly down the stairs. At the bottom of the steps, Sir James pressed a hidden button and the mountains disappeared from view as the windows were covered. Small emergency lights came on near the floor. "Once I cover the windows, it triggers the entire home into emergency status. From the outside the house looks just like the rest of the mountain if someone looks from across the valleys from another mountain."

As they walked down the hallway toward the kitchen the lights behind them shut off. They reached the kitchen and Sir James pressed another button that caused a steel door to slide across the door they had just come through.

"We have some time to get water and supplies together." He opened cabinets and pulled out canvas satchels and a large wheeled freezer chest. Mary didn't need any further direction and immediately began opening cabinets and placing food that wouldn't perish quickly in the satchels. Celine seemed at a loss momentarily as to what they were doing, but then opened the refrigerator. Within minutes they had filled the satchels and the mobile freezer.

"I think we are fine now. They might even try to wait us out, if they find out they cannot get through, or they will be waiting for the plane to return. Either way, they are going to be very aggressive and they understand that we are their enemy. Are we ready, ladies?"

The two women nodded and they lugged and pushed the heavy satchels through the hidden door into the planning room. As soon as they were through the door the kitchen went dark and the door automatically sealed. The house was silent. The heat had already lowered in the main house. While the pipes were kept warm against freezing, the action of shuttering all the windows automatically cut off all normal services of the house.

The planning room had its own heating system, as did several other areas that were sealed and hidden from the main house. If anyone was able to access the house, they would be certain the house was deserted and had been for some time, based on the level of cold that was now permeating the living areas.

Sir James asked the women to sit while he took care of the computers in case someone located this room. But what no one knew except Sir James was that the hidden doorway was now booby-trapped. He knew that these people whoever they were would not let a small explosion stop them. They would let the expendables take the lead and would follow to step over the pieces and reap the rewards.

Sir James had always known he would be unable to move all of the computers in the room in case the home was invaded, but he quickly downloaded everything onto the memory sticks and wiped the hard drives. "Mary, you have had plenty of practice in caring for information, so I'm giving you a duplicate set of these memory sticks. Guard them in the safest place you can think of. I have two more sets, one that I will hide later and another, that I will keep should we need the information that is on them.

"Let us move now, ladies. Please follow me and stay close. Unfortunately, here we must walk. Where we are going there is transport, but not from this direction. The halls are very narrow, and there are some tight turns. As long as you stay with me you should not be disoriented. I would say that it will be several hours before anyone might actually set foot in the house at all, but I would prefer to be well situated before that."

Before they left the planning room they placed the food satchels and freezer on two rubber wheeled dollies that they pulled along silently behind them. They walked along for several minutes before Sir James stopped in front of a rock wall. He walked right up to the wall and stared into a retina id, then moved over to the left and placed his hand onto the wall.

Celine and Mary both registered surprise when instead of a door opening normally, which is what was expected, the wall slid upwards just high enough to let the three in with the food dollies and closed immediately with a hiss. They walked on for at least another ten minutes in what felt like a circle, the lights near the floor turned on just ahead of them and turned off after the silent wagons moved past.

"Welcome, to our new home." This time the door slid sideways silently into a wall pocket. Lights turned on as they walked in, and the door closed behind them with a barely audible click. They were surprised to see a home that spread out apparently on one level. Comfortable couches and chairs were arranged in the living room, they could see right through to a dining room and a kitchen that opened up on the left.

"There are bedrooms and baths down the hallways to the left and right, ladies." He looked at the two women for a moment, as if he was assessing their strengths. "I have to leave you here for at least an hour. Please do not leave this place, because once you do and that door closes behind you, you will not be able to reopen it and return. This is a very safe house. So you will be very safe here. Do both of you understand that your safety is at risk if you leave here?"

"Of course, Sir James," Mary answered immediately. "But do you think it is safe for you to leave here?"

"Thank you, Mary, I will be fine." He turned toward the entrance then turned back toward the quiet Celine. "I would suggest, Celine, that if you have some way of communicating with Philippe without using the computers or a cell phone, that you do that. Let him know that the mountain is being invaded. Depending upon their numbers it could take an hour or a few days for them to either make it to the house, try to destroy it, or be defeated. Tell him they need to stay away from here for at least five days or until you let Philippe know that it is safe to return.

"So, can you do that?"

"Yes, Sir James. I have been communicating with him all along. Do you wish everyone with him to know what is happening?"

"Yes, Celine, have him tell everyone what has happened and that we are all safe." Sir James left the room and the door closed behind him so quickly that the women could not hear his footsteps moving away down the passage.

"I guess we should put the food away." They rolled the carts into the kitchen and began filling up the cupboards and refrigerator. When they had emptied everything, Mary said she was going to find a bedroom and take a nap.

"For some reason, I feel exhausted. It's probably just the suddenness of the move and the stress of walking blindly for so long."

"Go ahead, Mary. I'm going to wander through here and find out more about this home." The two women went in opposite directions down the hallways and Mary found a bedroom just steps away.

As soon as she entered Mary realized that there were no linens on the bed, so she began opening the built in drawers and was soon rewarded with sheets and blankets. She found pillows and a comforter on a shelf in the small closet between the bedroom and bath. She threw the bedding on the bed, not worrying about making it perfect and snuggled in between the sheets.

Celine walked into a small room that had been set up as a gym. One wall contained a flat screen television and two pictures intended to look like windows, in front of three pieces of workout equipment. She moved on to the next room, a large office, divided into four cubicles, each with its own computer, across from that was a full bathroom, then two more bedrooms.

At the end of the hallway was a door. Celine turned the knob, but the door didn't open. More of Sir James secrets, she thought. The man continued to surprise them. Philippe had been correct in his assessment that the Englishman was much more dangerous than Vanderlin. Apparently, Sir James had been preparing for something to happen for decades. But, it seemed some things were happening that even he had not expected.

The President left yet another meeting of the world leaders and still they had not reached any decisions. All of them were wondering at the sudden silence from those that had contacted them. But at least there had not been any new disasters. His head was down as he walked the corridor toward his bedroom, thinking that it seemed as if all of them were waiting for something. It was just too quiet.

"Sir, Mr. President."

He looked up to see Saunders, the head of the White House Secret Service. "Yes, Saunders, I was just thinking."

"Ah, sir, could we speak in private for a moment?"

"Yes, of course." They had reached his bedroom suite and he led the way into the sitting room. The President had always thought that Saunders was one of the most non-descript looking men he had ever met. Average height, build, brown hair just beginning to recede, but he was incredibly organized and highly intelligent. The man could easily be lost and unmemorable on a street. But he was reliable and so the President paid immediate attention.

"So, Saunders, what is happening?"

"I've just had a call from a friend of mine. He's a professor at Cal

Tech. He does a lot of research. I guess you'd say he's a little geeky. We grew up together outside of Chicago, in Evanston. You know, next door neighbors, always in each other's houses. Get in trouble together, first double dates." He paused for a second. "Anyway, he was upset, very upset. He said the oceans are rising. Not slowly like an inch or something, but in feet. Because it's winter, a lot of people aren't realizing that there's suddenly less beach."

"Why would he call you with this information?"

"He knows I work here. He's done work for the government. Special projects here and there, so he has a certain level of clearance."

"So he wanted you to tell me this?"

"Yes, Mr. President."

"Did he give you any details? Something we can work with?"

"He says it's occurring all over the world. The glacier melt has picked up to a level that has spurred an increase of two feet in the last month, and it's continuing."

"There was an earthquake a couple of days ago in the Arctic. Did that have something to do with it? Did he mention anything about that?"

"Yeah, that's why he called me. The geologists have determined that it wasn't an earthquake. He said they studied all the seismic charts, and found that unlike an earthquake there wasn't any depth. Everything that happened skimmed along the surface, sideways. They flew over the area. Glaciers were shattered and floating southward."

"That means shipping dangers as well as rising waters, Saunders. Did he give you a time frame before things become critical?"

"He just said he called me right after the meeting they had to discuss the findings. They are going to have a press conference in the morning. Of course, that's West Coast time."

"I'd like to talk to this fellow. What's his name?"

"Ted, Ted Varney."

"Okay. Can you get him on the phone?"

Saunders pulled out his cell phone and punched in the number. "Ted. It's Gary. The President wants to talk to you. Are you alone?" He listened for a few seconds. "Okay, here he is."

The President took the phone from him, "Hello, Mr. Varney. I understand that the world is in trouble." The President's face as he listened to the voice on the other end told Saunders that perhaps Ted was going into even more detail. Then he suddenly reached out for the nearest chair and sat down heavily. "Mr. Varney, your discussions today. Was there talk of how far inland the encroaching waters will move?" He looked up at Saunders and mouthed the words, 'paper and pencil'.

Saunders brought over a pad and pen from a small writing desk in the corner. The President began scribbling quickly. "Italy? Australia? Russia? Mr. Varney. I have people from these countries here tonight. They need to know. Can you or do you have paperwork that you can upload to us immediately from your colleagues and yourself?" He loosened his tie and got up from the chair, walked over to a window and stared into the night as he listened.

"All right, Mr. Varney, I'm returning the phone to Saunders, he will give you the address of my computer. I'll be waiting for it. Thank you for your service to this country, no, your service to the world, Mr. Varney, your service to the world."

The President tossed the phone to the Secret Service man and left the room. He took the stairs at the end of the hall down to his secretary's small office. He walked in and looked around expectantly. "Marge?"

His secretary quickly emerged from the copier room. "Yes, Mr. President. I thought you had retired for the night, I was just trying to get everything ready for tomorrow."

"We have another emergency. There is a document coming in from the West Coast. I want you to make copies for everyone here and bring it up to the meeting room as soon as you're done."

He started to leave the room, then turned around and walked over to her. "Marge, you can read it. After you do, you'll need to make a decision. Just let me know what you decide." He leaned down and kissed her forehead. "Thank you, Marge," he said and left the room.

The President mounted the stairs to the meeting room two at a time. He walked into the small room, his face was grim, his mouth tight as he looked around to see who was still in the room and who had to be called back. He picked up a phone and called Saunders and gave him the list of who needed to be rounded up.

"Gentlemen, ladies, we are going to have to have another meeting. We are awaiting the arrival of the others who had already left to retire. Unfortunately, this is something that cannot wait until morning, so please bear with me while we wait for the others."

Three White House staff came in to remove and replace glasses, bottles of water and left off trays of quickly gathered snacks. They left quietly, just as the rest of the delegates began to return to the conference room. Saunders poked his head in, signaled that everyone was now here and pulled the door shut. Suddenly a door behind the President opened and Marge came in with a stack of papers, which she laid on the table in front of the President.

The President stood and cleared his throat and began to address the group. An hour later, the first limousines pulled up to the front gates of the White House. Delegates climbed in together and as each of the limousines was filled they left at top speed for Dulles International Airport.

Air traffic controllers and airport security were on high alert, as the delegates own personal staff rushed each one to their own planes. The media kept a very close eye on the White House, some had staff following the delegates to the airport, while others stayed where they were outside of the iron fence. Stapleton knew that the reporters would be hesitant about breaking speculative stories. But it wouldn't last for long, once they got wind of the real story.

He sat in a wing chair near a window of his bedroom, lost in thought, as he thought about his own next step. No night calls from a military liaison from the basement on this one. No traitorous Secretary of Defense or Homeland Security offering their rumors, lies and whispers seeking to ingratiate themselves even further with their bosses.

The President picked up the phone beside him and dialed a number. "Sam, sorry to wake you, but I need you here. Not next week. I know you were planning to come then. I'm going to send a car to pick you up and fly you here immediately. A helicopter will land you on the lawn.

Ask for Mr. Saunders when you step out. He'll bring you up, and Sam? Thank you."

He hung up and walked over to his bureau and began to rummage around in his top drawer and pulled out a business card. He turned it over and nodded as he walked back to the chair. Again, he dialed a number, this time referencing the back of the business card. "Barney. It's me, Jack. You said if I needed you to give you a call. I need you, now. Tell me where you are, I'll have you picked up and flown here."

He listened a moment. "Great! Drive straight here then. When you reach the guard, tell them Mr. Saunders is expecting you. I'll see you in about an hour then."

As soon as he ended the call he buzzed the Secret Service man. Within two minutes the man was standing in front of him. "Two people will be coming here within the next three hours. They will say your name to whoever greets them. Please instruct everyone to get you immediately and you bring the two people here."

"Ah, Sir. I'm sure you know these people, but things are dicey right now and bringing two strangers, I mean civilians into this could jeopardize the security of this building."

"The two people that you will bring in are crucial to the security of the world about now, Saunders. I need to speak with them personally. They are on their way. I want them up here within five minutes after they say your name."

"Yes, Sir, Mr. President, sorry, Sir, I was just concerned about....."

"I understand, Saunders. You are doing your job." Stapleton clapped the other man on the shoulder and went into the bathroom and closed the door.

Sir James walked quietly into the secured rooms and stood just inside the door as it closed behind him. Edward's wife was sitting on the couch staring at him.

"So you finally decided to come and visit the prisoner?"

"No, I decided to come to see you and find out if you felt like talking with me about your part in what has been happening in the world over the last several months."

"Apparently you have decided I am totally responsible, so I'm here all alone."

"Well, I've never been absolutely certain, Evelyn, that you are totally responsible. I am unsure as to whether you have been duped because of your father or if you have knowingly caused the tragedies that have been inflicted upon the world and actually were telling him what to do."

"So if you don't know, Sir James, why did you put me in here?"

"Because I believe that in some manner you were communicating with our unseen enemy.

"Evelyn do you remember your mother?"

"No, as a matter of fact I don't, I was really young when she died. I've tried to remember before, I can only remember, some lady taking me to my grandparents. But even that is kind of foggy. What does that have to do with anything?"

"We'll discuss that later. Right now, you and I have somewhere else to go, Evelyn." Sir James opened the door and held it for her.

Just outside the door was a small golf cart type vehicle. Sir James punched in some numbers on the dimly lit tiny dashboard.

"Please hold on tightly we are going to be moving rather quickly and there are no seatbelts on this little runabout." As he spoke they began to move silently and Evelyn gripped the metal bar next to her.

Charles Barton stared out of the office windows, but he wasn't looking at the crane that was building the third tower of their home office. The way things were going the crane operator would be out of a job real soon leaving a hollowed out skeleton of steel looming over piles of concrete. The premise had been to keep the world unaware of the underlying plan until control had been wrested from the separate political powers and placed under the shield of his people.

He hadn't thought they would be able to pull Vanderlin out of his home as easily as they had. A shame about the nurse, and the rest of his people, but then liability was something that they were accustomed to dealing with. Now he was recuperating, but they would only use him if they really needed him to bring Sir James under control. Vanderlin himself would be eliminated if he tried to wrest control from his bosses.

There was a knock on the door that brought Barton out of his reverie. A man walked in, tall, broad shoulders, his black suit jacket fastened over a blue striped tie to hide a small paunch. He strode across the room and sat down behind Charles's desk. Barton looked around disconcerted, wondering what he was expected to do.

"What are you doing here, Mr. Skinner? I thought you were out in Colorado or somewhere managing the situation with Sir James."

"Actually, my dear Charles, I've decided to visit you here to help you operate our home offices more effectively. Tell me, do you really know who you have working for you?"

"What do you mean? Of course I know who I have working for me out there. I recruited them personally. They show results, they get bonuses. They fail and they are permanently out of work."

"Right, so they work harder to make sure all you know about are results."

"Stop beating around the bush and spit it out!" Charles shouted.

The other man's tattooed left hand smoothed his black hair back from his pale forehead, while he stared at him quietly before responding, "Barton, I think you've gone over the edge. This project has gotten the best of you. You are part of a group. You were chosen to lead the group on this project. Unfortunately, not everything has gone as expected, as team leader you should have planned much better for contingencies. You didn't."

"You're wrong! I planned for problems. How were we supposed to know that Sir James had some sort of fortress and help from outsiders? I believed the information I was given to be up to date and correct. We didn't have the information that we needed to make the right decisions. As far as I knew from the intel, once we blew up his mansion that should have completely isolated or killed him."

"It didn't, Barton, it didn't. Why? Because you failed to discover where he was, where his daughter was, before you chose to attack. No one was on the premises, not a cook or maid. He had given them all a vacation."

"Do you think he knew you were planning an attack? I don't think the man is psychic, I think the man was told. We grabbed one of the maids, she said they were given time off over a week before you blew up his place and told to stay away for at least two weeks."

"You think we have a leak? No. No, we couldn't possibly have a leak. Everyone has been with us for years. No one would even think about discussing plans or talking to strangers about what we do. Besides, despite what you may think, no one, no one is ever told in advance about what operations are imminent."

"So, Charles, how do you think they caught on to Seth? He was our best, yet they not only found him, but, he sustained severe injuries before he was dispatched. In other words, he was tortured, quickly and painfully. You have an explanation for that as well I'm sure." The man said sarcastically, the leather of the chair creaked as he leaned forward on his elbows and tented his fingers on the desk. As his sleeve moved up, the tattoo seemed alive as it coiled around his wrist and glistened under his watch as it picked up the vivid colors.

In the silence following the remark he suddenly he stood up, went to the door, and turned as he opened it. "Your services have been terminated, my dear fellow. We cannot afford any more blunders. Sir James is making us look like amateurs. This office has been closed."

The man left the office, closing the door softly. Barton stared at the closed door wondering what he was supposed to do now.

Outside of his office, although it was the middle of the day, the offices and cubicles were deserted. There was not a sound of a printer or fax machine to be heard. The chime of the elevator door as it closed echoed from the floor lobby. When the elevator arrived at the main floor, the man who had been in Charles Barton's office left it, walked through the enormous glass doors, turned a key in the lock at the bottom and strode across the sidewalk to a waiting limousine.

On the thirty-fourth floor of the Crown and Shield Insurance building, Charles Barton stood at his desk, staring at the closed door, pondering what he should have said. Thinking he should have presented a stronger argument for his situation of what he had been up against. Then trying to figure out what he should do with his life. His entire working life had been here since he'd been recruited out of Princeton University.

He was just about to sit down when he felt a vibration in the room. He knew immediately what had happened. Skinner had placed one of the silver tubes in his office. Charles grabbed his briefcase and ran from the office, shouting for people to run from the building. His shock at seeing the empty area caused him to halt momentarily in mid-stride.

The exit stairs were to his left and he could feel the vibration increasing as he slid, jumped and ran down the staircase. He was at the fourth floor landing when he felt the building shudder and he knew he would never see daylight again. But the will to live kept Barton running downward even as pieces of concrete, grout and pipes began cascading down and around him and finally stopped him, burying him at the bottom of the second floor stairwell.

Sir James entered the deeply hidden rooms, left Evelyn standing just inside, turned right down the hall entered an office and closed the door. The automatic door closed behind her with a click. Mary Fleming and Celine came around the corner from the kitchen and walked over to her.

"Thank God, I'm not alone here." Evelyn said quietly, and then sank to her knees on the floor sobbing. The other two women helped her over to a sofa.

"Celine, what has been happening? What was I doing? What happened to me in Malta? Celine, tell me. What happened?"

Celine stood up, "I cannot say what happened, because I do not understand what you mean. What has happened to you? Why did Sir James hide you away?"

"He believes that I might have some sort of implant and was giving away information somehow. I would never have done that. I don't have any information to give. I kept doing things that didn't seem like me, but nothing seemed to be wrong."

Mary looked from one to the other before speaking. "Evelyn, you were constantly sitting in the window staring out at the mountains. They believed you to be upstairs and instead you were there. It happened very frequently and because there were almost immediate consequences to things Sir James had planned. Things that could not have been known outside of this compound he felt that perhaps you were responsible."

"You mean that he thought that I was transmitting his plans?"

"Yes."

"How could I transmit plans, I was never around him, the others when they were meeting? How can he think this?"

"There is more, Evelyn. Mary, I realize you don't know that Evelyn is actually Vanderlin's daughter."

"Evelyn you are the Leader's daughter? Ilena's sister?" Mary sat back against the cushions, her hand covering her mouth in shock.

Evelyn stared at Celine a moment before speaking. "I hated being that butcher's daughter. My grandparents told me that my father was a very famous, very wealthy man. They took care of me, raised me from the day I was brought to their home from Mexico. They took his money to make sure I had the best of everything. But I put myself through college. I refused to take that man's money."

"Why didn't you tell Edward? Sir James?" Mary asked her.

"I am me, not him. I never knew him. I heard my grandparents talking one night. I was ten. It was a couple of days before Christmas. My grandmother was crying so hard. She said 'That bastard Vanderlin had killed her after all, just because she left him and had her child somewhere else. She never even had a chance to see her grow up.'

My grandfather kept hugging her saying, 'At least Evie is with us, her family. He sends us the money to take care of her. You've got to admit it helps out.' Evelyn was crying. "I made up my mind then as soon as I was old enough I wouldn't take a penny from him. I researched and read everything I could about him, I worked hard and when I went to college, I made sure I went with scholarships and on my own, so I wouldn't have anything to do with him.

"I met Edward and never looked back. I introduced him to my grandparents he had no way of knowing. I've done you all a disservice, by not telling you my father is Vanderlin. I feared at times for my own life, thinking he would kill me. At other times I wondered if he knew who I was, where I was, and would go after my husband."

Celine looked at her for a moment. "You've never met your father?"

"No, I never met him, Celine. I wouldn't be caught in the same room with that butcher. I know from things that all of you talked about that he was behind the devastation in Bermuda. I'd kill him myself if I could. I know that Sir James thinks that I was working with him, but I wasn't and I'm not. I wouldn't work with that, that.….God, there are no words to describe him.

"I said some things, I remember, earlier, when Sir James was questioning me. I don't know why I said them. I was angry with him, I wanted to hurt him for suspecting me and yet, what I said even hurt Edward. I felt like I was set apart from myself.

"Perhaps Sir James is right about an implant. That could be why I had a headache for so long when I was in Washington. It lasted nearly a month. I went to a doctor, they gave me something, but it didn't help. The headache finally went away on its own."

"Thank you, Evelyn. I think you have cleared up quite a few things." Celine walked away from them down the hallway, pressed her hand against her temple as she knocked on Sir James' door.

"Do you want something to eat, Evelyn?" Mary asked her as she took the woman's hands in her own. "It will probably be only a sandwich and some juice, but at least it will keep your strength up."

"Yes, yes. I could definitely use something light to eat. This is another of Sir James' bunkers, isn't it, Mary?"

"Yes. I must admit that I am amazed by the ingenuity of the man. He seems to have planned for any contingency. But my concern now is for everyone else. Everyone in the United States and heaven only knows what other countries are targeted by whatever these people are trying to do."

The force had been divided into eight groups of ten. Each group had rope for rappelling, explosives strapped to their back packs, along with rocket launchers, rifles and handguns. Some of the men had their own secret specialty weapons stashed in various places around their bodies. They had been told that there was a building or fort within this mountain and they had to locate, notify, and enter it.

The first team to locate and enter would receive a one hundred thousand dollar bonus each. That gave all the teams a little more incentive to push forward. They were climbing like ants over and around the mountain, but they were nearly blind as the terrain maps had not arrived for them to check out like they ordinarily did. Each team was moving up and across the mountain by inches in the brutal cold.

Progress was slowly being made when one of the men on team three transmitted to the group leader that he noticed something that looked man made just ahead of him. He began moving toward it when the metallic shrieking and vibration began. Everyone's automatic reaction was to cover their ears. They had been hanging on the side of a mountain and they dropped screaming into the cliffs and darkness below. Those that managed to resist suddenly realized their ears were bleeding and their eardrums had been ruptured by the noise and they dropped next, driven by the pain in their heads.

In all over fifty men fell to their deaths within seconds of the possible sighting of something man made in the middle of a mountain. Twenty miles away, their handlers, shocked at what had occurred, called the remaining men back and began to work on another plan to invade the mountain fortress. In the meantime they wanted to send a helicopter into the area to check for any survivors.

The handlers were huddled around a small table as the survivors of the failed attack straggled in bleeding and limping. Three of the men at the table had the thick tail of a snake slithering from under their shirtsleeves. They were berating the others on their stupidity, when the man Charles Barton knew as Skinner walked into the room. The others looked up and some blanched at the face they had grown to fear.

"Good afternoon, gentlemen, I believe I have arrived just in time. I have been monitoring your progress, or should I say lack of progress. You have apparently had yet another setback at the hands of our English friend. Well, I think we will have some help in entering his little hide away." He turned around and snapped his fingers, and a man and woman were pushed into the room.

Both of them were at least in their sixties and obviously frightened. "Well now, Mr. and Mrs. Stillman, I understand that you do the caretaking for an Englishman, is that true?"

Both the husband and wife nodded their eyes wide behind glasses, as they looked around at the others in the room. "Don't look at them, look at me. I want to know how you get to that house?"

"It's very simple, we drive up in our pickup, we walk a ways and then we take the elevator." Mr. Stillman said, staring now at Skinner.

"Here, here is a map of this county, show us how you get there." Skinner threw the map open onto the table, and pushed the old man toward it.

Mr. Stillman stumbled then righted himself and looked at it for a moment and then said, "The road is right here, it's more like a driveway, really. It isn't on this map, but it is right here, it goes on for about ten miles and then you can't drive anymore. You walk down the path for, oh, at least a mile, till you come to the door. That door is the elevator."

"Good. Mrs. Stillman you can have a seat right here. Your husband will be going with us to look at the Englishman's house." He gestured and three men who had been standing beside the door moved over to hover near Mrs. Stillman, whose round face was pale with fear.

"Roger, please be careful."

"I will, Molly, don't you worry."

"Don't worry, Molly, as long as your husband takes us to the house, he'll be just fine." Skinner said sarcastically, as he pushed the elderly man out the door.

They left the ramshackle building in the middle of the abandoned town. Outside the four Humvees's and three Jeeps were started up and headed out to the road that Roger Stillman had pointed out on the map.

The young woman walked through the parking lot between the three hundred year old buildings to reach the wooden walkway that led to the harbor and the near empty slips. It would be at least four months before people would begin to put their boats back into the water. She passed a couple walking hand in hand, engrossed only in each other, as she walked down the ramp to the end.

A small squat building with one window held a weathered sign stating that it was an office, gave her a sheltered place to stop and observe. Clothilde realized that she had arrived just in time. The two men she had been instructed to find were walking together down another walkway barely fifteen yards away, toward slips that held several large sailing vessels, but only one caught her eye. The trawler sat dark, dirty and sinister in the middle of the pristine white of the large sailboats.

The two men were older, heavy set and casually dressed, talking intently as they continued walking until they stopped opposite the squat trawler. A third man was suddenly with them as if he had risen from the walkway itself. He must have been sitting down on some sort of bench that she couldn't see.

Clothilde watched the three, noticing that the men were talking very animatedly, no handshakes, no visible greetings at all. She noticed a fishing pole leaning against the railing of the deck. Ah, the third man was ostensibly fishing while waiting for the other two. Oddly, the three could have been brothers as none of them were over five foot ten. All three were overweight, and looked well over fifty years old.

One of the men turned, walked back up the boat ramp toward the shops, with a thick yellow book with the markings of a telephone book. The other two stayed where they were, one picked up the fishing rod and showed it to the other. Then he gathered up a backpack and they headed down the slip and up the short ramp onto the trawler.

Clothilde left the shelter of the tiny building, glanced at the heavy gray sky, as she walked back the way she had come. Once in the parking garage she used her cell phone, texting the information to her father as he had requested, Even though she didn't know what it meant.

She had been in Newport for the last two weeks waiting for that dark ugly boat to show up. She had begun to think her father was getting senile or getting paranoid, but all that changed when she walked down that ramp again today at the specified time and there it was. She had enjoyed Newport but now the weather had turned, it was wet, raw, not really raining, just a heavy drenching mist. The warm clothing she had brought served her well as even the gray sky resembled England more than New England. Well, she could leave now she thought with a sigh as she started up the rental car and drove to the renovated mansion out on Bellevue Avenue that was now a bed and breakfast.

She relaxed in one of the club chairs, browsing through a magazine, while she waited to see if her father had any new instructions. If not, she would be on her own. She often wondered when her father asked her to do things every so often what the reasons were, but he would say he just needed her to look after a couple of his private interests. She wondered if his private interests were the reason she no longer had a home to go to, everything she'd had growing up had been blown away. Even if her father rebuilt the manor, her childhood possessions were no longer there.

Clothilde didn't have to wait long. She was still sitting in the common room of the bed and breakfast reading when she felt her cell phone vibrate. She pulled it out of the pocket of her jeans, opened it and was surprised at her father's message.

She ran upstairs, threw her things in a carry on, went downstairs and informed the manager that she had to leave suddenly for an emergency back at work. She drove the rental back to the local airport and was able to get a flight to Newark Airport that was leaving within the next half hour.

Clothilde had entered the United States on one of the passports her father had placed in her private security box in Manchester, England several years before, as Jane Mayfair. Once she left the plane in Newark, she used the one he had marked for her as the second one for her to use along with two credit cards, and as Sarah Palmer she rented another car. She was becoming more concerned about what was happening, but she felt sure that her father was trying to protect her from whoever had blown up their home.

She was happy that the car contained an onboard mapping system, so that she wouldn't need to constantly stop and check her route. She had a full tank of gas and after entering the address of where she needed to go, was well on her way an hour after she had left the plane.

It was after eight o'clock at night as she drove down the New Jersey Turnpike on her way to the Pennsylvania Turnpike. Her father had warned her not to talk to anyone and to stop for food only when she had to stop for gas. Definitely, he thought someone was trying to get to her to get to him.

Some twelve hours later she was driving down a two lane road, listening to the now annoying computer voice tell her to watch for Tyne Road. The morning was overcast, her eyes ached and her neck hurt from turning this way and that to see the small street signs. There it was, the fork in the road and Tyne road went to the right. Her eyes strained as she searched for the small driveway, with a bridge that went over a brook.

Despite a speed of less than twenty miles an hour she overshot it and had to back up. The drive widened slightly after it crossed the brook then it began climbing and curved sharply to the left. The trees hid the rest of the driveway from the main road as it continued to rise up the hill, curved to the right and there suddenly was the front entrance of a small home. An open garage was in front of her and she pulled the car into it.

Clothilde slowly walked out of the garage, holding her overnight bag and purse in one hand and pulled the door down with the other. The gravel of the drive ended at the two steps up to the front door. The keys she took from her pocket had been with the passports, she tried one and then a second which turned easily in the lock.

She knew better than to turn on a light as she stepped inside and closed the door behind her and turned the bolt. The envelope in her pocket held instructions to arm the alarm system, but she had to find the keypad. A tiny key chain flashlight helped her locate the keypad and she immediately pressed in the code. According to the instructions this would alarm not only the house, but would sound a warning if someone was driving or walking about the long driveway.

A rough hand drawn plan of the house told her that the master bedroom suite was to the right of the front door. There was a closed door on each side of the foyer, she chose the door on her right, walked down a corridor lined with closets and an entrance to a bath and there, soft and inviting, was the first bed she had seen since the previous morning.

Much as she wanted to collapse across it and sleep, she knew she had to look through the house and contact her father. Then, and only then, could she get some rest. Clothilde walked through the master and into a large study. Unlike the bedroom which only had a king bed, two dressers and a chair, the study had two desks, an old couch, filled bookcases overflowing with loose papers and file folders, several file cabinets and a couple of floor lamps. All of the furniture seemed to have been rescued from a jumble sale.

She closed the door on the mess and moved into the tidy, fire-placed living room. Worn, overstuffed couches were arranged within the large space, which, unlike the darkness of the study was flooded with light from the sun poking through the clouds and streaming through the French doors near the entrance to the dining room. Just as Clothilde was entering the kitchen the alarm in her hand vibrated. She looked at the screen that showed a car was coming up the drive.

She immediately texted her father that she had not only arrived but company was coming. He responded immediately telling her to watch for an old friend. If she saw him it was safe. She shook her head and quickly moved into the second bedroom and kept watch through the small crack between the white shutters that covered the windows, instead of blinds.

A large white limousine came slowly around the curve, into the parking area and stopped in front of the door. A young woman got out first then, a tall handsome blonde man opened the driver's side, followed by four more men who exited the rear doors of the car. They were all looking around at the trees and landscape. Clothilde gasped as she recognized her old boyfriend, Richard. That's what her father meant. But who were all of these people?

She left the bedroom went down the hall and opened the front door to the group. "Richard, what a surprise, I haven't seen you in years."

"Clothilde, gosh, you are a sight for sore eyes. How did you get here? Oh, these are all, um, friends of your father's. Can we, may we come in?"

"Of course, of course, I'm really surprised. I just got here myself."

Tino said quietly to Edward, "I think I better start patrolling down that drive, you know, make a couple of traps. We got up here pretty easy."

"If I know my father this place has security, Tino. Let me check with him to see what we need to set up. I don't want you alone. We will need more than one person if this place has to be patrolled."

The group stood about in the foyer momentarily as Clothilde looked from one to the other. "Um, I'm not sure what is happening, Richard, or who lives here, but I've only found two bedrooms and a study. I don't know if there's room for everyone."

"Don't worry, Clothilde, we aren't going to stay here very long." Richard said quietly. "Where were you that you just got here?"

"I just got in from Newport, Rhode Island. I've been flying and driving since late yesterday afternoon." All of a sudden she realized that

Michael was with the group. "Michael you're here too. What on earth is happening? Does this have to do with our home?"

"It does, Clothilde. I'm very sorry about your home. I guess someone was angry with your father."

"I know he can be a bit stuffy at times, but I can't believe that anyone would try to hurt him."

Ilena and Tino had gone rummaging in the refrigerator. "Whoever lives here doesn't eat a whole lot, or they eat out a lot. The milk is out of date and the bread is moldy." Ilena called out to them.

Michael said, "I don't think we'll be here long enough to eat anything. Everyone stay in here for just a few minutes, I'm just going outside with Edward and Tino." He started back out the door when he looked back and asked Philippe to come along as well.

The four walked around the car and into the surrounding woods before speaking. Then Michael told them what he had just learned from a text from Sir James. "There is a group trying to invade the house in Colorado. They're all safe as he's moved them but apparently a large group was killed when they tripped one of the devices. But they've kidnapped the old couple that has been acting as caretakers. They've got an assault force moving with the old man showing them the road."

"What does he want us to do, Amigo?" Tino asked. In Felipe's car we can be there in no time."

"This might be a battle with the ones we've been trying to find." Michael answered. "They're going overland so it's going to take them some time to get close. But those devices won't know that the old guy is a friend. We should split up leave Richard here with Ilena and Clothilde. Tino, Edward and I will fly back to Colorado with Philippe. Do you think you can maneuver the plane to get the old man out, Philippe, and then get back here?"

"I can try, but I don't know how successful I will be. Celine is not with me. But she will be close, so perhaps, just perhaps we can do it."

"I'll sit up front with you, Felipe. You know, ride shotgun?"

Michael nodded. "Sounds like a good idea, Tino. I don't care how you have to pull that old guy out of there, but Sir James doesn't want him hurt. His wife is back in the abandoned town we flew over that last time we dropped so fast we could see it."

"Do we have to get her too?"

"Unfortunately, that's what he wants. If we had two of these cars we could do it, but with only one. I don't know."

Philippe looked at Michael for a minute then said. "You know I think Sir James has been looking for a test of Celine and I think this just might be it."

"You're probably right. I know I wouldn't want to try this one. With the communications the way they are, as soon as you grab one the other could be killed."

"I know. Tino, if you're ready, we better get going. I just need to let the others know what we are doing."

"Bueno, Amigo."

The men came out of the trees, Michael continued on into the house as the others got into the car. Philippe deftly turned the limousine around, and they waited for Michael's return.

When Michael went in without the others, Richard immediately asked what was happening. Michael looked at him and the others and said to Clothilde, "Your father needs us to take care of something for him. Hopefully if all goes as planned we will be back soon." He drew Richard aside and told him the last message from Sir James.

"It looks as if he is bringing things to a head, Michael. I'll manage things here. Clothilde has a car here so, if we need to move, I'll call you."

Michael went out the front door and slipped into the rear of the limousine, Philippe immediately drove down the drive and just as they rounded the curve they were airborne.

Edward sat at the rear of the plane while they flew west and punched in a number on his phone that he hadn't called in several months.

President Stapleton had his eyes closed. He wasn't sleeping just resting, waiting, wondering what the next hours would bring. Sam and Barney had both arrived within minutes of each other. He had needed to talk to someone other than the people who had been feeding him information. He had needed to listen to someone besides those that had been telling him what to do. Samantha Pelham and Barney Young helped him keep his perspective. Each of them worked for the government with their own very high security clearances, but neither wanted public office.

He had spent several hours with them talking, even laughing every so often. Till they all finally grew tired and he told them thank you. Made sure they got back home safely and he had gone into his bedroom and collapsed into his favorite chair. His private cell phone buzzed and he looked at it thinking it was Marge. Only one other person had this number and he hadn't called it in months.

"Gately?"

"Yes, Sir, Mr. President, can you speak freely?"

"Yes, I'm alone."

"The person and the group that has been trying to assist you and the other countries is himself under siege right now. In fact, Sir, I can give you the coordinates of the place where several of the higher echelon are presently located. These are some of the people who were involved in the Bermuda disaster. The coordinates are for an old ghost town in Colorado, northwest of Boulder. Be very careful about whom you share these with. As there are corrupt people where we least expect, Sir." Edward waited while the President read back the coordinate numbers.

"Are you all right, Gately?"

"Yes, Sir. I'm fine, just tired."

"Good. I know what you mean by tired. I hope this mess will be over soon."

"I do as well, Sir."

"Good night, Gately and thank you."

As soon as the president hung up he rang for Saunders. When the Secret Service man came in the president realized that the man also seemed strained and tired. But they weren't finished yet.

"Saunders, are you familiar with Colorado at all?"

"Not really, Sir. I've driven through parts of it on the way to somewhere else, but never stayed more than overnight."

"Yes. Well, I have some coordinates here in Colorado. Apparently at these coordinates we can locate the rest of that group that caused the Bermuda disaster. In fact, from what I gather, I think they are running some sort terrorism operation from out of the ghost town at these coordinates. We need to run a completely covert operation to get these people.

The biggest problem, Saunders, is who and how many can we trust?"

"If we run a totally Secret Service operation we would be within bounds as they were also responsible for somehow invading your war room."

"True, so, how many can you gather immediately and get there without any notice at all? No inkling to the press, any politicians, no brothers, sisters or wives. This would be a completely secret operation. Can you do this?"

"The way things are going right now, Sir, everyone is on the alert looking for anything. We have several agents here on site, but if we move them all at once it will be noticed."

"Use the underground tunnels. I think you should have at least two hundred men with as much fire power as you can muster. I want those bastards and I want them dead. That sniveling Romanian, sitting right here, pretending to be concerned with people dying, when he was one of the killers. By the way where is the little weasel?"

"He is in a Marine brig under heavy guard, Sir. I understand that paperwork has been started to extradite him back to Romania for trial."

"Excellent. Let me know as soon as the operation is ready to roll. I want you to be in charge from here. I think your sidekick may be the right person to lead the group, what do you think?"

"I think he would jump at the chance, his parents were on one of the cruise ships that went down in Bermuda."

"God! I had no idea. Try to have them on their way within the next two hours."

Saunders almost gasped, but cleared his throat to cover it up. "It might be somewhat longer, Sir, but I will hustle them along."

The Secret Service man left the private suite and took the exit stairs directly down to the Secret Service offices below the first floor. Foster was sitting at the console checking the screens.

"The boss has a job for you and a few others. Requisition all of the fire power you can find. He just gave me the coordinates for the rest of that tattooed snake group. He wants us to handle it since they infiltrated the White House."

"I'll be ready in minutes, you going?" Foster went over to the couch that he used to sleep on grabbed a small duffle bag, he checked his Glock, bent over and checked the Beretta he kept on his ankle.

"Nope, I'm staying back here to keep things coordinated and moving and quiet. No talking to anyone, other than you, I'm not telling anyone the coordinates. You don't tell anyone except once you are in the air and give them to the pilot." Saunders looked up as Foster broke down his favorite Armalite rifle that he kept hanging behind the couch.

Saunders silently began pulling up names, calling them and sending them to the military airbase for immediate take off. Foster checked over the list that Saunders handed him. Then he wrote up the requisition and Saunders signed for the weapons for all of the men. Fifteen of the men were leaving directly from the White House with Foster.

Within an hour two SUVs left the White House and Saunders advised the president that exactly two hundred men would be meeting at the air base within the next half hour and taking off soon after that. He would let him know when they were in the air.

Sir James and Celine had been in the office for a while watching various screens that fed back information as to what was happening outside the mountain fortress. He had always been worried about the ghost town because they were the closest structures to his home. Even though he owned the property, Sir James hadn't wanted to change anything in the area, so no one would know that anyone lived near there, but he'd had hidden cameras strategically placed overlooking the main street. One camera angle was facing the saloon, which was one of two nearly intact buildings.

Celine let Sir James know that Philippe was on his way, he said Tino is riding 'shotgun?' but they need to be able to come in safely in order to pluck Stillman away from his captors.

"Celine, let Philippe know that they have to wait until the group is in the open, walking on the path toward the house. I'll be able to see when they have left their cars behind."

"They are twenty minutes from the ghost town, Sir James."

"Excellent! Tell Philippe that he should look like that helicopter he used near my home. No United States markings at all. Have him tell Tino that Mr. Stillman is short with grey hair. He usually wears overalls, a straw cowboy hat and a tattered old shearling coat in the winter. That way they will grab the right person."

Celine silently relayed the message to Philippe who responded that he understood.

Sir James gave no inkling of his concern about having to orchestrate this dangerous rescue operation. But he owed it to the couple that had taken care of his house for years. He knew their children and had seen pictures of their many grandchildren. They were an active, healthy couple but he didn't know how this rough treatment would stress them out.

"Celine, tell Philippe now, they are out of their cars and they have about a ten minute walk time before they reach the first device."

Seconds later, the helicopter appeared on the computer screen flying in low at an almost impossible angle. Celine made every effort by watching the helicopter on the screen to bond with her husband to protect the machine. There was a jumble of motion on the screen, then the helicopter took off fast and dropped behind the next peak. Back down on the ground, several bloodied people were slowly picking themselves up, checking out their companions and looking skyward.

"Tino got him. The man is shaken, just wants his wife, he says."

"That's your husband's next mission, Celine, we have to find Mrs. Stillman. I know she's in the ghost town, but I have to keep the communications down. Ask Philippe to make one of those military vehicles they were using, the Humvee. No, no, wait. I don't want him on the ground, not when they have Mr. Stillman."

"No, it is better that they keep the helicopter look. That will bring them out. I'll let you know where I think she is being kept." Sir James looked away from the screen momentarily. "Ah, the cavalry, as they say, is coming, my dear."

Celine looked at him, noticed that he was looking at his cell phone, and returned her attention to her husband's efforts. "He has located the ghost town and is flying low over it right now.

"I knew I should have placed more cameras in that damn town. In the center of the main street there is the old jail next to the saloon. Those would be the most likely buildings they would be using. They are the only ones with windows and roofs still intact."

"They are being shot at from the roofs. He's had to break away from the town." Celine spoke quietly, her voice not betraying any emotion, as she watched the vehicle evading the rifle fire.

"All right, tell him he cannot land anywhere near here. He should pull away northwest, into Wyoming, wait about an hour, and return from the south, as if he is coming up from New Mexico. We need to see how quickly our reinforcements can be here."

Philippe and Tino looked grim as they turned away from the town. While Sir James and Celine only saw a blur as the plane moved behind the mountains, the group inside had not felt any change at all in the speed.

"Damn! Bloody screw up." Michael was angry. Edward put his hand on his shoulder.

"Nothing else we could have done, Michael. We can't get Mrs. Stillman back if we're all dead."

"We're not done yet." Philippe said. "I have another trick up my sleeve that I think will work. Sir James reminded me when he had Celine tell me to come in from the south. But I think all of you should be sitting down. Edward, can you come up here, I need you on that side."

Mr. Stillman was looking out of the windows of the plane, back at the mountains that were receding. "My wife, I thought you were going to get my wife. She can't stay there. She'll be worried about me. Please go back. Don't leave her."

Edward brought the man forward in the plane. "It's all right, Mr. Stillman. We're working on getting your wife back to you safely. It's just going to take a little longer. We want to make sure she doesn't get hurt."

"Sure, Sure, I know, I don't know how you even managed to get me away from them. I'm just worried about her. Once they find out I've been rescued they might really hurt her."

Edward kept trying to soothe the worried man. All of them were now seated closely together in the front of the plane. Philippe guided the plane through the clouds, well above and west of the last sighting. He was concentrating as he connected with the plane and his mate far below. At last, he had found the harmonics and through the connection with his wife he stabilized it around the plane.

All on board felt the sudden dive as the white plane left the clouds and flew in over the ghost town hovered momentarily, with the rotors of the helicopter kicking up the sand and blurred the vision of those on the ground. Philippe rushed into the saloon, grabbed the frightened elderly woman, and dashed back into the vehicle.

They were suddenly airborne again and away from the mountains flying east into the darkness. Edward and Michael were staring at Mrs. Stillman and back at Philippe in disbelief. They both knew the amount of time it would have taken either of them to rescue the woman, Even with the distraction of the blowing sand. Both of them knew they would have been in a firefight and been killed as well as the woman. Philippe had just saved all of them and Mrs. Stillman while they were trying to figure out the logistics of dropping out of the helicopter.

Michael spoke up first, "Philippe, I have never in my lifetime seen anything like what you just did."

"To be truthful, Michael, I have never done it before. I don't know what a toll it took on Celine, because she bore the brunt of that exercise. I am not able to connect with her right now. So I am unsure how she is. We have both been aware that it is possible, but we have never tried it before. There are people on earth who have performed similar feats. It is the most extreme use of adrenalin.

"However, we are able to focus and enhance it, but in this case we were doing so many things at once, that it became even more difficult."

Sir James was shocked by Celine's sudden slump into the chair. She had been standing beside him one moment, telling him that she and Philippe were going to attempt something and it would be difficult. Then she gasped and fell into the chair. He went out to the kitchen and retrieved some bottles of water.

When he returned with it, Celine was still sitting in the chair, but she was sitting up. However, she seemed to be having difficulty keeping her human form. "I need to rest. I will be unable to assist you for several hours, Sir James." She whispered. He could barely hear her. He put his arm around her waist and helped her to the nearest bedroom, and left the water beside the bed should she need it and closed the door.

When he returned to the office, he checked to see if he had missed any communications, but nothing had come in, nor had his cell phone buzzed in that few minutes. Now he was worried for the first time. He didn't realize how much he had come to rely on the two aliens. Despite his misgivings he had let them work alongside and assist him in regaining control of this mess.

Two hours later the white limousine rolled up the driveway through the trees in North Carolina. Philippe, Tino, Michael, Edward and the Stillmans left the car just outside the garage. Richard opened the door and was shocked by the visible strain on their faces. All, except Philippe, looked as if they hadn't slept in days.

"It looks as if you really had a successful mission." We've been able to get some food in the house and set up some places to sleep. Richard closed the door behind the group, locked it and set the controls to arm the house alarms. Then flicked another switch that he had put in while the others were away to alarm the driveway entrance.

Philippe hovered near the door, watching the others settling in. Ilena was showing the Stillmans around. Michael looked over at him from the kitchen doorway, hesitated a moment and then walked over to him.

"You're worried about Celine?"

"I cannot really call it worry. That transfer that we made I know caused a weakness in her. She has not yet recovered. We have never tried anything like that, we had always been warned of the potential risks."

"What kind of risks, Philippe?"

"If she is not given what you might call a 'charge' she might expire."

"Can Sir James do it?"

"No. It would be difficult even for me to do it. That is why after I was injured I had to leave and go home. When we are injured, even though we heal, we are severely weakened. A charge from one to another strengthens us again so that our healing is complete and we are whole again."

"I'll get Edward." Michael hurried away through the French doors onto the back slope where Edward and Richard had gone to check out the rear perimeter of the land. Minutes later when they returned, Philippe was still standing by the front door.

"Come on, Philippe. Let's go. Michael has told me what is happening. The two of us will go back to Colorado. We'll get in somehow. The others will stay we can't take a chance on everyone getting killed." Edward clapped a hand on his old friend's shoulder as he spoke.

The two went out the door. Seconds later the white limousine was around the curve and airborne again, chasing the sun.

Sir James cell phone buzzed only a second before he answered, anxious for word from the others.

"Dad."

"Edward. Thank heavens you're safe, where are you?"

"Philippe and I are on our way back to you. How safe is it to land now?"

"I've been monitoring things since you rescued Mrs. Stillmann. There was a lot of fighting for a couple of hours, it seems the entire group that was in that town has been rounded up or killed. There is no sign of our adversaries."

"How soon do you think you will be here?"

"Philippe is concerned about Celine, we can be there in about...." Edward stopped and looked at Philippe, who gestured for one hour, "about one hour, Dad."

"I will be able to send you the coordinates in a few minutes. I have to put some things in place. But be careful because if some have been missed they may try to shoot you down. I have no way of actually knowing until they are airborne if they are outside the perimeter of my security."

"Right, Dad. We'll keep a sharp eye out."

Fifteen minutes later, Sir James voice broke into the silent cockpit of the plane. "All right here are the coordinates. However, you will have to drop in like a helicopter. There is no room to taxi in this space."

"We should be there in just under forty-five minutes, Dad."

Forty minutes later a small white helicopter showed up on Sir James system net, and dropped like a stone onto the floor of a tiny canyon. As soon as the skids hit the red x and the rotors slowed, the entire floor moved into the side of the mountain into darkness.

The two men stretched and waited while lights came on and they saw the arrow showing them the way further into the mountain. They left the helicopter and Philippe rushed down the narrow passage, after a couple of turns the tunnel looked more like the hallway to a home than a rock hewn cave.

A door opened and there was Sir James. "Dad."

"Sir James, how is Celine?"

Sir James put his hands out to both men, as he suddenly realized just how much strain and stress he had been under for the last few days. He needed to rest himself. But he smiled and said to Philippe, "She is very weak and resting. I am not exactly sure what occurred, she just said you were going to try something, and then, she collapsed into a chair."

The older man led Philippe to the bedroom in which Celine was resting, "She's in here, Philippe."

When Philippe closed the door he saw Celine lying flat on the floor. Her skin had the healthy gold tone of their species and the lids of her eyes were lowered to cover most of her face.

Philippe raised the four fingered hand in his own and she opened her eyes. "I couldn't retain my human form. Sir James helped me to get in here."

"I know. But judging from your color you should be all right soon.

I thought I might have to take you home to recover when I could not hear you."

"I couldn't think or speak. It was as if I had received some sort of electrical surge throughout my body."

"How are you feeling now?"

"I'd really like to stay here for a few more hours, so if you need me later I will be able to help."

"Good, good. Can you try human form again?"

"Not yet, I don't want to fade in and out. Right now I still feel drained."

"I understand." Philippe then also returned to his true nature and his gold tone was much deeper than Celine's. He placed his body next to hers on the floor, they both closed their eyes and with a displacement of the air around them they merged for seconds. The golden glow strengthened and filled the room then Philippe drew away from his mate.

"That will help you to recover more quickly and strengthen you. I will make sure the others leave you alone." Philippe stood up and was again the tanned, blonde man that Edward knew.

He left the room and went in search of the others. He found them in the office with Sir James. "How is she, Philippe?"

"She will be fine. Thank you so much for helping her, Sir James. She needed to be by herself at that time."

"I'm glad she will be all right. Now, we can concentrate on the situation that we have on all fronts.

"The town has been cleared. Apparently the Secret Service completed that action alone, without any other agency involvement. However, I believe that they did not get the head man."

"I made a phone call," Edward said quietly, "and a couple of the guys they picked up were very eager to tell all they knew. They said the head man is still out here somewhere. He is some insurance guy named Skinner."

The man awoke, looked up at the peeling paint of the ceiling and walls and remembered. He lifted a scrawny arm, and saw his wrist circled in a leather band, linked to a chain that was attached to the wall. Despite the shackle he managed to push himself up in the bed. He looked in disgust at the filthy sheets that surrounded him and knew that his power was no more, he had been kidnapped, but who would have dared to try this.

His thoughts whirled, Sir James, Seth, or could it be one of the people on the phone, the people whom he had never seen, who sent orders that always seemed to conflict with each other. Somehow, he had managed to always keep things straight, but he had angered someone. Well, he thought, he had angered many people. But he never knew who these people were, but they always knew what he was doing, how and when he did it. They had warned him, particularly one man. Yes, it had to be him.

A voice spoke, "Well, its damn well time you woke up, old man. You have work to do. Sir James has caused quite a stir and you are going to bring him in and stop it."

"I don't know what you are talking about." His voice was a croak,

299

barely above a whisper. How long have I been asleep? He wondered to himself.

"You'll know soon enough. Get him out of there, cleaned up and brought to me."

A minute later, a door creaked open and two men came through, both dressed like medical personnel, one was pushing a wheelchair. They unlocked the chain from his wrist and helped him carefully into the wheelchair. The taller of the two began pushing the chair so fast down the hall that he felt like he was going to fall out of it and his hands hurt from gripping the arms. They got on an elevator and went up. He looked at the numbers and realized he had been in a basement. He wondered what day it was, how long had he been kept here. The last thing he could remember was being dragged from his bed and that infernal nurse getting knocked to the floor.

The elevator stopped, the wheelchair was roughly jogged over the uneven threshold and they turned left down another hallway. This one was painted green, there were windows at the end of the hall and the sun was shining through. Sunlight, he thought, never realized how beautiful that was. I must be getting senile. I don't know what use I can be to these people. I must have had another heart attack. I guess I'm lucky to be alive.

They pushed him through another doorway into what looked like a reception area and then turned right and went into a large conference room. He looked up to see a tall bearded man walking toward him. The tattoo on his left hand, Seth had a similar one only smaller, but it went up his arm under his shirt like this one did.

"Ah, no more guile from you, Vanderlin. You recognize my tattoo. Yes, I am the 'Hadi Skupina', I am the owner of Crown and Shield Insurance. So now you know where you are, you are with friends, like-minded people, Vanderlin.

"We have joined our extraterrestrial friends to make sure that the world that they want and the world that we want will be under our control. Not those petty politicians that everyone hates. We have our fingers on the pulse of the world, with all of the policies that people have to buy? We know where and how much we can lose, and we will still make a profit. Flood insurance is going to go through the roof." He chuckled as he watched the frail man try and shift his position in the uncomfortable chair, walked over and sat down in one of the conference chairs close to the wheel chair.

"Well, I have a job for you again, Vanderlin. You need to talk to Sir James, and get him to, aha, come down from the mountain."

"I don't know what you are talking about, whoever you are."

"Oh, I'm so sorry I didn't tell you my name. I'm Gregory Stulov Skinner, the man from whom you take orders. We really made a good penny after the Bermuda disaster. I have you to thank for that, a really well run operation. The losses of money paid out were well distributed as planned, but now corporations are clamoring for insurance for all those beautiful hotels, corporate headquarters and homes they built so close to the oceans. I've been able to make billions from these new contracts. Great work, yes, indeed.

"So your next brilliant move is to get Sir James to come to you. He's responsible for the loss of many of my workers, and it's time that stopped. He has undermined my plans and has almost finalized the countries working together. I think he knows what is being planned for our beautiful planet."

"I don't know where he is. He visited me in the hospital that was it."

"Yes, well no worry there, Vanderlin, we know exactly where he is, you only have to talk to him, and arrange one of your usual late private meetings at a place of our designation. He'll come running."

"All right. I'll make the call."

A cell phone was shoved at the old man and he entered in the number.

It rang for a few seconds and then was answered. "Yes?"

"James?"

"Yes."

"This is Anthony Vanderlin."

"Really?"

"We need to meet to get things back on track."

"Where?"

"Perhaps the last place we met, at 2 in the morning as usual."

"When?"

Skinner mouthed the word Wednesday.

But Vanderlin said, "Ah, Thursday morning."

"2 in the morning Thursday. Place 3."

"Right."

"Good-bye, Anthony Vanderlin." There was a click.

"Excellent, you did a wonderful job. Thursday will be all right, it will give us plenty of time to set things up. So you let me know where place 3 is and we will get you all dressed up for the trip. But for now these fellows will make sure you get something to eat and we will wait and see how the meeting turns out."

The two orderlies, rushed him back down the elevator and back into his basement room, but now the sheets were clean and there was a tray of food on a stool next to the bed. They lifted him out of the chair and sat him down on the side of the bed and again shackled him but this time by the ankle.

"Just making sure you're still here in case the boss needs you again."

He nodded. He knew that once Sir James showed up at the meeting house, they would both be killed. But he had given himself two more days. Perhaps that would give him a chance to figure his way out of this mess.

Sir James looked around the room as he hung up the phone. "Well, Son, I think we have a way of getting rid of whoever is in charge of the opposition."

"What do you mean, Dad?"

"That phone call was from the Leader."

"The Leader, we thought he was dead."

"Yes, Philippe, we did. But I always knew that man had nine lives. He sounded very weak, so I am sure someone has him stashed somewhere and is using him to get us to stop the world union. Edward, this is the address where the meeting is to be held. Can you let the cavalry know the coordinates? The time is two a.m. on Thursday morning. That will at least give them some time to plan.

"I do not have any intention of leaving here to join that meeting. So if Vanderlin wants to attend he will be caught as well. I'm going to rest."

Edward and Philippe stared at each other for a moment. "I think this is it, this will be the end, Edward."

"It may be the end of the fight, but we still have to find a way to stop what they have placed in motion with the ice at the poles melting."

"Once these people have been stopped, and Celine is well again, I believe we can place some of our knowledge in your hands to stop the calving and the seas from rising any further at least from where they are now. We won't be able to make them retreat, but we can stop further intrusion."

"Good, Good. Let's do first things first, I'll get these coordinates. I think we might want to be on the east coast for this, do you think Celine will be well enough to travel by tomorrow morning?" He talked while he entered the address and logged the coordinates.

"Yes, I think she will be fine by then. She can continue to rest until we are needed to act again, even while traveling."

"That's what I was hoping to hear, Philippe. Edward called the president for the second time in days.

"Good Morning, Sir. A meeting has been set up at these coordinates for Thursday morning at two. Here are the coordinates, 39.514932° by 79.2858246."

"You're kidding, two in the morning?"

"Yes, Sir, the head of the other side has given us the time and place. But I think that there might well be a last minute change or some sort of booby trap to this. If I may suggest, Mr. President, that two teams be used, one for the primary meeting place and another ready for any last minute change that they might spring on us."

"Good idea, Gately. It sounds as if this might get to be a skirmish situation, do you think that might happen?"

"Yes, Sir, I do believe that we are going to be in for a fight or we might be in danger of their favorite weapon, the explosive. So we have to get your teams the particular detector that locates their weapon ahead of time. We will try to get them to you by tomorrow."

"That's too late, tomorrow's Wednesday. People have to learn how to use them, what to look for, how to disarm the explosive."

"It can't be done sooner. I'm nowhere near you and we don't know who or where other agents of these people are located. All I can say is watch for the snake on the left hand. I've got to go now, Sir."

"I hope his private phone isn't compromised, even though the call was scrambled and bounced around we may have been on the line too long."

"I was timing it and you were just under sixty seconds, Edward."

"That was too long. I had to let him have some idea of what to expect. I had to let him know that there could be casualties. Somehow we do have to get them that detection device. Those people will probably blow that place up as well, once everyone is there. Who knows the device may already have been planted."

"The rest are already on the east coast, how far are they from the meeting site?"

"Just a few hours ride. They have a detector with them, but we don't have a secure way of contacting them."

"Sir James might be able to contact Michael in some way. I'm sure after all this time they have worked together."

"You're absolutely right. As soon as he wakes, we can have him send Michael with the detector."

"I would say Tino would be the best. He is unknown to the others and could easily be overlooked by them. Michael and Richard have both been seen and are known."

"Well, there is nothing to do until he awakes."

"I will be making several more devices, there is enough here that I can put them together, and I have two with me that I have already made.

The President stood at the windows of the Oval Office staring out at the light snow falling on the lawn that was still covered from the last three storms. Twenty-four hours and this mess could be over. He had talked with his counterparts from several of the other countries, who were burying their dead and planning on evacuation of coastal areas. He knew that they were all thinking that these continuing crises had brought the countries closer together, but unity? One government? That was still very doubtful.

Well, once this next operation was complete, perhaps, they would be able to present a cooperative front to this extraterrestrial threat, if not a totally unified one. They had shown that they could work together pretty well when faced with global problems. It had opened up a more honest and direct dialogue if nothing else.

A double knock, followed by three on the door, let him know that Saunders was entering with someone. He turned around and Saunders walked in followed by a short, powerful, Latino looking man.

"Good Morning, Presidente. I have been told to give you something that you were promised. I was told to ask for Mr. Saunders who would bring me to you."

"What is it that you are bringing me?"

Saunders was hovering just behind and to one side of Tino, ready to bring him down if necessary.

Tino chuckled, "Don't worry Señor Saunders, I mean you no harm or the Presidente. Here, Sir." He pulled a small, rumpled paper bag from his jacket pocket and placed it on the ornate desk. "This will let you know if those little bombs are around, give you time to get away. They are only four inches long and look like silver or chrome. As long as they are cool no problem. If they are warm and glowing, run like hell."

The President looked in the bag at the device. "Just one, can we get more?"

"I don't know. That is the only one we could get to you this quickly, Presidente. I have to go now, Señor."

"Thank you for bringing this, Mr.....?"

"No names, Presidente." Tino smiled, rocked back slightly on his heel as he turned to leave the office.

Saunders escorted him out of the White House, down the drive and to the gate. He watched while the man blended into the tourist crowds and disappeared. No car meant there was no license plate to track. But then these people were careful and obviously they had to be.

He hurried back into the building and returned to the oval office. The smooth black device didn't look like anything he had ever seen before. Other than the little wire on the end which seemed to rotate, obviously an antenna there wasn't anything movable or a place for batteries. How could they duplicate this?

"Sir, the only way we could make another one of these is to break this one open, which will render it useless, I think."

"I agree. We use it as is. Hopefully they will be able to get us another one. Do you think this is outer space technology as well?"

"Since we are looking for something that sounds like an extraterrestrial device, I guess that would be the only thing that could find it."

"Do you have people out there all ready?"

"Yes, Sir, they have been onsite for almost eight hours. They are scouring the terrain around the only house at that location. I've got some pictures they've sent along on my phone."

He leaned over and showed the president some of the pictures of the house, a good size ranch, with a gravel drive, surrounded by large trees.

"Does it look as if anyone has been there recently?"

"Not to the house, there weren't any tire tracks in the snow. It is pretty tough to get to right now. Its five miles from the Interstate, a State road for a couple of miles, then a small county road for another two miles, then turn onto a nearly hidden gravel drive. Since they planned the meeting, I think they might plan on plowing later today. So I've had everybody dig in now to be ready for that. That might be when they plant something. The thing is can it be triggered remotely?"

"Let's hope someone contacts us to let us know. I feel like we are missing something. Wait, Saunders. Remember, they used the same device for that house in England that they did in Canada. Have you searched to see if it has been used anywhere else? You know they talk about signatures?"

"You're right, Sir. They may have used it for other bombings. We have gotten so accustomed to things blowing up that we always assume terrorists bombings with the ordinary C4. The ATF will have the signatures. I'll call them immediately."

"From here, Saunders. I want to know."

"Yes, Sir." Saunders scrolled down his phone and pressed the entry. "Clark? It's Saunders at the White House. I need to know something."

The President paced back and forth behind the desk, his hands in his pockets, head down. His brown hair was now heavily laced with grey, which went well with the lines that had etched themselves in his once youthful face. Recently, his eyes had acquired dark circles that belied those who slept little, but the news media had had no access to him since the Bermuda crises, so they couldn't babble about it. Although reporters were camped out in mobile trucks encircling the White House, other than a long range camera view as he stood in a window, or walked briefly outside before the last group of snow storms made that impossible, they were kept at bay.

Saunders had been nodding and making notes during the entire call, but saying little, when he finally hung up he looked at the President and said, "You were right, Sir. Two days before we went to Colorado, there was an explosion of a building in Omaha, Nebraska, Crown & Shield Insurance headquarters. It had all of the markers for the type of explosion that was seen in England and Canada. There have been several over the past three months in almost every country in Europe, Eastern Europe, South America, the Middle East, China and India, as well as the Arctic explosion."

"Well at least they are not playing favorites. Go on."

"Survivors have been few, but they have all told of vibration and a type of shock wave that precedes the actual blast. Only one person was killed in the Omaha explosion. The entire staff had been told to take a holiday the day before. The only person killed was the CEO of the corporation. Oh, he had an interesting tattoo, a snake, coiled from left hand over his shoulder and down his back."

"My God, those people are everywhere. With so many people tattooed these days, no one even notices anymore."

"I'm going to get this out to the site. After they plow, about midnight, and every half hour, we will check the house with the device and see what happens. I'd prefer to catch these people and bring them to trial then having them all dead."

"It may not be possible, Saunders. When are you leaving for the site?"

"I should have everything ready to go in about an hour."

"Keep me posted and thank you. If I hear from our friends with any more information, I'll get in touch with you."

Saunders was opening the door to leave when Stapleton's private phone rang. "Wait."

The president picked up the phone and said, "Yes?" He listened for a moment and then, "I have received it, but we could use more if at all possible."

Then silence as the person on the other end continued. "Thank you, I appreciate that." The president said and hung up.

"They are going to try and get you two more but it won't be until this evening. Meet at the Walmart parking lot on the county road, same messenger.

"Saunders, are you sure this room isn't bugged?"

"I check it myself, Sir. Three times a day. The last time I found something in here was the day that fat guy from Romania turned up."

"He probably put it in here."

"Right, so our friends are going to be pretty close tonight. I hope they don't get caught in the net when we pull the noose. We only know one of them now and we don't know who he is. I did get a couple of quick photos, that we are running, but so far no matches."

"But, I'll be meeting him out in the open tonight, maybe then, I'll get a name or more information."

"Don't press it. We don't know who is watching or where our adversaries are at anytime."

"I'll play it safe, sir. I better get going."

The large white limousine was an unusual sight as it drove up the narrow road in North Carolina on a cold late winter afternoon. It turned in between the low stone markers and drove over the little creek and up the drive. The alarms had been planted under the markers and blared loudly in the house, awakening the Stillmans from their nap in the guest bedroom.

The others had been camping between the living room, study and master suite, leaving only the dining room and kitchen free of blow-up beds, lap tops, and tossed clothes.

The Stillmans knew that they had to remain in their little area when an alarm sounded and held each other, frightened not knowing if this was just a delivery or trouble. They had seen the guns and other weapons the men had, but the two young women had worked to make them as comfortable as possible.

"All clear you two." They recognized Clothilde's British accent calling through the outer door, and peeked through the white shutters to see the same large white limousine in which they had arrived here.

When they came out it seemed as if everyone was talking at once. They were introduced to Celine and then Mrs. Stillman said she would put something together for all of them. Her husband followed her into the L shaped kitchen and left the group behind in the living room.

Edward and Philippe explained to the rest that tonight was going to be very busy. Tino, had not yet returned from Washington where he had passed along the one detector that the group in North Carolina had. Edward looked around the group, and wondered if Clothilde knew yet that he was her brother and chuckled inwardly as he thought about Ilena and Evelyn. This had really turned into a family affair. But it was going to be a very deadly family affair if tonight didn't end well.

Clothilde still didn't know about Philippe and Celine or what the nature of the job was that they were doing. So while Philippe was talking, Edward whispered into her ear if she could help the Stillmans. She gave him an odd look and walked out of the living room, through the dining room and into the kitchen.

While they were talking and planning Edward's cell phone buzzed. He looked at it and said, "My father. I'll put it on speaker."

"Hello, everyone. First of all, the President has requested more detectors, Philippe has had a chance to take care of that. Tino will be delivering them at the Walmart, County Rd. So you must be ready to leave the house as soon as he returns. We want to take as many alive as possible, and we want all of you and the cavalry alive as well. This is a major mission. Be careful, all of you. Ilena, please stay with Clothilde and the Stillmans. You must keep them safe, no matter what. I don't know if they have found this house as yet. Good luck and God speed."

A minute later, Clothilde walked out of the kitchen and stopped in the dining, her phone to her ear. She looked up, her mouth in an 'O' and stared at Edward, as she continued to listen, and her eyes widened and she sat down in the nearest chair. Even though Edward understood what was happening, he thought it best not to go to her. When Richard started to go into the dining room, Edward put his hand on the man's arm and shook his head. Richard frowned but stayed where he was, and waited. Clothilde walked into the living room and into the master suite and slammed the door.

Richard looked at Edward who responded, "I think my dad just told her I'm the older brother."

Richard grimaced, "I guess that didn't go over too well."

"He had planned to tell her in person, didn't get the chance."

Mrs. Stillman called out to them, "Come and get it," as she and her husband brought out a steaming platter and dishes filled with food and placed them on the sideboard. They could smell the fresh brewed coffee and they started in on the buffet.

Minutes later the alarm went off, and they went to their posts, weapons drawn. The rental car pulled up and Tino bounded out. They all sighed and opened the door for him.

"I smell food, you started dinner without me?"

"There's plenty left for you, but you better be quick, cause we have to get back on the road or uh the air, my friend." Michael said as he clapped him on the back.

Half an hour later, they had loaded up the limousine and were saying good bye to the Stillmans and Ilena, when Clothilde came out of the bedroom.

"I guess all of you are leaving for whatever it is that you and my father are doing."

Edward answered, "Yes, Clothilde. We should be back in the morning if all goes well."

She looked at Edward for a minute then said, "I hope you all come back safely, I need to get to know my brother."

He grasped her hand for a minute and said "Thank you, thank you."

They left. Ilena had on a large belt with a gun in the holster, and a rifle in her left hand as she waved goodbye.

It was already getting dark and the limousine made the first curve down the drive from house and took off into the air. They had to reach the Walmart in Maryland as quickly as possible.

Celine and Philippe were up front the others were huddled in the back, going over the maps of the area, tense with the need for action, yet concerned that there was too much that was unknown.

An hour later, Tino walked out of the Walmart restroom and into the parking lot. He slowly walked toward the right side of the store then down the aisle of cars to a large black SUV. He opened the door and jumped inside.

"Hello, Señor Saunders. We are able to give you a few more. I hope this helps. We will be there as well, to assist, but behind you, not in front. That is all I can say, Señor."

"Tell your team, whoever they are, we thank you, we all thank you."

"Si, Señor" Tino jumped out and slowly sauntered back to the Walmart, went in and returned to the restroom.

Foster looked after him, "That is some weird guy. I would not want to mess around with him. I mean he looks fat and out of shape, but, most of that is muscle."

"Yep, I know just what you mean. Okay, let's get these to the teams. They are going to need them. When you hand them out, just tell them, put it out in front of them, if there is something, they'll know. The little wire faces away from them."

At seven o'clock that night two large plows started up the mile long driveway. By nine o'clock they had finished clearing the drive and the gravel parking area in front of the house and plowed their way back out and drove away to the next job. One two man car had been assigned to follow the plows to see where they went and to stay with them. They drove on to the next town, Suitedale and plowed out a couple of small parking lots next to churches, then the town hall. It was eleven o'clock and the two plow trucks drove further away from the ranch house to Groveton, stopped in a diner for coffee, and started on the churches there. The men watched them go from church to church, and keep heading west until they were almost fifty miles away. At that point the two, started back to the ranch house in case they were needed.

At one o'clock in the morning the watching teams saw three large vans stop on the road and then noticed several people with bags and pieces of equipment slipping into the area around the house. Moving stealthily around the outbuildings and garage, four were seen to climb trees. All were dressed in white camouflage. The others surrounded the house digging their way into the snow. A count went out among the surrounding Secret Service men of twenty to twenty-five.

Three of the group broke off and entered the house through a rear door and they came out in under a minute. The agent stationed at the rear aimed his detector at the house and it began to buzz. The man reported to all, "The house has been armed. I repeat the house has been armed." Five minutes earlier it had not been.

It was one forty-five in the morning when three cars drove up the driveway. They turned the cars around so that they would be headed back down the drive. Then doors started opening. Two men walked up to the front door, unlocked it, pulled guns from holsters and went inside, bent low. In minutes, the lights were turned on and the men returned to the front porch and waited on each side of the door. The rest of the group left the cars, one man was being held by the elbow as he seemed to shuffle along, obviously either very old or ill.

Everyone, but the two men by the door was inside. Figures could be seen moving back and forth as if searching for something. Then quiet returned to the area. Nothing was seen, but long range cameras had been trained on each face that entered the house and computers were churning silently, searching for names to match all the faces.

The president was sitting alone in his upstairs sitting room, wishing that his wife were still here. But she had been working that beautiful Tuesday morning in September 2001 on the seventy-fifth floor of the south tower. Their plans for a romantic getaway for their fifth anniversary just finalized, when his life changed forever. He had buried himself in his work and silently vowed he would make all terrorists pay, if ever he had a chance.

He had studied everything he could about how terrorists worked, planned, plotted, and just this once, just maybe, he could make these homegrown and worldwide terrorists pay. He was waiting for word from Saunders, at nearly two o'clock in the morning. What was happening? Had it started? There was no way he was going to be able to sleep.

Saunders had just started to receive the names of the people who had entered the house. Gregory Skinner, Owner, CEO, Crown & Shield Insurance, the old man was Anthony Vanderlin, American multimillionaire, Tobias Wentworth, British multimillionaire, owner of several corporations, Jonas Maitland, suspected of orchestrating several financial scams in Europe resulting in just a few deaths, the list went on, well to do people, from all over the world, a dozen in all. Now they were waiting it seemed. It was almost two o'clock.

Saunders heard a metallic voice in his ear, "Large white limousine driving down the county road, turning in to the driveway." Right on time, he thought.

Two people got out of the limousine, a man and a woman, both tall, slim, blond. They went up the steps of the house and he just barely heard the clicks of the camera. As they passed the two guards it looked as if they touched each guard. The men seemed to stand straighter, but when the door closed both men fell forward on their faces.

"What the hell?" Saunders breathed.

He watched the lit windows intently as people seemed to be violently moving about, then suddenly movement stopped, and the door opened. Vanderlin and Skinner walked out with the man and woman who had just entered and they drove off in the white limousine.

He heard a shaken whisper from the rear of the house, "The armed device it is going to blow."

Saunders ordered immediate silent retreat. Gately who had been monitoring the exchange signaled to everyone to move back to the rendezvous point. Michael and Richard knew they had about five minutes, which gave his people and Saunders people enough time to get out.

They were standing at a bus stop when the limousine pulled up and they all got in. An ill appearing Vanderlin and Skinner were already seated and handcuffed in the rear of the vehicle and seemed startled at the group's arrival. Seconds later they were airborne and watching the look of shock on the face of Gregory Skinner.

"Do you know who I am? Why are you taking me hostage?"

"Yes, we do, Mr. Skinner. You are a terrorist and a collaborator." Gately answered, as he moved forward to speak with Philippe.

"We have to get rid of these two."

"Yes. Can you have them meet us somewhere?"

"How about an industrial waste plant, one not far from D.C?" He looked up the one he was thinking about on his phone and gave Philippe the address. "What did you do to them in there?"

"Just made them freeze, temporarily interrupted muscle movement. It only lasts about fifteen minutes. They'll have a few aches and pains if they get out before the place blows up."

"I don't think they'll have time to get away, it should be going up right about now, according to what Michel and Richard think."

As if in response they felt a slight turbulence. "I'd say that was it."

The President's phone began to buzz and he responded immediately. "Yes?"

"Mr. President?"

"Yes, Saunders."

"It's over, no shots fired. But I don't understand what happened. Anthony Vanderlin and Gregory Skinner left with two people and for some reason the bomb was triggered. We got out in time but the others who had gone in the house didn't run out or anything. We don't have Skinner, Sir."

"You will be picking him up. Go to Industrial Way, in Baltimore the two of them will be waiting for you."

"Who are those people? A man and a woman walked into the house and walked out with them."

"Did you get their pictures?"

"Yes, Sir, we are still searching, but so far everything has come back negative, unknown."

"All right, they are apparently working with our friends. They must be, since they are handing this Skinner over to us. Take Vanderlin as well. He is also responsible for Bermuda, I believe. Once we have them in custody, we will get it sorted out."

"Yes, Mr. President, we are all together, we'll pick them up."

"Good night, Saunders, good job."

"Good night, Sir." Saunders thought to himself, we didn't do anything.

Two hours later Saunders found the shivering Skinner and Vanderlin alone, shackled together and then to the rear of an empty freight car.

The blast at the house off County Road in Maryland was being investigated by the ATF, several morgue wagons and ambulances were on site ready to go once all the bodies had been processed and released for autopsy.

Saunders got a call from his friend Clark on the way back to the White House. "Did you know there was going to be another one of those blasts?"

"Nope, I'm as surprised as you."

"Yeah, I'll bet. We are still digging body parts out of the walls. There isn't one body either inside or out that is intact. The ME is going to have a field day trying to match them all."

"How many bodies total?"

"We're not sure, possibly thirty."

"Well, thanks for the information, Clark, I owe you one."

"Yep, don't forget I will come around to collect."

"Yeah, I know. No problem."

Sir James was sitting in front of the computer for hours, monitoring the operation from the mountain hideaway, when Mary walked into the office.

"Sir James, you need some rest. You've barely eaten anything. You can't keep up this pace."

"Thank you, Mary, for your concern. I was just thinking that I need to get some sleep. Almost everything is done now. We just have to find out what is happening with those upcoming visitors. But I think I have time to get some rest as you suggest."

"Good. You'll be no use to anyone falling asleep in a chair."

"I understand that only too well, Mary. I just have to let my son know what is happening and I can get some rest."

Mary left the room and walked into the kitchen to find Evelyn rummaging around in the cupboards. "Not much here to eat."

"No just the basics, Evelyn. We didn't have much time to pack a lot."

"Has he told you where my husband is, Mary?"

"I don't know for sure where anyone is, but they are all together working on something or other."

"I wonder if our marriage will survive this. It survived all of the years we were away from each other, but, thoughts of betrayal? I'm not sure." Evelyn sat down at the small table on one side of the kitchen, her short brown hair, always so perfectly neat was growing long with strands of gray shining in the artificial light. She opened up some cracker sandwich packs and began nibbling away. Her skin which had tanned in the Maltese sun had faded and she seemed pale and wan.

Mary realized that the last few months had taken a toll on all of them, but she just said, "Well, you had many years together and that takes a tremendous amount of commitment, so you have a firm foundation. It will probably take time but you have your past to build on."

"You're right, Mary. It will take time. I just hope Ed will be open to taking the time."

Everyone was sitting around the dining room of the house in North Carolina, except for Philippe and Celine. The Stillmans had made sure everyone had a good breakfast and they were relaxing for a few minutes over coffee.

Gately had been in touch with his father who recommended that they start back after eleven in the morning and it was just ten. "Well, it looks like now all we have to do is to wait and see what all the countries are going to do against the extraterrestrials. I'm sure once we get back to Colorado, my father will have it all figured out. But I don't think we will have much to do with that. The stage has been set, so to speak."

Michael was shaking his head, "Sorry, Ed, I think we may still have a fight on our hands with these invaders."

"Sure, but that will be up to the Armed Forces, not us, Michael."

"We have great weapons, all the countries are armed, but not like those silver explosives. Who knows what else they might have?"

"I agree with Michael there, Ed. We are sitting ducks, it's not like we can move the planet and get away from them." Richard said.

"Well, it's not up to us. So we might as well get ready to get back there. Where are Philippe and Celine?"

"They went into the study."

Ilena got up and went over to the door of the study and knocked. When the door opened a golden glow lit up the entire study. "We had to strengthen ourselves after last evening. I hope we didn't startle you?" Celine said.

"No, ah, we were just wondering where you were, we are just about ready to leave."

"Good, good, we are ready as well." Philippe came out of the study looking if anything younger and more tan than ever.

The Stillmans had already cleaned up the dishes and the house was neater than it had been when Clothilde had first arrived weeks ago, but it was still cluttered. The group pulled together their jackets, and extra clothes they had acquired as well as their laptops and other personal items and got in the limousine.

Clothilde had to return the rental car so the limousine followed her down the road to the rental office and waited for her to complete the transaction. She then crowded into the back of the white car. They drove down the small town road and onto the highway. Philippe found the first highway access road, pulled off onto the gravel, drove past the transportation service buildings and went airborne. Clothilde gasped as she had never been in the car before. Ilena laughed. "Yes, I agree it is a shock, Clothilde. You'll get used to it though."

Tino chimed in, "Sorry, Ilena. Me? I'm still not used to it."

Edward had already contacted Sir James to let him know they were on their way back and would need guidance on landing.

About an hour into the trip, Sir James told them to return to their original or first landing coordinates. Philippe set the memory of the plane to the correct date and the coordinates came up. Forty-five minutes later the plane landed on the strip in the mountains and was retracted into the mountain. A mechanical voice welcomed them with instructions, "Please follow the lights when you leave the plane. If you have forgotten anything on the plane you cannot go back to retrieve it. So make sure you have everything you need when you leave."

Richard and Michael helped the Stillmans from the plane and the grouped trouped in line through the dark tunnel following the glowing white lights on the floor. A wall suddenly loomed up in front of them with a handle, Michael pushed down on the handle and they walked into the living room of the mountain mansion. "Well that was unexpected. I thought we would be in the kitchen."

"Well, we have guests, and my daughter certainly wouldn't expect to come home through the kitchen."

"Father!" Clothilde ran to her father and put her arms around him. "Oh, thank heaven. I've been so worried about you."

Sir James put his arm around her and smiled. "Well, you're here now, nothing more to worry about, dear. Mr. and Mrs. Stillman, please let me apologize for your having been drawn into this, ah, problem. I will definitely compensate you for your time and all of your help in keeping my team well fed, as well as, what we like to call hazardous duty pay.

"I think that it will still be awhile before you can get home, but I'll get you back there as quickly as possible. Now, we have a lot to do, a lot. Clothilde you will find your room upstairs the last one on the left. Mr. and Mrs. Stillman, you can go to the suite you always use when you stay here." Sir James pointed down a hallway that opened up opposite the staircase. He turned to find Clothilde staring at him.

"Ah, you want to talk. Yes. I'll meet the rest of you in the planning room." He put his arm around Clothilde's shoulders and drew her over to the window seat overlooking the surrounding mountains.

"Father, why didn't you tell me about him? I mean, all these years? Where has he been? What is this house and who are all these people. I know Michael and Richard, but the rest? Tino? Where on earth did he come from?"

"One question at a time, my dear. I had to protect you and Edward. When your mother died after you were born, I had already sent Edward to be raised separately from the manor. He was twelve when you were born. No one knew when he was born as we were in the United States at the time. My friends were desperate for a child and they were more like relatives than friends to your mother and I. Besides your mother was not well after he was born. She was young, we were both young. So when we returned to England, just the two of us, no one said anything, it would have been inappropriate. People assumed she had miscarried.

"Then, years later she became pregnant again, we thought she was older, stronger, she would be fine. But again she was ill after you were born, and as you know she died before you were even six months old."

"I know, but why didn't you bring your son home? You left him alone, abandoned all of these years?"

"No, dear, no, I saw him frequently, he knew who he was. He always did. But he knew that I had to protect him from people who might try to do harm to him. You remember meeting Anthony Vanderlin?"

"Of course, I remember. He was your old school and college friend. What about him?"

"Well, we are members of a group. In fact your grandfather, his father, and as far back as we can remember have been members of the same group. However, Anthony Vanderlin, who was its most recent leader, has been out of control, ruthless, and dealing with people who do not have the best interests of the human race at heart. Greed and power are his only allies."

"So why didn't you just leave the group?"

"You cannot just leave the group, you are born into it. Your brother was born into it and Vanderlin thought you were."

"I was able to ensure that Edward was brought up knowing how to deal with him, which I could not have done, because Vanderlin would be hovering over him as he tried to with you."

"Yes, he came to my school. He was always asking what courses I was taking. He acted more like a relative, an uncle than your friend."

"Well, I needed to turn things around that he was doing, make the world a better place instead of butchering people. Then I found that he had sold his leadership to others, terrorists so that he would have even more power.

"But enough. There isn't much to do here for you right now, but hopefully you can just relax while I talk to the others. We have much to do.

"All right, for now, Dad. But I hope that I can help you with whatever is happening."

"You already have, my dear. You already have. I meant to thank you for letting me know about that small ship. They work for me and have been able to keep me aware of some important changes."

With that, he got up and headed toward the kitchen and slid through the hidden entrance into the planning room.

"Edward, have you heard from the President?"

"Yes, Dad. Based on tattoos found on the bodies they feel that those killed in the house were all members of the Hadi Skupina."

"So, their numbers are dwindling."

"Philippe, Celine, did you set the device to explode?"

"No, Sir James. While we were subduing those in the house, one of them triggered it before we could stop him. As we told Edward, we merely made them incapable of movement for fifteen minutes. The man who triggered the device, we made him incapable of moving seconds after he activated it."

"He probably thought he could get away."

"All right, then. We are going to contact all the government leaders once more. I believe that this time we have a firm foundation and can prove to them that we can get things done and effectively help them deal with the extraterrestrial invaders.

"So now we or maybe I should say I, have other questions for you, Philippe, Celine. What can you tell me about the others who are here from your planet?"

"If there are others here, Sir James, they have come here independently, they are not with us and as of now we are unaware of them."

Edward walked over and stood in front of Philippe. "Please, Philippe, tell my father the truth. I believe there are two people in the White House, even now, as we speak."

"Why would you think that?"

"The glow that you two emit, I saw the same glow from two men walking down a hallway in the White House last year. I saw each of those men alone and there was no glow. I only saw them together once."

"They might be hybrids."

"Hybrids?"

"Many of us have come here over the years. Some have returned, while others like it here and have stayed to become a part of the community."

"So what happens when a father dies?"

"They don't, they just disappear. To the people they know and love, it is like they wandered off, they disappeared, never to be seen again."

"Edward," Celine asked, "what positions did these people in the White House have?"

"Both of them were on the President's Secret Service personal detail."

Celine nodded, "Protection then, they would be well suited for that." She said quietly.

"They probably don't know they are hybrids. Most would not. They would just realize that their stamina, ability to be awake for long periods is better than the average and just put it down to genetics."

Sir James cleared his throat. "Well, now is not the time to tell the President he has alien hybrids on his staff. We need to find out if they are coming together or not."

With that, they turned on the successive scramblers and called the various world leaders.

"Good Evening, everyone, it has been some time since we have spoken and events have been most enlightening during this time. We have been able to place many of the terrorists in your hands for you to question.

"We are now faced with the imminent arrival of extraterrestrials that plan on making this world a water world for them to inhabit. There have been very recent independent studies on the rising of the oceans around the world which will bear out the work that these terrorists and their cohorts have already initiated. We need to stop them before they reach here and stop their work to eliminate us and flood the planet. The question before you is can you all work together as a cohesive unit to face them? This time I will be back with you within three hours. There is much work to do as, no matter what your answer is, there will be a fight for the very survival of the earth as we know it."

The transmission was cut off and Sir James looked around at all of them. "I am neither trying to scare them or threaten them. I simply told them the truth. You have discovered these facts through your travels. I believe that they also know something unnatural is happening just from the explosions in the Arctic. We all know what the world is up against."

The group stood around silently looking at each other. They had all been so busy, working to stay alive, flying from one place to another, fighting when necessary that they had lost sight of the final goal.

"Sir James, Edward, might we speak with you?" Philippe looked at the father and son, realizing that it was now or never. They had played all of their hands and he and Celine knew that they could no longer hide their role.

Edward and Sir James looked at each other and then at the pair that Edward now thought of as the 'golden ones'. Sir James nodded. "I was wondering how long it would take."

"The rest of you, go, get some rest. We are in for a long fight."

Michael and Richard stood at the entrance to the kitchen after the others had left. "It's all right, Richard, Michael. You can stay in the kitchen or get some rest." Sir James wearily sat down at the conference table, waiting for whatever the tall blonde couple might have to say.

There was absolute silence in the room. A sense of apprehension mixed with excitement was almost palpable in the room. They were all seated, Sir James and Edward across from the handsome couple.

"We were manipulating Vanderlin. We knew what was needed to meet the oncoming threat. We knew about the Hadi Skupina, and that it was tied to the insurance company. The world has allowed insurance companies to operate with few regulations, to say no, or yes to everyone, everyone, no matter how powerful. Skinner knew that and used that to gain not only the finances, but the property, the people, everything needed to undermine the world. Through his company he insured other insurance companies thus owning even the world's government buildings. Everything, whether educational, medical, political or business ultimately flowed through Crown and Shield. We knew that, but no one in the world realized that Crown and Shield was the silent operator. We thought that if Vanderlin could bring the countries of the world together he could force Skinner to stop. But Vanderlin was himself infiltrated through Seth and the Hadi Skupina. That is where the Bermuda business came from, from them.

"He thought he was in charge, but he wasn't. He was receiving orders from Skinner as well as from us. Only Skinner frightened him, threatened him. He didn't know who either of us was, he had never met us. But he felt he could pull off the Bermuda deal and still manipulate us and people like the General Anders' of the world.

"That is why we came to you, Sir James. We knew you were trying to stop what had been set in motion, and we knew you wouldn't allow this total annihilation to take place. The Hadi Skupina have been working with the 'Others' and obtained the silver devices, but now with Skinner no longer meeting with them and some of them lost on that other plane, we believe that they have escalated their plans and will invade more quickly than planned."

"So Philippe, Celine, what have you planned now?" Sir James asked quietly.

"We have asked for assistance."

"Assistance? Assistance from where?"

"Our planet. Our People."

"Wonderful! Now we will have a war in space and we can barely fly above our own planet."

Celine spoke up. "This all depends upon the answer of the governments. We make every effort not to interfere with your governments, your wars, your situations. We observe, and we assist only, by giving hints of technology to, your geniuses, who might be hybrids in some cases. We are here to assist. As we have done throughout your operation. We have tried to assist where and whenever you needed us."

"You have, you have." Edward spoke for the first time, "But I need to know what happened to my wife? What did you do to her? What was done to her?"

"We do not know. We know that her behavior changed when she was with us. We were bringing her to you. She was on her own when I found her," Celine went on, "in the Co-operative Cathedral down where the knight's crypts are, under the main altar. We left, went to her place to get her some clothes and when we left there she kept staring at me. She would turn away and then turn back and stare again. I don't think she realized I knew she was looking at me."

"Evelyn said that your eyes had changed color and it was confusing to her. She thought perhaps you had on colored contacts."

"Oh, yes. There are times when my eyes will change. Normally my eyes are brown, when I am relaxed, but when I have to move quickly, I'm working at keeping everything together, my eyes do become their natural deep blue. I usually wear sunglasses, but if it is overcast I don't."

"I think she had an implant of some sort." Sir James said as he stood up and began to walk around the room, absently tucking chairs into the computer desks. "Possibly adrenalin triggered. She said had intense headaches for a few months while Edward was away. Right now she and Mary are keeping each other company in another part of the house."

"But there is more, isn't there Philippe?" Sir James looked at the tanned younger man with narrowed eyes.

"Yes."

"Correct me if I am wrong, Philippe, but I believe you and your planet's rulers have been manipulating us, playing the puppet master in all of this for centuries. Moving us forward, with technology, perhaps faster than our human environment could keep pace, but that was all right because the hybrids would help us to catch up with our technology. I'm not angry with your assistance, but I want to know the reason behind it. What if any, is your, their, ulterior motive, Philippe?"

"Yes, there is an ulterior motive, to help you move forward into space. I of course reported back to my planet when I first arrived and was surprised by the adaptability and general intelligence of the people here. That is the ulterior motive. To save this planet, your people. But if these invaders overcome the earth, all of our efforts will be in vain. So again we have to help you. This is all that there is. What I told you before, that we came to see, that I, came to the earth out of our planet's curiosity, is the truth. I, we, realized what you could become and I've stayed to help. I'm still here to help. Our planet is committed to help."

"Finally, I have it all. Thank you, Philippe. Your help has been invaluable, and yes, your help is accepted. At least by me, I cannot speak for the rest of the world. But I think if there were some way for the hybrids to join with you they might be able to push forward some of your capabilities if needed.

"We should find out if our invaders are close enough to be seen, perhaps the Hubble can scan for them. At least we are not without some eyes in the sky."

"I believe, Sir James they are still too far out for the Hubble to spot them, by next week they should be able to be seen according to our assessments."

"All right then, we have work to do and about an hour before we call our friends.

The President had taken the first hour of the time to rest and asked Marge to call him at the end of that time and have a large coffee ready for him. He walked into his study and there was the large steaming hot mug of coffee on his desk, with a full pot on a table nearby.

He began making calls, talking to his counterparts, as well as members of the Senate and Congress that he had decided to listen to. It looked as if at least for this effort, everyone, even China and India had decided to work together. North Korea continued to posture and threaten that this was another ploy on the part of the West to undermine their government. Iran had shut down its borders, with a final threat that should any infidel from above or the earth come cross their skies there would be nuclear retaliation.

Stapleton had finally called the man who had stepped into the Vice Presidency, Norman Donellen, when he had become President. He didn't care for the tall, overweight man, with the white hair and loud voice, and kept him at a distance during the last two years. But he knew he now had to brief him on the present situation before the next call from the unknown person. The President thought he knew who the person was, but he was not going to reveal his suspicions. He felt everyone was ready. Yes, there were a few holdouts, but for the most part they were going to get together for this fight.

"Good Evening, everyone again. I realize that it is late in the evening, so I will only keep you a short time. We will take a quick poll on who will be joining in the World Government to keep the extraterrestrials from flooding the world for their own uses. I will begin with the United States."

Sir James went down the list of countries large and small, north and south, east and west. As expected North Korea said no and cut off communications. China said yes and swore they would bring North Korea around to show some sense. Iran had not answered the call. After an hour it was done. The unified government at least temporarily was formed. Whether it stayed together or not would have to wait until the present threat was eliminated.

"Before I sign off this evening, I need to let you know that by next week you should be able to see the invaders through the eyes of the Hubble telescope. The original timeline they gave us has been shortened because they know we have discovered their plan. I will check back with you in four days to see if you need help with anything." They were again disconnected.

The president immediately called his secretary, "Marge, that was the longest they have ever been on the line, see if you can trace the call this time."

"Sir, I tried, but it was impossible. The entire time it seemed to be rotating through several satellites, and from several coordinates. It wasn't a steady line."

"I figured something like that would happen. He knew he would be on for a longer time and had it all set up to change places. The guy is smart, you've got to give him that."

"Are you sure you can trust him?" Donellan asked, his normally jovial face frowning with concern.

"With what he's done so far? You better believe I trust him. We have the brains behind the Bermuda disaster and the head of the Hadi Skupina, who owned Crown and Shield, which has just about bankrupted every insurance company in the world with their manipulations. He has reached into our very midst and pointed out traitors. All he is asking is that we work together."

"Well, you know if it sounds too good to be true it usually is."

"This is not too good to be true, because we are still doing the heavy lifting as far as I can tell."

"Yes, that's true. All the defenses of the world are facing outward. What about the ISS, the International Space Station. Do you think they are vulnerable?"

"God, I hadn't thought of those guys. Let me get on the horn to NASA and see what we can do to keep them safe. We might have to bring them home and shut down the station. Thanks, Norm."

The nations of the world were finally working together. Their leaders were now sanctioned to meet at the United Nations building and plan their moves so that all the defenses were mobilized outward. China finally convinced North Korea to join the group until the invaders had left. Then they could go back to pouting and threatening everybody else.

The group in the mountains had finally had a chance to rest and eat more than sandwiches. Richard and Tino had gone out in a pick-up truck with the Stillmans to buy fresh food and Mrs. Stillman cooked a turkey and a ham along with all of the fixings that went along with it. During their shopping trip the couple stopped by their house and found that it had been thoroughly ransacked, with furniture broken, holes in the walls and floors of every room.

There was another earthquake in the Arctic Circle, centered close to the same coordinates that they had flown over the month before. When Sir James heard of it, his face flushed. "They are still here, someone is still moving around, they have not all been caught. We need to get to the Arctic Circle."

"We can bring up some satellite imagery, so that we can see what happened up there, without flying over it again." Richard said. His hands flew over the keyboard, linking with a search engine's imaging system to see if he could see what had happened. Ilena was researching any information she could retrieve from geologists regarding what kind of earthquake had occurred, and if possibly it was not an earthquake at all but another explosion.

The President had been apprised of the situation in the Arctic, and an hour later he was informed that it had been determined that it was an explosion not an earthquake. The ATF facility in Alaska had monitored the geological tracings and compared it with the previous explosion there, as well as the others in Canada, Great Britain, United States and around the world, and determined that it must be the same type of device as the signature was exact.

The four days was almost up and the unified government was still having growing pains, the Arctic explosion only intensified their fears. They needed direction other than ordering an immediate call up of all troops and placing the world on a war footing. Food supply distribution was increased to all areas of the world, fuel storage areas were placed under twenty-four hour armed security, grocery stores were stocking shelves as fast as they could, the big appliance stores sold out of freezers, generators, and gun shops had to close due to decimation inventory. As expected, civilians were panicking in part because they were afraid of the invader and partly because they didn't trust their governments, united or not to protect them.

The United Nations had decided to place a non-habitable zone of twenty-five miles around the country of Iran, to ensure that no one would accidentally trigger a nuclear response from the isolated country. Check points had been set up manned by U.N. forces, while humanitarian groups began clearing all civilians away from the small villages within the zone.

"It has not been a good four days. I have to call and see what they need. That explosive melted even more ice and the waters are still rising. But I was able to find out that they are arming the International Space Station. They sent an unmanned supply shuttle with all sorts of weaponry."

The astronauts on the International Space Station had been given the option of staying or leaving, but the six crewmembers said they would stay. Their reasoning was when the enemy showed up, the astronauts wanted a chance to defend the earth as well. The crew would make sure the aliens knew they weren't welcome.

"Let's hope they don't blow themselves up trying to use the weapons, Dad."

"Hopefully they have been trained in how to use whatever they have been sent."

"Most likely they got shipped instruction manuals, since it was an unmanned shuttle. Plus they won't have the luxury of getting in some practice. But it's better to go down fighting then just being a sitting duck."

Everyone was now together in the planning room, even Mary and Evelyn who Sir James had personally brought back to the main house. He had taken Michael with him and they had restocked the place that Mary and Evelyn had been as well as a few other places around the mountain. Sir James had taken Edward down one day to a different secret area, as well as shown him various places around the mountain that could be armed, he had shown Michael, Richard, and Edward how to use the armament system in the mountain that they had heard used when the planes had come in behind them or the helicopter had gone down for coming too close.

The elderly man felt more relaxed now that he had shared his knowledge, but he still felt that he had to be the one to really work out how to save the world from this invasion. He also knew that he had to rely on Philippe and Celine. He hated this aspect, but he knew their personal capabilities far outweighed his own.

He looked at the expectant faces around him. They were silent waiting for him to make the global call.

"Good Afternoon, everyone. The four days is up and I was wondering how things are progressing and if you need help."

The babble started immediately. "I cannot help you if you all speak at once. I will call back after you have designated one of your number to speak for all of you."

He abruptly hung up. "We shall wait for fifteen minutes. What doldts! How do they expect to get anything done if they are all speaking at once?" Sir James got up from his black leather chair and walked around the room, circling the group that now feared to say a word. He may have been Edward and Clothilde's father, but they all looked to him for his unflagging leadership, his concern not only for their well-being, but that of the world.

He had been trying for years to bring pressure to bear on all countries of the world to understand that their constant bickering both internally and with other countries set the entire world up for failure. A failure was now looming over all of them, and it could well be too late for them to understand what fighting with each other might do to their lives. He had obviously lost his temper now that this same problem could cause the elimination of everyone on the planet.

"Mary, could you get me some wine, or better yet for everyone. I would rather have something stronger than water when dealing with these people.

"Of course, Sir James."

"I'll help you, Mary." Evelyn got up and the two women slipped out through the hidden door and ten minutes later were back with a tray of glasses and bottles of both red and white wines already opened.

"Well, it's time. Let us see if they have sorted themselves out."

"Good afternoon, again. Have you selected someone to speak for you?"

"I am Prime Minister Fairwell. I have been chosen to speak for everyone here."

"Thank you, Prime Minister. Now, do you need help with anything?

"We believe that if we could launch successive satellites around the world, beyond the ISS to form a grid of protection. The satellites would contain a net, we would still have sunlight, but neither the invaders nor any projectiles sent by them could get through this net. Is this something you could help us with?"

"Excellent! You have a plan. How many satellites are you capable of launching within a forty-eight hour period and what are you planning to use for the net? Also, how soon do you think all of those countries capable of launching satellites will be able to launch?"

"We are preparing all of the satellites as we speak. We believe we will be able to get at least three hundred into orbit within the time line or at least within seventy-two hours from the first launch. The netting makes use of a new type of clear filament similar to a fishing line. Although it is clear, it has both strength and elasticity, we are hoping that any device shot at us will be snapped back at the invader. We have tried this on a small scale and it has proven viable."

"All right. I have to discuss this and I will be back to you in approximately one hour, to let you know if this plan is feasible and if we can in any way assist you with the launching or placements, we will let you know."

Sir James again cut the connection. "It seems as if human ingenuity has really stepped up to the plate here. I like their idea. Not only is it protective, but it is far enough outside of the earth's atmosphere. The simplicity is novel, using a sling shot effect like David and Goliath. Well, any thoughts?"

Philippe was the first to speak. "Sir James, Celine and I can help by ensuring that all of the satellites reach the proper orbit and deploy all the nets. We can also assist by making sure that the invaders once repelled, leave the area."

"Excellent! Any other thoughts on this?"

Michael looked at Philippe and Celine, "Sir, does this mean that they have a ship somewhere?"

"Michael you have been flying in it all along." Philippe said.

"So, the car, the plane, it can go into outer space?"

"Yes, the vehicle is capable of performing any utilitarian mobility needed. That is why we have it."

"Can we go on the ship as well, into outer space?"

"Yes, Michael. In fact we plan on arming the ship and would need you to assist us in fighting these invaders if you wish."

"A question here, Philippe," Richard spoke up, "normally when we, meaning astronauts go into outer space we have to wear pressure suits, we are in a pressurized cabin. You know like the ISS. They live there but they are weightless when not wearing their suits. I don't see how we can be of much use if we are weightless."

Celine laughed, a soft musical sound. "Remember when you entered the car after being injured in Canada?"

"Sure, I hurt everywhere. Michael was a mess, we were bloody. Our skin was in ribbons."

"Then be assured you will be just as safe."

The others had been listening to the exchange.

Tino who rarely spoke when surrounded by the others seemed barely able to contain himself. "You are talking, Señor Felipe, of fighting in outer space? Like Star Trek?"

Now everyone chuckled. "Pretty much, Tino. In order to complete what the countries have started, they need some back-up. That will be up to us."

"Well, Philippe, Celine, it seems as if you will be arming your plane. How long do you need and can I provide you with any resources?"

"No, Sir James, however, we will need complete access to the vehicle over the next few days, so it will be ready. But we will also need Michael, Richard and Tino, if they want to help. That way they will learn what they need to do, how things work, so they can help us do this."

Michael shook his head. "Sir, I think I should remain here with you, just in case."

Edward looked at him for a second realizing that Michael's allegiance was to his father first. "That's all right, Michael. I'll help Philippe and Celine."

Sir James sat in silence, thinking carefully about the plan, the acknowledgements of Philippe and Celine's capabilities and the vehicle's extraordinary flexibility. He got up from his chair, "Philippe, Celine could you come with me, please?"

They followed him out of the planning room and into his study. He looked at the small brass clock on his desk. They still had a half hour.

"Celine, Philippe, I have seen how you look in your true nature. Your color is the purest of gold. My mind is rebelling still against trust, feeling that in all of this you have been pulling the strings and we, the inhabitants of this planet are merely marionettes at your bidding.

"Yet you have helped us, you have saved lives, you have taken lives, you have warned us, and you say you are willing yet again to help us. Do you know enough about human beings to understand my reluctance to trust?"

Philippe answered slowly as he sat down at the desk. "As we told you, I have been here for thousands of your years, Sir James. I have pushed and prodded your ancestors to build, to find, to learn, to seek and humans are intelligent, fast learners. I have known many, many humans down through the years and considered them as friends, like your son. I do not want to see all that I have done, that I have given my life to doing, lost to greedy, mindless invaders. Yes, you may see me and Celine as well, as puppeteers overall, but you are who you are and you have this mountain and all that it contains, because we, I, have been here all along. I am willing to fight for the human race, are you willing to allow me, us to do that, Sir James?"

Sir James stood up, tall, erect, the dark circles beneath the blue eyes belied the strain and sleepless days as he stared at the couple in front of him. He put out his hand, Philippe raised his to meet it and they shook hands. "I believe, Philippe, you should call on your own people, because as wonderful as your vehicle is, I believe you will need more than just yourself out there.

"An invading armada can be daunting and we have no idea how long our little net will hold off a sustained attack."

"Sir James we have many on the way. They have been monitoring through our ship and your satellites and have seen the invaders on the way and have slipped around beyond your sun to come in behind them once they are within range. We are hoping that when the invaders realize that they are not just going to fly in, land and take over, and my people are behind them, they will turn and run.

"We will of course chase them out of the galaxy."

"Then I will inform the countries that we will assist. What about satellites that misfire, or can't get off the ground? Not all of these countries have been successful in launching satellites or always reaching appropriate orbits. I know there are a few that this will be their first launch ever."

Celine spoke then, "I will be able to help some of them here and there. I am aware of those that are having problems and will help them reach the goals that have been set."

"All right, I guess it's time to call them."

They left the study, and returned to the planning room.

Sir James immediately made the call. "We will be assisting you in whatever manner that we can. We feel that the plan is an excellent one. When do you think you will begin launching the first satellites?"

"We plan on launching the first twenty-five satellites tomorrow morning at eight, from the northern hemisphere, and fifty at eight in the evening, from the southern hemisphere. We will be remotely deploying the nets overnight and then the other satellites will be launched to fill in around the center of the net at approximately every eight hours after that for seventy-two hours."

"All right we will check in with you after tomorrow evening's launch and again the following evening."

Sir James cut the connection. "All right everyone. That's it. Get some rest. We are going on a war footing like the rest of the world. The launch time tomorrow is at eight, so we have time to get some things done here. Philippe, Edward, I would like you to come with me, we have somewhere special to go."

The three men left the planning room, the kitchen, went through the living room and back into Sir James study. Sir James walked over to the bar, leaving Philippe and Edward standing just inside the closed door watching the older man. He ran his hand under the lip of the bar and pressed a button, the bar swung out and the back wall opened revealing an elevator.

"Let's go," he said beckoning them.

They rushed forward to join him on the elevator. "By the way, the study door is now locked, and no one can press the button to open the elevator door, until the elevator is returned to the study."

"What if the electricity is off, Dad?"

"This is on its own generator."

"Sir James, you have thought out everything over the years. How have you managed to keep this place such a secret?"

"I hire men from various countries to do different jobs. Very few speak English. They are here for a specific job, told exactly what needs to be done, fed well, paid well, and sent home, before the next workers arrive. That is why it has taken over forty years to build it. Each time new technology has come out, I have added it, each time I felt some security item needed upgrading it was done. None of the workers could say anything about where they were except that they had landed at Denver and went into the Rocky Mountains to work for a private corporation."

The elevator hissed to a stop and they all got out. The lighting was based on their movements on the soft carpet as they followed Sir James down the hallway, chiseled out of the mountain like all the other cavernous hallways they had seen. They turned left as the floor slanted downward and they could see the double steel door in front of them. Sir James pressed his right ring finger in the center of the handle and the door swung open. Lights came on automatically.

"This is my very private office. However, there is something here that you both need to see and know about." He walked over to the back wall and took away a panel, revealing several objects in the space behind the glass sealed into the wall. But one immediately caught their eyes, Philippe and Edward looked at it and they both gasped at the same time. The golden statue was at least three feet tall, slim, the eyes were painted deep blue, the hair was painted yellow, and the skin was gold. The slim handsome face looking back at them was Philippe's.

"How did you find that, Sir James?"

"Then you recognize it?"

"Of course. That was done in Egypt. It was supposed to be hidden in the Valley of the Kings."

"Philippe, it looks just like you."

"Edward, that is because it is me. It was sculpted so long ago by those who thought I was a god. I had helped them learn to build their shelters, their temples. I had a vehicle with me, much smaller than the one I have now, but it was primarily for the purpose of helping humans learn to build. So I helped them."

"This was found under the right paw of the Sphinx, Philippe."

"Yes, I know."

"Did you place it there or did someone else?"

"Someone else, the sculptor, after the Sphinx was built, she sculpted this of me saying that if ever it was found under the paw, the world would need my help again."

For the first time, Edward saw emotion in Philippe. He must have cared deeply for the woman who had sculpted this.

"I knew it had been found many years ago, but I couldn't locate it. It has an element in it, something from my home world, which would help me trace it should anyone find it. How did you find it, Sir James?"

"The Egyptian Antiquities people were again working to keep sand from reburying the Sphinx. I was with a visiting archaeological group there to assist them. It was a windy day, the sand was blowing everywhere and something was gleaming up at me. I returned at night with my work jeep and retraced my steps and was able to wrestle it out of the ground, despite the security. I could not believe that no one else had seen it. They had been there as I had every day working. So probably my placing it here kept you from locating it."

"The nature of the stone in this mountain blocked its signal. I did feel a tingling when you opened the steel doors, but I was not expecting this."

"I'll keep it here if that is all right with you, Philippe. Edward, this was taken a long time ago, before the rules were so stringent about foreigners removing things found there. I could see that the clothing depicted did not have any bearing on what the ancient Egyptians wore."

"Yes, Sir James. Yes, you are correct. This is why you kept questioning us, me. You were trying to make sure."

"Yes, Philippe. Now, Edward, there are other things here as well. You can go rummaging about at your leisure. But Philippe, if you want to come back down here, only Edward can bring you down or myself."

"I know where the statue is I no longer need to concern myself with it. It is near me and safe. Thank you, Sir James."

"Well, we must return to today's world and prepare to fight for our freedom and humanity."

They retraced their steps and returned to the study. As soon as they stepped off the elevator they could hear someone banging on the study door.

Sir James chuckled, "Probably Michael worried about me."

He walked over and opened the door and there was Michael. "Sorry, for all the banging on the door, but Richard and I couldn't locate you."

"That's all right, Michael. Edward, Philippe and I had some business to take care of.

"Now let's get some rest. That includes you, Michael."

Philippe was in the vehicle with Celine, Michael, Richard and Tino. The men were shocked at the number of unfamiliar armaments that the two were lining up for them to learn about. They had been expecting gun types of weapons, but instead were shown screens similar to video games, with levers, buttons, and joy sticks. Philippe was keying in and listening to humming sounds that the vehicle was making while they were working.

Tino asked him, "Señor Felipe, why is she singing. Does she talk?"

"No, Tino. The vehicle is being covered in a protective shield that keeps it from being so visible against the sky in space, as well as keeps it safe. It's almost like a safety blanket. The humming sound is the shield sliding across the outer skin."

"Ah, Si, Señor. She will be warm out there with her blanket on." Tino commented quietly, nodding.

"Yes, it will keep her warm." Philippe said as he looked over at Tino for a moment, surprised at the feeling in his voice for the vehicle. 'Humans, always continue to amaze me,' he thought to himself.

But Celine had heard his thought, and echoed back 'They are truly amazing people, Philippe.'

They kept working, making sure that all of the weapons that the vehicle had available were up and running. While Philippe settled down to teach the three men how to go to war in space, Celine returned to the house and retreated to a small room where she reached out with her mind to help the various engineers that needed it. Sir James had wondered about that capability in the extraterrestrials and would not have been surprised at the amount of assistance that surged around the world. Technicians and engineers working through problems suddenly had the proverbial 'light bulb' come on and fixed their satellites and launch devices in time to meet the time table.

The Stillmans had gone to two different grocery stores and picked up all the food their pick-up truck could carry, knowing that they would be helping Sir James and the team fight a war. They weren't quite sure who the fight was against at the beginning, but the television had told them that the world was arming for a visit from outer space and the visitors did not have earth's best interests at heart.

For once they were glad that they weren't at home, but they were concerned about their children and grandchildren. Sir James had talked to them and assured them that he would make sure they would be all right.

He had Ilena and Mary go down the mountain to each of the Stillman's children's homes with food, check on what was needed and make sure that they knew that their parents were just fine. They had set up a Skype system in the Stilllman's suite and the families were able to stay in touch while everything was going on.

Edward knew that he needed to know how to work the weapons as well and went down to Philippe's vehicle. "Permission to come aboard."

"No permission needed, Edward. Do you want to try these weapons systems?" Philippe asked.

"I think it would be wise to know as much as I can. I need to help as well." They worked for the next several hours. Michael was rubbing the back of his neck and Edward was rubbing his eyes.

Philippe checked the training logs and realized that the men's accuracy rate had fallen in the past hour. "I guess you all need to take a break. I always forget that."

They shut the vehicle down and went back into the main area to get something to eat. Michael walked over to Richard. "We need to take turns sleeping. If we are going to master those weapons systems we have to be at our peak. I'm exhausted."

"I understand, I'll keep an eye on everything you go get some rest."

"Thanks, mate. It's the first time that I think I actually might be able to get some real sleep in months."

Michael mounted the stairs, followed the hallway to the end and around the curve of the mountain to the right and walked to a room at the end. He had chosen it because it was quiet, away from the stairs and he knew if he needed to get to sleep quickly there wouldn't be any noises.

Sir James, Mary and Ilena had been monitoring the news and scientific reports for any word that the Hubble telescope had picked up the invaders. They were now at forty-eight hours into the preparations. The satellites and nets were being placed as planned with some mishaps. Every country had had difficulty in keeping up the pace of launching the satellites and getting them into the proper orbit. Then the remote launching of the nets proved to be more difficult than originally thought.

While the men were resting, Celine and Philippe had worked tirelessly above the earth, linking and stretching nets, pulling errant satellites into their needed orbits, and then getting the nets launched. The final launching was due to take place within the next eight hours and the men needed to be back on board before that time.

It was nine o'clock on a Tuesday evening, when the Hubble caught sight of the invading fleet. Ilena yelled, "They're on their way. Everyone, we can see them."

The launches of the satellites were taking place at the same time. The eyes of the world were on the skies. People everywhere were watching the sky some with binoculars, and backyard telescopes, others were glued to television sets and the news channels. They knew they couldn't see them yet, but everyone wanted to know. They had to be a part of this fight.

Philippe, Celine, Michael, Tino, Richard and Edward left for the vehicle that had just returned from pulling all but two satellite nets into place. When it launched out of the Colorado Rockies with such speed that the vibration could be felt in the mountain and the sound barrier was broken less than a mile away.

They completed the last linking and pulling of the two satellites into place that completely closed the net. They knew that they would not be able to return themselves until it was over.

Celine turned to the others, "We want you all to know that our 'cavalry' is coming. They will be here in about an hour. Edward, your father knows about them. They will not make any effort to go through the net, but one group will surround the net with us. The second group will be coming in behind the invaders. We are telling you this so that you will understand how we are fighting this battle and so you know your targets.

"You can continue to practice while we are waiting. If you have questions about the weapons, how to recharge the systems, or anything please ask us now. We will be busy once the fighting starts and will not have time."

Michael said, "How will your cavalry show up on the screen, Celine?"

Celine smiled, "Don't shoot any angels."

"Great, we'll just shoot the devils." Edward said.

They hung motionless in the sky above the Arctic Circle watching, waiting. Then Tino whispered, "Madre de Dios, they are angels."

They were glowing a deep gold as they flew together, but as they moved apart to encircle the netted earth they looked more like blue discs with gold halos. They deployed just in time as the armada of invaders came into view and found the way to their destination blocked.

Philippe and Celine's vehicle stayed in the same place they had been hovering previously but now they were side by side with others. By keeping just enough distance from each other the gold halos touched each other to completely surround the planet.

The invaders slowed, the gray tube ships shifted around from their arrival pattern into a wedge like fashion. Their battle line hung in space from the Arctic to the Antarctic along one side of the slowly revolving earth and began to mount their attack. Celine called "Commence." They began to press the buttons on their levers or joysticks, and immediately holes were blown in various areas of the wedge of invaders. The concerted attack of moving side to side then up and down on the wedge caused the invaders to begin to retreat. Even while they were beginning to retreat they were still being hit hard by the glowing defenders. Flaming pieces of debris floated throughout the dark area of the battle. Large chunks of the destroyed invaders ships were struck again by both incoming and outgoing fire and obliterated.

The retreat was short lived and the invaders realigned into several lines, each rising just higher than the previous one and began to move forward this time at a much higher rate of speed toward the glowing field of ships in front of them. Unfortunately for the invaders this maneuver simply opened up more of their ships to damage as the blue ships fire power strafed the enemy from side to side.

The golden glow reflected the hits taken from the enemy as black smudges which rolled down the surface of all the ships and into space. The force field was holding, but the heavy constant bombardment was felt inside the disc ships and there were injuries from falls and from being too close to the point of impact.

Meanwhile, deep holes were seen in the invading ships onslaught, apparently as practiced aggressors they had not seen the need for any protection against weaponry. Parts of exploding enemy ships were flying everywhere, and in some cases interfering with visibility to targets. But buttons were pressed and levers moved from side to side again and again, continuing to cause severe damage. The invaders retreated again. But the second time, they couldn't retreat far, because behind them glowing blue ships moved up to block them. Those that had surrounded the earth now moved out and began to surround the invaders who were caught within the golden glow that brightened and compressed the enemy within.

Philippe and Celine moved back and began to circle the earth checking for damage to the net or breakthroughs by the invaders. But the net was clear, there was no damage. The blue discs began to break away from the earth, while still compressing the invaders remaining gray tubes within their golden glow. But five of them flew in to surround the vehicle that Philippe and Celine were flying.

"They want to meet you all, Edward. This is their first time meeting humans. They have helped other races as they helped you today and would like to know if they can meet you."

"You mean a delegation? Do they just want to come aboard or what?"

"They want to meet Sir James and the people of earth. They want them to know that they can be called upon at any time."

"Wait." Edward tried his cell phone. "Dad, the battle is over. But the people, they are like Celine and Philippe, they want to meet you and the government of earth to let them know they are available to help from here on with invasion problems or….."

"Yes, son, yes, it is time. But ask them to wait. We don't want the ISS or anyone thinking this is part of the invasion. I have to let them know."

The people of earth watched in shock, as the battle unfolded, and was streamed live to every home, phone and electronic device. The net that surrounded the earth could not be seen, but the satellites that held the net could be seen by those with their telescopes trained on them. Those hobbyists were all watching the skies like the Civil Air Patrol did during World War II. But the golden glow that followed the final placement of the net could be seen by everyone.

That glow of protection as the media called it, spread around the world and once complete seemed to be alive and moving in place. Still the cameras could see through the glow, The Hubble telescope cameras had been remotely moved to follow the battle playing out in the skies.

It photographed the large tube like ships of the invaders as they moved across the dark space headed toward earth. It also photographed the nearly flat disc shaped blue objects which encircled the earth, and glowed while in near contact.

But more importantly the Hubble photographed the first space battle in Earth's history as it took place. President Stapleton and Prime Minister Fairwell were watching it, along with several of the other heads of state. NASA had sent the live feed from Hubble directly to them. So they knew immediately that those discs were fighting for the world, and when they finally pulled together and surrounded the enemy, and drove them from the solar system and into deep space beyond, a cheer went up, not just in that room, but across the world.

An hour later a call came into the UN council room and various heads of state to say that a delegation of leaders from the other planet wanted to meet with the leaders of earth, there was little discussion before a unanimous agreement.

Sir James then said there was some caution as the ISS astronauts, might not realize that the battle was over. "We will make sure they know. Please have the visitors wait a couple of hours. Most of us are together and we would like to properly greet them." President Stapleton said.

Then Prime Minister Fairwell broke in, "We would like to meet you as well, and your team, we know you have helped us, helped the world through this."

"That won't be possible, Sir, though we do appreciate the invitation. We will be retracting the net in a small area over the Pacific in an hour, Sir. We will keep that as a permanent doorway through the net, but keep the net in place and close the doorway in case there are future problems."

Sir James turned off the scrambled communications and spoke to his son, "Can you have Philippe retract an area of the net over the middle of the Pacific, large enough for all of you to come through? Fly north over the poles and stop here, I would also like to meet their people."

"Philippe, you heard him."

The small group of glowing discs flew in formation to the two satellites that hovered over the central Pacific Ocean, and hovered there while Celine began the retraction maneuvers. Minutes later they flew as directed and dove down over the Rocky Mountains to land.

The metallic voice than asked that all who wished could simply follow the lights down the halls. The months of stringent security measures had been relaxed.

The team walked down the lit hallways, Celine in front of the small delegation of their planet's people and Philippe came behind. This time the halls took them directly into the living room.

The large group of tall slim blonde young men and women stood around, while they resembled each other, there were differences in height, and actual facial features.

"Sir James, they felt it safer to look as humans, so as not to upset anyone. This is how we have always looked if we go to a planet with humans."

"There are definitely other planets with humans?"

"Yes, there are, at least five that we know about."

"But we know you are not humans, so I believe that our human race would expect you to look different."

"That is true. Well, everyone is here, so let us see with a small sampling."

With that all of them retreated to their true nature. Still humanoid, but the beautiful deep gold now, they moved together and the golden glow expanded to fill the room. The peace and happiness felt throughout the room at that moment was palpable. Tino's eyes had gone wide, Evelyn who had been looking at Celine when the change occurred put her hand to her mouth as tears flowed, while Clothilde and Mary just sat down on the nearest chairs in shock.

Then, they changed back to human beings again, but stayed

close. Sir James was the first to speak. "Your golden glow is more than protection it is also a projection of feeling as well."

"We are believers in peace. There is no need for protection if there is peace."

"True, quite true, Philippe. All right, head to the meeting, I can assure you, you will have your pictures taken. Our world is media hungry."

One of the newcomers spoke, "We know, Sir James. We are happy to meet with you and we would like to talk with you again after we have formally met the leaders of this earth. There is much to do to ensure that other invaders do not come to harm you."

"Well, I'm getting a little old for this. I don't think I have another fight, maneuver or battle left in me. So you would do best in talking with my son, Edward."

The man nodded, "We understand."

The golden group headed back to their ships as Philippe and Celine led the group to meet with the world leaders.

Sir James looked around the room taking in the exhausted faces before him, "You have all done a great service to the world, but I'm afraid no one will ever know of your efforts or mine on their behalf.

"All of you may consider this your home as long as you like. I do intend to rebuild my home, but until it is finished, I shall be here. There are still many things that must be cleared up in the meantime."

With that he left the living room and walked down the hall in the direction of his study.

It began with a trickle of words on the social networks, than it was widely reported that during the hours that the golden glow had spread around the world prior to and during the battle in space, crime had dropped. In the hours since the battle, there had not been one single act of aggression against another. The incidence of drug abuse halted, and people began to overwhelm the rehabilitation centers to seek help for their addictions. The tobacco companies reported a week later that not a single pack of cigarettes had been sold in the world since the battle in space.

Iran sent a request to the United Nations to discuss the present situation of isolation and how the country could, as they put it 'stand down' from the nuclear footing it felt was overwhelming to Iran's well-being. North Korea meanwhile opened up talks of trade with its neighbor to the south.

People were sleeping better. Shows on television that depicted raw violence were no longer being watched in favor of shows that depicted people helping others. But one important change in everyone was that people were aware of who their neighbors were, who needed help. People's lives changed and they smiled more.

When the delegation completed their meeting with Earths' leaders, they said that they would leave some of their numbers here to learn more about life on earth and establish their own embassy. They also invited open travel to their own planet for education and leisure. The group flew back to Colorado to meet again with Sir James and the team. This time the group's stay was much longer as they began to build several vehicles for earth.

Over the next month, Edward and Evelyn moved from the main house into one of the bunker 'safe' houses as they began to rebuild their marriage. Edward began a daily commute through the tunnels to work side by side with Philippe and Celine on the prototypes and other innovations the aliens were giving them.

Mary and Tino decided to stay in Colorado, along with Richard and Michael. Clothilde went home to begin the work of negotiating with architects and contractors to rebuild the family home in Britain.

Philippe and Celine shared another of the safe houses that Sir James had built. One evening soon after they had begun spending time working with Edward in the hangar, they returned to their new home. Sir James would no longer recognize it due to the changes they had made. They sat together on a curved sofa and toasted each other.

"We did it, Celine. What we have worked for since the beginning. The countries of earth are finally able to work together."

"Do you think they will ever realize what has been done?"

"Maybe, once they travel outward, meet others and understand that each and every planet must act as one and then group to other planets. They would have been decimated years ago had we not stepped in to save them."

"They have more independence then many of the people we work with, that and their various God based faiths kept them separate, Philippe."

"Those chords around the earth are like puppet strings, we must lose them and let them be free again."

"Soon, I hope."

"Yes, once we are certain they are safe from themselves and can work to repel other world intruders."

Philippe kissed her as they watched the Maltese sun set on the opposite side of the room.

Printed in the United States
By Bookmasters